ETCHED *in* FROST

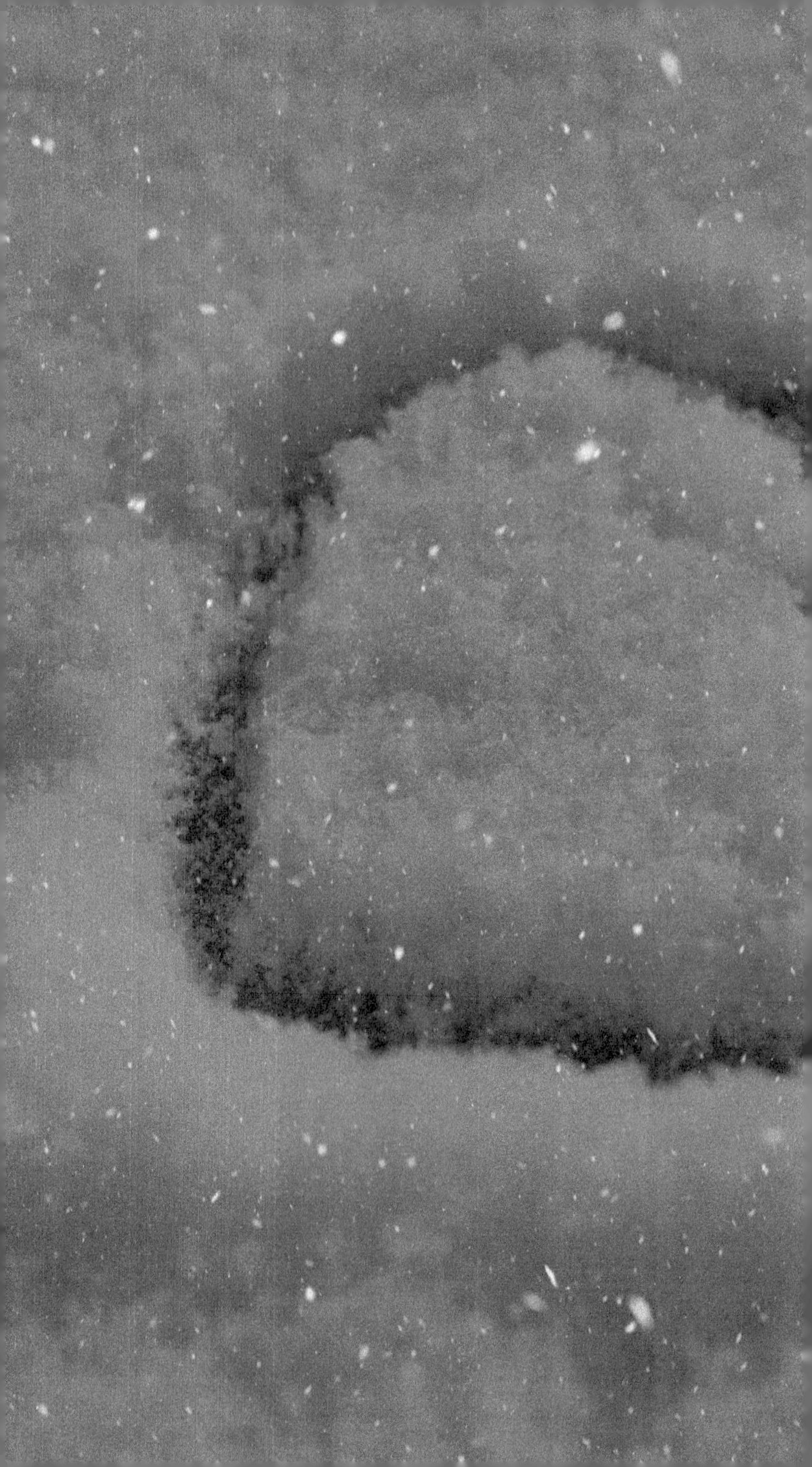

Content Warnings

<u>Content:</u>

Explicit language, on page descriptions of sexual acts (solo play, MF), voyeurism, public shenanigans, magical sexytime, icy toys, knotted/textured/pierced MMC, knotting, and a version of a heat cycle (note: this is not considered an omegaverse).

<u>Potential Triggers:</u>

Themes relating to grief and mental illness, injuries, gentle stalking, on page death, sacrificing your mortality for immortality.

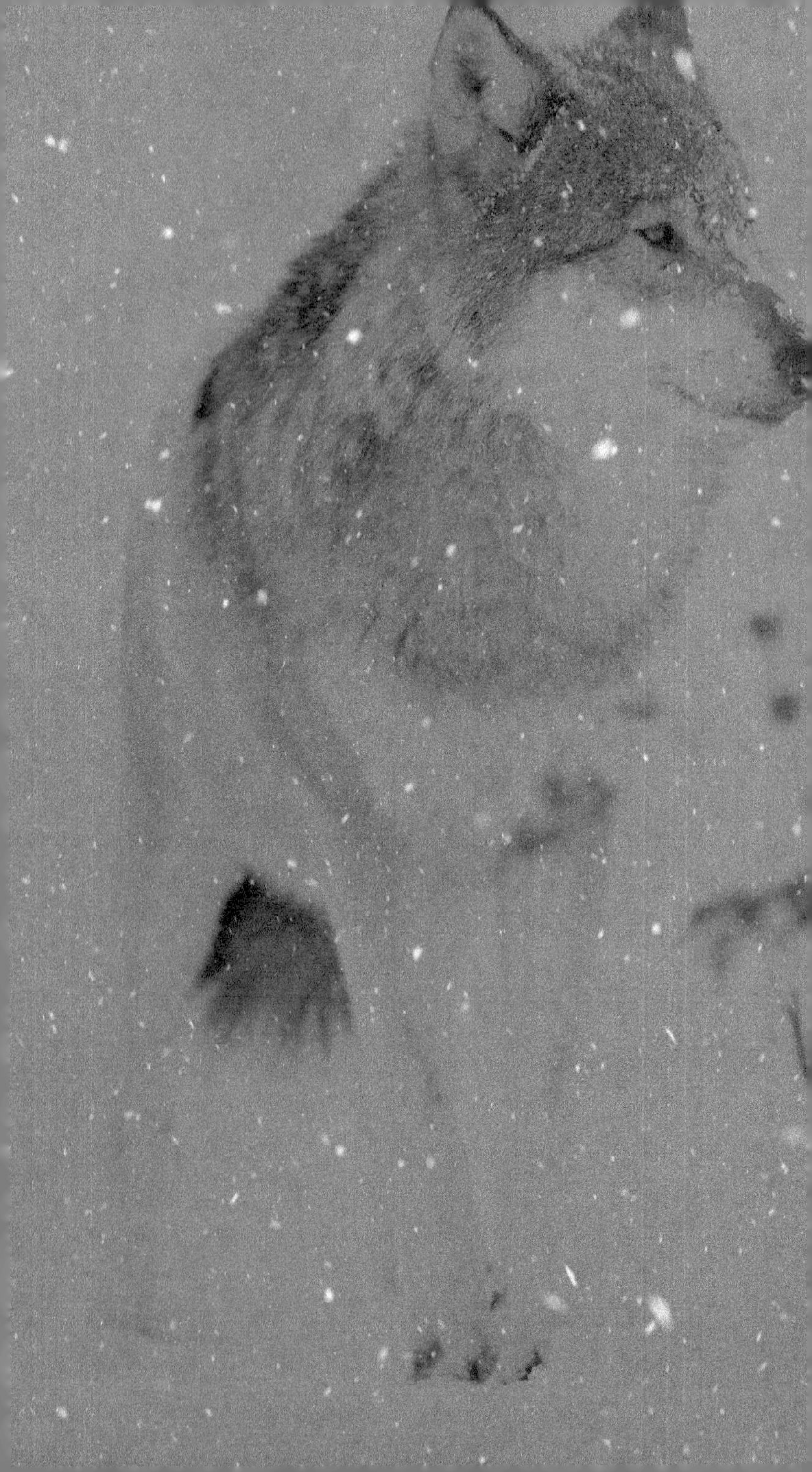

Playlist

Dancing After Death - Matt Mason
Dark Blue - Jack's Mannequin
The Bolter - Taylor Swift
Winter Song - Leslie Odom Jr. feat Cynthia Erivo
Snowman - Sia
Don't Forget About Me - CLOVES
Ghost Town - Benson Boone
Home - Catie Turner
Half Life - Livingston
Kiss Me - Jason Walker
Circles - Post Malone
Ice Cream - BLACKPINK with Selena Gomez
Something to Remember - Matt Hansen
Afterlife - Hailee Steinfeld

Glossary
OF BALLET TERMS

Adagio: Slow movements performed with fluid grace.

Arabesque: A position where a dancer supports themselves on one leg with the other straight behind it, raised up to 90 degrees.

Bourée: Quick movements of the feet that can be performed on pointe or on demi-pointe and are meant to make the dancer look as if they are floating across the floor.

Corps: short for corps de ballet, the members of a ballet company who dance together as a group. The lowest ranking members of the company.

Grand jeté: A long horizontal jump, starting from one leg and landing on the other, creating a split in the air.

Pas de deux: "Step of two"—a duet, traditionally performed by a female and a male dancer.

Piqués: traveling turns executed by one leg stepping out to become the supporting leg as the other is lifted to where the toe sits behind the knee.

Pirouette: A non-traveling turn on one leg, of one or more rotations.

Plié: A smooth and continuous bending of the knees outward with the upper body held upright.

Port de bras: "Carriage of the arms"—a controlled movement of the arms as they move through set positions.

Principal: A dancer at the highest rank within a professional dance company.

Relevé: Rising onto the balls or toes of one or both feet.

Révérence: A bow, curtsy, or grand gesture of respect to acknowledge the teacher and the pianist after class or the audience and orchestra after a performance.

Soloist: a dancer in a ballet company above the corps de ballet but below principal dancer who perform the majority of the solo and minor roles in a ballet.

Tendu: Extending the working leg until it is pointed, to the front, side, or back, where only the toes are touching the floor.

Variation: A dance typically done solo.

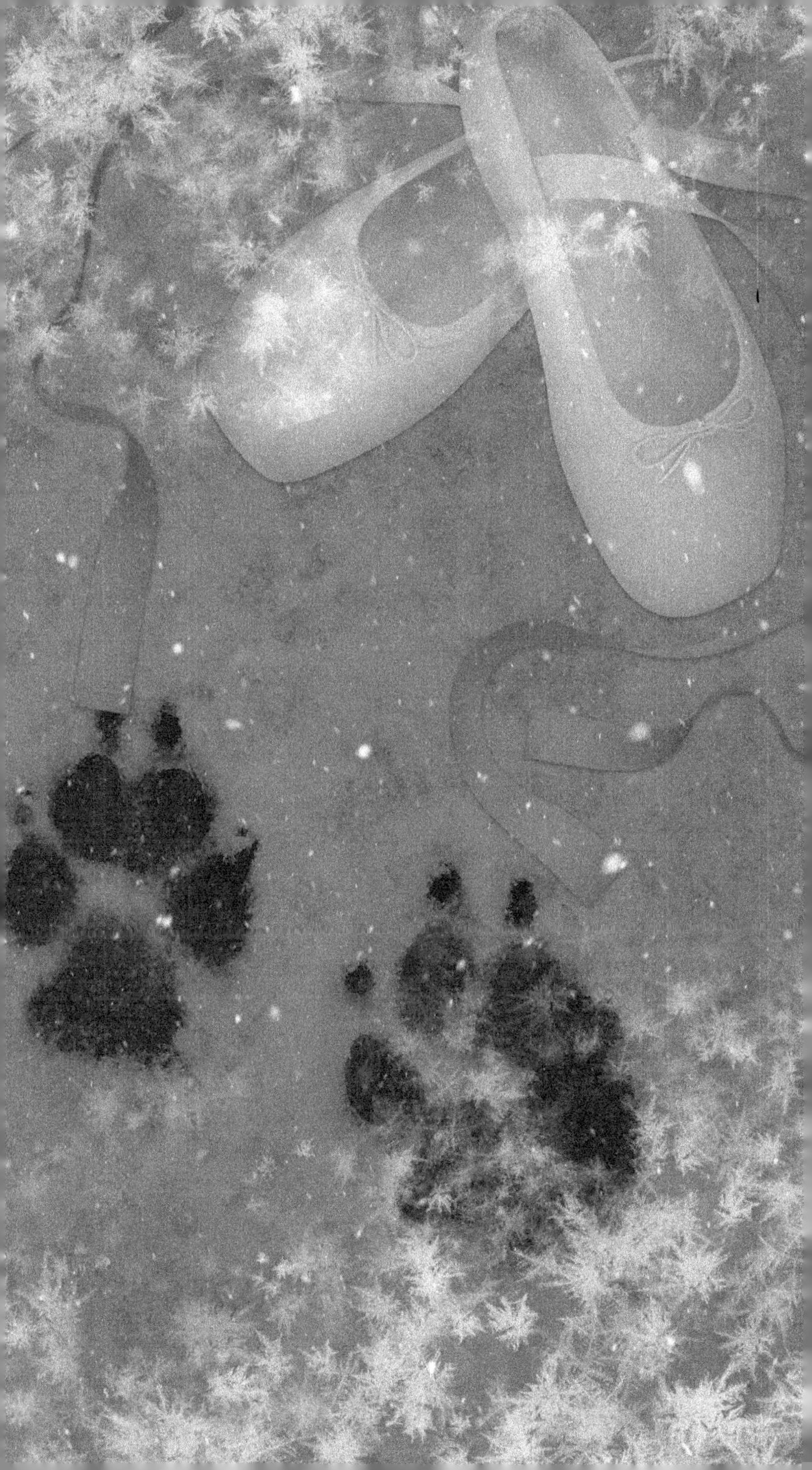

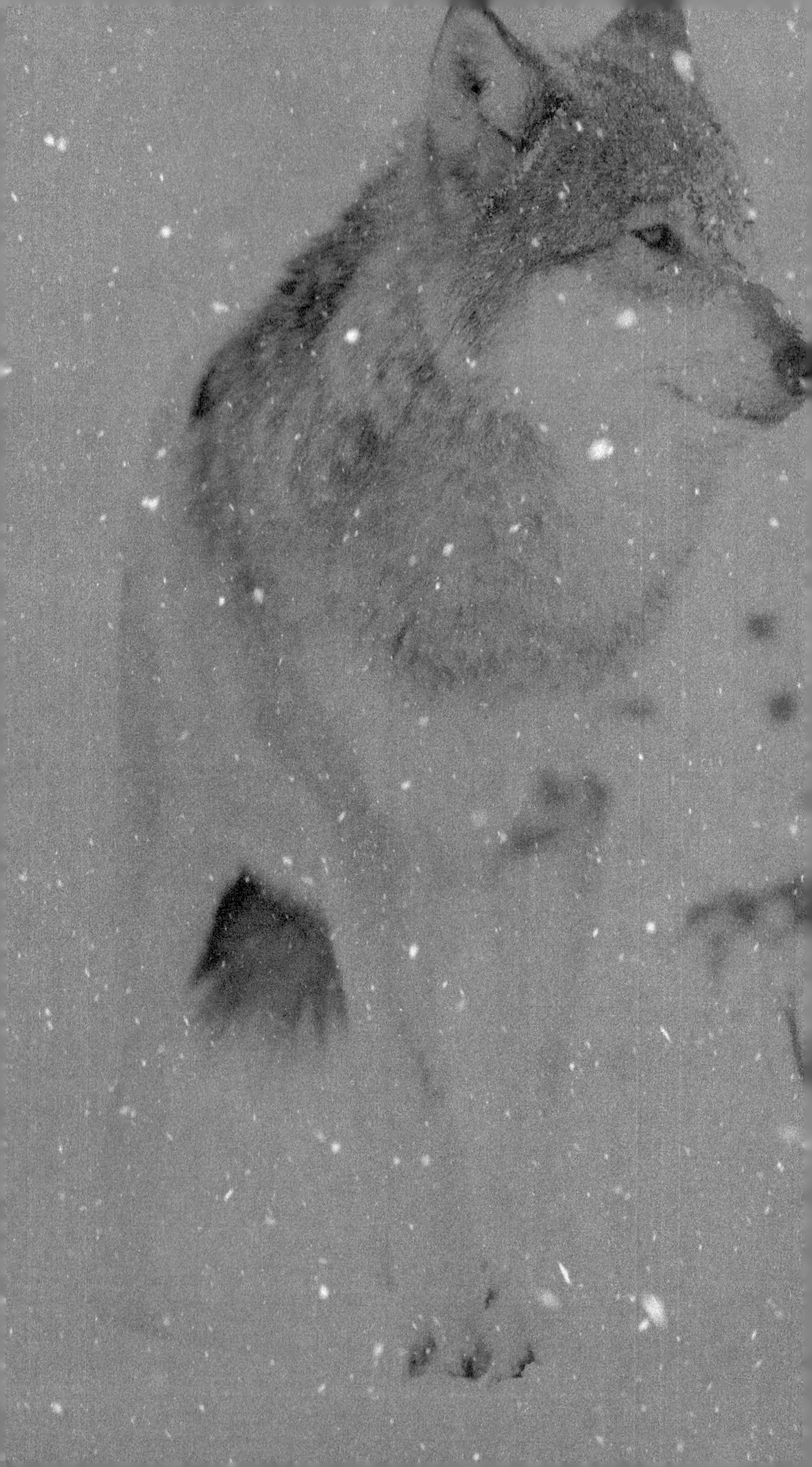

How the HARBINGERS' SEASONAL CYCLE WORKS:

For all the times you felt invisible or wasted energy wishing the wrong people would take notice.

I'm here.

... And I see you.

The crescent scar glints down at the boy. Faint but familiar.

It's the mark his little brother got when the neighbor's dog became territorial over a stuffed swan. A rascally bulldog. It had snatched the toy out of his small hand in haste, red dripping onto the frost-tipped grass.

Grabbing his brother around the waist, the boy picked him up and rushed home. They were both in tears, certain their parents would scold them. Instead, their mother pulled them in for a hug while their dad got mugs from the cupboard. They spent the rest of the night watching the snow fall outside and drinking hot cocoa while their mother tended to his younger brother.

Years later, the tiny, pale scar remains. A memory carved into his brother's palm. It stares back at the boy now, outstretched and tense. Grasping.

Reaching.

Cracks fissure the ice in hundreds of fragments. Some float along the rippling surface, others obscure the sliver of light pouring between frozen shards.

The air rips from his lungs. His limbs no longer flail. He's forever reaching for his little brother, sinking farther from the last drops of sunlight.

The hand grasps frantically. More join it. But it's no use.

They're too late.

Darkness curls around the boy's body in a final embrace. Skating through his veins, the cold seeps into his bones, settling in his marrow. Its chill is unforgiving. Unyielding. There is no fighting this. He gives in and surrenders to its pull.

Fate.

She's there in an instant. Getting to him is no issue. The frigid water, the scald of magma, the scrape of sand... Such things do not disrupt Fate.

She stares at the unmoving boy, his wild, straw-colored hair flowing with the current. He's another beautiful tragedy, lost to this world much too soon. But there is more for him. The stone she clutches says as much, and yet she hesitates, understanding the costs all too well. There's no other way, though. With her palm pressed to his chest, she plants a gentle kiss on his temple and her magic sinks into his skin.

Then she waits.

And waits.

Hours later, glittering irises peer up at her. The silver brows framing them are etched in confusion. "Wh-where am I?"

Combing through the disheveled blue and white strands of the boy's hair with her fingers, she gives him a gentle smile. The others are already gathered, whispering as the eldest pair skate forward. The boy eyes them warily, not that it discourages the couple. They are used to this by now.

Fate helps him to his feet.

"Everything's going to be okay," she reassures the boy. His hand quivers in hers, but he doesn't release it, clutching her tighter. Lowering her lips to his ear, she whispers softly, waving her hand toward the sea of shimmering strangers.

"Welcome home, Jax Frost."

January
OCTO
MO TU WE TH
3
10
17 18
24 25
31
2 3 4 5 6
9 10 11 12 13 14
16 17 18 19 20 21
23 24 25 26 27 28 29
30 31

Chapter One

JOLIE

I huff up the metro stairs and out onto the frigid city streets, puffs of white filling the air. The cold whips at my cheeks and bites my nose with each step, but I don't dare slow my pace. It's so early that black blankets the sky aside from a handful of stars peeking out.

It's got to be close.

My gaze drops down to my phone, and I swipe to the map to make sure I'm heading the right way. A few blocks in the wrong direction around here can make the streets shift from luxurious to dangerous—not something I want to worry about before DC traffic picks up. There aren't many folks out, but I wanted to give myself extra time to navigate a good route this morning.

My legs are nearly numb under my leggings, though the chill doesn't stifle the pain streaking down the back of my thigh. At least if I arrive early, once I find the darn studio, I can warm up and collect myself. The last thing I want on my first day is to show up red faced and stiff from the cold. I'm sure they're already theorizing why the famed District Dance Institute didn't bring me back after my allotted sabbatical. And since they'll be quietly sizing me up as if I have a scarlet letter pinned to my leotard, I don't need to draw any additional attention to myself before class even starts.

If that isn't enough fodder for their gossip, the deep scars along my shoulder and back will no doubt catch their notice once the warm-up layers come off. Eleven months have passed and even I still find it hard to ignore them when I see myself in the mirror.

The alarming swoop of my guts. The screech of tires. The crackling of ice before it splinters—

I shake my head.

Save it for the therapist, Jolie. Not right now.

I need to be on my game. Make the best first impression. Today will set the tone for the rest of the season—and potentially my career.

I push open the door and pass the posters decorating the walls with beautifully poised ballerinas, all principals at Ballet Potomac. There are some I recognize, a handful I don't. We had similar pictures posted up at the Institute—a lot more of them, in fact, from decades of being the premiere company in the nation's capital. I used to peer up at them each morning while I ran to class as a reminder of my goal.

Now, they just remind me of how far I've fallen.

My stomach ties itself in knots, screaming for me to turn around and run out the door. Maybe coming back to this makes me a masochist, but I refuse to give up on my dream.

You can do this.

The receptionist—a pale woman with a thick, red perm and false lashes—keeps her attention on the computer screen as I approach the desk.

"Hi, I'm Jolie Wilder," I say, mustering my most friendly smile. A smile that says I'm approachable even though I know you've all been judging me since before I stepped through the door.

She nods but doesn't lift her gaze. I glance behind me to see if I can figure out which room I'm supposed to go into, but the few dancers who've arrived this early trickle into different studios.

Guess I need to tweak my definition of *early* if I want to be one of the first ones here.

My fingers tap nervously against the counter until the receptionist finally looks up.

"Ah, yes. The director told us you'd be coming today, Miss Wilder. Studio B." She points to the door at the farthest end of the hallway, denoted by the big, bold *B* painted on it. A poster for this year's Ballet World Summit is plastered below it. Every year the ballet festival takes place in a different part of the world, showcasing various companies by invitation only. Too bad if Ballet Potomac gets an invitation, I won't be making the cut. That's a soloist and principal opportunity. And honestly, as a lesser-known company, the likelihood of them being invited is fairly slim for an international event as big as the Ballet World Summit.

"Thanks," I say to her, not taking my gaze off the picture of dancers leaping against Sydney's stunning backdrop.

"Welcome." Her tone is clipped, attention already back to the computer.

It isn't exactly the greeting I'd imagined. She didn't even give me her name, though the golden nameplate across the desk says Ms. McCormick.

Guess that's it, then.

I turn back toward the lobby. Normally someone shows you the ropes on your first day. But today isn't technically my first day, is it?

I follow blonde and brunette buns down the hall,

passing another room of dancers chatting with each other. Their voices drop once they notice me, and for the first time that I can remember in my dance career, I wish I was invisible.

Scurrying toward studio B's open door, I peel off my jacket and layers, hanging them on the hooks outside the room before I enter. My gaze darts to the clock, and I suck in a breath. Not as early as I'd planned, but I still have time to get on my shoes and warm up before the ballet mistress arrives.

A few of the other dancers look up from either stretching or chatting among themselves, shooting me curious glances before returning to their pre-practice activities. No one makes a move to introduce themselves. If anything, they seem to retreat further among their fellow company members. This room holds close to twenty other people, and they're all huddled in little clusters, leaving me starkly alone and standing out.

Exactly what I don't want.

I grew up dancing with some of these girls, but then we headed off in different directions, some going to college before auditioning for companies, and others, not wanting to waste those precious years at school, looked for work right away. I'd left Virginia to study at NYU's Tisch School of the Arts before coming back to the area to be closer to my mom. After working my way up the rungs of the District Dance Institute, I thought I'd dance with them until I retired. Maybe teach. Now those plans were gone and here I was, back at square one.

Luckily, one of Ballet Potomac's benefactors is the spouse of one of my former instructors, and they were nice enough to put in a word with the director. While I've been demoted back to the corps, the ballet company's ensemble, at least I have the opportunity to dance again.

Dragging my bag over to me, I unzip it, grabbing out my pointe shoes and setting my pads in place. They've barely been touched in months and the boxes are chilly and stiff.

I take my time tying up the ribbons, flexing and pointing my feet to ensure they aren't too tight or too loose. This used to be second nature, like putting on a second skin. Now my fingers are clumsy, fumbling over the ribbons.

Once I finish lacing my shoes, I stand, adjusting my warm-ups over my leotard. I leave my shrug on, checking the other dancers to see if they still have on their layers. Most do and I exhale for what feels like the first time since I walked through Ballet Potomac's doors.

At least they won't have to see my scars yet.

I spent more time than I should've concealing them with makeup this morning, uncertain if they had rules about leaving on layers for class. It's not like they're a secret, though. If I had to guess from the way the other dancers are scrutinizing me, some of them already know what happened. The accident was in the papers, after all.

Plus, in a world as small as ours, there's always gossip.

The other company members have already managed to space themselves out along the edges of the studio with five in the center on a metal barre. I scan along the barres for an empty space. Silently, a petite blonde with a cream-colored leotard and a blue boat neck sweater waves me over, stepping back to make room for me next to her.

"Thank you," I whisper and shuffle to snatch the open spot. "I'm Jolie."

"Evelyn. I recognized you from ABT's summer intensive." She had looked familiar, but I couldn't place from where. She turns toward the barre, putting her leg up on the top one and shifting her hips back to stretch her hamstring. "Welcome to Ballet Potomac."

Before I can thank her for making me feel less other on my first day, the door clicks and the room hushes. Mistress Maral, whom I recognize from the company's website, enters. Tall and slender with chestnut hair tucked into a perfect twist pinned at the back of her head, she wears a loose, wine-colored sweater over a black ballet skirt with leggings and appears to be in her mid-forties. After retiring as a principal with the Joffrey, she'd moved with her husband to instruct at the newly opened Ballet Potomac.

Everyone remains silent, but instead of addressing the class, she turns away from us, setting up the sound system.

"First position," she begins, marking through the plié combination. We all adjust into place at the barre and follow along in time with her. The movements flow smoothly from everyone. Everyone except me. This must be some pre-choreographed barre they're accustomed to and I'm expected to keep up. When we get to tendus and I'm struggling to memorize the combination, Mistress Maral lets out a sigh, seemingly annoyed that I'm holding up the class by forcing her to actually instruct. When my eyes meet Evelyn's, she gives an apologetic grimace.

Alright, Jolie. Time to sink or swim.

As soon as the music comes on, and the other company members hit each brush and stroke of their foot in time to the beat, it's clear I'm firmly in the sinking category.

Sinking. Sinking. Sinking—

My throat dries and I can't seem to suck in air as memories threaten to drag me down.

Focus, Jolie!

I grip the barre tightly to center myself in the present. I can't afford to be distracted. This opportunity is my only life raft. One I'm desperately clinging to. If I want to keep my place in the corps and be promoted back to soloist, I need to be flawless. There are dancers poised at these barres vying for the same spots. Ballerinas who've spent years working their way up here, just like I had done at the Institute. They don't want their promotions going to a newcomer, no matter how illustrious my previous company was.

With a flick of the ballet mistress's finger, the intro to the instrumental comes on, and I follow along, grateful it's slow and there are bodies moving seamlessly through the combination around me. Mimicking the other dancers out of my peripheral, I brace my core. My knees bend into my grand plié, and I grit my teeth into a frozen smile to conceal the pain slicing up my left thigh as I come back up from the floor. Mistress Maral eyes me with hawk-like scrutiny.

They may know about the accident and that I wasn't asked back to the Institute, but they don't need to know about this. Never about this. Not even this injury can hold me back from making the most of this second chance at my ballet career.

Pressing up onto the balls of my feet into my highest relevé, I find my balance and then glance at the mirror, checking my alignment as I release the barre. My shrug accentuates the curved line of my arms floating through the port de bras. I follow my fingers with my focus—

A flash of movement from outside the window snags my attention.

Two prismatic eyes watch me intently.

A silver-and-white wolf peers over some park bushes across the street. The more I look, the less I believe it's a wolf. It couldn't be, could it? Must be a large dog. A very, very large dog. Maybe some sort of husky mix? Whatever it is, its intense stare pinches between my ribs. Wobbling, I nearly lose my balance, recovering at the same time Mistress Maral exhales a disgruntled huff.

Shit on a snowflake.

Flashing an apologetic smile, I blink away the distraction. When the music ends and we move into the next combination, I sneak a glance at the window, only to find swirls of delicate frost creeping along its edge.

The beast is nowhere in sight.

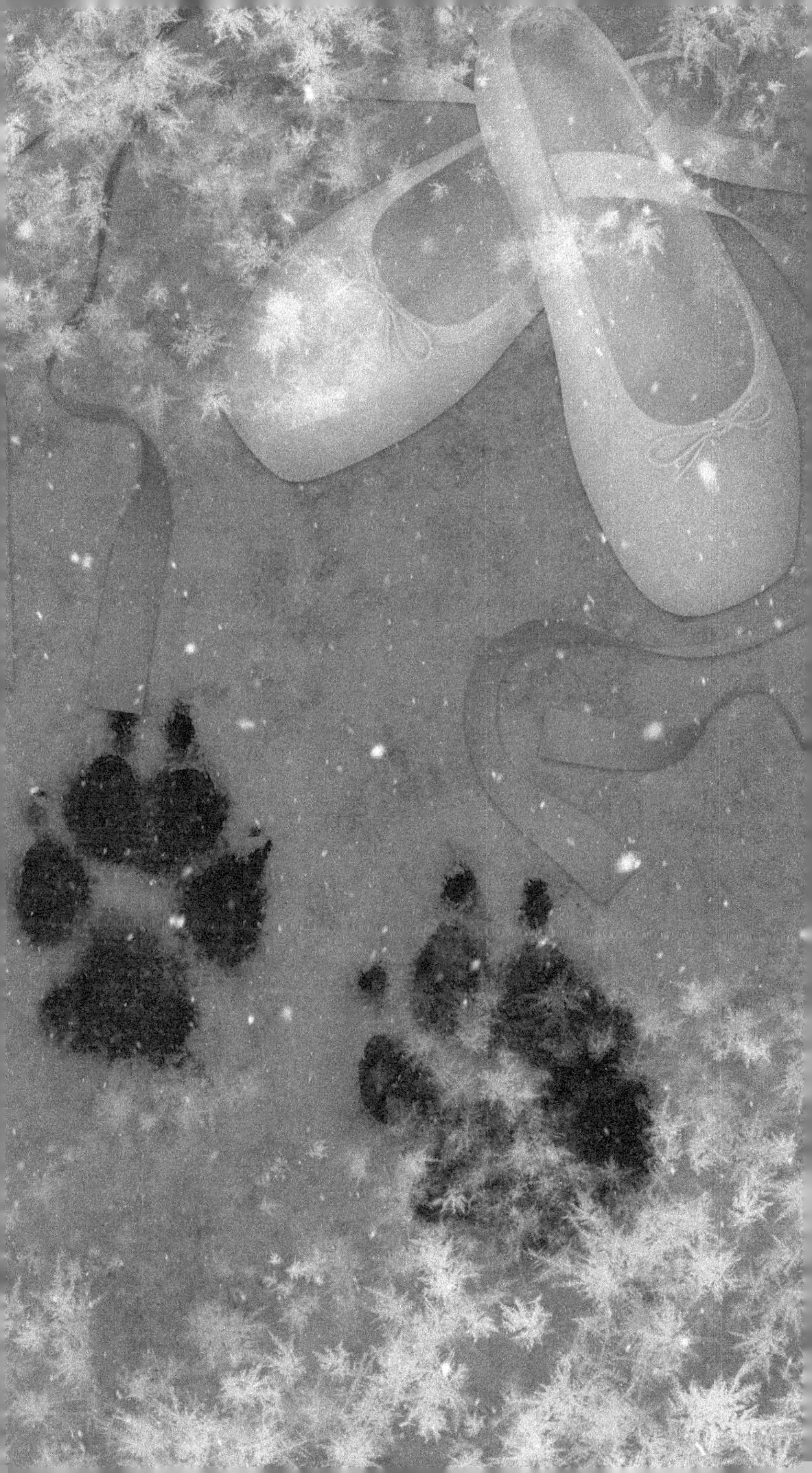

Chapter Two
JAX

Thump-thump.
Thump-thump.

I watch her dance as the pulse between my ribs kicks up, beating beneath a tuft of silver fur. The one covering my mark.

My fellow Frosts, immortal harbingers that bring winter to the world, had always said how much it hurt when Fate etched it into our skin. But the moment I awoke from my hibernation, it was already there, seared into my sternum.

It was odd. Even in hibernation, there were periods where we were somewhat lucid. I would have thought I'd have felt it happen. But there was no pain.

Once I'd reached adulthood among the Frosts, my fathers had sat me down and explained that one day Fate would bring me an immortal mate. As two of our Lead Albiduses, it's their responsibility to ensure all Frosts in their care understood everything about harbingers. According to them, first would come the mark. Then we'd be able to find them with just a touch.

Mates were treasured among my kind. Some immortals went centuries without one, only to suddenly feel the mate mark carved into their flesh. I'd inspected myself weekly for years, combing over every silvery mark marring my body. Waiting. Hoping there was someone out there who was mine.

The day I awoke to my mark, I touched the silvery swirl and closed my eyes, and my nerves jolted through my fingertips as I was transported. When I looked around, though, I was no longer beyond the veil that shielded Nivea from the mortal realm. I thought, perhaps, that they were a fellow Frost who'd headed out early to their harbinger assignment. I scanned the tree line...

Thump-thump.

Thump-thump.

Thump-thump.

My mate was nearby.

Could it be one of the Frosts I'd grown up alongside? Maybe even someone I'd been with before, enjoying each other's company until we were lucky enough for Fate to bless us.

Just as I was about to descend to shift to chase them down, a pair of blue eyes startled me from the other side of a windowpane. It was her.

My mate.

She had long, brown hair, pale-pink lips, and was staring right at me. My chest and chin lifted as I beamed at her through the glass. I'd imagined this moment a hundred different ways over a hundred different seasons, and here we were.

"Hello." I waved at her, trying to tamp down my excitement so I didn't look like an idiot.

I held my breath, waiting a few moments while she continued to stare. But then, instead of waving back or saying anything in response, she turned away from the window.

My brows furrowed.

Thump-thump.

Thump-thump.

I swept in through the window quietly, a few stray whorls of white marking the glass. She didn't notice any of that. She didn't notice me. The room began to spin. I clutched my chest and zipped backward, flying out the window as I stared at her, brows furrowed, hands shaking at my sides, flecks of snow flurrying from my palms. Realization began to sink in, but I didn't want to believe it.

She couldn't see me because my mate, the one I'd waited my lifetime for, destined to be mine, was *mortal*.

The pain of that moment still haunts me, even now, but it doesn't stop me from coming here whenever I can.

I have to leave soon, refreeze the partially melted rooftop icicles so it looks like I've done my job before the others notice I'd wandered off. This has been the steady rotation for over a month, and I still don't understand how I ended up with a mortal mate. It's not supposed to be possible.

No one seems to have any answers for me. Part of me wonders if letting me out this season was to stop me from asking more questions. Anytime I've tried, I've been met with a clipped response, sent off to do another task, or reminded how I am so close to earning enough frost marks to become a Lead Albidus like my fathers.

They took me in as a young Frost, raising me as their own alongside other new Frosts until we were ready to be on our own and serve the mortal world. That's a large part of what being a Lead Albidus is, helping immortals adjust to their afterlife existence. I want to pay forward what their guidance and kindness did for me. Training the next generation of Frosts, it's everything I've been working toward.

Of course, I've been a little distracted, but so far I've been good, not missing a chilly mist or leaving a snowflake out of place.

While there aren't many rules when it comes to being a harbinger, there is one very important creed we must follow: Never interfere with the affairs of mortals.

It doesn't stop me from envisioning what it would be like to be seen by her. To know her.

Whatever I do, though, I can't risk banishment from the mortal world. Not when that would cut me off from her. Not when she's finally within reach.

There's just one problem...

She doesn't believe I exist.

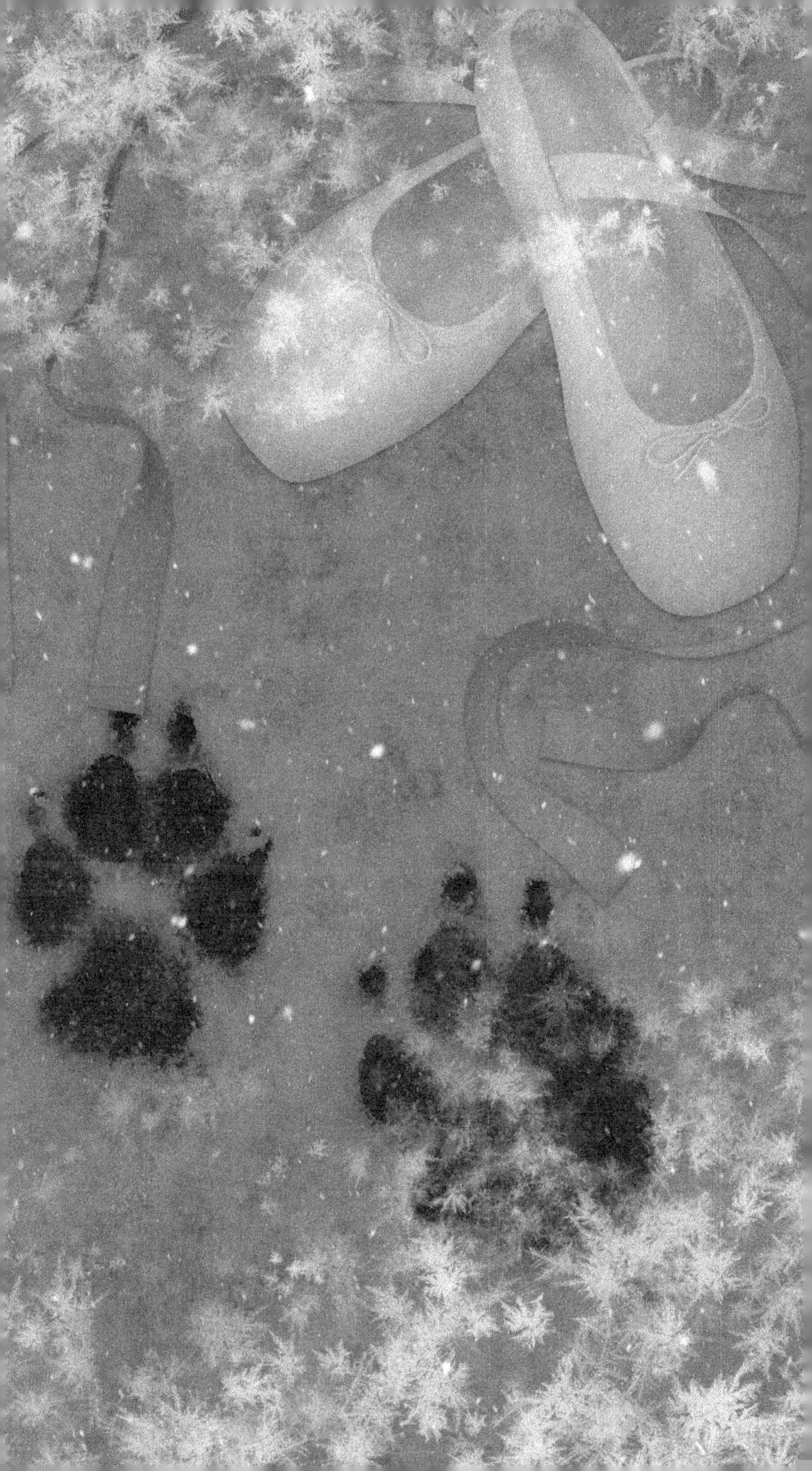

Chapter Three

JOLIE

I'm exhausted.

By the time the day is over, pain streaks steadily down the back of my leg. My feet sting, blistered and bleeding, scraping against my wool socks as I trudge through the snow. The only benefit of the white stuff flurrying around me and heaped on the ground is that soon my toes will be numb. That'll spare me some agony until I can get to my pain relievers and soaking tub.

After an uneventful metro haul and three blocks of walking, I reach our corner apartment building. There's an eerie heaviness to the air. The whole trek home I scanned my surroundings for some sign of that strange mutant beast, unable to shake the feeling of eyes on me.

My thighs ache with each climb up the stairs toward our fourth-floor apartment. *Stupid, broken elevator.* A thin sheen of ice coats the railing, so I shove my hands into my coat pockets, cursing myself for forgetting gloves. Hopefully I don't slip. Last thing I need at this point is another career-hindering setback.

Eleven months was much too long of a break for my body. I'll be feeling today's classes for a while. While I shouldn't have skipped out on the recovery room, I was nervous about being all too visible to the other company members. Better to give them some proper time to gossip about me behind my back. Besides, I can squeeze some stretching in after a nice warm shower.

Just the thought of the scalding droplets fills me with renewed purpose, and I pick up the pace, ascending the final flight of stairs.

Fumbling through the front zipper of my dance bag, I find my key and slide it into the hole, pressing my whole body against the door. It won't open otherwise. I jimmy it, growling at the cold nipping at me. When the knob finally clicks, I twist it open, sighing. The relief is short-lived, though. My body sears, every appendage burning when I enter the apartment, adjusting to the swift temperature change from the icy chill outside.

A clatter comes from the kitchen, and I round the corner, spotting Lark throwing ingredients into a stock pot. Her girlfriend, Delilah, curls around her, helping her stir as she leans down and whispers in her ear. Lark's deep tan cheeks pinken.

I'd puke if they weren't so freakin' adorable.

"Jojo! I was hoping you'd be home in time for dinner. It's sweet potato bisque." Lark lifts the ladle out of the pot, thick, creamy orange dripping down and splashing back into it. "Delilah even brought some of her mom's incredible sourdough to go with it."

"Sounds amazing. Thanks. I'll grab a bowl after I get changed and shower real quick." My mouth waters at the savory aroma filling the room and my stomach gurgles. Thank goodness for a roommate that cooks. Peeling off my coat, I hang it in the closet and kick off my boots with a hiss.

I forgot how annoying it is to build up calluses and the necessary blistering part of the process.

"Sure thing," she says, returning to her stirring.

As soon as I shuffle to my room and shut the door, I pull my sweater off and toss it into the hamper, followed by my warm-ups, leotard, and tights. My fingertip traces the faint silver scar between my ribs. It glints under the dim light, feathering out in a whorl.

It's the only one I have that I consider beautiful.

I hurry into the bathroom, turning the knob to the hottest it will go without burning me, and let the water run. Steam billows over the shower's sliding doors until fog paints the glass.

Tap, tap, tap, tap, tap.

I barely hear the sound over the running water. I grab my towel and wrap it around myself, but when I open the door a crack, no one is there, just the sound of Lark and Delilah's laughter filtering down the hallway.

Tap, tap, tap.

A shiver skates along my collarbone, and I whip my attention toward the sound. A branch knocks into the window. There are tiny flecks of white scattered across my desk and a thin layer of snow draped over Snip, my pale-green succulent. I don't remember opening the window today, but small lapses in my memory aren't as unusual as they used to be. I've been a bit distracted trying to get my life back together.

The breeze lashes at me, sending goosebumps skittering along my skin. I cross my arms, rubbing up and down for warmth, then latch the window shut, ignoring the frost spinning at the edges of the frame.

Ping!

My cell lights up from within my open dance bag, and I

grab it, checking the message and time before tossing it onto the bed.

THE PRINCE:

Be there in one hour.

One hour. Plenty of time to warm up in the shower, stretch, enjoy dinner, and hang with Lark and Delilah. Prancing into the bathroom, I shut the door behind me. With each inhalation of the thick steam, my lungs clear and my body relaxes. Hot water pelts down in a forceful stream. It's a sting I welcome.

The throbbing along the back of my leg eases, and I place the ball of my foot onto the base of the shower seat, leaning forward to stretch my calves one at a time. I need to be ready for tomorrow, both physically and mentally, especially since they'll be announcing the upcoming ballet.

Usually the announcement of the next show is something I look forward to. Not this time, though. My thoughts pirouette over the fact that, at twenty-eight years old, there will be no soloist role for me. Not that there's anything wrong with the corps. They're an integral part of the ballet in their own right. It just sucks when I've spent years paying my dues already. If I hadn't been so close to promoting to principal, this wouldn't hurt as much. I don't even know if I'll get the opportunity to be promoted again.

While I'm grateful for this second chance at my dream, there's a little voice in my head that nags at me. How long will my injury allow me to continue to do what I love? The idea of not dancing again, not experiencing the warmth of the lights beaming down on the stage, the thrill of the curtain pulling back to an audience swathed in darkness, there to watch me share my craft...

I lean back against the cold tile, trying to catch a full breath that seems just out of reach.

Stop it, Jolie.

I won't let those thoughts linger.

When Blake shows up, I can't be in a sour mood. It's been two weeks since I last saw him, and I can finally give him a dance-related update after months of it being a one-sided conversation while I tried to hold back the disappointment of no longer working for the Institute with him.

I get out of the shower, dry off, and apply my scar gel before I dress quickly, throwing on bandages and a pair of thick, fuzzy socks to warm my battered toes. While I do some final stretches for the night, I grab my journal and dump all the negative thoughts that have managed to creep in today. At the end, I make sure to jot down three wins. Anything I'm grateful for. It's the one thing Dr. Tanner requires of me when I do this—to always finish with three positives.

1. Survived day one.
2. I'm still moving.
3. Blake's coming over.

Throwing the journal into the top drawer of my desk, I head out into the living room. Lark and Delilah are already sitting on the couch, watching a rerun of *Gilmore Girls*. I grab the bowl they've set out for me on the countertop, along with a plate piled with two thick sourdough slices, inhaling the thin slip of steam wafting the air with sweet potato, ginger, and other spices.

They drape part of the plaid blanket over my legs when I sit down next to them, and we watch an episode we've seen at least ten times in the last four years of living together. I'm firmly in camp *Rory should have picked Jess*, and Lark is team Logan, so we sit and debate as usual. It's the first time my mind is silent today and I savor it. I'm here in the moment, not living in the loop of a memory I'd rather forget. A loneliness I find myself tucked away in all too often.

Knock, knock.

Lark's brown eyes snap to the door and then to me. "Tell me you didn't, Jojo."

My cheeks flush with heat, but I ignore her glare as I head for the door. When I open it, Blake stands there with his elbow resting against the frame, a brilliant smile pulled across his lips. Rich brown eyes stare down at me, warming my insides. He smooths back one wayward blond strand into his perfectly coiffed hair.

"Missed you, beautiful."

Lark mutters something unintelligible before the word *fuckboy* from behind me.

"Come on in," I say, cutting her a quick glare of my own. She might not like him, but they are colleagues. It's the only thing stopping her from speaking her mind in front of him. I cock my head at her, and she clamps her mouth shut. Avoiding Lark's stabby stare and Delilah's half-apologetic grimace, I take Blake's hand and lead him down the hallway.

Lark's lecture will no doubt come with a side of coffee in the morning. At least caffeine's involved.

Once we get inside my room and I've shut the door, Blake drops his jacket, scarf, and gloves onto the chair at my desk before striding over. Just as he's about to touch me, he quivers dramatically. "Brr. Do you always keep it so cold in here?"

He walks over to the thermostat which, admittedly, is a few degrees lower than what I usually set it at.

"That's odd. You can turn it up a bit."

"We can keep each other warm in the meantime," he says with a waggle of his brows. Blake taps the screen a few times before coming back over and trailing his fingers along my shoulder. My skin flushes beneath his touch. "Rehearsals aren't the same without you."

"Really?" I ask, trying to downplay how much that means to me, though my voice cracks. I swallow my nerves, hoping to sound charming instead. Casually unaffected. "I heard you got Prince Siegfried."

"I did." His smile widens, chest puffing up a bit.

These last two seasons, without fail, Blake's been cast in some princely role or another. Always leading-man material. And he's here, with me. I might not be the star of the ballet, but I'm the one he seeks out. When we dance, our bodies moving together, it's almost hypnotic. His hands on my body, powerful arms lifting me into the air, the chemistry we exude when partnering is mesmerizing. We never got the chance to do it officially, only after hours when we'd both stay late to rehearse.

"Wish you would have told me instead of me hearing from Lark." Fingers finding his, I look up at him. "You know you can still talk to me about the Institute."

"I know, baby," he says. "It honestly has been just such a whirlwind between coming off Don Quixote and then heading back into auditions, rehearsals, and conditioning. You know how it goes."

I *do*. That's what stings so much.

"It's amazing. I'm so proud of you." I sweep the edges of my lips up into my best smile, trying not to think about the crappy first day I had and what might await me tomorrow.

"Wish you were there, of course." One hand wraps around my waist. The other lingers on the band of my sweats. There's no reason to dress up when he comes over. Most of the time we've spent together has been at the Institute or right after rehearsals. Even while I was on sabbatical the last eleven months, he's only seen me in sweats... or out of them.

"Of course," I agree, crossing my body to take off my baggy shirt, leaving me only in my lacy bra. I swallow the lump at the back of my throat when his stare instantly goes to the scars that begin at my shoulder and shred down my back. Not that they're easy to ignore. There are three long gashes, one deeper than the other two, and I hate that I feel ashamed of them. That my instinct is to turn away from his gaze.

His brown eyes dip to the small peaks of my breasts, and the smirk he gives me has my belly doing backflips. My nerves float away, replaced with want, when he grips my waistband and peels my sweats down to my ankles. He kneels, as gracefully as he does on stage, with his attention pinned to me. I step out of my pants but leave on my fuzzy socks. Ballet blisters do not mix well with foreplay.

He gives a knowing chuckle but doesn't say anything about it. "I can't stay the night—"

"Rehearsals," I say at the same time he does. "That's fine."

It's always disappointing that he doesn't stay, but I get it. For both of us, our dance careers are the priority, and right now, we're getting into our new rehearsal routines. I can't fault him for that.

"Yeah, schedule is killer. I'm just glad I could squeeze in a visit. You have no idea how bad I've needed this." He stands and tosses his shirt to the side. Every ridge and trimmed muscle is on full display. Blake's body is beautiful and strong, and he knows it. Unzipping his jeans, he pulls them and his briefs off in one swoop before climbing with cat-like grace onto the bed. One hand gripping his erection, he tugs it from the base while I remove my bra and panties and join him on top of the comforter.

"Baby, look how hard you make me." My skin flushes under the compliment. He clutches himself and gives a few more rough strokes. Leaning over to my nightstand, he opens it to grab a condom without even turning his attention from me. Ripping the foil packet, he puts it on with a devilish smirk on his face. "Come here."

I gasp as he drags me to straddle his lap before bringing his palms to my breasts. My nipples pebble beneath his touch. Then his hands slip to my waist, guiding me onto his dick with a satisfied grunt. We've clearly gotten this choreography down pat.

"So good," he hisses out.

I preen at his attention. Blake's a principal dancer of one of the best ballet companies in the world and I am the one he's with. When he looks at me, I'm not just some girl in the corps—not the baby's breath meant to surround the roses. I'm the rose.

He holds on to me, head dropping back with each rise and fall of my body bringing him closer to the precipice. My leg aches, my hip straining in this position. I slow my movements, and Blake's attention snaps to me.

"Sorry. I'm a bit sore from class today." The last thing I want to do is mention my injury, so I try a different tactic. "Can we...switch?"

His chest heaves, and he gives my waist a little squeeze. "I'm so close. Don't stop."

I nod, splaying my hands across his pecs to support me. I'm stronger than the pain anyway. Both in dance and in here. All the screwups of class today drift away, replaced by this moment. The hurried eagerness of him responding to my body, his breathy pants, having him come undone from what *I* do to him.

"God, you're so fucking amazing, baby. So fucking amazing. I'm c—" His neck strains, veins bulging as he grits out a pleasured groan.

Hip twinging in pain, I take a moment to catch my breath before I climb off of him.

"That was perfect," he says, and moves to discard the used condom. Releasing a lazy sigh, he relaxes back onto the comforter, hands coming to his forehead. He smiles up at the ceiling, then his attention finds me again. "Was it good for you?"

I bite my lip as I hunt through the rumpled covers for my underwear.

"Of course." It's not a lie exactly. I always enjoy our times together, but I never come. Ever. Not with the few guys I've been with. Part of me wonders if I'm just not wired for it. Some women aren't. Every time I start to feel something, I always seem to lose the sensation. But that isn't a big deal. Blake and I share a passion much more intimate than sex. *Dance.* It brought us together one steamy night post-rehearsal three years ago, and we've been doing this bedroom pas de deux ever since.

Unfortunately, it's frowned upon to date within the company, so we kept our relationship under wraps, not wanting it to impact our respective roles or upcoming promotions. Even after the accident, we continued to keep it a secret since I was planning on returning to the Institute. Lark knows because she lives here. She's up for promotion to principal, and Blake has some sway with the Institute's board, so despite being annoyed by his presence, she puts up with it.

We haven't talked about it officially, but now that I'm with a different company, we can finally go public. I'd planned on asking him about it tonight, but as he returns from the bathroom, already pulling his clothes on, the question sits on the tip of my tongue. I let it linger, unanswered, and before I realize it, he's giving me a swift kiss goodnight on the cheek and heading for the door.

Chapter Four

JOLIE

The window's stuck.

Water is everywhere. It pours through the slat as I try one last attempt to roll it down. Leaning back, I slam the heel of my boot into it. The force of the water spilling in works against me, its chill pounding into my limbs. I reach behind me and shake Mom, who's slumped over the steering wheel's deflated airbag.

She doesn't move. She just stares at me.

My pulse skyrockets. If I let reality sink in, I'll stop moving. Stop fighting for breath. Soon the car will be fully submerged, taking me with it. I need to think of something. There isn't much time.

But Mom...

Agony claws at my chest.

I can't leave her. Not like this.

I pop the glove compartment, searching for something sharp to wedge open or crack the window. Items explode out from the force of the water. I grab a small window scraper and try to lever the window down. When that doesn't work, I pound on it. The strength behind my strikes wanes and I'm desperate for air. I lift my head just above the water, face squished against the ceiling, gasping.

With a final slosh, I'm submerged. Pain radiates through my chest—

Light catches my attention from outside.

Two bright eyes stare back at me, silvery with winking flecks of iridescent blues. They glitter like shattered glass, so beautiful that I can't look away.

The space between my ribs sears, pinching as an overwhelming rush of bubbles bursts against my skin.

My lungs fill with water, those eyes the last things I see before I'm swallowed by the lake's dark grasp—

I wake with a gasp, grappling with my comforter and clutching my chest, as if I can somehow physically drag the air into my lungs. Reality crashes into me.

I'm not there. I'm here. In my room.

With that comfort comes the weight that threatens to drown my waking hours.

I'm here but Mom's not.

She never will be.

I shiver and hug around myself. It's freezing, as if the temperature of my bedroom has somehow blended into the nightmare. I jump out from under the covers and turn up the thermostat before I run to my desk and grab my journal. I write down everything I can remember, scribbling quickly across the pages. Flipping through the previous entries, I check if I've learned anything new. Some clue to understand what happened. Unfortunately, most of its contents are nonsensical. Splatters of ink across a canvas I don't understand. A full picture I can't see yet.

Maybe I never will.

Regardless, I comb through the words, weighing what matches against what I can piece together. I still don't know how I survived the crash. At first, I figured I was able to smash open the window and lost consciousness as I floated to the surface. My therapist believes I'm repressing the traumatic memories of my mom's death and the accident. When they were able to finally fish the car out of the lake last spring, all evidence said the window had been smashed from the outside. From the gashes, now thick pink scars, the investigators guessed I was pulled from the wreckage.

But by whom?

The police ultimately chalked it up to some good Samaritan who wanted to remain anonymous. But the water was freezing, and they would have had to cross the ice beneath the bridge we'd skidded off of. Who would go to those lengths only to vanish?

I stare down at the colorful sketches of eyes spread through the pages. No matter how I try to draw them, I can't get the shades right. They're always too silver or too blue, and they never glitter enough. Not that they could be real…

Nevertheless, they haunt me.

I'm sure Dr. Tanner will reassure me it's a coping mechanism. That I'm looking for answers in my past instead of focusing on gratitude for my future.

I glance over at the clock. 3:55 a.m. I still have another hour of sleep I can snag before it's time to get up and prepare for the long day ahead. Climbing back into bed, I stare up at the ceiling, trying to fall asleep but unable to think about anything other than the day ahead at Ballet Potomac.

In the corps, it's important to build the visuals, stay in sync with the rest of the dancers, and keep our lines as consistent as possible. It's a different mindset for me now, purposefully trying to blend in versus adding my personal touches to stand out. I'll have to save my flair for class. It's something I miss desperately about solo work, the magic that comes from letting a variation sink into your bones. A choreographer could set the same piece on twenty different ballerinas and they would all do it slightly differently if allowed to get lost in the music.

We spend hours perfecting our craft, studying every placement of our body, and that all pays off when we get on the stage. Under the warmth of the spotlight, we come alive, moving through the piece as if it's second nature. Embedded into our soul. By the time it reaches opening night, it basically is. The beats and our bodies carry us through. Despite wanting to showcase to the hundreds of people in the audience, there's something intimate about letting go to the music. A few minutes of defying the gravity holding us back. Of freedom.

There's nothing like it.

It's what I miss most. That and having my mom out there, supporting me. My biggest fan.

Dread sinks in my gut thinking about how different this first season back is going to be.

Focus on the positives, Jolie.

I've paid my dues before. I can pay them again. Hopefully, this time around won't take as long to reach soloist. Every year is another year closer to retirement, especially with my injury. I understand how to excel in the corps with the experience I have—there's a reason why every dancer begins their journey there. I just need to use that to my advantage. Show them I can be a team player but also my value as an individual if they are willing to give me a shot.

My thoughts twirl and leap in and out of focus, each wanting to be at the forefront of my mind. At least I'll be seeing Dr. Tanner soon to talk through it. We've moved to bi-monthly appointments, and while I'm glad not to have to go weekly, I find myself itching to see her when it's a few days out.

By the time my mind slows its cadence, I glance at the clock. It's twenty minutes until my alarm is set to go off. With a groan, I head into the bathroom. I'll just get a jump-start on the day. Taking out my scar gel, I peer at the mirror from over my shoulder, applying it to the streaks of deep pink raised on my skin.

My fingers linger over the thick ridges, reminders of the accident and all the things I still don't understand about that night. I should hate them, and sometimes, when I catch them in the mirror, they make me self-conscious. But every time those feelings come, a stronger one falls into place—I'm alive.

It's a force that keeps me going, a second chance I refuse to waste.

I brush my teeth, wash my face, and put on my makeup. My blue irises pop against the dark liner winging out from my lashes. Wetting my brush, I pull my hair up and secure it with an elastic tie, then I feed my ponytail through my bun maker, tucking the dark-brown strands around the mesh before covering it with a hair net. The bobby pins scrape my scalp, my signal that they are in tight enough to not fall out during rehearsal. I spray it in place, the overly floral scent mixed with aerosol clogging my nostrils, before using a few more pins to hide my wisps.

Perfect.

When I return to my room, I cross my arms, rubbing my shoulders. My gaze darts to the window, double checking that it's fully shut so I don't come back to a repeat of yesterday's snow-covered desk.

It is.

I almost think that it's all in my head when I glance over at the thermostat. It's down a few degrees again, and I bump it up to where it should be.

Strange.

I'll have to see if Lark is having the same issue. Maybe we need to contact the super.

I dress as quickly as I can, then lean over my journal to dump a few thoughts and doodles onto the page.

"Coffee's brewed!" Lark's too-cheery-for-5:30-a.m. voice calls through the door. I sigh in relief. I need some caffeine after that night of sleep—or lack thereof. Throwing extra clothes into my dance bag, I turn off the light and beeline for the coffee pot.

"I can't believe you invited Blake over last night," Lark groans from behind her steaming cup of coffee. I pick mine up and take a sip before setting it down on the table in front of us. Lark can't stand Blake, both at the studio and outside of it. She's made it very clear she doesn't enjoy his regular visits to our apartment. "I'm just grateful to be immune to his charms. Watching everyone moon over him is gagworthy."

"I didn't invite him over. He asked to see me."

We are both busy, both building our careers, though his is leaps ahead of mine. As a man, his ballet career is set up for exponentially quicker promotions. The reality is there are not as many of them, which creates a higher demand for strong male dancers. Despite her personal dislike for him, Lark can't deny that Blake is a phenomenal performer. He had his pick of companies, but he chose the Institute because of their illustrious reputation and they'd all but guaranteed him an accelerated track to principal.

Lark sips her coffee before setting it on the table, then she places a hand on my knee. "You deserve better than being an asshole's booty call."

"He's not an asshole."

She cuts me a glare.

"Well, sometimes he can be a bit of a prima donna, but he doesn't think of me like that." We might not be ones for fancy date nights or prophetic declarations, but when he looks at me, it might as well be a spotlight beaming down.

"Oh really?" Lark nods at Delilah as she emerges from her room in an oversized t-shirt and heads over to the coffee pot, pouring herself a cup. "What did you talk about for the whole hour he was here before he quickly cut out?"

"We talked about plenty of stuff." My mind goes blank when I try to recall, but I'm sure we did. "We talked about rehearsals."

It's a vague enough answer. We always chit-chat about dance, though less than we used to since I took my sabbatical. While I was on leave, I avoided talking about myself much—what was there to say? I was grieving, dealing with recovering from the accident, and avoiding everything that came with all...that. Now that I'm at Ballet Potomac, I'll have more to share with him.

"Are you at least getting off?"

My face heats, and I'm glad I wasn't mid-sip because my coffee would have been sprayed everywhere. Lark's lack of a filter is something I love about her...as long as it isn't directed at me.

"Th-that's private."

"That's stress relief, which is important."

Grabbing my coffee, I quickly bring it to my lips, taking a big gulp.

"So, no," Lark replies for me, and she and Delilah exchange smug *that's-a-man-for-you* glances.

"I'm not talking about this with you." When I realize how harsh the words come out, I take a deep breath and another sip of coffee before adding, "But I appreciate that you care."

I know her concern isn't really my sex life. We've been best friends since we danced together in high school. Even after going our separate ways, her training with the Institute when I went to Tisch, it was easy to settle into the familiar rhythm of friendship when I moved back.

"I don't want you to get hurt, Jojo."

"And I love you for that, but Blake makes me feel like I'm not some broken ballerina who will never see the spotlight again." He never pitied me after the accident. Never mentions my injury, though I'm sure he has noticed it. He treats me the same even with not being invited back to the Institute. What we have is the one constant, other than my friendship with Lark, that still remains all these months later. One part of my life that hasn't shifted despite the scars I've accrued, both visible and unseen.

Lark's hand squeezes my leg, and I flinch, not at her touch, but because her thumb presses on the spot where I'm most sore from yesterday's rehearsals. She brings her voice down to a gentle whisper, laying her palm flat on my leg. "You will see that spotlight. But that has nothing to do with him and everything to do with you."

I sigh in frustration, the sound grating at the back of my throat. "I hate starting over. It's like all those years of work were for nothing."

"They weren't for nothing. Now you understand what's expected ten times better than those other girls. Soloist and principal may be closer than you think."

With my luck, I'm not counting on it. I have no guarantees I'll even make soloist at Ballet Potomac. I'll be competing against those who have been paying their dues there since the beginning of their ballet careers. Dancers who are hungrier and haven't been exhausted by the toll this career can take on you mentally and physically.

"Yesterday was awful." I'm already dreading going back there and having Mistress Maral or some other instructor look down their nose at me. "*I* was awful."

"It was your first day. Give yourself some grace," Lark says, standing up and taking her coffee over to the sink to rinse out the mug. "It's going to take some adjustment."

"You're right." *But it still sucks.*

Lark heads for the door, rifling through her dance bag before throwing on her coat. "Why don't we meet after rehearsals one day this week?"

"Sure. I can bring coffee to you from Java Joe's?" I offer. It was our favorite spot when we danced at the Institute together. Standing up from the couch, I go wash out my mug and leave it on the drying rack before turning back toward my room. "It'll give me an excuse to visit everyone."

Something flickers in her expression. "You sure?"

"Of course." She's probably worried about me getting depressed being back at the Institute. I'm sure it will hurt, but I miss them. I miss the familiar. Besides, seeing Lark, Stasia, and Denise will be fun. I might even get a peek at Blake, if he's not too busy.

"That sounds great, Jojo." She tugs on her gloves and wraps her scarf around herself before flashing me a smile. "You've been missed. Everyone is always asking about you."

"It'll be great." I return the smile, though I don't feel it fully. "Just text me your order from JJ's and what day works best once we get our schedules. I'll grab it on the way. Then I can say hi and we can catch the metro back together."

"Sounds like a plan," she says, giving me one final wave before she's off.

I trudge back to my room, anxious about the day ahead. I just have to focus on each rehearsal as another chance at reclaiming my career. Today's class can't be any worse than day one's, right?

I'm not sure I want to find out.

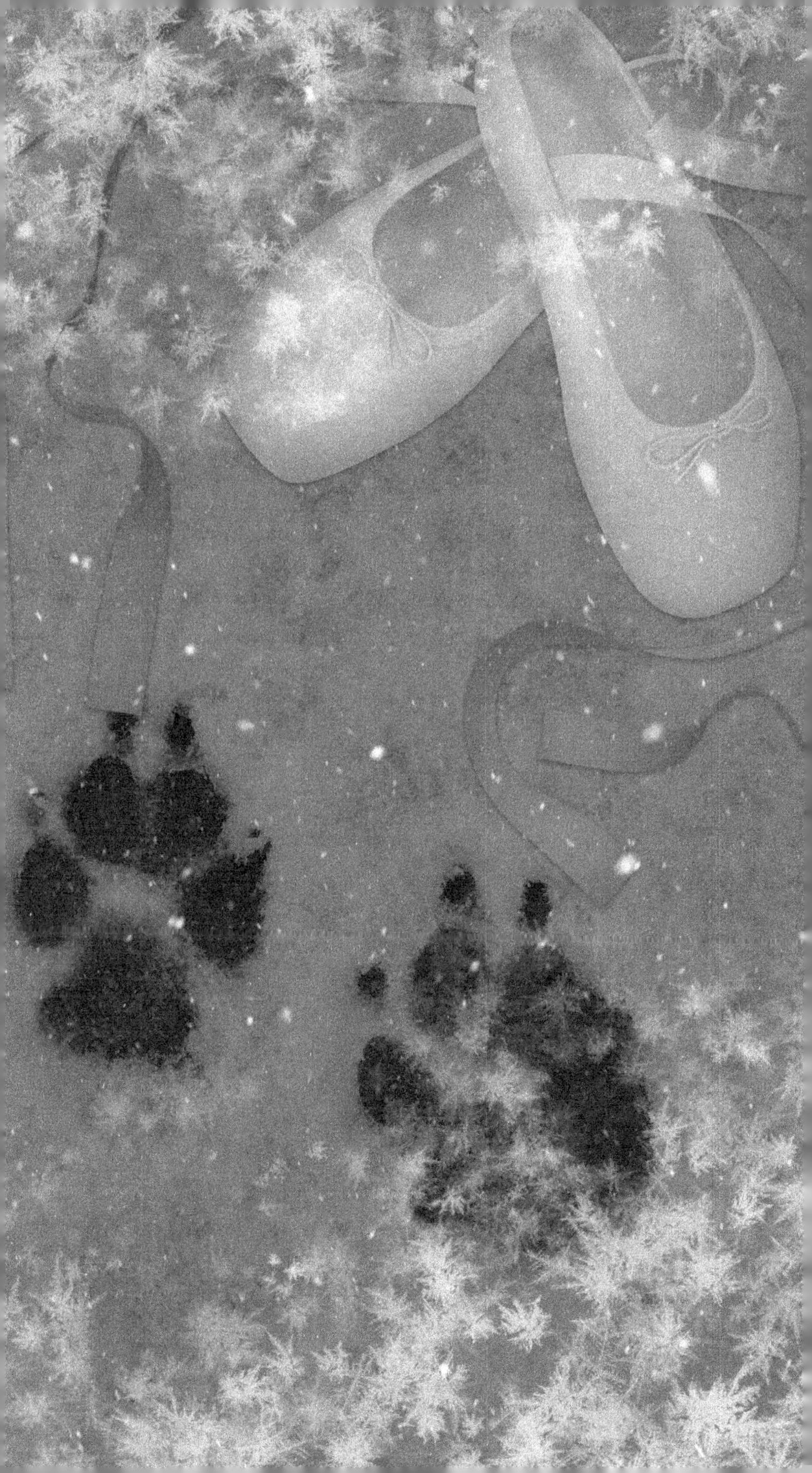

Chapter Five

JAX

I trace my fingertip over the letters, savoring the dip where pen met paper. Two words pierce my chest with a weight I don't fully understand.

I'm alive.

I've served over fifty winters outside hibernation. Waited decades. And by some horrible stroke of luck, I've been bewitched by a mortal.

Jolie Wilder.

She's *everything* to me and she doesn't even know it. Someone I can't have for a multitude of reasons. Not that it stops me from zipping here every chance I get. I don't think I've had a more productive winter to date.

I know better than to interfere, but every time I return, I try to learn as much as I can about her. Every fragment of information I glean shoots a boost of serotonin through my veins. She's a compulsion I can't shake. An addiction I'm desperate to feed. A high I never want to come down from. The farther I am from her, the worse I feel. That usually comforting flutter, like two fairies pulsating within my sternum, amplifies to the beat of dragon wings.

She's inescapable.

My hand trails over her journal. She's left it out today, something she normally doesn't do. I shouldn't read what's within its pages. We study mortal customs in our lessons to better understand the world before we are sent into it. Diary reading is frowned upon. But this may be the closest I ever get to her...

With a quick flick of my wrist, I flip through the pages one at a time. Maybe there's something in here that can help me find out how to reach her. It's a hollow hope I shouldn't push, but the urge to show her I exist, that I'm here—hers—is too strong to ignore.

I wish it wasn't. Things would be much easier for the both of us.

No matter how far I go, though, I always end up back here. And I will keep coming back, satiating my need for her, undetected. As long as I keep doing my job and don't break our only rule, I should be fine.

Scattered across the pages are a mix of memories, musings, and quick sketches. Most have a numbered list at the bottom.

I glide through her room one more time, scoffing at the discarded penile cover in the corner trash can. Frustration coils in my chest, making my fists clench. I slipped in despite knowing better. I should have left when she brought that lowlife back to her room. I normally do... Well, maybe there were times that I watched in agony from the windowsill. But he hadn't been back in a few weeks so I was hoping they were through. Then he showed up last night, and like some sort of masochist, I remained in her bedroom.

My body responds despite the pain of knowing she was

with someone else. Her *prince*, as he's referred to in her journal. In reality, he's some jerk who doesn't even deserve her attention, much less her devotion. While I desperately hate him and would love to slip some ice wherever he's walking, harming him would only bring me temporary joy and would get me swiftly benched another winter. I can't afford that after missing the last one, placed on extended hibernation. I still have no clue what I did to be benched, but I'm grateful to be here now. And I refuse to fuck this up.

I sigh, staring up at the ceiling, and lie on the bed, one spot over from where I was last night. Entranced by the way she moved. Every curve of her body. The way her nipples hardened, begging for me to tease them with my hands. My tongue. To taste every inch of her. To cover her body with my own, painting her skin in my frost.

How I wish it had been me beneath her.

Not *him*.

I'd have her whimpering, bringing her to the edge until her breaths grew ragged and she quivered in ecstasy. How incredible would it be to have her eyes locked with mine, her tight heat clenched around my knot.

I'd fill her over and over.

According to my mated siblings, there's no better pleasure. No truer fit. And while I've been with others before, I've always wanted my mate to be the first and only to ever take my knot.

I get up from her bed, taking deep breaths, wrangling the discomfort of denying myself.

Stop letting your imagination go wild, Jax.

Snarling, I fist my hands at my sides, ignoring my tented trousers. The physical need to be with her is ever-present. And the worst part is that when solstice approaches at the end of winter, it will only intensify. It's a time when immortals are drawn to our mates. When our craving for them is insatiable. Unbearable. Mates spend a day, or three, as close as possible, filling each other with pleasure, devotion, and love.

It's something I've looked forward to, seeing others pair off at the end of each winter—an inexplicable level of ecstasy I wish to share. With her.

Spending my first mate-blessed solstice alone is a very real possibility. I'll be the first Frost it's ever happened to, and I need to figure out how I will survive the pain of it. It's lonely enough to wander this world each season, hours and weeks of delivering invisible tender care to the world that goes unnoticed. Unappreciated.

My soul is tied to someone who doesn't know I exist. It's torture. Even to just be seen by her, to be able to hold her through the night, to feel how it would be to have her skin pressed against mine...

I'd give anything, pay any price, for that.

Come spring, I'll be tucked away in hibernation, unable to get to her. I don't know if she senses our unsettled bond as a mortal.

Why did we have to be the exception?

After a few steadying breaths, I drift to the window and scan the room, double checking that everything is in its place. It'll be as if I was never here. Because to her and the rest of the world, I'm not real. I'm a myth. A fanciful idea people joke about a few months out of the year.

Disappointment floods my veins. I couldn't give a fuck about the rest of the world. But her? I'd give anything to be seen by her, if only for a moment.

What would she see?

I spend so much time alone, or in my beastly earthside form, it's easy to forget what I look like. We don't use mirrors in Nivea, only catching quick glances of our reflections in the ice.

I glide over to the bathroom and stare at myself. Fractured irises glitter back at me. It's hard to believe I once was mortal. How different must I look now?

My form shimmers, pale blue and silver frost marks adorning my arms and chest, starting to skim my hip. Each winter I earn more of them, a badge of honor among the Frosts, each one a step closer to Lead Albidus.

I just need to focus on that. On doing my duty.

Don't interfere, Jax.

Heading back to the desk, I stare down at the three lines that, based on the first entry's instructions, are things she's grateful for. They're on every page, feeling just as forced as the prescription to do them. Maybe one day I'll be able to show her how beautiful she is, and she'll fill these pages with her joy—not scribble them half-heartedly at the end of a spiral of doubt and self-deprecation.

Over the next hour, I read every entry, piecing together the fragments of her like a puzzle I'm desperate to figure out. I need to understand how they fit. How she can possibly fit *with* me. She fucking has to. Wading through the sadness that fills these pages is enough to drown me. I'm close to giving up on answers when the shards finally converge. I freeze at the four words scrawled large on a page.

Where did you go?

Eyes are sketched in the corner, mosaicked irises with stars littered within them. I flick through the pages again. There are different variations of them strewn throughout the journal. Each one makes heat creep up my spine.

I bolt to the bathroom, giving my reflection another

glance. Two glittering irises peer back at me from the mirror. The truth is like a sharpened icicle to my lungs, puncturing my ability to breathe.

Those eyes she's been sketching over and over?

They're mine.

It's the sliver of hope I've been begging for. One that has my hands shaking. My fingers reach up, and I wonder if I'm about to help Fate along or doom us both.

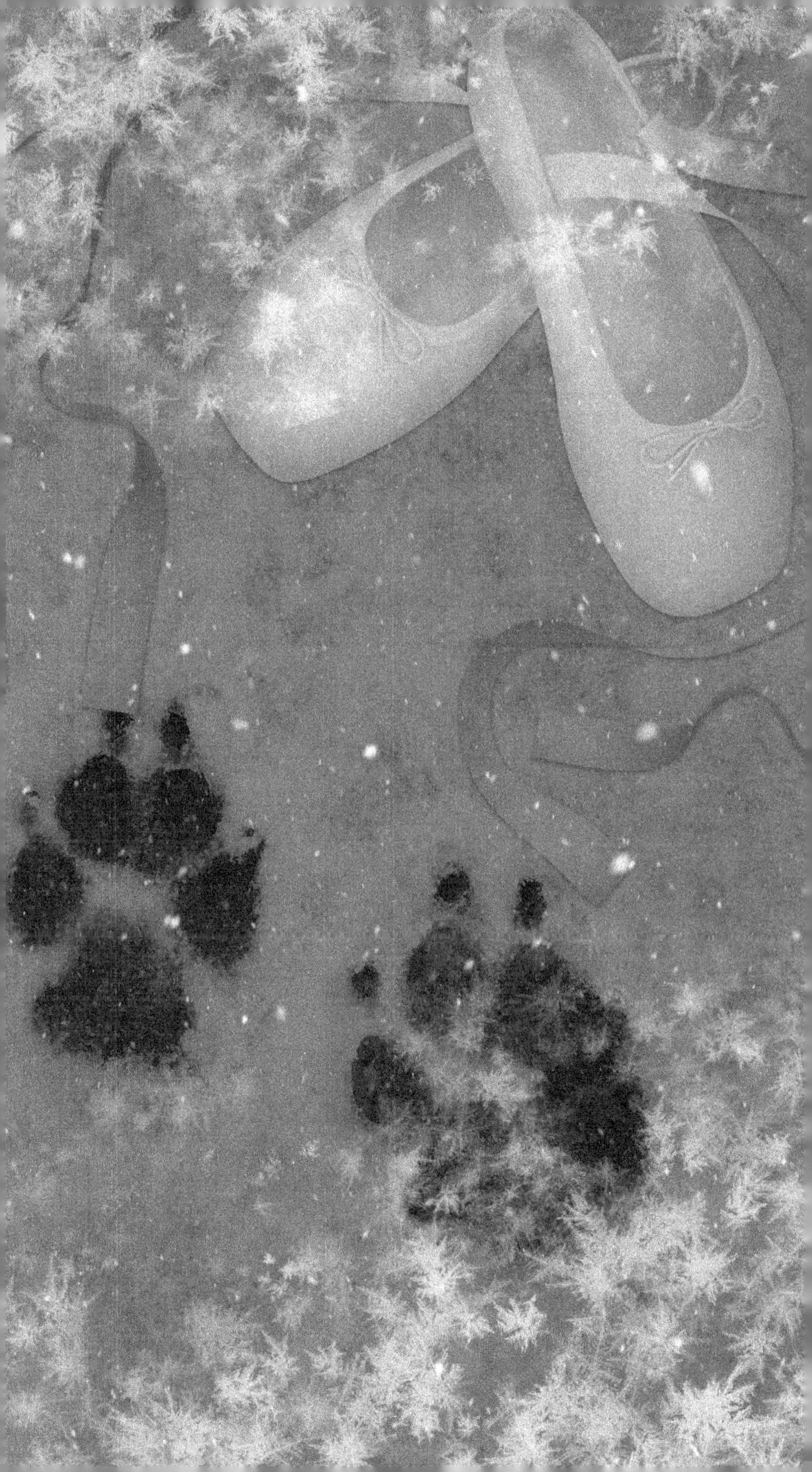

Chapter Six

JOLIE

"Jolie, I'd like you to stay after today," Mistress Maral says as soon as we finish our révérence. A lump catches in my throat.

After completing barre wobble-free and keeping pace with an especially arduous grand allegro, full of leaps and quick jumps in rapid succession, it was beginning to seem like I could hold my own here. Now the small pile of confidence I amassed is washed away by the stern look on Mistress Maral's face.

My mind races over any mistakes I could have made. I'll admit, I'm not a fast learner. It takes me a day or so to get choreography into my body, but I thought I was doing well. Surely it's not expected that my comprehension is fine-tuned the day we learn the variation?

As soon as I get home, I'll immediately practice in my room, visualizing the piece with Adolphe Adam's compositions playing on repeat.

Just as I'm getting carried away with my plans, Evelyn lays a gentle hand on my shoulder and gives it a squeeze. "Join us in the recovery room after?"

"See you there," I reply with a tight nod.

While ice baths are the favorite tradition of the dancers here, I'll be stretching out my legs on the nearby mats. Evelyn's been encouraging me to give the frosty plunge a shot, as a way to spend time with her and a few of the other girls in the corps. *No, thank you.* There's no way I'll be submerging myself in an icy tub. As much as I'd love to build some camaraderie, the frozen surface of the basin is enough to send tremors through me.

I used to love the cold. Winter. Now it brings me back to last February. To the night of the accident.

A pair of fractured irises peer at me from the recesses of my mind. My body chills and my eyes dart to the window, half expecting to see the large dog there again. After a minute of scanning, I finally exhale, shaking my head at my own paranoia. It's just the usual DC hustle.

Add this to my notes for my next session with Dr. Tanner.

The other company members exit the studio while I rummage through my bag. I'm not sure what I'm doing. Killing time? What does she want from me? I could have sworn I did much better in class today. I leave my shoes on just in case Mistress Maral wants me to demonstrate something for her.

My body aches, hips resisting my forward bend as I roll my leg warmers back up my legs. Once the room's empty, I head to Mistress Maral, who's standing by the sound system. I swallow thickly, bracing myself for whatever she's about to say. "You wanted to see me?"

"Yes." Her thin lips pull into a line, her gaze scanning over me. "I wanted to know how you think things are going."

"Um..."

Is this some sort of test? I've had my share of stern ballet instructors growing up, even one from Russia who always called me Josi, never taking the time to learn my name, but something about the way Mistress Maral scrutinizes me when I dance is like being put under a microscope.

"I think they are going well." My voice is higher pitched than I intend. When she mutters under her breath, I quickly add, "I know I had a rocky start yesterday and I'm still catching up. Today seemed like an improvement, though."

I hold my breath, waiting for her to say something. Anything.

When she lets the silence linger between us, I continue, "I'm sure I could be doing more."

"Yes, you could."

Air lodges in my throat and I'm frozen in place. My body's so stiff that I'm certain if I exhale it'll splinter my ribs.

"That's why I wanted to talk to you." Her tone relaxes a bit, but I'm not ready to relax with it.

"Oh." *Don't cry, don't cry, don't cry. Maintain professionalism, Jolie.*

I need to show her and the rest of Ballet Potomac that I can take criticism. No one wants a prima donna who isn't open to feedback in their company. While there are many out there, it's not what you want to be known for in a world as small as ours.

"To be frank, I was hesitant to bring you on when the director told us he'd invited you."

I blink rapidly, trying to stifle tears. It's not some great revelation, but it stings, nonetheless.

Mistress Maral crosses her arms, shifting her weight and sticking out her hip. "While the others voted in support of giving you a shot, I did not. And based on your first few days, you are proving my assumptions correct."

"I don't understand," I croak, rubbing my palms on the sides of my leg warmers. "What am I doing wrong? I really want this, Mistress Maral. I don't expect every instructor to like me or want me here, but I am trying my hardest."

"That's the problem, Jolie. You're trying too hard." *What?* "Do you know why I left the Joffrey?"

Her question catches me off guard. I was ready to defend myself. Now I'm filing through what I can recall from the company website and gossip—which, admittedly, I haven't been here long enough to know much about.

"You moved here with your husband. I assumed he had a job here or something," I reply with a shrug.

"He did. But that's not all." She waves me over to sit on her chair. I hesitate, but at the end of the day, I'm too intimidated by this woman not to listen to her. "I retired because I couldn't dance any longer. About five years into my career, I injured my ankle. Back then, injuries were seen as a weakness—an easy way to be replaced. I didn't tell anyone, worked my ass off, and that ultimately ended my career."

"I'm sorry." My heart breaks for her. The idea of my career ending has been an all-too-close reality. One I'm doing everything to avoid. At least I thought I was...

"Don't be sorry. Take the lesson." She bends down and inspects my right hip. "I know about your injury." She continues to assess me, scrutinizing my leg as if drawing a line of my pain down the back of it. Like she can *see* it. "When you dance, I notice every wince. I asked around about you before you arrived, about why you weren't invited back to the Institute. The *real* reason."

My body stills, pinned under her attention. "And what did you learn?"

"They also knew of your injury. The one you were trying to hide before the accident."

"I—"

"Let me finish."

Shit.

I'm not sure where this is going but if I stay in this room much longer, I won't be able to hold the tears at bay. They prick at the backs of my eyes, making me blink rapidly.

"Being injured isn't a weakness, but being careless with your wellbeing is. I expect you to be in PT tomorrow with Heather after class and follow whatever course of action she prescribes. I will be keeping personal tabs on your progress. Do you understand?"

"Yes, ma'am." It's all I can get out as I sit in shock. I'm bare. Exposed. Seeing my scars when I'm in just my leotard is one thing, something I mentally prepared for knowing I could only hide beneath makeup and ballet shrugs for so long... Spotting the pain underneath that, an injury that's only worsened from my lack of care, it's too much.

Now I'll have PT *and* therapy appointments. Being prodded from every direction with everyone's attention on what I lack. Viewed as broken on the outside as I am on the inside.

"You miss one appointment and I will go to the director with what I know and get you pulled from performing."

"I understand." My fists ball at my sides.

"Good."

"Thank you, Mistress Maral," I manage to toss out before I stand up.

"Don't thank me... And don't mistake this for generosity —you will find none of that in my class." She walks over to my dance bag and brings it to the door, silently dismissing me. "Your lack of self-preservation is a liability to this company. Get yourself together or you'll find yourself starting over again somewhere else."

"Yes, ma'am."

She opens the door and taps my shoulder as I move to

exit the studio. "Don't forget that Heather will be giving me regular reports."

"Of course." I keep my gaze trained to the Marley floor, following each gray streak along its grain. "See you tomorrow, Mistress Maral."

When I get to the dressing room, I take my time, mulling over the conversation. I need to get out of my own head before I have to be social with the others in the recovery room. There's no doubt in my mind that they'll be curious as to why I had to stay after to talk to Mistress Maral. If she's been able to spot my injury, have they?

People underestimate how cutthroat the ballet world can be. They see graceful, delicate, poised dancers. In reality, there is always someone waiting in the wings, calculating if your failure is their next opportunity. There are girls in the company who are understudying for ensemble positions in *Giselle*, the ballet we will be performing. They could easily see my injury as their chance to swoop in and snag a spot in the corps.

My pulse eventually slows, and I exit the back of the dressing area that's connected to the recovery room. There are three ice baths set in a line across a tiled area in the corner. On the floor, oversized mats are situated with bins full of stretchy bands, foam and textured rollers, and various sized balls for getting out knots and working through tense spots with trigger point massage.

"Hey!" Evelyn calls over to me. She's wrapped in a towel with tiny water droplets scattered across her shoulders. "Just finished up in the ice bath, but if you give me five, I'll come back out and stretch with you."

"Sounds great." Relief washes through me. At least now I can chat with her without feeling bad about turning down her ice bath offer again, making myself more of an outsider to the rest of the company.

Finding a spot on the large mat, I pull out a textured roller with jagged edges, rolling it up and down the backs of my legs between stretches. Evelyn and two of the other girls from the corps, Sara and Veronique, grab their recovery toys of choice and plop down next to me. My chest clenches, trying to decide what I'll say if they ask about why I was kept after class. It's Veronique who kicks off the conversation, only it's not in the way I expect.

"You know, I saw your Lilac Fairy performance a few years ago." A smile peels across her lips. "It was stunning."

Veronique is one of the youngest in the corps and came straight from Ballet Potomac's training program. Her father is a French diplomat who works at the embassy. I don't think she's even twenty yet. Her thick raven hair is pinned up in a messy bun, her big, brown eyes conveying something akin to admiration. It surprises me, along with her compliment.

My cheeks heat. "Thank you."

"I bet you were amazing," Evelyn adds. "What was it like being a soloist? If you don't mind us asking."

I think back to the piece, how many hours I spent honing the control and flexibility to get my lines to where I wanted. It was after those rehearsals I'd started to feel the stiff twinge of pain at my hip, the one that later began to radiate down my leg. The beginnings of my injury. I'd smiled my way through the Lilac Fairy's variation, earning a riotous applause from the audience.

I craved it. Devoured it.

But the moment I got backstage, I found a dark corner, sobs racking my body as the ache surged through me. Lark scooped me up after she realized I hadn't come back to our dressing room, stretching out my leg and sitting with me until I could gather myself up for the rest of the performance. She's the only one I've ever talked to about it, other than my mom.

"Do you have a recording of it?" asks Sara. She seems... genuinely excited.

It's odd how they are staring at me. It's how I stare at Blake and the other principals at the Institute.

While some of these dancers might be threatened by my very presence, seeing me as the competition, there are also dancers who want to be friends. Dancers who respect what I've done through my career thus far. The three women in front of me remind me of myself when I started years ago. They're hungry for their moment to shine, when the spotlight will shower them in its intoxicating glow, even if only for a few minutes. Where all eyes are on them and their craft.

"I can shoot you the link later if you really want."

"Yes, please!"

My chest warms, chin lifting. "And it felt absolutely incredible. I definitely miss it."

We continue to chat about each other's backgrounds as we finish stretching. While their questions about my career press on a past that stings like an open wound, there's a satisfaction that's layered on top. A balm to my soul.

For the first time since I put my ballet career on pause, maybe there's a place for me. Somewhere I'm a little less alone and ashamed of what I've lost.

AFTER AN HOUR of recovery and grabbing tea with the other girls, I head five blocks to the metro and ride it home. There's a coat hanging on the hook and a dance bag tucked into the corner of the room. Lark is home.

I press my ear to the door and the sound of her showering spills from the other side. After removing the layers and layers of winter gear clinging to my frigid body like a wooly second skin, I wobble on sore legs down the hallway to my room.

After the chilly metro ride and trek home, I'm more than eager to warm up in the shower. I turn it on, then head back into my bedroom. Steam billows out from the bathroom, mist spreading next to the bed. I pull out my phone to jot down the notes into my journal and send Sara the recording of my Lilac Fairy performance from *Sleeping Beauty*.

I watch the video three times. The nostalgia is bittersweet and I can't help but reminisce over what my body was capable of only a few years ago. A time when it was at its prime, thirsting to be pushed and challenged. I could dance for hours, then come home and rehearse in my bedroom or in my head until I passed out, before starting the routine all over. I can't move like that now. But if I take PT seriously, like Mistress Maral wants, and keep working hard, maybe I can get back to that point again.

I strip off my dance clothes and toss them into the hamper. I spot my journal still out on the desk. *Odd.* I'm normally pretty careful about not leaving it out, but I was in a hurry earlier.

Two eyes peer up at me from the page, striking deep in my soul, along with the words that accompany them.

Where did you go?

Something I've wondered countless times. I sigh, shutting it and sticking it back into the drawer before I head into the bathroom. Thick streaks on the mirror catch my attention, and I cross my arms over my naked body before I rip the towel from its hook. I wrap it around myself, glancing into the bedroom. A chill spins down my spine. My heart races. I manage to take a deep breath and turn my gaze back to the big letters outlined in fog.

I'm here.

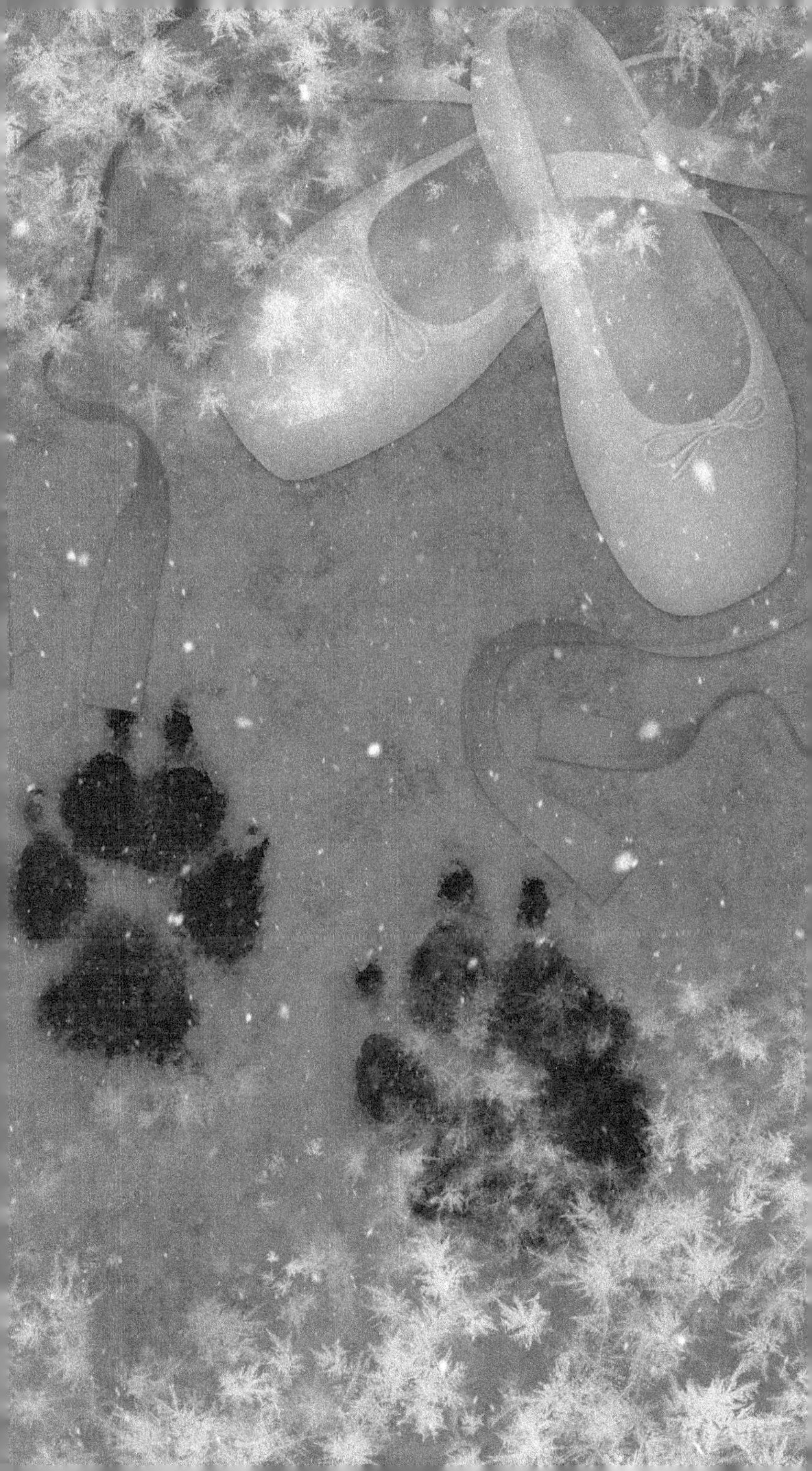

Chapter Seven

JOLIE

I'm here.

"Hello?" My voice quivers, hands shaking at my sides as I stare at those two words. Is this some sort of prank? A practical joke Lark or Delilah is playing on me? They aren't really the type, but how else can you explain writing on the mirror in your bathroom? Nevertheless, I text Lark.

> Haha very funny

LARK:
> I usually am, but what did I do this time?

> Were you in my room earlier?

LARK:
> No. Why? Is there something juicy in there for me to make fun of you for?

I'm pretty sure if it was her, she wouldn't act like she has no idea what I'm talking about.

> Never mind. I'll leave you to get ready for tonight.

A shiver sneaks up my spine. The thermostat is low

again, not as low as before but still lower than what I set it to by more than a few degrees. When I'd asked Lark earlier about hers, she'd said she hasn't had any issues…

Cold air. Strange messages. The goosebumps streaking my arms. The way-too-weird-yet-obvious answer is standing in front of me: My room must be haunted. I blame Lark for making me watch too many supernatural reality shows.

"Hello. Mr.—or Mrs.—Spirit." I swallow, trying to fight the dryness of my throat. "Are you still…h-here?"

I wait, ignoring the way my pulse ramps up, thudding over the silence.

There's no response, but I'm officially creeped out.

I text Blake. Lark would chastise me for this, but there's no reason for her to ever know. She and Delilah already have plans, so they won't be here to glare at him for the short time he'll be visiting. Maybe I'll be able to convince him to stay the night this time. There's no way I can be alone right now.

I wipe away the writing on the mirror, double lock the windows, and shower quickly. Every few minutes, I poke my head out of the curtain, checking to see if there's a new message or anything else out of place.

As I step out of the stall, frosty air lashes my skin. I wrap my towel around myself tightly, eyes darting around the room, half expecting to find the window open. Tiptoeing to my dresser, I grab some leggings and an oversized gray sweatshirt. It's cut along the neckline with *The Tempest* scripted across the chest, the Institute's logo emblazoned on the back. It's something I used to rock at rehearsals. Now it's just another addition to my pajamas. Something I can't wear outside these walls.

Not anymore.

Slipping on a pair of blue fuzzy socks with white

snowflakes scattered across them, I leave my room. Lark and Delilah have already left, so I sit on the couch and wait for Blake to respond or just arrive at my door. I'll take either option at this point.

After twenty long minutes of fidgeting with it between my fingers, my phone buzzes. I swipe off the lock screen, wondering how far out Blake is.

THE PRINCE:

Hey, roads are a bit too slick for me to drive
over tonight.

My stomach lurches.

Metro?

THE PRINCE:

You know how I feel about public
transportation.

I promise I'll make it up to you.

Okay. How about a night out this weekend?

Is this a little desperate? Maybe. But Lark and Delilah will be away for a wedding. I don't want to be alone with this Casper wannabe.

THE PRINCE:

…

I stare at the tiny dots. Waiting…

THE PRINCE:

Can't. Traveling to NJ to see the fam.

I'll text you next week once I'm back.

Okay. Sounds good.

Disappointment sinks into my gut, a stone of unease whirling into a surge of nausea. The wind whistles against the balcony door, as if searching for a way in, and I shudder, trying not to think about the strange message left on my mirror or whoever left it.

I pull up my phone, typing in "how to spot a ghost"—

Thwap!

I jolt off my ass, dropping my phone onto the couch. What just slammed into the window? I should have gone out with Lark and Delilah when they'd offered.

Grabbing the phone from between the cushions, I clutch it tightly in my shaking palm, ready to use the emergency setting if some intruder is somehow magically chilling on the balcony. I turn on the flashlight and aim it out the door, making sure no one is standing in the small four-by-four space. Darkness engulfs everything aside from what's lit by streetlamps and the moon. Unlocking the door, I slide it open, the wind helping me along instead of meeting me with the resistance I expect.

My arms wrap around myself for warmth. The evening chill nips at me, tousling my hair like a gentle lover, the air crisp with the scent of pine and nutmeg—the remnants of the holiday season carried on the breeze. I inhale it deeply, ignoring the cold's bite. I used to love this, the beauty of winter. But now it's something I try to ignore...knowing it also brings the anniversary of the accident.

I take a deep breath. Strangely, I'm comforted by the way the wind trails my skin, tiny goosebumps rippling along it. I pop my back and hip, enjoying the release of pressure on the joints, my exhales painting the dark sky in muted grays.

A glorious numb settles into me. I should head inside, but some pull, no matter how illogical, keeps me lingering.

After a few beats of silence, the wind whistles past me. I

shiver as the trees rattle against the building. When I turn to slide open the glass door, spicy pine gusts into me, herding me the rest of the way inside.

My body is slammed by the warmth radiating within the apartment. My fingers are stiff and purple as I wiggle them before rubbing my frost-kissed nose. I glance once more outside the window, latch the lock, and listen to the brush of wind against the glass.

My mind swirls back to the mysterious message on my mirror...

And a crazy idea begins to form.

Chapter Eight

JAX

I didn't think Jolie could steal my breath away any more, but her brushing against me outside tonight knocked the wind from my lungs. Playing with her long, dark tresses, skating along her exposed skin, my magic's starved for her as much as I am. For the first time since I felt that nagging thrum post-hibernation, I'm at ease. Satisfied.

I could sway with her for hours. For eras. There's nothing more beautiful than the way she spins under my chilling spell.

My tempest.

The word drawn across her chest fractures me, sinking deep between my ribs, giving it new meaning. Jolie's a storm of motion threatening my very delicate ecosystem.

I want her all the more for it.

My willing yet unknowing partner. Can she sense our connection through the veil keeping us apart?

When her fingers turned blue, I ushered her inside as best I could. I must keep my mate safe, even if she doesn't acknowledge that I'm here.

I follow her, keeping my distance as she moves quickly down the hall toward her roommate's room. Has she seen my message? I'd left it hastily before arriving in Mass-achusetts, blowing my way down the East Coast, stopping just past Philadelphia, and then finally returning. Apparently, my extra visits haven't gone unnoticed. Weather reports of extended cold fronts have finally caught up with me. Now we've been ordered to do extra duty up north and avoid this area. *Oops.*

Jolie heads past me, something wooden and rectangular clutched in her hands. She moves straight for her desk, setting the box on it and rifling through it.

I slip into the bathroom and find my words erased from the mirror. Had they even been there by the time she'd gotten back? *Shit.* It's probably for the best, considering I'm not supposed to be interfering. Disappointment claws at me, nonetheless.

Jolie glances around the room over her shoulder. I freeze in place—no clue why since I know she can't see me—but when I look back to where she is staring, it's at the empty mirror.

She did see!

Hope drifts through the air like gossamer flurries, fragile and gone far too soon. I zip into the bedroom and over to the corner by the desk, careful not to blow any of the papers in her journal. Her eyes are back down on the rich mahogany board with fancy lettering.

"Eww-I-jah," I sound out slowly, reading the single word carved at the top. *Ouija.*

Peering over her shoulder again, she rests her fingers on the curved triangle atop the board. Her hands quiver the tiniest bit. "Are you here?"

I take a closer look at the board. It's nothing I've seen before, but that doesn't stop the excitement that streaks through me.

This is something I can work with.

Using my magic, I blow wind out of my lips along with a few flecks of snow that catch on the strangely shaped apparatus. It moves toward the *YES* at the top, and I inch it farther with another gust. Her fingers shake atop the plastic and her body shudders. "Why are you here?"

I sweep my breeze to shift the triangle across the board, spelling out—

YOU

Her hands lift, body stilling. *Crap.* My brows furrow as I continue to move the plastic device around the board, sensing her fear.

YOU ARE SAFE

She exhales loudly, a puff of white floating from between her mauve lips. I can't help but imagine them against mine. "Wh-who are you?"

A howl comes from outside, and both our heads snap to the window. Jolie pops out of her chair and rushes over to it. I scoot out of the way, watching her intently. Does she think it's me?

I can't tell if she's more scared or curious. Curiosity I can work with. Fear won't do. I've observed enough seasons to know that far too many people rely on fear to get what they want. I never will. Not when it comes to my mate. But you better believe if her *prince* comes back here, I won't hesitate to scare him off. Even the thought of it has me giddy. There's only so much torture a harbinger can take.

"Maybe it's the wind," Jolie mutters, as if reassuring

herself. Her gaze cuts back to the board where the circle encases the letter *J*. "This is crazy."

I quickly swipe the triangle across the board to *NO*. Once she sits down again and I know I have her attention, I carry it over each letter to answer her question. She says each one aloud, her brows scrunched together.

"J – A – X."

I halt my movements and wait.

Just say it. Please. I'm fucking begging.

"Jax?"

Frost blasts from my lips, and the Ouija board flies across the room, cracking in half against the wall.

"Oh my god!" she said, cowering.

I swirl some snowflakes in the air, hoping it'll ease her mind. Her gaze darts around, following them, and she bites her bottom lip.

Shit. I couldn't help myself, though. While my full name is Jaxon, the idea of her calling me Jax, like I'm something close to her, *someone* close to her, does something to me. Her pulse flutters within my rib cage, and it gets me all the more excited at the prospect that she could believe in me.

See me.

Want me.

I sigh in relief when her shoulders relax. Her pulse slows. Taking a pen in her hand, she writes my name in big letters across the next page of her journal.

My heart twists in my chest. The sensation is painful and equally glorious. It's everything. Every-fucking-thing. If only she could see me.

I imagine floating with her on the breeze, dancing with her. Claiming her. Then the only invisible forces between us would be the bond and our love. Not this veil hiding me in plain sight. I'd take her into my arms and love her beyond this world, beyond time, beyond a fickle fate that keeps her away from me.

There has to be a way. There just has to. Maybe they'll make an exception for us since my mate is mortal? I haven't gone back since winter started. We aren't really supposed to...but I'm desperate. Anything has to be better than this agony.

My fingers brush the skin on the back of her hand, and she drops the pen, eyes following the white flecks drifting toward her windowpane. With another breath, I cover the glass, scrawling my name with snow.

She stands from the chair and slowly approaches my message. Her delicate fingers trail the frost, and every stroke of them against my magic is as if she were touching me directly. My body hums under the attention, and I will my excitement to get ahold of itself. She knows my name. That I'm here for her and she's safe. I'm so close to reaching her.

Her eyes dare a glance at the cracked board and her face falls.

No.

Retreating quickly from the window, she fumbles behind herself, grabbing her phone and bringing it to her ear. I move in front of her, waiting for her to see me. To acknowledge me. To find me.

Us.

But she continues to stare right through me, at *Jax Frost* spanning the window at my back. "Dr. Tanner, I know I'm only supposed to use this number in case of emergencies. But this is an emergency. I think I'm...seeing things."

She goes silent, and I'm too focused on the strain in her jaw to eavesdrop on whatever the feminine voice on the other line is saying.

"No. I don't think I'm a harm to myself or anyone else."

My brows scrunch together and I clench my fists. I'd freeze the world before she could anyway. No harm comes to my mate. Not ever. I'd trade my immortality before that would ever happen.

"Okay. I'll be there at 12:30. Thank you."

She hangs up, phone shaking in her hands as she backs away and climbs into the bed, pulling the covers around her. Her breaths release in shallow pants. I follow her, halting by her bedside table, hating to see her fear. Fear over *me*.

White puffs slip in the space between us. When she sees them, her panic only grows, and a tear streaks her cheek. It crushes something inside me, and I transport myself to the park and shift, my paws crunching against the grass.

And then I run.

And run.

But no matter how far or how fast my feet carry me, I can't outrun the fear that thrums in my chest...and the painful realization that comes with it.

Convincing Jolie I'm real might be the worst fate I can give her.

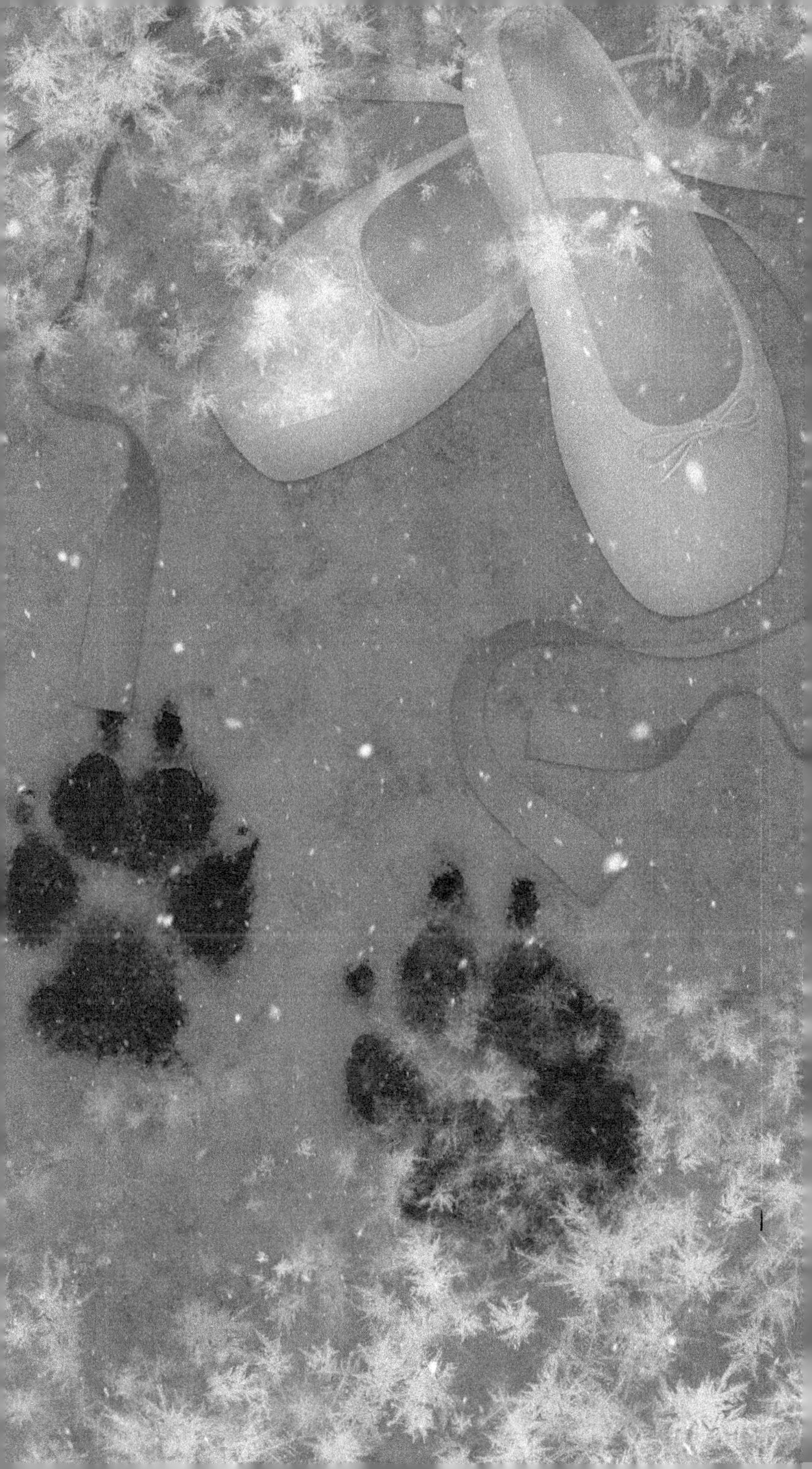

Chapter Nine

JOLIE

I keep my head down during rehearsals, focusing on not letting my mind wander to my midday appointment with Dr. Tanner or the eerie events of last night.

Not that I know what I'm even going to say when I see her.

I shouldn't have been able to drift off to sleep last night. I should be more unsettled. Logically, this is the stuff of nightmares. If this were a movie, someone would be calling me and breathing heavily over the other line. I'm the girl that decides to go into the haunted house alone. A sitting duck, ready for the taking.

A smart person would have immediately left the apartment and called Lark. A smart person would have called Blake, demanding to stay at his place for once. A smart person definitely doesn't keep thinking about *Jax Frost*.

My curiosity will be the death of me and there's no one to blame but myself. I mean... Jax Frost? Isn't that the little sprite that flits around for winter? A made-up story used to sell holiday movies? Not a real...whatever. Being.

"You ready to talk about why you called me last night?"

my therapist asks, tapping her purple pen a few times against her clipboard. Her green eyes glint beneath tortoise-shell glasses, and she tucks an ash-blonde strand of hair into her bun. Then she waits. And waits. And waits.

"Do you ever have patients that, um...see things?" Once the words are out, I try not to panic, though there's no good segue into *I think I'm getting messages from a ghost that may or not be a childhood myth.* "Like ghosts or something?"

Dr. Tanner takes a few beats before she responds. "Well, sometimes our grief can manifest in different ways."

"So you think this is just my grief?" Would grief be able to throw something across the room and break it? I don't think so, but I also don't want to sound any nuttier than I do already. Of course, Dr. Tanner's professional enough not to say I'm crazy to my face, though I'm sure *delusional* is now somewhere on that chart.

"I really don't know, Jolie. But I think it's important we explore this and find out." Anything she says afterward is a blur as my mind reels over if I made up the name on my window, the strange wolf, or the broken antique Ouija board. While I'm grateful she doesn't make me feel more insane than I already do, she's also reinstated my weekly sessions.

That's telling in itself.

I can't dwell on that long, though, because before I know it our session is over and I am hauling ass back to the rest of rehearsals to dance until my feet blister and bleed and pain streaks down my thigh. My next physical therapy session is tomorrow, and I'm oddly looking forward to it. My therapist, Heather, reminds me that each time I go is a step toward progressing my career. I repeat that to myself over and over like a mantra, and it helps. Plus, I notice Mistress Maral is glaring at me less during rehearsals. That's a huge improvement.

By the time I finish, it's 3:30. I skip recovery bonding time today in lieu of meeting Lark at the Institute. I didn't see her this morning before I headed to class. Honestly, it was for the best. I still need to search for her replacement board.

Every step toward the metro, I glance around, the ice and snow surrounding me like a personal taunt even as it glistens within the cracks of the bustling streets. The cold may have left the area, but it rattles my bones, culling a dissatisfied ache in my chest. I slide onto the seat in the metro and run through all the strange things that have been happening, half expecting to find the glass on the windows frosting over with another message.

No matter how hard I try, I can't think of anything else.

After the metro ride, I hurry to JJ's. The owners give me knowing smiles and immediately begin pouring our usuals even though it's been months since I've been here.

"Long time no see. We've missed you," Emily says from behind the counter, fitting the lids onto the to-go cups. When her gaze flicks up, she gives me a tight-lipped smile.

"I'm hanging in. Doing much better."

"And you're not returning to the Institute?"

"No." I shuffle from foot to foot. "They were not happy that I extended my bereavement leave and filled my spot." Though now it seems like they used it as an excuse to let me go after my hip injury continued to deteriorate. Sure, the accident and time off made things worse, but the pain that radiates down my leg on a daily basis came long before the crash. My body just showcases more of the pain now. The gashes that go down my back from my shoulder and the one along my knee...

"Shame on them," Emily tuts.

"It is what it is." I shrug, keeping my eyes on the floor. I don't disagree with her, but there's nothing else to say. "I'm dancing with Ballet Potomac now."

"Ah! When's your next performance?" Bryon asks with a grin on his face. I miss seeing them before rehearsals. If I could squeeze in a coffee, I loved starting my day with JJ's. They are the sweetest couple, and it always brightened the mornings on the gloomiest of days. "We'd love to come see you."

"It'll be in March. We're doing *Giselle*."

"*Giselle*? I don't think I know that one," Bryon says, his brows scrunching together.

"It's not as well-known as some of the others."

Emily glances up while she pours some foam atop my latte. "What's it about?"

"A peasant girl who falls in love with a duke who's betrothed to another. She goes mad and dies of a broken heart, joining the wilis." Trying to explain a ballet in a few sentences is pretty much impossible.

"Who are you playing?"

"I'll be one of the wilis." When they stare at me with confusion, I clarify, "They are the lost spirits of betrayed women that haunt the forest, luring men to dance to their deaths."

"*Oh*," Bryon croons, raising his brows a few times. "Sounds fun."

"It will be." And I actually mean it. I've danced this part before, years ago with the Institute. Thankfully, gives me a slight advantage. I know this ballet and its variations like the back of my hand. I'll just need to translate that mastery into something that will impress the director.

"Well, keep us updated and put us down for two tickets

for opening night." They come around the counter and give me hugs before handing me the coffees and walking me to the door. My chest aches a moment as it sinks in that I won't be needing a ticket for my mom this year. She always went around like the Institute's personal saleswoman, getting everyone she knew to buy tickets to my performances. She'd been so proud of me, especially after my promotion to soloist. We'd made plans to go to the Ballet World Summit once I became principal. We spent hours watching videos of the showcase while I was growing up.

I guess I could still take the trip someday, but it wouldn't be the same. Seeing the poster for it every day when I walk into class is a not-so-fun reminder.

The bell rings behind me when the door shuts, frosty breaths leaving my parted lips. Across the street, the Institute's big sign is aglow. I inhale deeply, heart racing at the sight of it. Nearly every morning since I joined the company started with this view...until that terrifying night.

The coffees keep my hands warm as I cross the street, my gut churning with each step. I've been anticipating and dreading this since I woke up this morning.

It doesn't help matters much that they are rehearsing for *Swan Lake*, a ballet I've been dying to perform since I saw the show at the Kennedy Center when I was ten. My mom took me as her date shortly after she and my dad separated. We dressed up, went out to Jean-Paul's for a nice meal and then went to the ballet. Box seats. She had won them in a silent auction for some charity she was on the board of.

I'd watched, enraptured, as the dancers bour\u00e9ed gracefully across the stage. Delicate and fragile yet strong and poised through every movement. While I already enjoyed going to my ballet lessons, that night changed my life. After that, I focused on honing my craft. I practiced for hours, listened closely to my critiques, studied every facet of my posture, perfecting my technique so I could have my big day. Not a wedding, like for most girls, but *my* big day. The day every ballet dancer dreams of when they get fitted for pointe shoes. From the moment I slipped them on, tying those ribbons and fastening them at the ankles, I knew this was my fate. Dance is the love of my life. There's nothing else that even compares.

The night of *Swan Lake* also had been the night I realized that my mother and I would be okay. That it was us against the world, even if my father had left and decided to *start fresh* somewhere else. As if we'd never existed. Mom came to every performance, paid for training—she gave everything to see me make my dream come true. That night, it had become *our* dream. A dream I had to make happen for both of us, even if she'd never see it now.

Of course, after years of waiting for the Institute to decide to showcase it, they are finally doing *Swan Lake* without me.

The familiar sage awning looms over me as I stare at the entrance. The District Dance Institute is in bold block letters on the sign next to the double doors. How many times did I walk past this sign and barely give it a glance? Now I'm noticing every tiny crack in its lettering while I avoid taking the plunge and opening the door.

The alleyway next to the studio would be the perfect spot to hide out and text Lark that I can't make it...

I shake the thought off, mustering up the courage to go inside. I tuck one of the coffees into the crook of my arm and use my free hand to pull open the heavy door against the wind threatening to slam it shut. Quickly slipping in as the door smacks into my dance bag, I stumble forward, clutching my caffeine tightly. Brown spatters my jacket and scarf, my coffee spilling from the cup.

Great.

It's only made worse by the fact that everyone in the lobby is looking in my direction.

I'm unwrapping my coffee-stained scarf when murmurs flow out the door opening from studio A. Lark is out the door with a flurry of other corps girls, a few new faces, but when Stasia and Denise shoot me a smile and wave, it feels like I'm back home.

I try not to let disappointment get the best of me when Blake is nowhere to be found. He likes to stay after and practice before taking a few hours in the recovery room. So did I, once upon a time. To be fair, I didn't text him ahead of time that I'd be coming by. It's not like he's expecting me. Just when I think that maybe I should pass by the doorway to get his attention, Lark shoots me a look like she already knows what's going through my mind.

"Principal meeting."

I know better than to interrupt that. Things are usually tense the weeks following when the ballet is announced. Aside from the excitement, there are the nerves that come with casting—not that Blake has ever had to worry. He's their best principal. There was no way he'd get any role other than Prince Siegfried.

God, he will be brilliant at it. Makes me all the more envious that I won't be able to watch him rehearse. The way he moves to the music stirs something within me. The few times we've partnered after rehearsals, well...let's just say that's how things truly began. His tight grip on my hips, hungry eyes roving over me, moving in the dimly lit studio... We hadn't even made it home that first night, our bodies coming together quickly in the alleyway I'd just been considering hiding away in.

There wouldn't be any more nights like that, but knowing we could finally come out about our relationship outweighs the disappointment. While going to the preview gala and opening night will be hard for me, the idea of being on Blake's arm ignites me. I might be stuck in the corps at Ballet Potomac, but Blake's spotlight is bright enough to shine on us both. Who knows? Maybe once I make my comeback and become an established principal with Ballet Potomac, I'll be able to return to the Institute? We can finally dance together *and* be together out in the open.

"Earth to Jojo," Lark says, snapping her fingers in front of my face. "Where'd you disappear to?"

"You know me, always a dreamer." I laugh it off and hand her the coffee. We chat together in the lobby, and I get sporadic hugs from familiar friends as they head out. In some ways it feels like nothing's changed. Then there are moments when they talk about the ballet or ask me about Ballet Potomac and a line feels drawn between us, skating along discomfort.

Studio C opens, and my breath catches in my throat. A few of the principals ignore me or give a quick nod before leaving. Blake comes out, talking to Nina and Beth, who are set to play Odette and Odile, the white and black swans in the ballet. The roles hold an elegance I dream of. I imagine myself clad in ivory feathers and delicate satin, lights warming me from above while a full audience watches me share my craft.

I stand up from the couch, and Blake pulls me in for a hug. "So good to see you, Jolie."

"Yeah, Jolie," Nina says, lips flattening into a thin line.

She's about three inches taller than me, but something about her makes her always feel like she's towering over me. Her champagne bun is slicked back, and when she hugs me, it's as ass-out as it can get. She never warmed to me when we danced in the corps together, or even when we were soloists. She was promoted to principal last year. I envied her then, and I do even more so now. "We've missed you."

Uh-huh, sure.

"We have," Blake agrees, shooting me a charming wink.

"We're running to the juice bar, then we have to go through more choreography," Nina says.

"Sorry to have to run."

"Sorry to have to run."

"No worries." I look up at him from beneath my lashes. While I don't want to seem too enamored by him in front of everyone, I'm disappointed he is on his way out already. I clear my throat, wrestling away my sudden shyness. "I figured things would be busy."

"I'll shoot you a text later." He gives me another squeeze and a swift kiss to my temple. I follow him with my stare as he reaches the door, but it's the white blur across the street that ends up snagging my attention.

Two iridescent eyes peer at me. The beast halts there, licking its lips. A glint of sharp teeth keeps me pinned beneath its stare. Silvery-gray spots are mixed into its white fur. A terrifyingly beautiful *wolf*.

I blink a few times, and in a flash, it disappears.

Maybe this is all in my mind.

Thirty minutes later, after I've visited with my former company mates, Lark and I head out to go home.

"Hey, let's cross the street real quick," I suggest, wanting to get a closer look at where the wolf was. I need to know if it's my mind playing tricks on me. Besides, Dr. Tanner said to explore the things I was seeing. A giant, unexplainable beast seems like something to look into.

Especially when it has those eyes that have haunted me for months.

"Um, sure." Lark squints across from us for whatever has me wanting to go there. "Any reason why?"

"Just feeling adventurous." Pretty sure "I keep seeing a wolf with sparkling eyes" won't win me any sanity points right now.

Lark shrugs, then presses the button at the intersection. "If your adventure doesn't involve making moon eyes at Blake, I'm all for it."

"Why do you hate him so much?"

"I don't hate him. He's just not good enough for you." She grabs my hand and we cross the street, watching the light count us down before angry DC drivers honk at us. It's one of the many reasons I've stuck with public transportation around here. "Please tell me you're at least putting your birthday present to good use since the boy doesn't strike me as one to know what he's doing, which you only confirmed for me the other morning."

My birthday present, aka a massive vibrator she named Buzz.

I groan. "Not this again."

"Stress relief is important," Lark says with a smirk, giving my side a nudge with her elbow. "He's obviously not relieving it."

I don't make eye contact. If she says anything about me blushing, I will deny that it's due to anything more than winter's chill. "Dance is the only stress relief I need."

"Says someone not getting any other kind of *relief*," Lark grumbles. She gives me a strange look when I step onto the snow-covered grass. "Ignore your prince and take a night to yourself. And Buzz." She winks. "Delilah and I will be out on a date."

"Okay." But my attention is pinned to the very large paw prints in the snow leading toward the woods.

"What the hell are those?" Lark asks as I follow the tracks. "They're huge."

My face snaps to look at her. "You see them?"

"Not sure how I could miss them." She trudges after me, keeping a few steps behind. "What are you doing?"

I'm too busy trailing after the wolf's prints to respond. I'm certain this is its tracks, as certain as I am that the sky is blue and the seasons change. We walk, and walk, and walk some more into the tree line.

"Jojo, did you hear me?"

My legs are sore from rehearsal, numbing pain spreading down the back of my thigh until it's wobbling. But I don't stop, too focused on each pawed imprint in the snow. I'm a fish on a line, reeled in by some unseen force.

Three steps later, they vanish.

They don't even taper off. Just *poof*—gone. Like the wolf disappeared in the wind.

Before I can investigate further, Lark catches my wrist. "Hey."

My attention finally snaps back to her, and she releases her hold, pulling her beanie over her ears. She scans the park's clearing that's just a blanket of white with peeks of frosted grass. "What are you looking for?"

"Something. Nothing." My brows furrow. "I'm not really sure."

"Well, can we head back home before we freeze our asses off? I'm not built for this cold." She loops her arm in mine, shivering against me.

"Of course." I huff out a laugh, gray mist wisping in front of us.

As we walk in the direction of the metro, I can't help but glance over my shoulder. There's no way more than one wolf has eyes like that. How can I be seeing it on the opposite side of town? And why do I get the feeling this won't be the last time?

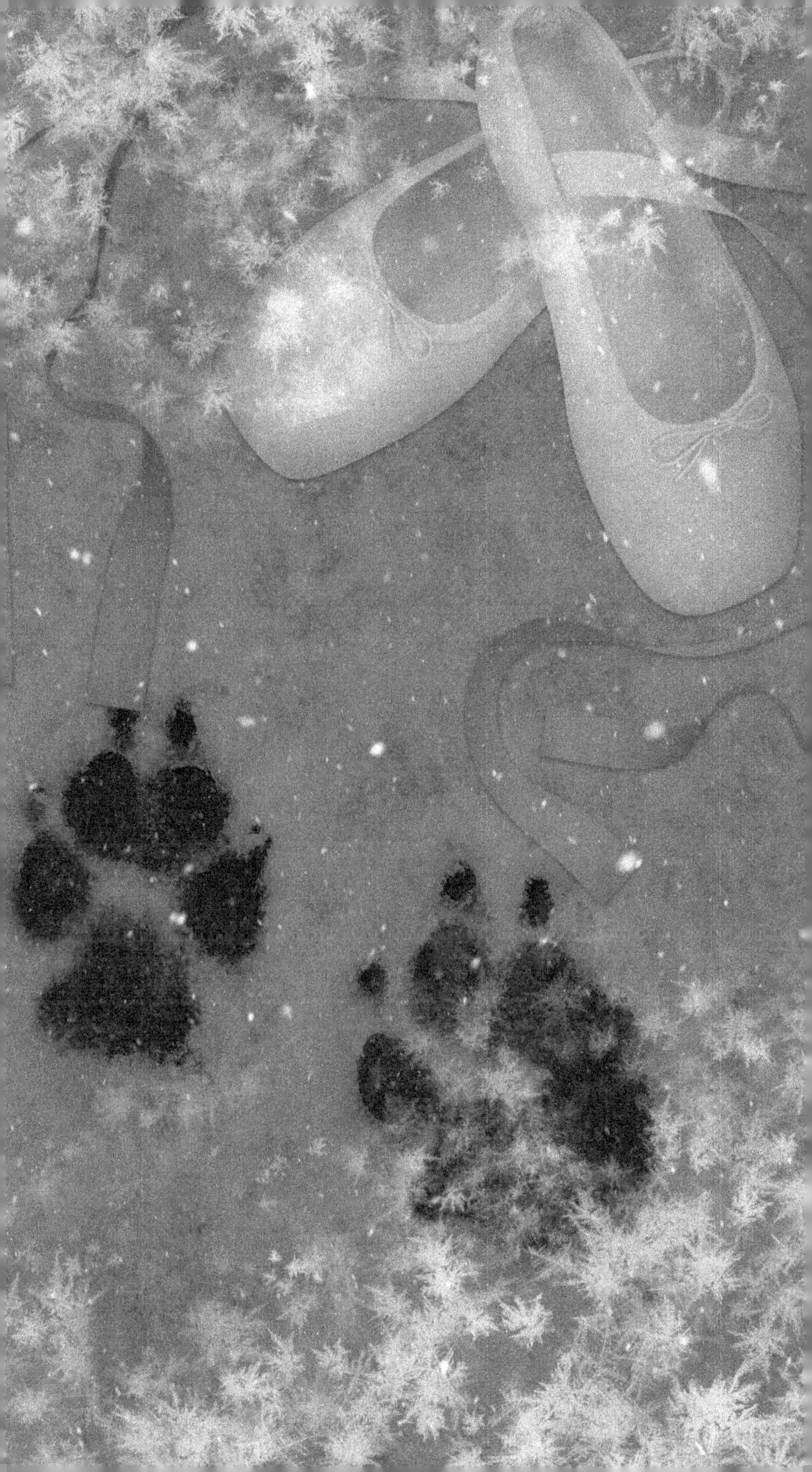

February

Most people use an empty apartment to listen to whatever music they want, throw on their guilty pleasure TV show, light a candle, dance naked, masturbate.

I'm not most people.

It's been a week since I saw the wolf outside the Institute. I have no clue at what point I decided to tempt fate and try to contact my ghost—or whatever—but I've been counting down to Lark and Delilah leaving for the night ever since. Technically, I'm listening to my therapist's advice. *Exploring* what these strange things I'm seeing could mean. Though I'm certain she doesn't believe there's anything happening beyond my subconscious swirling in my grief, especially as the anniversary of the accident looms closer.

Narrowing down a way to lure my mystery messenger has been the hardest part. Do I write on the mirrors and windows? Leave an entry in my journal with questions?

About an hour after Lark and Delilah leave the apartment, I dig in my Caboodle and pull out some deep-pink lipstick, then head into the bathroom. Uncapping its lid, I twist the base until enough has emerged to write with. Its pointed tip has been curved over from all its use. Pressing up to my tippy-toes I write across the highest point of the mirror in bold letters.

Hello?

I stare up at the pink streaks and lean against the bathroom wall.

Last time they used the steam to write into, didn't they? I quickly twist the faucet and turn on the shower before shutting the bathroom door. Steam billows around me in a cloud of gray, and my pulse taps at my sanity while I wait.

And wait.

And wait.

Popping the lid off the lipstick again, I scribble down another line. Shoving the lipstick into the back pocket of my sweats, I go back to resting against the wall. Steam collects around me, and I use the time to stretch out my hamstrings, hips cracking as I move through some exercises while my body is warmed by my homemade sauna.

Are you here?
Jax?

I do the same on the window, sweeping my finger against the frosted glass. After I wonder for a half second how weird it would be for someone living in the apartment across the way to see this, I decide I don't care. Apparently, my desire for answers is greater than my desire for sanity.

To kill time, I go through the stretches and exercises Heather gave me, then I sew ribbons onto my extra pairs of pointe shoes. I hiss when the needle pierces the pad of my finger. I forgot what a pain this is. When it's been about fifteen minutes and there's no response, I try not to be disappointed.

The questions spin like ballerinas doing piqués across my mind. I sit at the desk and smooth the paper beneath my fingers, pen poised over my journal in my other hand. As each thought twirls into view, I jot them down.

> *Is your name really Jax Frost?*
> *Are you a ghost?*
> *What do you look like?*

I draw the wolf to the side with a question mark next to it, then circle it for emphasis. With each press of the pen, the pressure in my skull abates, somehow feeling lighter.

> *Have we met before?*
> *Why are you here?*

This is ridiculous.

There's no way to logically explain this. Maybe I'm crazy. Maybe this is all in my head. Either way, I continue to write, getting the words and doodles down until the page is filled. Each line and curve unclenches the tightness in my chest a bit more until I finally release a sigh, staring down at my handiwork.

Those eyes stare right back.

After I twiddle my fingers for a few minutes, I peek up at the window. The frost embraces each stroke, preserving it within the delicate flecks. By the time the sun rises tomorrow, my window dressing will be gone. Out of sight, but definitely not out of mind.

Scooting my chair out, I get up and move far enough to peek into the bathroom. The leftover fog is gone, leaving behind only smudged lipstick decorating the mirror. Maybe they are off haunting someone else right now.

More likely, I'm losing it. Or maybe...

I unlatch the window and open it a crack. "Jax?" My voice quivers as I say his name, trying to stifle how crazy I feel. "J-Jax Frost?"

The cold wind smacks me with its icy palm, stinging my skin. Shivering, I scan the room, waiting for something to happen.

I wait.

And wait.

And wait.

I'm not patient enough for this.

Just a week ago, *Jax Frost*, or whoever this entity is, visited me after I'd been outside. As far-fetched as this seems, I head for the balcony, retracing my steps. Like the last time, the breeze almost assists me when I slide the glass door, something that usually takes much more effort. A chill dances across the ice-blue ballet shrug that crisscrosses over my chest. It comes down low, a peek of the silver scar beneath my leotard showing.

Admiring the thin glistening layer streaking the railing, my gaze follows how it expands out to icicles hanging at varying lengths. They'll no doubt be dripping come morning. According to the weather report there's supposed to finally be some sun. For the first time in days I might not need to bundle up like a human marshmallow to leave my apartment. Each year, winter seems to grow shorter and shorter, but this one has been unseasonably frosty. Where it's usually just a handful of especially frigid days, this year there's been weeks of it.

The ice is smooth as spun glass, entrancing me with how it encases the iron railing. I reach forward, trailing a finger along it. After the initial shock to my skin, the pain skims into a numbness I find myself leaning into. I've missed the warmth of sunlight lately, but there's something magical about being surrounded by such a white winter. As if on cue, Leslie Odom crooning "Winter Song" spills out of one of the apartments a few over from ours. The beat vibrates through me, thrumming with each gust against my body. It's like the wind itself is whispering *dance with me.*

Could this be my phantom?

"Jax?"

My hair lifts in a silent, playful response. Music kisses my skin, echoing through my soul. Swaying to the rhythm, I let the billowing breeze sweep me through the movements. My arms extend up, reaching for the stars, a glittering audience spread among a sea of black.

"Are you here?" I whisper along the wind as I continue to dance.

Snow appears as if from nowhere, flurrying with the lines of my arms, tracing all the way to my fingertips. Every brush of it against my skin sends goosebumps pebbling beneath my shirt, but it's less chilling and more invigorating than anything. There's no choreography to retain, no one else to judge my timing or technique. Just my body and this wind moving in eerie harmony.

The moon shines on me like a spotlight set from above, and spicy notes of pine and juniper swirl around me like a cozy embrace. It's one I never want to leave despite the wintry sting that streaks through me. When the music ebbs and I slow my movements, I'm hit with the burn searing into my uncovered fingertips.

I shiver and the wind scoots me toward the sliding glass door, then assists me to open it.

Steadying my breaths, I try to stay calm while nerves jolt deep in my belly. I slide the glass shut, locking it into place, and wait for any movement, wondering if he's still here...

I wait.

And wait.

And wait...

Nothing happens. Even the wind has receded outside.

When I finally slink back into my room, I notice that the window is no longer open. Did my ghost shut it? My words from earlier are strewn on the glass, still legible enough to read.

With each passing minute it feels more likely that it all was a dream. And the only dream I have time for is ballet. *Giselle* rehearsals need to be my entire focus. Even if I know most of the steps by heart, that only intensifies my need to perfect them. I should shine within the corps, but it wouldn't hurt to rewatch the solo variations. While most dancers would rather suffer through injuries and illness than give their spot to an understudy, there's no harm in being prepared.

Grabbing my laptop, I climb into bed and set it off to the side while I get cozy under the covers before resting it on my knees. Maybe this will kill some time and my ghost will come back. My gaze darts to the thermostat, which is at its usual setting, and my lips pull into a thin line. Clicking ahead to the famous mad scene from Act I, I settle against the pillow behind me. It's one of the most gut-wrenching moments in ballet that takes skillful acting, transitioning through so many emotions in one scene. The principal in The Randolph Ballet's 1996 production, Stasia Sylvane, performs with a broken grace that's absolutely captivating.

The heroine, Giselle, collapses to the ground after learning the true identity of her love, Albrecht: He's no peasant but is actually the duke and already engaged to a noblewoman. The audience witnesses her heartbreak, and she dances by herself, twined around an invisible force as she relives her whirlwind romance. Conveying an echo of a love that was a lie, she showcases her disillusionment through a series of steps interrupted by pauses and jarring movements, slowly losing her grip on sanity until her heart fails.

I scan through about five or six other productions, replaying my favorite moments. Pausing the performance, I glance between the window and the thermostat, hoping for... I'm not even sure.

Would it all make me less or more crazy at this point?

Chastising myself for my own irrational thoughts, I train my gaze back to the screen, visualizing myself swaying and falling apart with the music, conveying the final moments of Giselle's humanity before she's summoned to the woods to become one of the ethereal wilis. Doomed to dance for eternity, luring men to their deaths.

The act closes on the seventh video, the instrumental replaying in my head, strumming over and over like a sad lullaby. My eyes flutter. I glance at the window, finding it empty of anything other than my words. I groan. 4:30 a.m. will be here before I know it, and I need to be at my best and most rested. Curling up in a ball, I pull the covers over myself, settling my head on the pillow. I manage to force myself not to look at the window again and try to get some much-needed sleep.

Chapter Eleven

JAX

I've tried my best to stay away despite the way my chest aches with the constant thrum of my connection to the beautiful mortal asleep on the other side of the windowsill. Lines mark the glass, and I blow on it, slips of white and silver curling around the letters.

?ereh uoy reA
?xaJ

My brow wrinkles in frustration. This is no language I've learned in my harbinger studies.

Then I notice the backward squiggles. Question marks.

Duh.

I chuckle to myself before gliding into her room and spinning around to read the words:

Are you here?
Jax?

She's trying to talk to *me*. Hope rumbles through my chest. Does she crave my contact as much as I've craved hers?

Doubtful.

The only thing that could make this moment better is if I'd been here when she'd done it. When she didn't try to contact me, I kept my distance, watching her from afar. Last night, though, when she came out onto the balcony, I couldn't resist the opportunity to be near her. Our moonlit dance was the only thing I could give her—too scared to frighten her again until I was certain she wanted me around.

Maybe I would have seen her write this, but I was summoned to help some Frosts brew a big blizzard at the tip of Burlington. I hated having to leave her, especially after holding her beneath the stars, but I still can't risk getting banished. Not when I'm already skirting the cardinal rule.

Fuck, I've got it bad.

The glass gently squeaks as I write into the frost.

YES, TEMPEST.

I admire my handiwork, then notice her journal sitting open, deep grooves etched on the blank page facing me. I wave my hand, flipping to the prior entry. A dozen questions are spread across the lines, curves of black and white sketches surrounding her words.

Is your name really Jax Frost?

I chuckle to myself. She wants to know about me. That's encouraging. Maybe a way to each other isn't as far out of reach as everyone keeps telling me?

Taking a deep inhale, I exhale a thin layer of frost on the windowpanes. My fingertip scratches into the perfectly pristine layer, answering each question. That is, until I come to the last one:

Have we met before?

My nail hovers over the ice-coated glass. Something snakes through the back of my mind, slithering and coiling around whatever it is I can't see. No matter how much I want to reach in and grab what's hidden, I can't.

That's...odd.

Before I get frustrated, I breeze through the other pages, staring down at various renderings of my eyes, my wolf. *Me.* I'm spread throughout her journal, reflections that hold a truth I don't understand.

But I want to—and more than that, I want *her*.

Jolie shudders, and I spin away from her desk to face her. The comforter crests and falls with each breath. So peaceful. I could watch her for hours. For days.

Let's face it, I have.

I sidle up next to her, and she squirms, tugging the blanket tighter as white ghosts from between her lips. She's so fucking beautiful it hurts. I reach out and brush back some of the hair strewn in her face. Her nose wriggles and her body shivers.

Adorable.

I'll spend the next week along the northern tip of the East Coast, unfurling flakes and dripping icicles across four states. Slowing the meltdown for spring. I hope winter isn't cut short. Not this year, if I have any say in the matter. Which I don't, but a harbinger can dream. One day I will be a Lead Albidus, like my fathers, and have some sway when it comes to these things. It's all I've wanted since I graduated from the harbinger's academy over twenty seasons after my arrival, and each winter I serve the mortal world brings me closer to that milestone. Of course, I'm a bit distracted now by the only thing that could eclipse my duty to the Frosts.

Jolie.

I need to do something about this desperation for her that constantly overtakes me. Each day is harder for me than the last. While no one has ever been bonded to a mortal, there has to be more to it. Fate wouldn't have tied me to a mate only to have me pine over them for an eternity. Would she? The answer to that is something I must know.

And now I'm angry I missed this. She's been thinking about me. That's *everything.*

My cheeks warm as I look up at the window covered in answers, all written from the inside.

She'll know for certain I was here.

That thought fills me with pride, ice rushing through my veins to *every* part of me. Jolie squirms again, and I swallow down the way my body is eager for her. To caress each soft curve, thick strand of hair, raised pink scar. How I wish I could. In a way, I'm not much more than a ghost. The apparition she believes me to be, haunting the one I wish would see me most.

My very own form of unfinished business.

I peel myself from the bed, going against every part of me that wishes to soak up this closeness, one that she'd shudder away from if she were awake. At least until I can make her understand.

Hopefully, my responses will help her begin to and that small wintry mix up north will be enough for me to take a few days off without sacrificing winter's reign. The last thing I need is for those sneaky spring Blooms to think that the East Coast is ready for them.

It's not.

I'm not.

I need more time with her, but first, I need answers of my own. When she's ready to listen, I want to know what to say. I truly didn't want to interfere, didn't want to scare my mate after that broken message board fiasco, but I can't give up now. I refuse to. Not when she's so close to finding me.

Once I'm outside again, I press the heel of my palm over my heart and close my eyes, envisioning my destination like I've done a hundred times before. I normally don't make any trips back to Nivea midseason, but I can't wait until winter's end. I need to figure out how to reach Jolie without punishment or come to terms with denying myself. Solstice draws closer with each passing day, and I already can't get her out of my head. Something tells me that is just the tip of the iceberg when it comes to our bond and this desperate call to claim her.

Love her.

I don't know how it's possible to have someone make you feel alive when you haven't even spoken a word to them, but that's what she does.

She's become my heartbeat. The only one I have now. She pulses with a certainty that is etched into my skin and sinks deep into my bones. If she were to claim me as hers, as I long to claim her as mine, the world itself would come to life, full of color and possibility.

With each frantic step down the long, winding staircase that leads toward our city, my resolve solidifies. When I reach the landing, ice coating the ground in all directions, I summon my skates, gliding over the whirls of tracks spinning through Nivea's frozen streets.

"What are you doing here?" Aneira asks, popping into view and giving me a quick glance up and down. "You're not due back for another..." her periwinkle eyes dart up to the dial beaming down from the icy tower in the center of town, ticking off the timeframe on her fingers before lifting a hand in front of my face, "four weeks, if Fate's little pet isn't so lazy this year."

I ignore the thick divot carved into the icy timer signifying solstice and the shift change. The time when I'm meant to be claiming my mate, filling her full of pleasure, of me, before we go into blissful hibernation together.

"Well?" Aneira crosses her arms, brows lifted.

Her question has already slipped my mind.

"What are you doing here, Jax?"

Oh, that's what it was.

"I think you know why I'm here, Ani."

Aneira is one of the hardest working Frosts. She only works every other winter with me, though. A few spots in the world need tending to on the off seasons and she volunteered for it. Now she's taking this winter off to replenish her powers. If she didn't need the rest, she wouldn't. Her frost marks curl around her neck, swirling partially down one arm. The other shoulder, the one that's bare, is covered by thick waves of platinum hair. She always styles it that way, and I can't help but wonder if that will change once her marks begin to feather over there.

I'm looking forward to spending my next winter with her in the mortal world. I always enjoy her company, and she's so set to prove herself that I never have to pull her weight like I do with some of the others.

Speaking of... Crispin, her mate and one of the laziest Frosts of the family, makes his way over, powerful legs pushing against the ice, hips twisting sharply to break. Tiny flecks of frost kick up from his blades. He loops his arms around Aneira, pressing a kiss to the top of her head.

He's incredibly handsome and, therefore, most of the

unmated Frosts have happily picked up his slack in prior seasons, influenced by his charm. I'd be lying if I didn't say he'd won me over a time or two. But now that he and Aneira have claimed each other, I doubt he'll be getting the same assistance. Not that it really matters, Aneira is happy to help her mate.

Mate.

A divine blessing and my greatest curse all wrapped up in one four-letter word.

I groan internally thinking about spending my next winter with them, watching them together while my chest continues to fissure over a mortal I can't be with.

"I know you're struggling without your mate being here, but you know the rules," Aneira says before biting her lip. "She's not meant to be with you. Not yet."

Not meant to be with you.

How is that possible? The very nature of mates is *meant to be*. Ordained by Fate's very capable hand.

"Then why do I have this mark? Why do I feel like I'm being torn from the inside every minute I'm away from her?" My voice shakes the icicles hanging around the awnings. A storm simmers beneath my skin, becoming more frantic the farther I am from her. "Everything is telling me that I need to stay close. That I need this bond like I need the breeze."

Crispin gives me a pitying look and places his hand on my shoulder. "I know it must be difficult."

"Do you?" I swat his hand away and skate back a few paces. "Because your mate is always within reach," I say, tracing over my mark. "There's nothing preventing her from taking you in her arms, from talking to you. Jolie won't even listen to me when I try... Not without—"

I think back to the worried furrow of her brow. The way

her fingers shook as she contacted her therapist, begging to be seen.

"What did you do, Jax?" Aneira asks, gliding toward me, but I skate out of reach, lifting my hands up to warn her and her mate to keep their distance.

"Nothing. Doesn't matter," I mutter. *She just thought she was crazy.*

"Maybe it would be better to sit out this assignment? I can swap in and cover the rest of winter for you and you can go into early hibernation. Get some extra rest before you're due for another season."

"No." Ice climbs my fists and lower arms, and Aneira's eyes slide straight to it. Crispin takes her hand.

I'm glad they have each other, but this fucking hurts.

After some steadying breaths, the white retreats, and I wiggle my fingers. "Never had that happen before."

"This isn't good for you, Jax." Her voice is quiet.

"It's not," I admit. "But neither is being *home* without her. I could still sense her before I even arrived here." I wave at the icy expanse around us, the collection of towering skyscrapers aglow with white light peering out from each small window. "I know you're just trying to help, Ani, but... don't."

"So you just want to be miserable, brother?" Crispin asks, tilting his head. He may be a lazy motherfucker, but I hate how perceptive he is.

Maybe they're right. Maybe I should give up. Wait. Figure out how to survive solstice alone.

Maybe that's what I'll have to do, but... "I'd rather be miserable and have a shot than give up on everything."

Aneira swallows any retort and says softly, "I hope you know what you're doing."

"I don't, but we both know that's not going to stop me." I

swivel away from them, looking toward the spiral drop to Fate's den. There's an entrance from each of the harbingers' cities but it's rarely used by anyone here outside of our leadership. I've never been. "I have to find a way. I'll plead on my knees if I have to."

"Just make sure you know what you want before you do anything hasty, Jax."

"I want her." I reply, clipping her off before she says anything else. She should understand the importance, especially with her mate by her side. "There has to be a way and I'm going to find it."

"I hope you do." She opens her arms, and I can't fight the pull to hug her. I don't hold her concerns against her. She just wants to keep me safe. Wasn't I the one to welcome and comfort her all those winters ago after she'd become so sick that Fate had swept in and brought her here? Now she was comforting me. "Good luck, Jax."

"I don't need luck," I say with a chuckle. "I just need Fate."

JOLIE

My peaceful sleep is assaulted by the *tap, tap, tap* of drums from BLACKPINK's "Ice Cream" blaring into my ear.

I jolt up from my covers. Whipping my head to the phone buzzing on my nightstand, my brows drawn tight. It's 4:30 a.m., as it should be, only that's not my alarm.

It's been changed.

I snatch the phone up, and it vibrates in my palm. I turn it off, swiping to my settings and changing it back to Dua Lipa's "Hotter Than Hell."

How did that happen?

The question vanishes when my gaze falls to my bedroom window, and my lips part on a sharp inhale. There, in the dew-covered glass, words are scratched into the pane. *Tons* of them.

But at the top is a response to my window-written question, big and bold.

YES. TEMPEST.

The answers beneath veer off into different directions.

They're huddled together in clusters, creating little clouds set against a frost-covered sky. I shiver and lift my phone to snap a picture. It's the proof I need for no one but myself.

This isn't all in my head.

I rise from the bed, slipping my feet into two puffy swans before shuffling closer. Wrapping my arms around myself, my teeth chatter, the chill increasing with each step forward. "What the fuck?"

My pulse stutters, throat turning to sandpaper as I trace a finger along the thin sheet of frost coating the glass—the *inside* of the glass. Jax was in my room.

How many times has he been around when I had no idea? A very large part of me doesn't want to know.

My attention snags on **Tempest**. Is that some weird thing he is calling me? I think back to the last few nights out on the porch. I had my sweatshirt from our production of *The Tempest* on then. It's confirmation that he has been here. He's some invisible presence. That both affirms my sanity and deeply unsettles me.

My gaze lingers over each huddle of words. They're answers to my questions, and I can't take my eyes off them. Reaching behind myself, I fumble around my desk until the familiar texture of paper is beneath the pads of my fingers. Hands trembling, I clutch my journal tight, alternating between my questions and starting at the top of the pane where the words **Yes, my name is Jax Frost** and **No, I'm not a ghost** are etched into existence. My legs shake, nearly giving out from under me.

I'm not crazy.

He's not a ghost.

He's Jax Frost.

Staggering back a few steps, I plop into the swivel chair at my desk and tuck my feet under my knees. I should be getting ready to get to the studio extra early and warm up before rehearsal, but beams of sunlight shoot through his words and the idea that I could come back to all of them erased pins me to the spot. I grab a pen and, with a shaky hand, jot down the answers next to each corresponding question, despite having photographic evidence.

Pausing, I double check that the image is still there, breathing a sigh of relief when it is. Part of me is worried that, like some vampire lore, his handiwork will magically disappear. Regardless, I want the words on the page, every affirming answer to account for the strange things that have been happening.

Jax is a harbinger, an immortal charged with bringing winter. I continue to log each answer, my pulse fluttering with every line I scrawl, especially when I come to the doodle of a wolf with the word *earthside*. Next to it is a stick figure and **true form**. Beneath it, in big block letters:

WISH YOU COULD SEE ME.

My hands press over his frosty admissions, as if touching them will somehow summon him here. The cold blazes through my palms, but I don't retreat. I lean into its chill. I wish I could see him too.

This should scare me. Some otherworldly creature-being has been creeping in my room, following me, and hanging around town as a giant wolf with glowing eyes. Every answer should be a signal to *run*. Instead, I'm rooted in place, hungry for more.

What the heck is wrong with me?

I step back, reading the final scribbled cloud, and glance at my journal.

The last question, where I asked if we've met, has been

left unanswered. Disappointment sinks into my gut. If he admitted to being the wolf I'd seen, the one with the eyes that have been carved into my subconscious ever since the accident, then there has to be some connection. There's no way that's simply a coincidence.

I check my phone for the time. 5:15 a.m. I've got fifteen minutes to get ready and make the metro with enough time to do a very abridged warm-up before class and rehearsals for *Giselle*'s second act, The White Act. I rush into the bathroom, running my hands under the warm water, shaking off this morning.

Nothing can send me tilting off center right now. Not even this.

Every rehearsal, every step, needs to be flawless. We are weeks away from opening night, and the director, my instructors, Ballet Potomac's benefactors, all their eyes will be on us. Judging each ballerina and determining our fate. They are the ones who hold my career in the palms of their hands. In order to make a comeback, I can't have distractions. No matter how intriguing they are.

I have the photo. The answers— Well, most of them. That will have to be enough for now.

Rummaging through my drawers, I grab my leotard, tights, a shrug, and fitted warm-up pants. Throwing an extra set of clothes in my bag, I quickly brush my teeth, apply some light makeup, pin up my bun, and head for the door.

"Hey," Lark shouts from behind me, bringing me to a halt.

"Hey! I figured you left without me so you could get to rehearsals early."

"I didn't need to get there *that* early."

Of course she didn't. She's not the one trying to prove herself at a new company. It hits me that she's only been leaving early so I don't have to walk to the metro alone. The sharpness in my tone softens, along with the tension pulled through my shoulders. "Thanks, Lark."

"Anytime, Jojo." She gets up from the couch, picking up the dance bag set in front of her, and tosses me a chocolate coconut bar. "Let's get going. You have rehearsals to rock and instructors to woo," she croons, reaching to redo one of the bobby pins in her hair.

Peeling back the foil on my breakfast, I take a bite, leaving the bar in my mouth while I use my free hand to open the door and hold it for Lark. I follow her down the stairs, ignoring the dripping icicles strewn across the railings. The whole descent, I wonder if Jax was the one to leave them there, where he is, and when and if he'll return.

As much as I need to keep my head on straight for rehearsals today, a very large part of me is counting down to his next visit and getting more answers.

I glide with singular purpose toward the drop to Fate's den, combing through how I will approach asking her what I need to.

"Jax?"

My head snaps to the left and I skid to a halt. Skating from City Hall, my fathers both wave at me with their free hands that aren't interlocked. They're everything I aspire to. Mated more winters than anyone can count, their bond has only strengthened over the centuries.

"What are you doing here?" Dad asks as they both stop in front of me, his silvery brows bunched together. "It's still wint—"

"I came to see Fate." There's no point in trying to keep this from them. They know more than I do, but I won't ask them my questions. Fate is the one who holds the cards— the one who can actually give me what I'm asking for—I won't put them in the middle of this. They've already given me so much.

As Lead Albiduses, they're always working with Fate to ensure every season is executed flawlessly and help rookie harbingers get acclimated with their new role. I had quite a hard time *adjusting* after my transition to immortality. I don't remember much about it. Like my mortal life itself, it's faded away. Only small shards of memory remain, glinting from the back of my mind when I least expect it.

"Son, you're so close to the end of season, and your work this winter has been impeccable," my pops says, a smile peeling up the corner of his mouth.

"It has." I grin back at them. I've made sure of it. Going above and beyond with my Frost duties makes it possible to see Jolie. It buys me every small moment I get to be with her, even if she's only just realized I'm there.

Dad's pale-blue eyes twinkle at me before darting over to his mate's. They are polar opposites in appearance. He's a few inches shorter than me with silvery skin, while Pops is tall and lanky with sky-blue skin, navy waves, and a beard to match. His swirling gray eyes watch me like a storm cloud. Every exposed inch of them, aside from their faces, is covered in the feathered markings of our people, a culmination of all those winters out in the world. Now they've earned the ability to remain here, helping us to do the same.

"I'm still getting my frost marks this winter," I add, wanting to make sure they remember how dedicated I am to our work. Being an Albidus, being able to help new Frosts, it's the perfect way to pay it forward after everything my fathers did for me. I've been working toward this role and having the power to oversee hundreds of Frosts, ensuring they thrive within our community, for more than two decades.

"And you've been staying away from the mortals?" Pops asks, his stormy stare making the air drop to an even more chilling level. My attention shifts to their hands that are still clutched but tensed, the veins on their wrists bulging beneath their markings.

"Yes," I say quickly, "I've been avoiding the mortals."

Now, a very specific mortal with hair the color of rich cocoa... not so much. But they don't need to know that.

"Good." Dad's shoulders drop and he releases a breath. "You have no idea how hard it was for us to keep you in extended hibernation through last winter."

"Keep delivering these outstanding winters and you'll be an Albidus in no time," Dad says, placing a hand on my shoulder and giving it a squeeze.

Pops beams with pride. "The youngest Frost to lead since Jack himself."

Ah yes, the first Frost harbinger and first to take the role of Lead Albidus. He spent centuries helping other Frosts, including the two standing before me. Now he's retired.

"You make us so proud, son." Dad takes his hand off me, resting his forehead on Pop's shoulder. Pop's navy waves fall in his face as he kisses Dad's temple.

"Thanks." I fight the drop in my tone, inserting a quick smile to offset it. My chest aches at the sight of them together.

Just another reminder of why I'm here.

Once I've earned my final frost marks, I'll be able to choose any calling within Nivea. Lead Albidus is what I'm destined for, and one day, I hope to serve as one with my beautiful Tempest by my side.

"So you're on your way to see the boss?" Dad asks, swallowing thickly.

Pops loops an arm around him—over what, I'm not sure —then his sharp gaze comes back to me. "Do you want us to go with you?"

I shake my head. "I need to do this on my own."

They'd only try to stop me, which I don't hold against

them. They love me. If I were in their skates, I'd do the same to protect the Frosts in my care.

"Of course." Pops gives me a small nod. It means everything to me that he's not trying harder to intervene. "You know where to find us if you need us."

Dad points over to their house, a large sculpted mansion that sparkles with icicles hanging off the roofs and wraparound porch. It's much larger than most of the other homes in Nivea, with plenty of space for the younger Frosts to stay until they are mated and on their own. "Stop by for a frozen cocoa before you head earthside?"

"Of course, Dad."

He and Pops pull me in for a hug before skating off together. The way they look at each other, like they see everything beneath the frost marks, staring at the core of the other... I want that.

Fate has the answers Jolie seeks. Ones I wish I could give her. When I see my Tempest next, I'll have them for her. No more pages filled with questions I can't respond to. No more self-doubt. She'll know everything I do. She'll know I'm real. Here.

Hers.

There are no secrets when it comes to your mate. I don't care if she's mortal, I'll give her every truth she desires. Give her *everything* in whatever way I can.

One day, she will see me. Fate has to know how.

She's the one that gifts us our mates, after all.

Fate's den is deep below where the harbingers live, a steep cavern with a dozen twisting coves extending in every direction. No one knows where all the paths land, aside from Fate, but each season's harbingers have a separate entrance. I assume some must go to her private quarters. Maybe some reach other ethereal beings like herself.

"I wondered when you'd come," Fate's silvery voice echoes through the chamber.

"You're Fate. I assumed you'd already know that."

Strings of flowers and leaves, branches, thick icicles, and beams of light fall from the ceiling, each element unique—as unique as the floor beneath us, carved to look like the dial posted on our tower in Nivea's city center. A watercolor pool swirls on its own at its center, and I stare into it, mesmerized. Fate sits on its edge, dress draped along the ground, stirring her palm within its rippling rainbow.

"Contrary to what you may believe, I cannot foresee everything."

"But you hold on to the strings?"

"More like tip the scale." She points toward an oversized one situated in the corner with small stones of different shapes, shades, and sizes piled on either side. Her rose-gold brows tighten while her arm is submerged in pinks and greens and yellows. "There have been times when I've even been surprised."

Her expression lifts as she sits upright and unfurls her fingers, showing me a tiny lavender rock, jagged at its edges and shining under the dim light. Clutching it tightly in her fist, she grabs her skirt to hold it off the floor with her free hand before waltzing with a few twirls that spin her glittering, rainbow-hued dress out from her. It's gauzy and matches the colorful swirls painted across her skin and peeking through her hair. Her body is nearly camouflaged by the streaks aside from her bare, unmarked, rose-gold feet. She leans over, blue and emerald strands of hair falling in her face while she assesses the perfect spot to place the stone within the pile. Lifting her arm, she repositions it a few times before moving her hand to drop it.

"Would one of those times when you were surprised happen to be when I was punished for breaking our rule?"

"In some ways, yes." Her brows knit in concentration as her delicate fingers stick the stone between a large blue and a sharp golden rock. Sighing, she sweeps herself in graceful paces in my direction.

"Can you tell me what happened?"

She halts midstep, multicolor eyes swirling with an emotion I can't place.

"I want— I need to know why you gave me a mortal mate."

Her lips purse. After a beat of silence, she sits down and pats the spot next to her on the ledge. "I don't know if that's wise."

I sit next to her, half tempted to touch the whirling colors within the pool. I've never come to Fate before. Not for anything. I've been grateful for my immortal life, and I don't want any special treatment.

Not until now.

"Please. There's something missing, something nagging at the back of my mind, and I think it has to do with my memory being wiped the last season I was out there. When I was punished."

"Yes." She averts her gaze, but I place a gentle hand on her shoulder, waiting until she turns to face me.

"There's something in the back of my mind—a memory I can't seem to recall," I begin, pointing at my temple for emphasis. "I'm sure whatever it is, you and my fathers hid it from me with good reason. Whatever got me benched last winter." I qualify that sentiment because I don't want her instantly on the defensive. "But my mate... She's out there. There has to be a way for us to be together, otherwise you wouldn't have connected our destinies, right?"

"It's a bit more complicated, Jax." Fate stands and turns toward me, then uses her pink-and-purple splashed fingers to crook my chin up to meet her rainbow gaze. "It wasn't our idea to erase your memories." She pauses, as if weighing whether to continue. "It was yours."

"What?" I rear back from Fate's grasp. "Why?"

"You're here for answers. I'm not unwilling to give them to you, but know that the truth of the past won't change who you are or what she is."

"She is mine, mortal or not," I growl out, the force of its reverberation shaking flowers and leaves down from the ceiling. An icicle shatters on the floor.

Fate winces, waving it away and tossing a new one up, as if it didn't happen. Her face softens. "You truly wish to rescind your request to withhold your memories?"

"Are they tied to her?"

"Yes."

"Then I rescind my request. I need to know."

"Once I return them to you, it cannot be undone." Her glittering eyes convey that this is the last time she'll ask.

"Yes." There is no hesitation in my voice, and I continue to breathe slowly despite the thrum of Jolie's pulse within me, calling me to her. I wonder if she's waking up. If she's gotten my messages. I want to be there to tell her everything, but I can't do that without doing this first.

"Show me."

Last February

The harbinger speeds through the trees, draping icicles along barren maple branches. He flies lower, spreading shiny verglas atop each rock in his path, the frosty breaths of two lovers bundled up in layers and kissing in the snow drawing his attention. Tiny mismatched flecks spring from his palms in shades of white and blue before he waves his hands. They drift down toward the couple, catching in her red waves and his dark beard. They laugh between kisses, their exhales painting the air white as they gaze in wonder at the flakes flurrying around them.

Admiring his work, the harbinger spins and skates off across the lake, water thickening into ice beneath his feet. Fifty winters finished, he's weeks away from earning more frost marks—

The wind is knocked from him, and a sharp, searing pain lances between his ribs. He shreds away his shirt, spotting ridges forming, carving line by line deep into his chest. This isn't like the frost adorning skin. It's an endless echo of terror.

Anguish.

A shocking pulse riots through him, vibrating so fiercely

it sends him staggering. Silver streaks glow from his sternum, and he presses a hand there, hoping to alleviate the discomforting throb. Even just a little.

Not once did he imagine this would be how it happened. The sensations are nothing like his friends described. The only thing he knows is he must follow its tug.

He clutches his chest, closing his eyes, begging to find his mate, but when he looks again, he's not back home in Nivea. He's still earthside, just somewhere further south.

Something's wrong.

He tries again, channeling the frantic rhythm overtaking his rib cage. His mind clears, wholly focused on finding them. While he doesn't understand this new connection fully, he knows his mate needs him. He scans the park. It's empty minus a few other Frosts doing their usual duty. None pay him any mind.

It's not one of them.

The bridge he sits on is covered in sheets of ice, blackened markings veering off toward the lake. The beat within his chest becomes less hurried, slowing...and slowing...

Panic claws through him, sparking every nerve as his gaze whips around the park. *They must be here. They must be.* Moving closer to the bridge, he peers down into the ice-covered lake below. Shards of broken ice bob in a gentle current, floating within a dark, gaping crack.

His heart seizes in his chest. That crack could swallow him whole...

There. My mate's down there.

This can't be right. He should be back home. His mate should be waiting for him with open arms. Finally finding each other thanks to Fate. He glances down at the stinging mark that's still forming a half-whirled semi-circle at his sternum.

None of this is as it should be.

Not wasting another moment, he jumps, moving through the thick layer of frozen water like its air.

To him, it is.

He's found a home in the cold. Its chill runs through his veins, coats his flesh. He freezes, coming face to face with his mate.

It's her.

He searches her wide eyes, focus dropping to her parted lips just beyond the cracked glass. Dark strands trail out from her, her vacant, pale stare gazing straight past him.

This is wrong.

She's leaving just as quickly as he's found her. Body floating next to the woman in the driver's seat. Silver starts to glow from her chest, and he's certain that beneath her clothes are swirls etching into existence that match his own. He brings his hand over his mark, already missing the pounding *thud*, the frantic beat that drew him here.

Never interfere with the affairs of mortals.

The harbinger creed rings in the back of his mind, but he's already using his icy power to shatter the window. The flutter between his ribs and the searing at his chest fades, and now the beat that drove him mad to get to her is the only thing he wishes for.

Please beat.

As she slips from this world, he's there, clutching her to him. Anger rattles his chest. Why would Fate allow this? He's found his mate—a moment he's looked forward to his entire immortal existence. Instead of excitement, though, the only thing spiraling through him is gut-wrenching terror.

Her limp body against his is a hollow reassurance. She

can't actually feel him. She can't feel *anything.* The skin pressed to him turns blue, icy streaks paint her hair.

Visions drift in and out of his mind, flashes of her life.

A little girl twirling in front of the mirror, dressed in pale pinks.

Walking through this very park, swinging between her parents.

Satin ribbons flutter into view. She ties them at her ankles before her fingertips fluff the tulle of her costume. Her lips are bold pink in this memory, not the silvery-blue they're turning now. She smiles, pressing up onto her toes with unencumbered glee.

She's older now, body and limbs long and lithe, reaching delicate fingers toward the audience. The harbinger can feel the warmth of the spotlight on her. It drowns out the audience in a sea of black, minus one person. The most important one.

The one currently strapped in the seat next to his mate.

Fear blows every memory away, and he sees his mate's final moments: the car skidding, the screams, the smash of steel breaking through ice, sinking, sinking, sinking, and the panicked push against the water's resistance.

A panic he recognizes.

The pulse of it is etched into his soul. Any tears the harbinger sheds are carried off with the current. Lost to him as quickly as the joy that flooded every cell of his being when the mate mark began to carve itself into his chest.

A hand grips his shoulder, and he jerks back.

He's not alone.

Fate's been there all along, looking on the scene with a somber expression. *"You shouldn't be here, Jax. She's meant to meet you in Nivea."*

Her voice caresses his mind, its comforting lilt all too

familiar. Too much like his first faint memories of her. Raw ones he doesn't like to think on much. Another shattering of ice. Another plunge into a chilling embrace. Reaching for someone else.

Too late.

His hands clench into quivering fists. *"This can't be right."*

"She is your mate." Fate's expression softens, looking at him as if pain is streaked across his flesh instead of frost marks.

"But she's mortal," he stammers, not understanding how this is possible. *"I just saw her life. Watched her—"*

"Her fate is already etched in Frost."

Fate extends a paint-swirled arm, the usual rainbow of it dulled by the frozen canopy blotting any light bar the strip where the car cracked it into shards. Swirls of glittering magic reach for his mate's chest. The space that minutes ago was filled with the blissful rhythm of her heartbeat now is filled with empty silence. What he would give to feel it again.

In every scenario he conjured in his dreams, none of them equipped him for finding his mate like this. Dying. He recalls her in the memories. Rich brown hair; shimmering blue eyes; warm, beige skin. So vibrant. So driven.

So alive.

And so much left to do.

"Stop," he says, wrapping his fingers gently around Fate's wrist and pulling it back. The magic searing his mate's chest is severed, leaving behind only the swirl of her mate mark. A sign of what could be.

"What will *be,"* Fate calls to him, answering his thought with the truth.

It's his mate's time to come home with him. To claim him and her immortality. He'll hold her close, make the transition better for her than it had been for him. He'll be everything for her. It's all he's wanted for decades: to have this bond and the harbinger attached to it to cherish for all of immortality.

"*No.*" He's seen her life, felt her dreams as if they were his own. They're now chiseled into his bones. Their existences are no longer separate. He carries her within him as much as she will one day carry him.

One day. But not today.

His story may have been cut short, but she deserves to see hers through.

He looks Fate in her prismatic eyes. "*Let her live.*"

"*What?*" Fate blinks, astonished, which is a feat. "*Do you know what you're asking? The stone has been set. Any shifts will create a ripple I can't see yet.*" Her hand fumbles over the skirts of her dress, floating out from her like watercolor come to life. "*Her death is an inevitability.*"

"*I'll take whatever you can give her. Hold me responsible, but let her live.*" The harbinger can barely fathom the words that escape him, but he doesn't regret a single one. "*I'm begging you.*"

"*You'd give up your mate to buy her more time...as a mortal?*"

"*Yes.*" His eyes sting, chest aches. There's no hesitation. Harbingers are those who were unable to live full lives. He may not have met her yet, but he knows her. Sees every wondrous moment she's had and every wish she hopes comes true. Taking her now would be thieving her of the dreams she has yet to accomplish. Ones she's desperate for.

"*You're sure?*" Fate hesitates, eyes darting, as if thinking over something she doesn't voice aloud. When her attention returns to him, her tone is firm. "*Giving back her life and seeing her goals come to fruition... You may never be reunited with your mate.*"

"I'm sure." Despite the stab of pain twisting through his gut, he nods for emphasis. He'll watch her each winter. He'll make sure she sees those dreams ignite. Even if he'll never be a part of them.

"Take her to the surface," Fate instructs. *"I'll do the rest."*

He's already shifting before she finishes. White and gray fur expands from his flesh. His nose elongates into his snout. Claws extend from his fingers and toes, his body contorting until he's in his earthside form.

The wolf wraps its maw around the neck of the mortal's shirt, pulling her through the partially shattered window. Crimson spreads through the water, trailing behind them. When the beast brings her body to the surface of the lake, he drags her across the ice until he rests her at its edge.

Where she'll be safe, as he's been promised.

Fate is there, waiting.

Her vibrant dress pools around her feet, swirls of vivid color creating a striking contrast next to his dead mate's pallid complexion. She flicks her wrist, unfurling her fingers to reveal a cerulean rock as thick as a puck. The wolf moves closer to inspect it.

"Last chance." Her hand lifts and lowers, as if testing the weight of the thing she's holding.

The wolf's attention is pinned to the stone in her palm. It's beautiful. Strong. It reminds him of the bond he longs to claim. The woman he could have loved.

Would have loved.

"Do it."

Fate places her hands on the shoulders of his mate, leaning down to press a kiss to her temple before her gaze shifts to the wolf. The rock in her hand crumbles, disintegrating and floating off on the breeze. Disappearing as if it never existed.

The wolf lies down alongside his mate, nestles his snout in the valley between her breasts, closes his eyes, and waits.

Fate bows. Her work is done.

A single kiss and destinies are rewritten.

Thump.

Thump.

Thump.

The faint flutter of her rekindled pulse rouses the wolf. He observes his mate. Her skin is less pale, lips no longer blue, chest no longer stilled. Her body warms against his, Fate's magic thrumming through her. Each passing second, her heartbeat regains its strength. It thuds beautifully, echoing between them.

Thump-thump. Thump-thump.

Thump-thump. Thump-thump.

When the wolf tilts his head up, Fate is gone.

Smeared streaks of dark red against the snow steal his focus. Though his mate's life has been spared, he needs to make sure she's safe. The last thing he wants to do is leave her, but he must find help. He must ensure the dreams he let crumble away like ash on the wind were worth his sacrifice.

In a flash, his claws retract, fur vanishing, body camouflaging into the wintry backdrop. He races through the park, hunting down the first mortal he can find. When his blistering wind doesn't urge the man in the direction he wishes, he reclaims his earthside form, growling and prowling with teeth bared until the mortal runs away toward the lake. Once he's out of sight, the harbinger follows, watching from the trees until blaring sirens wail in the distance moments before an ambulance arrives.

Once they've strapped his mate onto a stretcher and he hears their words that she's alive—*she's safe*—the harbinger places a hand over his unclaimed mate mark. He savors the beautiful beat of her heart against his palm. Holds on to it as he returns home.

Fate is waiting with his fathers. A cross of pity and disappointment spans their faces.

"You'll forfeit the rest of this winter and the next."

"You'll forfeit going earthside."

"You'll forfeit earning your frost marks."

The harbinger doesn't care, though. He'd forfeit it all to see the joy on his mate's face again. The vibrancy of her passion. His dreams may have ended much too soon, but hers don't have to. Each beat of her heart reminds him of that.

She's worth it. Always.

As the weeks of his miserable banishment pass, he curls up in bed, clinging to the comforting thud between his ribs. Clinging to *her*. While he'd never take back his choice, he mourns the colorful memories of an immortal life he may never get with her.

Speeding through the trees. Painting the world in ice and snow by her side. Spending solstice buried deep within her, claiming each other over and over again.

Never apart.

After a while—he doesn't know when, since he refuses to leave his room—he begs his fathers to bring Fate to see him. She sits on the edge of his bed, taking his hand in hers.

"I need you to do something for me—"

"I cannot undo this," she says, a tear streaking her cheek. "I'm sorry. Everything's been set in motion to balance the scale. You must let destiny play out as it's meant to."

"I know."

Fate's brows lift in surprise. Did she really think he would be okay watching his beautiful mate's life cut before his very eyes? As much as he loves her, he could never wish his own fate on another. It would have been something if he'd been tethered to another harbinger, but he couldn't stand by and see that happen to *her*. Not when he could do something to stop it.

Not when she had so much life left to live.

"I made my choice and I'd make it again."

The harbinger pushes himself up in bed. It takes more effort than it should, every part of him so weak. He half expects to crumble like that cerulean stone. How can he replenish his magic knowing she's out there, unaware of his very presence? Of their connection.

The heartbeat thuds wildly in his chest. Maybe it always will. But he cannot remain like this. It's too hard to bear. Too consuming now that he cannot reach her.

"What is it, Jax?"

It's his final request. The only way he can hibernate and rest before returning to his duty and bringing more winters. His eyes plead with Fate, his voice shaking with fierce resolve.

"Make me forget."

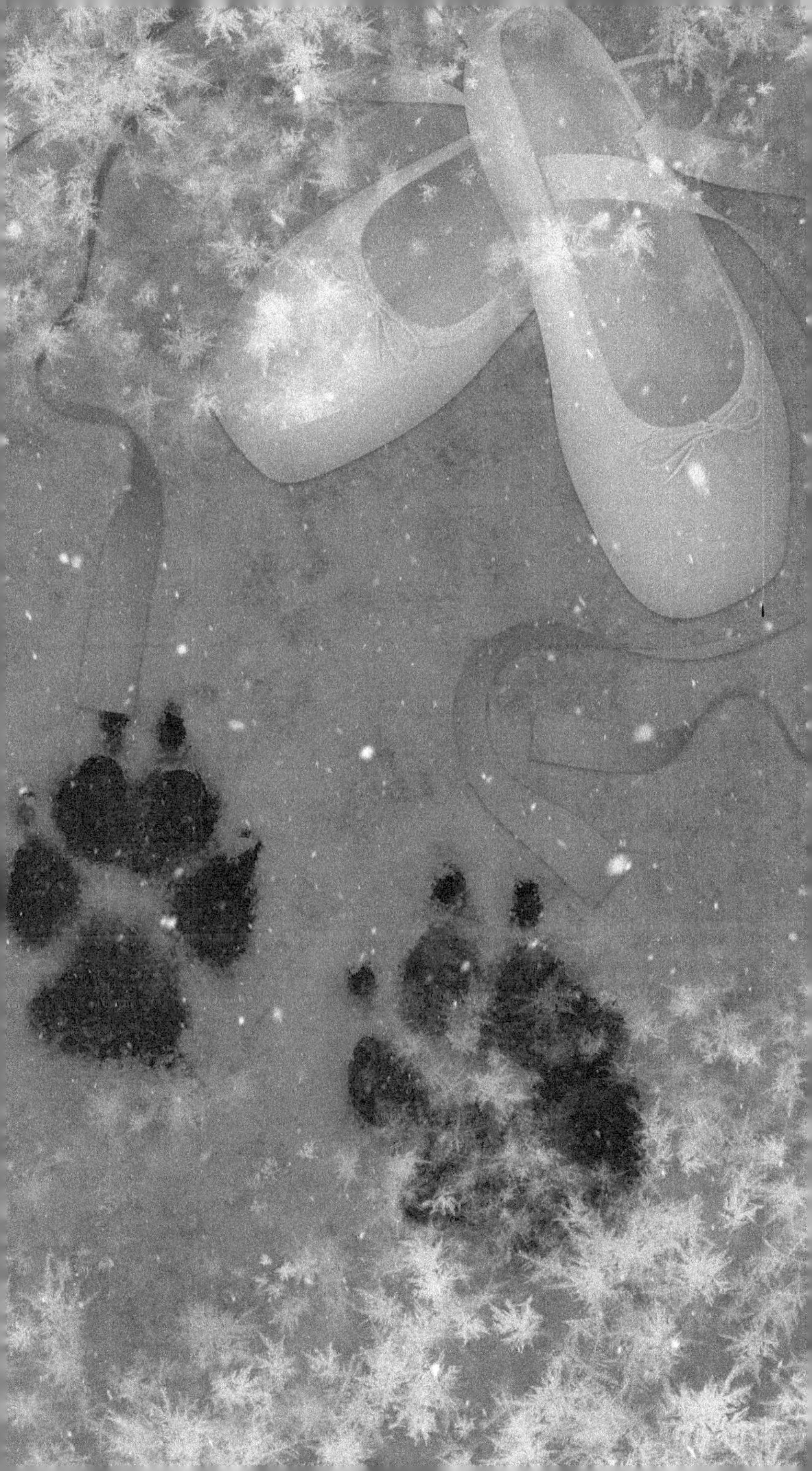

Chapter Fifteen

JAX

The storm surging through my mind is a blizzard of emotions that nearly send me stumbling into Fate's watercolor pool. I grip its ledge as she catches my arm. Her rainbow gaze scrutinizes me, and she makes no effort to let go of my shoulders. Not until I've caught my breath and tilted myself upright.

Though it feels like yesterday, it's been almost a year since I learned of my mate. That reality is unsettling. I bartered our immortal future so she could have a mortal one. Yet, as I brush my palm over my mate mark, I feel her pulse fluttering there and I'm struck with a fierce sense of pride. Nothing has brought me greater joy.

I chuckle, the sound echoing off the walls of Fate's den, shaking the strands of flowers and leaves dangling from the ceiling. The sharp truth of what I set in motion should break me, but I won't let it. Just as swiftly as the realization hits me, another one does: *our bond remains*. I've been able to find her even without my memories because I'll always find her. In any life. In any form.

For she is mine and I am hers.

I just have to find a way for her to see me.

"I know we're an anomaly but there has to be a way forward for us." It's not a question. It's a demand.

"You chose to keep her earthside." Her voice is full of pity and devoid of the hope I desperately clutch within me.

 "That was no choice," I say, gritting my teeth.

Jolie's limp body still in my arms.

Blood trailing across the snow.

Bits of crumbled rock floating away on the wind.

"No respectable mate would choose to let our other half die."

I'll never unsee the light leaving her eyes, unfeel the panic rioting through her pulse before it hushed within our chests. Any harbinger who'd willingly watch their mate's death and do nothing to stop it wasn't worthy of the tether they'd been blessed with.

"You weren't supposed to find her first, Jax."

"Well, I did."

"She is on borrowed time."

My body stiffens. "What does that mean?"

"She's going to die, Jax." Fate's voice is soft despite her harsh words, and she places a streaked hand on my shoulder. "No mortal escapes death. Eventually, her destiny will play out, and I can no longer guarantee her immortality." It's not an answer, but she presses her lips in a firm line, silently telling me that's all she's willing to offer.

"I will find a way to her," I growl. "She's *mine.*"

"Maybe so," she hesitates, weighing her words carefully, "but you cannot change what you both are."

"I know that," I grit out, "but if you know a way I can reach her, a way she could see me, could talk to me... *Please.*" I'm begging here. Hell, I could be banished for the rest of this winter just for asking because there's no way to reach her without breaking the cardinal rule of *interfering.*

But I think we both know, even if it's left unspoken, that I will always interfere when it comes to Jolie.

"I don't have any definitive answers, Jax. Nothing like this has ever happened in our history." She stands and strides toward the scale, fingers trailing delicately over the colorful stones. "We don't interfere with mortals because it upsets the balance. The natural order..." Her gaze narrows and she bites her lip. "Perhaps..."

"Perhaps what?" I stand and move toward her, inspecting the stones, large and small, sitting atop each surface of the scale. Every perfectly balanced bauble in its place. Dropping to my knees in supplication, I stare up at Fate, gripping her paint-streaked hands in mine. "Please. I'm begging you. I will do my best to maintain balance, but there has to be something I can do. Some way she can see me."

She sighs languidly, cupping my cheek. "In uncharted waters there are always ripples, Jax Frost. But I wish to help you."

"Then help me. Tell me what to do."

She flicks her wrist, and a small cerulean stone the size of a marble appears between her fingers. "Mortals are not able to view our true forms, not because it is not allowed, but because their minds are tethered to the physical plane of their world."

"Meaning?"

"If your mate believes in your existence, she will be able to see you. To touch you. In this form." Just the idea of that sends a shiver down my spine. Fate cradles my chin and gives me a small smile. "You weren't the first to be seen by a mortal."

"Who was the first?" I ask.

"That should be obvious," Fate says dismissively, flitting

back toward the pool and tossing the tiny bauble in. "The only other who's been seen by mortals is the very being they've spun into myth. The first ever Albidus. Our very own Jack Frost."

"So I just need to get her to believe in me?"

"You make that sound so simple. You know better than to think it will be easy. Mortal hearts are not quick to sway. I do not envy what is ahead for you, Jax," Fate says, dismissing me. With a wave of her hand, my skates glide me back up to Nivea.

If her words are meant to be a warning, that's not how I interpret them. If Jack Frost did it, then so can I. I've been working toward becoming the youngest Lead Albidus since his reign, after all.

I have one final stop—to visit my fathers as promised—before I return earthside. The idea of Jolie seeing me, hearing me, touching me, gives me all the encouragement I need. Pushing my skates into the ice, I speed as fast as my feet will carry me, renewed with a singular focus.

First, I'll help her believe.

Then, I'll make her mine.

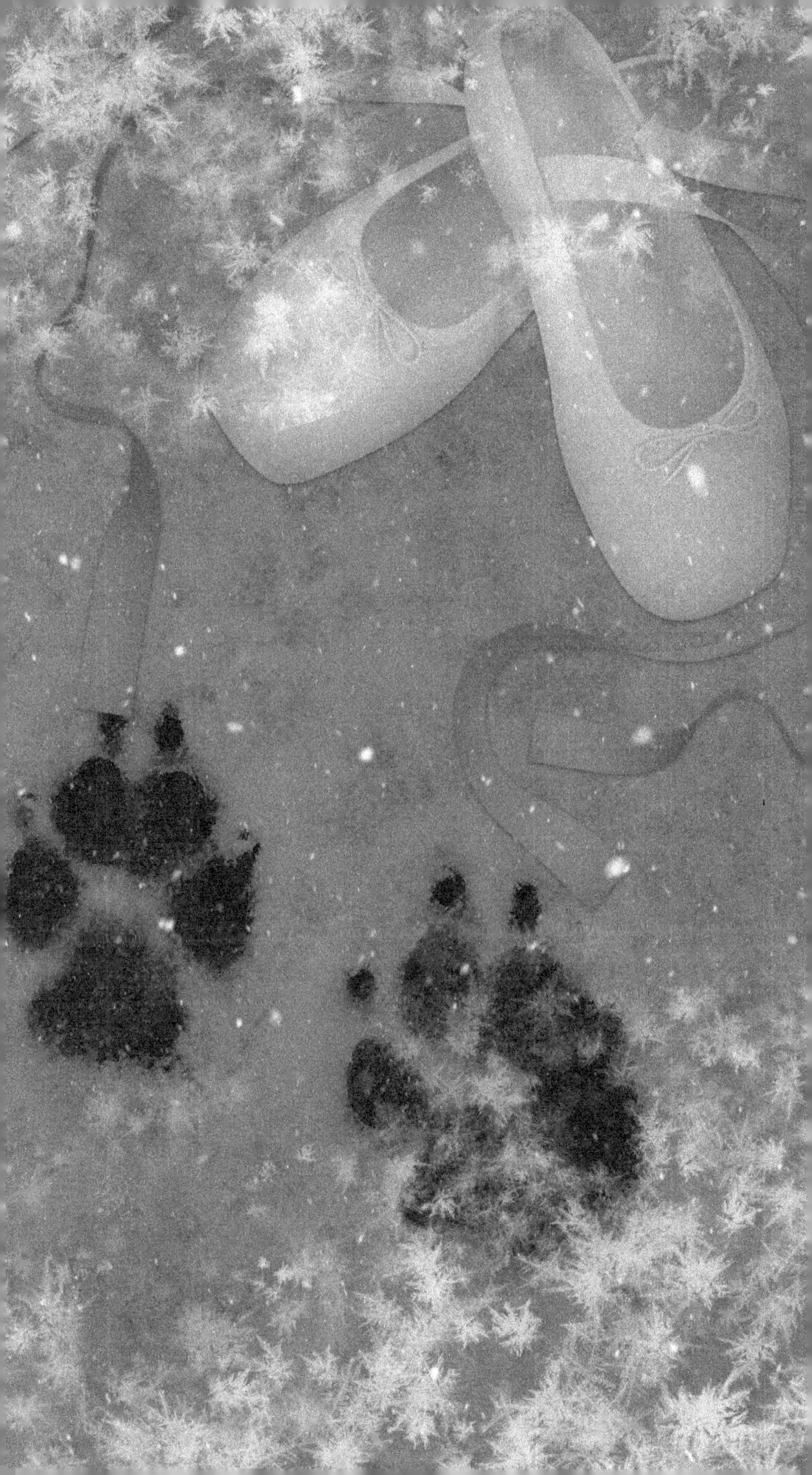

Chapter Sixteen

JOLIE

I get to class early and warm up. Evelyn, Veronique, and Sara haven't arrived yet, so I busy myself with reciting the barre combinations in my head. There are about a dozen other dancers in the studio, but most still haven't introduced themselves to me even though I've been here for weeks.

When Mistress Maral arrives and calls class to session, I'm poised and ready for pliés, my chest lifted and fingers wrapped around the wood. I move through each combination comfortably. Now that I've memorized the choreography, I can inject some personal flair—my favorite part. The subtle tilt of my chin. The float of my hand. Extending each line to complement the positions we move through. When the throb of pain shoots down my leg, I ignore it and keep going, refusing to let my unhappy hip come out victorious.

I'm in control, I'm going to PT, and I will prove that I deserve to be a soloist again.

Every time we switch sides, my gaze drifts to the window. Disappointment curls in my gut when I find it empty. There's no sharpened stare from Jax's wolf, just beams of sunlight pouring through the row of windows.

I rush out as soon as class ends, heading for my lunchtime appointment at Dr. Tanner's office. My mind leaps to every conclusion I can think of as to why Jax didn't answer that final question. Maybe he had to be somewhere. It's supposed to get warmer over the next few days. Maybe he's gone. The news all but predicted that good ol' Punxsutawney Phil won't be seeing his shadow. They claim the unnatural chill of this winter will bring an earlier thaw with spring.

A shiver sends goosebumps down my arms with each brush of the breeze. It's crazy to wonder each time if it's Jax, but I can't help myself. I flit back to my moonlit balcony dance, the sharp bite of wind against my skin. The answers he left on my frosted window.

Gripping the frigid door of my therapist's office, I tug it a few times until it opens. I have to squeeze through the sliver of space, resisting the gusts blowing outside until I'm able to whip my dance bag into the entryway. A lunchtime appointment is convenient, but the idea of how unsettled I usually feel afterward has my stomach twisting. I still have rehearsal after this.

Just breathe, Jolie.

I bounce my heels while I sit and wait for the receptionist to call me. He bobs to the music crooning through his earbuds.

"Jolie Wilder!" He calls it out like I'm not the only one in the waiting room. I even glance around to double check, finding only myself seated in the chair right in front of the desk.

As I walk past the desk, the catchy rhythm of Katy Perry's "Never Really Over" spills from his earbuds, and I have to fight the urge to dance toward the office. I'd rather express myself through movement than talk about my feelings any day. Not to knock the years of training and education my therapist has under her belt, but some feelings go beyond anything words can express. Full of joy or shattered into pieces, dancing gives my emotions an outlet. A way to release my anxiety and keep it from building up inside me. It calms the jitters begging to escape.

Unfortunately, it isn't socially acceptable to dance in public whenever I need to. That's why I'm here, seated on this dark-beige couch, tapping my toe against the wood floor.

Tap, tap, tap, tap, tap.

Dr. Tanner's green eyes trace down to my feet and I freeze. Crossing my leg over my opposite knee, I bring my hands to my lap, fingers fiddling as she grabs her clipboard and pen.

"How have things been going since our last session?" she asks, green eyes coming up from her paper to look at me.

"Good. Rehearsals for *Giselle* are keeping me busy." I nearly blurt out the words. My nerves ricochet through my body, eyes dart around the room, glancing over each picture hanging in the frames on the wall. Anything to keep my attention off her. "Mistress Maral is still keeping a close watch on me, but I haven't missed a single PT appointment."

"How are you feeling about physical therapy?"

"Frustrated," I sigh. Dropping my leg so my heels are flat against the wooden panels, I take a few deep breaths, refocusing on why I'm here. I don't want to waste Dr. Tanner's time or mine. "I don't enjoy focusing on what my body *can't* do. Makes me feel like I'm lacking."

She arches a brow from under thick tortoise-shell glasses. "Aren't injuries par for the course in your industry?"

"I mean, yes, but working through one at a new company where only a few people seem to like you is different from working through an injury at a place you've been forever."

"How do you know they don't like you?"

"Only three of them have bothered to talk to me. Most of the other dancers in the corps seem unsure of me since I came from the Institute and Ballet Potomac is not as established. And anyone who's a soloist or principal couldn't care less about my existence. I know a few of them from being at the same studio or within the same circles growing up, but it doesn't change anything."

"How does that make you feel?"

"Invisible." As soon as the word is out of my mouth, I want to shove it back in. It's one thing to think it, another to say it out loud. To have a witness to your shame.

If I could crawl into a hole right now, I would.

"I think that's understandable considering the circumstances," Dr. Tanner reassures, her voice filled with sincerity.

My chest unclenches. At least I feel like less of an idiot for admitting that. Even if the thought has crossed my mind, speaking it aloud is something I've avoided—as if somehow the admission would transform the shitty belief into reality.

Dr. Tanner cocks her head to the side, clicking her pen and jotting down a few notes. I wish I could see what she's writing, but it's probably best that I can't. "Is there any chance you might be making some assumptions about how they see you?"

"Maybe... I've never thought about it like that."

"Next time you are at the studio, really try to open yourself up objectively. Pretend you didn't come from the Institute. That you're just another member of their company without the baggage that comes from your old employer. See if the perception you have is truly there or a defense mechanism you've used to shield yourself as you start something new."

"Okay. I'll try to pretend." Not sure what good it will do me, but I'm willing to try anything Dr. Tanner suggests if it will help.

"How about outside of dance? Have you finally talked to Blake about going public with your relationship?"

"Um," I bite my lip, "I'm still working up to it." All I can hear is the scratch of her pen against paper. Not a good sign. "Next time I see him I'm going to, though."

"Okay." Dr. Tanner's attention returns to me, no longer pinned to the pad in front of her. "Why don't we practice?"

"Practice?"

"Pretend I'm Blake. What would you say to start the conversation?" She straightens and sets her notepad and pen to the side. The intensity of her stare sends my gaze to my tapping toes.

"Blake," I swallow thickly and roll my shoulders back as I meet fake Blake's eyes, "now that I'm not at the Institute and it doesn't impact our careers...what if we went public with our relationship?" Dr. Tanner opens her mouth to speak but I cut her off. "Sorry. This is weird. Can we just do something else?"

"Of course." She picks up the pen and pad again, jotting down a few words before tucking the pad against her lap.

Great.

I don't know why the exercise makes me so uncomfortable. She's just trying to help me get my nerves out. A dress rehearsal before the real performance. For whatever reason, I feel just as tongue-tied as I did the other night. At least I was able to get the question out this time.

"Is there anything else you want to talk about?" she asks, her pen poised in her hand.

Yes, but that doesn't mean I will.

"What about the messages and things you were seeing? Are you still seeing them?" Her question hangs in the space between us. While she means well, her tone is tinged with enough skepticism that I'm unsure if her instruction to *explore* these occurrences was sincere. It's more likely she pitied the delusions of a grieving daughter who'd been through hell over the last year.

Tick-tock.

Tick-tock.

Tick-tock.

The clock on the wall ticks loudly, and I wonder if therapists have some special shop they buy them from. If they're meant to be a constant metronome, counting out the beats of our session. Reminding patients that our time to get it out is limited.

Tick-tock.

My throat is dry and I rasp out, "I haven't seen anything else."

The truth isn't one I can give her.

She readjusts her glasses, as if killing time until I say something else. Sweat beads at my hairline, and I slick it back, taming the few wisps left there from rehearsals this morning. Between ballet, physical therapy, and these appointments, it's like I'm constantly being trapped and studied under a microscope. The lens may change but the scrutiny remains.

Can she tell that I'm lying?

I need her help and still have things to process, but there are things that go beyond her scope of practice.

Jax is surely beyond that scope.

Dr. Tanner purses her lips and her gaze slips to the clock. "Well, I think we made some great progress today."

Did we? "Try out the exercise when you go to the studio and let me know how it goes next session. If you notice anything else, jot it down in your journal, or if it's urgent, please don't hesitate to call the emergency line."

"Okay. Thanks, Dr. Tanner." I pop up from the couch, ready to get out of here. "Same time next week?"

"Same time next week, Jolie. I'll see you then."

Slinging my dance bag over my shoulder, I make it to the door in three strides and let myself out of her office. I give a polite nod to the receptionist on my way past his desk. He barely notices, just shoots his hand up in a quick wave while he continues to bob along to the beat.

I take a deep breath and push open the office door. Time to finish out the day of rehearsals. Hopefully, some answers, along with the person who can give them, will be waiting for me at home afterward.

When I get home, there are no messages and nothing is out of place. I spend fifteen minutes scouring my room before curiosity turns into frustration and eventually disappointment.

Jax hasn't been back.

I built myself up the entire trek home, mentally preparing myself to not startle when he visited again. I was ready for answers. Now, who knows when he'll return?

I undress and shower, peeking my head out of the steam every so often to glance at the mirror in case there's a message for me, worried he'll pop up any moment without warning.

While I rinse my hair, I wonder if he's been in here while I've showered. While I've changed.

What has he seen?

Once I'm done showering and getting dressed, I walk out to the living room. Delilah is out there watching hockey, and while I'm not a huge sports fan, I am a fan of Delilah. She makes Lark happy and humors us through all our ballet shenanigans. If she can't catch a Richmond Redhots game live, she'll record it so we can watch it together, preferring not to watch alone.

She sticks the big bowl of kettle corn mixed with chopped up Twizzlers between us. Her Redhots good luck snack. It sounds strange, but it's actually the perfect mix of sweet and salty.

"Get it together, Winston!" Delilah shouts, standing up from the loveseat and throwing her hands in the air. The Redhots are down by four. Delilah continues flailing her arms, so animated that I've stopped halfheartedly following the game. She's far more entertaining. Her red curls bounce around her shoulders as she jumps, grabbing at her crimson Redhots jersey. Proscella is in big, bold letters across the back, right above the number fourteen, matching the goalie sliding into the splits on the screen, blocking the puck from entering the net.

"Yes, Frankie! That's my boy!" She circles her arm in the air, rooting for him with hoots and cheers. I shovel some popcorn in my mouth, then take a bite of a Twizzler, enjoying both shows taking place before me. Lark comes out of her room in a robe, her wet hair wrapped up in a towel. When she sees her girlfriend, she chuckles, heading into the kitchen to grab some water.

An hour later, and about fifty glances toward my bedroom, the game finishes with the Redhots in the lead by one.

"I'm going to turn in. Big day of rehearsals tomorrow," I say, stretching my arms out.

"Night, Jojo." Lark tucks herself onto Delilah's lap, waving goodnight to me. They'll likely watch the last few minutes of the postgame show, but something else is consuming my mind.

Jax.

Could he be in there waiting for me?

I start down the hall, bracing myself for anything—

Knock, knock, knock, knock.

My attention snaps to the door behind me.

"I'll get it," Delilah says, shooing Lark toward her bedroom since she's in just a robe.

Hinges whine and the front door opens, but I can't see who's there. Not until Delilah turns around and rolls her eyes.

Blake steps into the entryway.

"Hey, baby." He shoots me a dazzling smile full of pearly white teeth, his blond waves bouncing with each step. He's still in his dance clothes, his bag strapped to his back.

"What are you doing here?" I ask, brows furrowing. He blew me off when I asked him to keep me company last week and now he's suddenly here in my apartment?

"Can't a guy just wanna visit his favorite girl?" He continues forward without hesitation, bringing his hand to the base of my spine and guiding me toward my room. His fingers trace back and forth along the valley of my low back. It's something I usually love, but right now, I'm just annoyed. I should be excited that he showed up, but I was really hoping to get some answers.

"I mean...yes, but—" I hold my breath, my hand hovering over the doorknob.

What if he opens the door and Jax has left me a message?

Luckily, I wiped down the mirror after my shower. No idea what he'd think seeing streaks of lipstick with some other guy's name. I don't see Blake as the jealous type, but I also don't feel like explaining these odd occurrences.

When I don't immediately open the door, Blake takes it upon himself.

"I hate that I never get to see you anymore, baby," he

says, twisting the metal. "No more stolen moments at the studio."

"Well, we're both busy with rehearsal, and we have early mornings ahead of us," I ramble. What the hell am I saying? I shouldn't be talking about an early morning, I should be asking him about taking our relationship public, like I'd practiced—or tried to practice—with Dr. Tanner.

My nerves scatter beneath my skin as the door creaks open. Following Blake into the bedroom, I peek over his shoulder, scanning every inch of the space. I heave a sigh of relief when nothing is different from how I left it an hour ago, though I can't deny the twinge between my ribs.

Blake tosses his bag in the corner, then wraps his arms around my waist. "Such a long day. I'm glad you were home."

"You are?" The words are out before I realize how awkward they sound. I'm just thrown off by his first unprompted visit and the strange things that have been happening. "I mean, I'm glad too!"

Glancing around the room again, I make sure Jax isn't here. I turn my attention to Blake, who's swaggering backward until he lands on the bed. He lies on top of the comforter, palm grazing it in invitation. I shove my hands in my pockets, swaying side to side. "How's *Swan Lake*?"

"You know, the usual." He cocks his head to the side, and I'm certain he can sense my hesitation.

Why am I hesitating? We've done this dance many times before. There's nothing holding me back—other than the possibility that the immortal ghost of a man could blow in here like a blizzard at any moment. Right now, all signs point to him being gone. Who knows if he'll ever show up again?

That thought stings.

And that gives me pause. I shouldn't care. I *don't* care. The desire to see Jax right now, to send Blake home, that has to do with the answers I want, the closure they could possibly provide. Simple as that.

Blake pushes up on the bed, scooting down to its edge before he extends a hand out to me. I take it, and he tugs me between his legs, his palms skimming up the outsides of my thighs. Why am I thinking about an invisible being when this man's right here?

Ask him, Jolie. Stop putting it off.

It takes me a moment to chase down a good segue.

"I'm looking forward to the showcase," I say, running a hand through his thick waves, playfully mussing them.

He glowers and gently guides my hand to his shoulder, training his blond locks back into place. "You sure it won't be too hard for you? If it's easier, I can just grab the recording and send it to you after."

It's like an ice bucket tossed on my momentary playfulness. An all-too-sobering reminder that I screwed things up at the Institute. "Do you not want me there?"

Way to sound super insecure, Jolie.

"Not at all, baby," Blake scoffs, almost too quickly. Does he know the real reason they let me go? Is he ashamed to be seen with me because I wasn't invited back?

I never spoke with him about my injury. Not officially. The times I mentioned the pain around my hip joint and the ones that shot down my leg, he just chalked it up to the usual things, reminding me that ballerinas put their bodies through the wringer.

It comes with the territory.

But the perfectly normal way we torture our bodies isn't as usual as most believe. These past weeks integrating physical therapy into my routine has shown me that. While my injury still persists, I am learning how to manage it better and adapt. My body is far less wrecked at the end of each day.

"Come here." He pulls me into his lap, tucking the wild strands of my hair behind my ear. "I just know how much you miss dancing for the Institute."

"I'll be fine," I reassure him. Maybe it will be hard, but I still want to support him and Lark. "I'm excited to come. Bet you're blowing them away with your performance as Prince Siegfried."

Besides, being there might show the Institute that I don't hold it against them for letting me go. That I'm still open to coming back. It's a long shot, but I want to get back there, be with my friends and reclaim my place under their spotlight. Even though things are going better at Ballet Potomac, it doesn't hurt to keep my options open. Who knows how long it will take for them to see me as a viable option for soloist, much less principal?

"I don't know about blowing them away, but I'd be doing better if I wasn't partnering Nina."

"I'm sure it's not that bad."

"Not that bad?" Blake scoffs, clearly aggravated by this production's Odette. "She stormed out right after rehearsal today. Wouldn't even stay to go over the final pas de deux after the director complained about us being out of sync. How are we supposed to be ready for the showcase if she isn't fucking there to rehearse?"

"That's tough. I'm sorry, Blake." I give him a sympathetic smile. For a moment, it's almost like old times. How it was before the accident, when we would commiserate about our long days at rehearsals. "Maybe she just needs the night to cool off and rest."

"She needs to get rid of the prima donna attitude and

practice, or the director is going to question our place in the company. I've worked too hard to go back now." His words slice into me, full of painful understanding before he tosses in a quick "Sorry."

"It's okay." I pretend they don't hurt. That they're a scratch, not something that pierces deep. "I get it."

"I knew you would," he says, his hand finding the hem of my shirt. The hard-on beneath my ass is a not-so-subtle clue where he wants this to go.

"Blake…" I begin as he lifts my shirt over my head.

Shivering in my bra, I watch him take off his own shirt, his abs drawing my attention.

Damn.

"I know we both have long days ahead, baby, but I'll make it quick." He says it like he doesn't always make it quick. He nudges me off him so he can remove his sweats. His erection springs free, and he grips it immediately, giving it a few tugs for emphasis. Then he guides my hand along his silken length.

Up and down. Up and down.

He groans, hips arching up into my hand. "I need this so bad."

Blake is beautiful. Renowned. The first time I saw him dance, he captivated me. I was still in the corps back then, and when his eyes met mine, it was as if he danced just for me. Of all the girls there, this rising star wanted my number. Wanted *me.*

I rub my thumb over the head of his cock, still miles away in the memory of how it felt to have him fawn over me afterhours.

My body should warm at the memory, but my veins chill. I should be into this. Instead, I just follow his rhythm, and he releases his grasp. He doesn't kiss me, doesn't look at me. Not really. It's like I'm not even here. Like this is less about us and more about stroking his bruised ego.

Years later, this is still the only thing we do together. A quick release and an even quicker goodbye.

I stop my hand, and Blake hisses. "Baby, I'm so close. Don't stop."

"Why don't we ever do anything outside of *this*?" My gaze drops down to his weeping erection, his chest heaving as he catches his breath. "Are you ashamed of me or something?"

"Why would you even think that?" He frowns, then cocks his head to one side. "You're incredible, but you know why we chose to keep things a secret."

"I know we *did*, but why now?" My voice shakes. "We haven't been at the company together for months. There's no reason to keep things under wraps."

This probably isn't how Dr. Tanner would suggest I go about this, but right now, I'm too rattled to care.

"You're right. There is no reason," he agrees, shaking his head quickly. "How about I take you out after the showcase? I'll text you where to meet me at the theater when I'm done, and we'll go on a real date."

"Really?"

"We'll be dressed up anyway. Might as well take my girl out." He flashes me a brilliant smile.

My girl.

My chest unclenches. "I'm sorry for overreacting."

I'm so stupid. I make a mental note to talk about my irrational insecurities at my next session with Dr. Tanner.

"No need to be sorry," he says, brushing my embarrassment away.

The vision of Blake pulling me into his arms after the showcase and kissing me in front of the company glides through my mind. No more hiding. No more secret rendezvous. He'd take me around, introduce me as his girlfriend to the Institute's benefactors as they greeted him. Then we'd spend the night dining and drinking and dancing. The next up-and-coming ballet power couple.

Blake's cock presses against my stomach. Guess I shouldn't leave him hanging. He is finally giving me what I want, even if the conversation to get there was a bit more awkward than I'd anticipated.

I grip around his shaft, and he jerks in surprise. "Damn, baby, your hand is freezing."

"Sorry," I say quickly, inspecting my hand. A few tiny white flecks drift onto my shoulder...

"You really shouldn't leave your thermostat so low in winter," Blake says, rubbing his hands together and blowing between them before encircling my own a few times. "I know they are calling for early spring, but the temperature drops at night."

It sure does.

Just not for the reason Blake thinks.

Chapter Eighteen

JAX

A low growl unleashes from my chest when I realize Jolie isn't alone. I have to remind myself that she doesn't understand what we are to each other yet, but I thought once she knew I existed and was curious about me that she would forget her stupid *prince*. Not only is that asshole here, but he's naked with his unimpressive dick out and eager for her.

My fucking mate.

Another growl reverberates through my chest, rattling the heartbeat cradled in my ribs. I stifle the urge to shift into my wolf, though it would be fun to scare the shit out of him.

A few flakes drift toward her, flurrying from between white knuckles. Jolie's gaze follows the snow hitting her shoulder, and she stills, her pale-blue eyes widening. The rhythmic pulse shared between us stutters before quickening its pace.

You know I'm here, don't you, Tempest?

I'm thrilled she can sense my presence, but when Blake brings her hand back to his shaft, that hope is replaced with rage.

Is this really happening? Is she truly going to make this pathetic mortal come right in front of her mate?

Of course, she doesn't know that. Even if she did, it's not like she'd understand the connection. It goes beyond space and time. Beyond mortality. She exists within me, etched so deeply that not even having my memories erased could tamp down my hunger to be near her. *With* her.

Consequences be damned.

The disgusting mortal sighs, using my mate's hand to stroke himself a few times, the movements hollow, devoid of the enthusiasm my mate deserves. "Come on, baby. I'm almost there."

It doesn't take a bond to see she's not interested.

It chisels at my already fragile composure.

My veins freeze and my fists tighten at my sides, a blizzard building within my grasp. The thermostat glowing in the corner of the room drops another few degrees.

I'm going to conjure the first recorded indoor snowstorm in history...

Jolie eases her palm off his cock and clears her throat.

Thank Fate.

Her lashes drop, cheeks stained the perfect shade of pink. "Sorry, hand cramp." She flexes it a few times, then forces out a yawn, wiggling her fingers for emphasis. "I'm so sorry, Blake. Can we just finish this, um...some other time?"

A slow smile spreads over my lips.

She's not cramping. Not really. Her every emotion is as open to me as the pages of the journal currently spread across her desk. Which is...odd. She usually hides it when he's on his way here. I glance over at my answers penned in her handwriting next to her questions from last night. There's no way she would want this out for him to see.

Either she's suddenly become very careless or... She didn't actually plan for him to come over.

That gives me a small sense of comfort.

"Seriously?" Blake seems completely dumbfounded. When Jolie shrugs in response, he huffs and tries to guide her back to his dick. She doesn't let him, though. Instead, she crosses her arms, eyes darting around the room.

Is she looking for me?

He reaches for her hand again. "Just one more minute. That's all I—"

Before he can finish his whining, I unclench my fists, frost flying into his balls. The idiot winces, hissing out a curse as he releases his grip on himself.

"She doesn't want you. Now get the fuck out." It feels good to say it aloud even though I know neither of them can hear me. It's clear she wants him to leave, and when it comes to my mate, I can't resist an opportunity to help her out.

Blake doesn't get the hint from her or me. "Come on, baby," he continues, grabbing for her.

Not on my fucking watch.

My body stirs and Jolie gasps. Thick paws pound against the floor, fangs stinging as they elongate until my mouth is full of sharp teeth. I happily show them off to the stunned idiot sitting with his pants down on the bed. I rear back on my haunches, displaying my glorious earthside beast with a low growl in warning.

The shrill cry that comes out of Blake before he scrambles off the bed, grabs his pants, and runs bare-assed out the bedroom door is all the reward I need. I didn't want to shift tonight. Had tried to control it. But the look on his face was worth the unintended intervention.

Oops.

I'm enjoying this far too much, trotting around the room in glee. Serves him right.

That is, until I notice Jolie frozen next to the door. Halting in place, I sit on my hind legs, looking up at her wide-eyed. Her hands splay against the wall, nails digging into the paint as if she's trying to get as far away from me as possible.

"Th-this can't be happening." Jolie's voice cracks just above a whisper.

Knock, knock.

"You okay? Did I just see Blake slam the door behind him with his pants halfway on?"

"Everything's fine, Lark," Jolie squeaks. "I needed to get some rest." She yawns dramatically. "Shouldn't you be happy he's not here?"

"I mean, yeah, sure I'm happy." Larks confusion is clear even muffled by the door between them. "Could've done without seeing his ass but, you know, I guess I'll take the wins where I can get them... You sure you're alright?"

"I'm great! Just tired."

"Okay. Night, Jojo."

"Night!"

Footsteps shuffle away from the door until there's only silence and me staring at Jolie pressed to the wall like she can somehow camouflage herself into it.

It takes everything in me to fight off the desire to get closer to her. To nuzzle her and show her how real I am. I don't want to scare her more, though. So I lie down, averting my gaze to my paws in submission. The idea that she could ever be fearful of me when all I've ever done or wanted to do is cherish and protect her cracks a fissure in my chest.

The floorboard creaks. I keep my snout low but glance ahead of me and wait.

She slowly takes one step closer.

Then another.

Then another.

Until two fuzzy, blush-colored socks stop just in front of my paws. Little mugs of cocoa hug around the ankles.

"Jax?" Her voice is brittle, like she's too scared to ask. "Is th-that you?"

Snapping up to standing, I can't contain my excitement. *"Yes, Tempest! It's me."*

I bow toward her, jumping from side to side, words bursting out of me even though I know she can't hear them beyond a series of barks and yips. *"You knew it was me!"*

In all my daydreams, she would pull me into her arms, and I'd feel her heart beating within our chests in eerily perfect unison. Beautiful acceptance.

Instead, her eyes are wide again, mouth slack. Not the reaction I'd been hoping for.

Shit. Stop scaring your mate, Jax.

Dropping to the floor, I glance up at her.

She shuts her eyes, dark lashes fanning over her cheeks. Her heartbeat flutters against my ribs. There's anticipation and a faint flare of fear.

I send a prayer to Fate that this works, then zoom to the window and blow some frost across it until it forms one word:

Listen

She opens her eyes and her attention goes straight to the message on the window just above me. If believing in me could manifest my true immortal form for her, then maybe if she opens her mind to hearing my words, she will.

"Tempest?"

"Holy shit." Her pale stare flicks back to me, and relief washes through my veins.

It worked! I want to go to her, rub my body against hers, comfort her with its soft warmth. It's so different from my usual chill, but something tells me that will only scare her more. So I stay still and wait, watching the rise and fall of her chest as she steadies her breathing.

Her gaze narrows and she crosses her arms. "You didn't need to chase him off."

"I know I didn't need *to. But it was enjoyable."*

"Not enjoyable." Jolie's voice is stern, but the corner of her mouth quirks. "Messed up."

"He clearly wasn't getting the hint. I just helped things along. Or would you rather I left him to guilt you into pleasuring him further?"

She bites her bottom lip, as if thinking it over, but the movement leaves me entranced. I wonder what she'd taste like against my lips, between my teeth. When we're finally together, I'll explore her for days, learning every inch of her.

"I could have handled it."

"I have no doubts that you could. Doesn't mean I didn't like doing it myself. Besides, he deserved it."

"How do you know what he does or doesn't deserve?"

"I know enough to know what you *deserve."* It's a better answer than admitting that I've observed them before.

Her arms remain crossed and her shoulders stiffen, almost imperceptibly. "And what do I deserve?"

"You deserve someone hellbent on loving you." The air sweetens, the pulse within me amplifying. I swallow down what the sensations do to me. *"You deserve someone who listens, wants to learn you and your body inside and out, sees your presence in their life for the gift that it is. You deserve someone who makes you feel alive."*

It was probably too intense of an admission, but it's one I need her to know, even if this somehow ends up being the last time she wants to see me.

"Let's just talk about something else. Like how a giant wolf is in my bedroom, talking to me." Her pupils eclipse the pale blue of her irises, but her lips are pressed in a firm line.

Shit. I said too much.

Although, she hasn't asked me to leave and her shoulders aren't raised or tense. They have lowered. The fear that flowed from her earlier has muted to the backdrop and lessens with each passing moment.

"I've been waiting for you to return all day…" She bites her lip again, and I clamp my jaw, not wanting to growl at how much I love when she does it. "Didn't know if you'd come back."

"I'll always come back." I can't ignore the way her admission vibrates through my entire being. Maybe she does still sense our bond. When is it too soon to tell a mortal that they are your mate? My words are clipped as I try to stifle my joy, not willing to get overexcited and scare her again. *"You were waiting? For me?"*

"Yeah. I still have questions."

Oh. So it's about what was left unanswered this morning. I huff, trying to not sound disappointed when I speak again. *"What do you want to know?"*

After hesitating a moment, she crosses the room to her desk. While she hasn't panicked as much as your average mortal would over a wolf appearing in their bedroom, it's clear Jolie's still wary of me. Not that I can blame her. She picks up her journal and plops into the chair next to it, then she sways side to side, tucking her legs under her. Pen in her shaky grasp, she taps at the page.

"Have we met before?" Her voice cracks, then she sucks in a breath, pointing to the two spots vacant of responses on the page. "I-I think I saw you—or your eyes, at least—the day of the accident. My mom's car crashed with us both inside of it. I know it might sound crazy... Well, probably not considering I'm talking to a giant wolf in my bedroom, but were you there?"

I inhale deeply, using the moment to carefully choose my words.

Don't tell her you're her mate, Jax.

I repeat it to myself a few times before I actually respond. *"Yes. I was the one who found you in the car that day, below the ice."*

Her brows lift. Then they furrow, creases lining her forehead, so adorable that I want to kiss every inch of them. "Did you pull me from the wreck?"

"I did."

Her gaze darts to her shoulder, and I know she's looking at the gashes there, where the glass clawed at her as I dragged her out after she'd died.

"Was there any way..." She pauses a second, then clears her throat. "Could you have saved my mom?"

The hurt in her voice is palpable, stabbing me right through the mark that welds me to her.

"She was gone by the time I found you. There wasn't time."

"Oh." Her disappointment tugs at my gut. As badly as I want to tell her the full truth of it—that I'll protect her for eternity—I don't. I can't say the words. Not yet. Though, there's nothing I want more than to share the beauty of what we are. Who she is to me.

My love. My mate.

My Tempest.

She's a storm that's swept me up and consumed me so

deeply that I'm both irrevocably broken and beautifully changed by her. Forever.

"Can I see you? Your *true* form," she clarifies.

We sit there in silence a moment as I hold my tongue, choosing my words carefully. Maybe, just maybe, she's more ready to believe in me than I'm giving her credit for. But I refuse to overwhelm her. To release our delicate truth into the wind just to have it come back and smack me in the face.

"Not yet. But soon."

Chapter Nineteen

JOLIE

My eyes water, my entire body frozen in place, attention pinned to the wolf in front of me. I'm too scared to blink and find him gone. If it's rude to stare this long, he doesn't seem to care. It's as if he's watching me as intently as I'm watching him, our gazes piercing into each other.

Not yet. But soon?

Why does it feel like this man—*being*—only speaks in riddles? I spent all day waiting for answers. Now that I have a few of them, I barely understand any more than I did an hour ago.

If anything, I'm more confused.

"What's swirling through that mind of yours, Tempest?" Jax's deep voice startles me back into the present.

Tempest.

The memory of dancing beneath the moonlight leaps to the forefront of my mind, recalling how I'd leaned into the caress of the wind as it carried my body to the music…

I rub my arms, trying to smooth down the goose bumps that have sprung up, realizing I'm still only in my bra. I spot my shirt and quickly snatch it off the floor, pulling it over my head.

"It's nothing I haven't seen before," Jax purrs.

I swear the vibration of his words shakes me from the inside.

What the heck, Jolie?

I clear my throat. "You know, that line isn't as cute as you think it is."

Though, his words don't exactly disturb me either. *But they should,* that logical little voice echoes in my mind. The one that still can't make sense of this, no matter how many answers I get. I straighten up, tugging the hem of my shirt into place. It's oversized, falling just above my knees, Ballet Potomac written across the chest in elegant script. Sitting on the bed, I tuck my legs under me, the chill in the room becoming more manageable. "I don't know about where you're from, but around here, that's more creepy than anything."

"I'm sorry. I'm not trying to be creepy." He chuckles, as if amused.

"How long have you been watching me?"

"Since I awoke for winter."

Over a month.

The silver-and-white wolf pads toward the bed. His snout lines up with my ribs before he sits back on his hind legs, cocking his head, those two icy prisms captivate my attention. Blues, whites, and silvers, with tiny flares of the rainbow glinting between the shades. It's the closest I've seen them since the accident. I could stare at them forever and not be any less entranced.

Not all in my mind, I remind myself a few times. *I'm not crazy.*

He's here and he has answers to the questions I've been

dancing around for months. I'm not going to waste time by not asking them. "Why?"

He hesitates a moment, then bows his snout, breaking eye contact. *"You're not ready."*

"Just like I'm not ready to see you? Well, the other you."

"Yes." There's nothing but firm sincerity in his words. *"Believe me, you have no idea how badly I want you to see me so you know, without a doubt, that I'm real."*

His eyes draw up to mine and he scoots closer until his snout rests in front of my lap on the bed. Whether I'm struck by his words or his puppy dog eyes, my hands reach out and scratch the small swirl of silver tufted between his brows. It's nowhere else on his head, but similar markings trail the upper half of his fur.

"What do you want from me?" I ask, stroking his snowy snout. He sighs, content, almost making me forget that I'm petting a large wolf. A large wolf in my bedroom.

"I want you to be happy. To thrive."

"Bit of a tall order," I snark. "There's got to be more to it than that. Why do you care so much about my happiness?"

"All I'll say is that your happiness matters to me. It matters to me a great deal."

My hands still, ribs pinching. "I'm not sure if that's supposed to frighten me?"

"I never want to frighten you. Though I understand why you might be scared. You don't fully trust it." The wolf's icy gaze drops to the floor, but I scratch under his chin until he's facing me again.

"Trust what?"

"Your mind."

He's not wrong. In fact, the most frightening thing about him is how well he seems to know me.

"It's hard to trust your mind when you've barely been

holding on for a year. Sometimes I dream that I'm still drowning. That my mom is there next to me. Dead." My eyes shift to my lap, and he nuzzles my hands that fidget there. I run them back through his fur. They quiver with each stroke, but the tension in my chest slowly uncoils. "How do you trust a mind that never lets you get past the most horrific day of your life? How do I even know that you're not just my imagination here to help me cope?"

"Do I seem imaginary?" He hums, the deep tone echoing through me.

"Well, no... But that doesn't mean much." I shrug and continue to brush his fur, scratching behind his ears. "Pretty sure anyone who walked in right now would have concerns. Who knows what's going to happen with Blake..."

I should text him and make sure he's okay. Being chased out by a giant wolf with glowing kaleidoscope eyes isn't something that happens every day. But grabbing my phone and dealing with him is the last thing I want to do.

He'd come here upset about rehearsals. I should have been there for him however he needed me. How long had I waited for the reassurance of making our relationship public without fear of it messing with our careers? I should be jumping for joy. Instead, I'm confused by the weight lifted off my chest from Jax running him out of the apartment.

What does that say about me?

His furry body moves with the reverberation of his chuckling, shaking the bed and rattling something within me. I shift, crossing and uncrossing my legs as I try to get comfortable. *"Don't worry, Tempest, your little prince will be fine."* His voice lowers, becoming serious. *"There's nothing I want more than for you to believe in how real this is."*

"I doubt that."

"Don't." He doesn't say more but the coarseness of his tone tells me that any questions I try to ask about the subject will only be met with silence and more riddles. And right now, I'm too tired for games. Too tired to deconstruct any of this.

It's already late, considering I need to be up at 4:30 a.m., but I don't want this night to end. If I go to sleep, who says Jax won't be gone when I wake up, taking his answers with him?

"Get some rest," Jax insists, as if reading my thoughts.

"Can you stay?" I ask, throat thick as I rasp out the words. Not that he can tell me everything. Not that any of this makes sense.

There's a beat of silence where only his bushy brows lift in surprise before he responds. *"Of course. So long as it doesn't creep you out too much."*

"It's only creepy when you aren't invited. Besides, I'm going to make you work for it." I get up from the bed and head toward the bathroom, leaving the door open while I brush my teeth.

"Is that so?"

The slight growl in his tone almost makes me choke on my toothpaste. I spit the rest out and then rinse my mouth, talking between swishes of water. "You seem to—know—a lot about—me." I pat my mouth and chin dry on the towel. "I don't know that much about you."

When I get back into the room, I turn off the light and cross over to the bed. Jax lies at the foot of it, and I tuck myself under the covers. The room is a bit colder since he's here, but there's a different coldness that settles in me because he feels much too far away.

"Why don't you come up here?" I suggest, patting the bottom of the bed a few times. When nothing happens, I tap it again. "Come on. If you're going to be in here making the room cold, the least you could do is keep my feet warm."

He hops onto the bed, jostling it. I yawn, stretching out my hip one final time before I curl around myself within the covers.

Jax's glowing eyes are the only things I make out in the darkness. They watch me with a soft curiosity far too gentle for his formidable beast. If his wolf is this massive, I wonder how tall he is in his *true form*. What does he look like? What is the daily life of an immortal harbinger? Where did he come from?

"You lured me here to ask me something. Out with it."

Lured *him*? As if I'm the predator and not the prey in this scenario.

Weighing where to begin, I bite my bottom lip. Jax growls so low I almost don't hear the sound, though the bed quivering would be impossible to miss. I clench my thighs tightly together. Clearing my throat, I try not to think on that too much, finally figuring out what question to start with.

Jax shifts on the bed, the warmth of his large, furry body sinking into my toes. Tugging the blanket around my shoulders, I lay my head on the pillow. "Tell me about yourself. And start from the beginning."

"Aren't you supposed to be getting rest?"

"I am, but I also like some background noise."

"My life story is your background noise?"

"Now you're just stalling," I tease, and his laughter jiggles the bed.

"Fine. You caught me... I'm not used to anyone asking about me." His soothing baritone whispers against the shell of my ear, but his words cleave a hollow ache between my ribs. He sounds...lonely. I dare a final glance at the bottom of the bed

and the hulking wolf lying there. Those prismatic irises break up the darkness with their unnatural illumination. *"Once upon a time, there was a young mortal boy who lived in Boston and loved wintry days full of hot cocoa and playing hockey…"*

I'm half asleep but somehow manage to cling to every word, as if they've been carved into my subconscious, deeper than any dream.

When "Ice Cream" startles me awake, I jolt upright, half expecting Jax to be gone. His chuckle is a welcome reassurance.

"Why do you keep changing my alarm?" I ask, tossing the blanket over his head and then ripping it back, teasing him.

"This song suits you better." He states it as fact, then adds, *"I know you prefer something upbeat. Wouldn't want you oversleeping."*

Nope. Wouldn't want that. Though if I could choose a day to do it, it would be today.

"When will I see you again?" I ask him, unwilling to leave it to chance.

"I'm not sure." His voice is a bit sullen as he pushes to sit upright on the bed, towering over me. *"But you can always reach me in winter."*

"I can?"

"Yes." His snout bows down, black nose moving toward my sternum but not touching. *"Just press on your mark and call to me. I'll come as fast as I can."*

My palm glides up over my shirt. My *mark*. Not a scar. And it somehow connects me to him. "Here?"

Jax nods, and I brush the fur spanning his cheek, taking a final look at those eyes. No longer a dream but a firm reality. Does he know today's the anniversary? I doubt it.

Sighing, I pull myself from the bed and walk to my dresser, picking out clothes for the day.

"I'm sorry, I need to go. Winter calls."

"Bye, Jax."

"See you soon, Tempest," he says, leaping from the bed and disappearing before his paws touch the floor. I busy myself and finish getting ready. The room warms within a few minutes of his absence, and while I should be comforted that my room's back to normal, I'm already missing the chill.

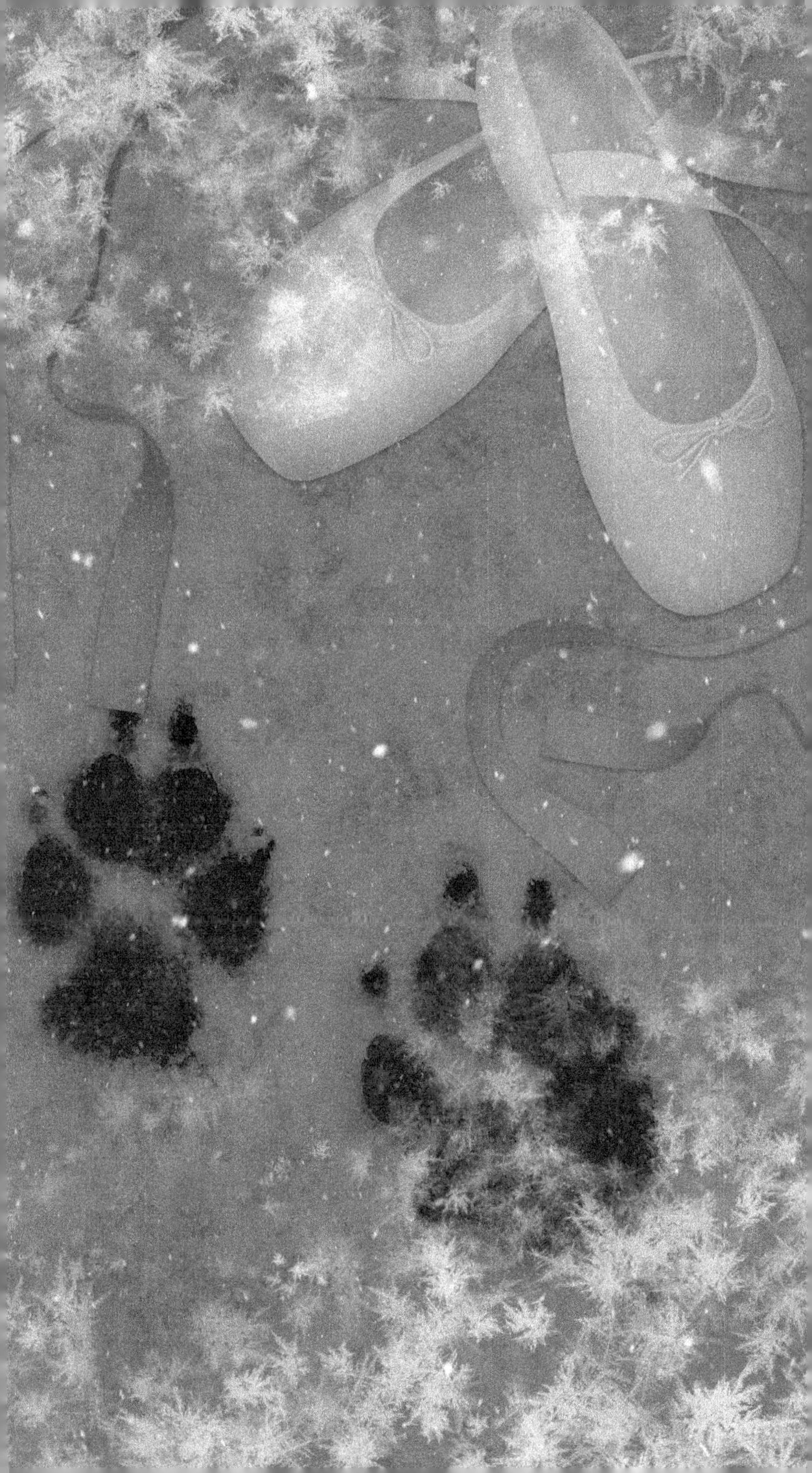

I ignore the tug, not wanting to leave Jolie a moment sooner than I need to. When I arrive at the meeting hall, a handful of icy eyes glower in my direction. Even Dad and Pops seem less than pleased with my appearance, or lack thereof. From the looks of things, the meeting is already far over.

Shit.

"Where were you?" Aneira asks, pushing through a cluster of Blizzard players. They're still in their hockey gear, metallic silver jerseys glistening in the dim light beaming between the stalactites above Nivea.

"Earthside." I don't say more than that, but from her expression, she knows what kept me there...or rather *who*. "What did I miss?"

A few of the hockey players snarl and mutter under their breaths from behind her. Probably because they already don't like that I've opted to play for the Polar Bears instead of their team my next season off.

I've always had a natural inclination toward the sport. It's one of the faint echoes left behind of my mortal life. I was young when I died, only fourteen when Fate claimed me. Many seasons have come and gone since, and each one that passes I remember less and less. Every so often I'll recall the silhouette of my mother stirring cocoa on the stove, my father carting me over his shoulder as a kid, making snow angels with my little brother.

I try not to dwell on the dimmed memories and be grateful for the ones I have. It brings me a strange sense of peace, despite the turmoil it's caused, that Jolie has gotten so much more time than me. That she'll have even more.

Aneira unleashes a snarl of annoyance that pulls me out of my head.

"You missed the whole meeting," she tuts.

"Am I in trouble?" Not that I care. I'm so close to Jolie seeing me.

"I covered for you." She elbows me and shakes her head, looping her arm through mine to guide us away from the crowd. "Told them I'd asked you to refreeze a few forests in New Hampshire."

I rest my head on her shoulder as we skate somewhere quiet. "Thanks, Ani."

"You're welcome. Good thing everyone believes you're a dutiful little Frost. They don't know better, but I do. You went to see her, didn't you?" I don't respond, giving her all the answer she needs. Stopping at an ice-carved bench at the edge of the city center, we sit side by side. Aneira's eyes dart around, her voice lowering with mirth. "I'll tell you what you've missed, but in exchange you're going to do something for me."

"What's that?" My gaze meets her piercing periwinkle irises.

"You're going to tell me everything about her." She breaks into a grin, voice giddy. "It's not every day someone has a mortal mate, and I want all the juicy details."

The fewer people who know about Jolie, the better. While I technically haven't done anything outright to interfere, I'm also not *not* interfering. I trust Aneira, though. Other than my fathers, she's the closest thing to family I've got.

"Someone's nosey."

She scoffs. "You bet your ass I am."

She's been so excited for me since I told her about the mate mark after finding Jolie this winter. I'm surprised she hasn't followed me to get a closer look at her. Though maybe she has? It's not like I'd notice. When I'm around Jolie, the world stops. Whether on a bustling city street or alone in her bedroom, she's all I see.

I chuckle, then stand and head over to drop a few frosted coins on the flavored ice counter, pointing at the pictures on the board. Grabbing the two cups, I skate back to Aneira, handing hers off after I sit down. She spoons out a heap of black winterberry and peanut butter, humming in approval.

"Fine." I inhale deeply, tapping the top of my red velvet treat, denting the icy flecks. "I'll tell you. What did I miss?"

"No surprise, Phil was too lazy to notice his shadow," Ancira says between spoonfuls. "Spring's coming early. The Blooms are annoyingly excited, as usual." She rolls her eyes.

"Of course they are." More spring means more flourishes, their own version of frost marks. Phil's been doing his gig for too damn long, not realizing that his simple decision surrounding his shadow is what can make or break harbinger careers. It only really affects the North American winter harbingers, though. It's also why Aneira and I refuse to work this as our only season each year. Most take on one season earthside, the next season they hibernate and then relax in Nivea the other two, repeating the process over and over. Unlike some of the other Frosts, Ani and I both have goals. "So when do we have to start reducing our workload?"

I shovel some ice into my mouth, savoring its sweetness.

"A week to begin peeling back, and maybe an extra few days until our earthside access will be revoked."

I choke on my flavored ice, nearly dropping the cup from my hands. "They can't be serious. That's not any time at all."

"It's a quick turnaround but nothing we haven't been able to manage before," Aneira continues, but I'm barely listening as she drones on about final preparations.

One fucking week to finish my work, maybe stretching it a few more days to see Jolie as much as I can. I'm so close, so *fucking* close, to her finally seeing me. Even feeling her run her fingers through my coat was a comfort. Anytime we are seen in our earthside forms, it usually sends mortals and wildlife skittering away. Easier to get our work done in the quiet. But my fearless mate invited me into her bed to warm her feet and scratch my ears. Just because she's beginning to accept my wolf, though, doesn't mean she's willing to accept the rest of me.

Of us.

I want to tell her about the bond, but how do you explain the unexplainable? The time isn't right yet, but it's melting away right before my eyes. Once spring comes, I won't be able to reach her for months. Even if I insist on delivering another winter, I'll be limited to that region experiencing the season. She seems so relieved she'll be able to call on me. Now that will only be for a number of days, not weeks.

"Hey." I'm elbowed in the ribs and brought back to the present, flavored ice dripping on my pants. Aneira's eyes soften with my attention, voice lowering, trying to reassure me. "Everything is going to work out. Fate's on your side."

Sure doesn't feel like it.

When I don't respond, weighing how I should handle my final days earthside, she adds, "Now, I got you caught up and covered for you. It's time for you to tell me about your mate."

I can't deny the smile that graces her lips. It pulls one from my own.

For the next hour, I tell her everything from the beginning, including what I discovered during my visit with Fate. After she's gotten the full update, I wait for her to tell me to be patient, that one day things will come together for us. That trying to get Jolie to see me is crazy and goes against what we stand for as Frosts. That I cannot break the cardinal rule we've been brought up to honor dutifully.

Instead, she just grins and asks, "When do I get to meet her?"

Chapter Twenty-One

JOLIE

My tights, leotard, and hair were all uncomfortable, as if too tight for my body, and no matter how well I did in class or rehearsal, nothing felt right.

Mistress Maral even highlighted me to demonstrate the adagio combination in front of the class. Normally, that would've had me grinning from ear to ear.

Not today.

It's the anniversary of the accident. One year since I saw my mom.

Today, ballet was a chilling reminder of all I've lost. It seems unfair to dance, leap, and spin without her here. But I know that's not what she would've wanted for me. Always my biggest fan. So, today I danced for my mother. In a way, I've danced for her every day since I walked through Ballet Potomac's doors.

"She'd be so proud," Lark reminds me back at the apartment after we've both showered and rinsed off a long day of dancing. I know she's trying to comfort me, but it doesn't lessen the ache sinking heavy in my chest. Pizza sits on the counter, chicken with peppers and mushrooms. A favorite that my mom and I used to split every Friday night.

I grab the movies I'd set aside, ones we'd loved to watch together, and Delilah picks out *Center Stage*, popping it into the DVD player. By about halfway through, Lark's snores echo in the background. It doesn't surprise me. She has to be exhausted from the grueling days of rehearsals. This week involves lots of late nights in preparation for the pre-performance showcase for the Institute's patrons, a way to get more money out of the benefactors and an exclusive opportunity for newspapers and magazine reviewers to preview the Institute's show and get the word out before opening night. Despite the fact that she can't hang through the entire movie, it means a lot that the two of them carved out time to spend with me.

When the credits roll, I wave goodnight to Delilah who's guiding a half-asleep Lark into her room. There's still one more movie set aside, and since I'm still emotionally wired from the day, I grab it and head toward my room.

With each step, my lip wobbles. Tears rim my eyes. As soon as I'm in my room, I plop on the bed and pull up my phone, listening to the last voice message Mom left me. One I can't bring myself to erase. She'd asked me to call her back when I was done with rehearsals, asking if I wanted to go out for brunch on Sunday. There's nothing profound tucked within her words, but the comfort of her voice makes it one of my most treasured possessions. Luckily, my voice messages saved to the cloud, otherwise it would have been lost along with my phone at the bottom of that lake.

By the time I replay the message a third time, tears are streaming down my cheeks. My hand shakes as I push the disc into the tiny TV in my room, one with a built-in DVD player, then climb into bed. Reaching over to grab the remote from the nightstand, I glance at the mostly empty bed and bite my lip.

I could text Blake. Rehearsals are done for the day, unless he stayed even later to rehearse the pas de deux with Nina. With stepping into her first role as a principal, I could see being easily overwhelmed. Soloist life was hard enough, and each promotion came with its own set of sacrifices. It was the price of greatness. A trade every ballerina would make with a smile on their face and bloody blisters beneath their tights.

I haven't heard from him since he ran out of my room. He knows what today is and hasn't bothered to text or call me, but I'm not sure I can hold it against him. Time and routines are thrown off during dress rehearsal week. Regardless, I still thought I'd hear *something*. It's disappointing, but I'm also grateful not to have to talk about his awkward and terrifying send-off. I have no idea how I'll play off the fact that there was a giant wolf in my bedroom. Guess I'll find out when I see him after the showcase.

I glance down, finding my hand hovering over the scar —*mark*—between my breasts.

Jax did say that if I called to him, he'd come.

What the heck am I doing? I'm pretty sure summoning otherworldly beings to your bedroom is the stuff of horror movies.

I drop my hand into my lap, then snatch the remote and press Play.

Now that the house is quiet and I'm shrouded in darkness—aside from the light coming from the TV—the loneliness brings an unsettling level of silence. I could ask Lark to stay in the room with me, but Delilah's here... Plus, she's so busy with rehearsals, I wouldn't want to wake her up just to keep me company. Not that I haven't done that plenty of times. After the accident, she'd insisted on staying with me for weeks.

It's taken me so long to put myself back together and I don't want her pity, another acknowledgment of how broken I still am. She knows. I need to pretend I'm okay, even if I'm far from it. There's something about other people seeing the ugly shards of my losses that makes me feel like I'll shatter beyond repair.

Knowing Lark, she'd just help me collect the pieces.

Picking up the remote, I pause the movie. An unfamiliar resolve strums through me, and my hand slides under my shirt. The pads of my fingers run over the delicate yet rough mark.

Am I really doing this? Do I want him to come here?

I inhale deeply, stomach clenching. Who knows if this will even work?

"Jax." I exhale his name in one breath.

I brace myself for a giant wolf to appear, half wondering if I've truly gone off my rocker. How else can I explain any of this? The wolf with glittering eyes, the dreams, the messages? But just because it's beyond explanation doesn't mean it isn't real. That *he* isn't real.

It's almost imperceptible, but a chill breezes beneath my palm, as if coming from the mark. He hasn't said how immediate he'll be able to answer my summoning. It could be minutes or hours, maybe even days. I grip the remote in my hand again—

"Tempest."

My chest unclenches as Jax's silvery wolf steps into view, breaths misting the air that flurries with tiny flakes. The room cools with his presence. The thermostat does its usual dip. He springs from the floor and joins me over the comforter, the bed wobbling with the weight of him. He lies down, tilting his ear to the side to look up at me. *"You're crying."*

"Tough day," I say between sniffles. "It's the anniversary —"

"Of the accident." His deep voice soothes me, despite it coming from a ginormous wolf that could easily fit my head in its mouth. I'm still adjusting to the idea that he's just chilling on my bed with me. *"I know."*

Of course he does. He was there, after all.

"I miss her." Tucking my hand into my *Tempest* sweatshirt, I wipe away my tears on the sleeve. The slips of white begin to slow as I catch my breath. "Can I ask you something?"

"Of course."

"You were mortal before…" His furry brows lift a fraction, as if surprised, then he pushes up to his hind legs so our faces are level. "Do you ever miss them—your family?"

"It was a long time ago. I don't even know exactly how many seasons have passed." His snout drops, voice etched in sorrow. *"I struggled at first. Over time, the pain has remained, though the specifics have faded."*

I stare down at my fingers in my lap, fidgeting with them. "Oh."

Silver and white sweeps under my chin, Jax's cheek resting at the base of my throat. I hug around him, running my fingers through his soft fur. *"Even so, I'll never forget my mother's smile. My brother's laugh. The taste of cocoa while my father told tall tales."* His body vibrates against me as he purrs, and a few of my stray tears soak into his coat. *"Some things are too imprinted to ever disappear, no matter how much time passes."*

Every day Mom is gone, she slips farther from my grasp. Dancing has helped me feel closer to her, one of the few things in my control that I can hold on to.

"Do you think she could be like you?"

"A harbinger?" His body stills beneath me. *"I don't know. Usually they are those who haven't lived full lives, assigned to live out immortality where it suits them best. I can try to find out, though we don't tend to interact much with the other paths or seasons."*

"You don't need to do that...just curious, I guess." My hands graze his ribs and his heartbeat is oddly in sync with my own, as if it's amplifying it. When the pulse quickens between us, I release my hold.

Jax shakes out his fur and turns toward the small television, sitting next to me. *"What are you watching?"*

"The Turning Point." I hold up the DVD case for him, flipping it over to show him the back. "Have you heard of it?"

"I haven't," he replies, shaking his snout side to side. *"What's it about?"*

"A young ballerina, her mother who was a former dancer, and her best friend. The choices they've made along the way. The paths they take or could have taken. My mom loved it. Figured I'd watch a few of our dance favorites tonight."

"Want some company?"

"Sure," I squeak out, a bit surprised that he seems genuinely intrigued. "That'd be great."

The next few hours we sit in silence together. Time slips by in a blur, and before I know it, the closing credits roll with Leslie Browne performing under the hazy glow of spotlights. I glance over at Jax. He's still watching, head resting atop his paws. I wonder what he's thinking.

"Why are you here, Jax?"

"Because you wanted me to come."

My hand lifts to cover my sternum, and he arches a furry brow. "If I pressed on this mark and called to someone else, would they hear it?"

"*No.*" His voice is firm.

"Why? What does it mean?"

He sits up, snout almost touching my nose as I tuck my knees under myself. "*It means we're important to each other.*" His voice is pure gravel, and my fingernails pinch my thighs. "*That's all that matters right now. You are important to me, so if you need me, I will be here.*"

Silence washes over the room. Somehow, his declaration sinks deeper than his carefully chosen words. There's more to it, I'm certain, but he won't tell me. It doesn't stop me from asking more questions, though. "But I won't be able to call you after winter's over?"

"*I might hear you,*" he says, voice lowering along with his snout, "*but I won't be able to come.*"

"Why not?"

"*For starters, our connection is...rare. I'm also limited where I'm permitted to travel during my earthside winters. Otherwise, I'm stuck in Nivea and cannot leave.*"

"I see." I think about it a moment, trying to figure out what he means by *connection*. "Does it have to do with when you saved my life? The night of the accident?"

"*It does.*" Everything he says is handpicked before he parcels it out.

I'm not sure I'm ready for the full answers he has to give. My emotions are already jumbled up tonight. But I don't want to always be left in the dark. "Will you ever explain it all to me?"

"*Someday. I just don't want to overwhelm you.*" There's a refreshing sincerity to his words, and his silver-and-blue stare gives me some quiet reassurance.

It's understandable, considering how crazy I thought I was when I started sensing and seeing him. "Will I ever get to see you outside of your wolf form?"

"*I hope so.*" He settles onto the bed, resting his head between his paws. "*I didn't know if you'd ever hear me and you made that happen.*"

"I did?" My curiosity piques. "How?"

"*You believed you could.*"

"So all I need to do is believe?"

"*You make that sound easy, but look at how you took my first message and all the times you still doubt yourself.*"

It's true. First, I thought he was a ghost, then a figment of my imagination. Some moments I still question my sanity, even as he sits here now. I reach out and stroke the silver swirl of fur on his forehead, then scratch behind his ears.

"Can I try to see you?" I have no clue how to make him appear, but I want to. As comforting as his wolfish form is, I'm curious what lies beneath.

"*Right now?*"

"Yes. Go into your other form," I insist, nodding toward the space between us and the window.

He pounces off the bed, nails never scratching the floor before he disappears. I sit in the darkness, squinting into the space where he was. Reaching over, I flip on my bedside lamp, hoping to see a sign of him.

"*Anything?*" his voice whispers, snowflakes flitting in front of me for emphasis. He's right there. Not even two feet away.

"No." My gut sinks.

"*It's okay. It's a lot to take in. I'm just glad we even have this,*" Jax reassures, still invisible. I can't explain it, but when he says *we*, it fills a hollow space within me. His tone brightens a smidge. "*I really enjoyed getting a peek into your world tonight, Tempest.*"

Is this his way of saying he's leaving soon? I need more time. "Will you stay again?"

I stare into the silence, wondering if he's already left. The room's still cold, but there are no flecks of white, no wolf appearing before me.

"Is that what you want?"

"It is." I nod for emphasis.

"Then of course." Relief washes through me at his certainty. *"Should I shift back?"*

"It doesn't matter to me."

Getting ready for bed as quickly as I can, I tuck myself under my covers. Even though I can't see him—the comforting chill that curls around my body tells me all I need to know.

He's here.

Chapter Twenty-Two

JOLIE

My heels clack along the pavement, and each time I put my weight on the ball of my foot, my blistered toes rub against the shoes, aggravating the pain shooting down my leg. My physical therapist would scold me if she saw me right now. I'll really be feeling this tomorrow when I hustle to the studio for another long day.

At least the strappy nude pumps complement the mesh base layer of my ensemble for the preview showcase and the gala following. The navy damask along the fitted mermaid cut hugs my curves in all the right places, its layered train currently clutched in my grasp as I rush toward the theater's glow.

I'd been waiting for Delilah to get home so we could head over together, but she texted to tell me that she'd been pulled into a conference call last minute. Now we are meeting at the theater.

I haul ass and pray my curls stay pinned up. My makeup setting spray better work the miracles it promises. Otherwise, I'm going to be sweating down streaks of foundation and rocking raccoon eyes.

This was not how I imagined tonight going. I was

supposed to be having my first official date with Blake, but I haven't heard from him since our wolfy interruption. Is he still planning on seeing me after the performance? I've been looking forward to finally going out with him, but if I'm being honest with myself, my mind keeps wandering to if I'll see Jax when I get home. Regardless of whether or not our date's happening, I need to talk to Blake. I'm not sure what I'll say, but I'll cross that bridge when I get there.

I texted Blake earlier wishing him an amazing showcase. There was no response, but it's normal to be busy when rehearsals and performances are kicking off.

The illuminated entrance comes into view, and I slow my pace, shaking off my stress. I lift my chin to channel my inner prima ballerina. The picture of poise and grace. I'll be surrounded by the Institute's patrons and biggest supporters, along with columnists who pride themselves in being career makers or breakers. Even though I'm not with the Institute any longer, I want to present my most elegant self to everyone I meet tonight. It's not just about my own career, it's also about Blake's. If we go public with our relationship, it will draw attention to us both from the company, my old instructors, and the patrons. It's already strange coming here after not being invited back this season—I don't need to add anything else that they can gossip about.

As promised, I make my way toward the back entrance to visit with Lark and wish her luck before the show, our signature pre-performance snack tucked in my purse. Gummy Peach O's—the perfect sugar kick to stave off the nerves.

Luckily, the stagehands recognize me, giving kind smiles as I pass them, a few exchanging quick pleasantries. I don't linger long, though, the curtain will be going up soon and everyone is focused on final preparations.

Passing Blake's dressing room on my way to the one Lark shares with our friend Sarina, I almost consider stopping by but think better of it. A few low grunts filter from under the door. He's probably busy wrestling with his tights or makeup. Besides, right now isn't the time to try to explain away Jax's supernatural interruption. I'll save that conversation for our date.

Knocking on Lark's door, I pull the little plastic baggie of candy out of my clutch, my lips peeling into a grin. She's being featured as one of the main swans in this production, something we'd always talked about doing together. I might not be by her side tonight, but I'll be cheering her on from the audience.

The door swings open, and Lark immediately lights up when she sees what I've brought. "You remembered!"

"Of course. Wouldn't be a show without them." I hand her the bag.

She tears open the zipper seal and shoves two rings in her mouth, one of them hanging over her lips as she gushes, "Mmm! So fucking good. You're a lifesaver, Jojo."

Lark hands me a few, which I dutifully enjoy. Sarina peers over her shoulder, eyes going wide at the treat.

"Want one?" Lark pulls out another one and holds it up for her.

"Hells yes!" Sarina snatches a Peach-O and scarfs it down. I'm not sure she even chews it first, it's gone so quickly.

"Wanna come in for a minute? We have to be at curtain call in five, but you're welcome to chill here," Lark offers, stepping back and holding the door open for me.

"Oh, that won't be necessary. I want to get back so I can get situated in my seat. There was a big line to get into the building." I give them each a quick hug. "Merde."

"Merde," they reply in unison before Lark plants a pink-lipstick kiss on my cheek.

You never say good luck. And "break a leg" is reserved for friends and family when they want to give you well wishes, but merde—*shit* in French—is saved for fellow performers.

"It's going to be a great one," I reassure them.

"I hope so." Sarina crosses her fingers while she reaches for another Peach-O.

I start to walk back toward the stairway when Blake's door opens. His lips are smudged with pink lipstick, matching Nina's, who's flushed, gaze lingering behind her as she readjusts the bodice of her tutu. When she notices me, she sticks her nose up, tone full of annoyance. "Oh, hey. Didn't realize you'd be coming tonight."

"Guess I'm just full of surprises." My attention's burning holes into Blake's guilty-ass face.

Nina heads off, leaving Blake and I staring at each other.

"We were just going over a few things before tonight," Blake says before clearing his throat. "You know, pre-perfor-mance jitters." His hand rests not so casually over the center of his tights, failing to hide the bulge there. The one he was probably using moments ago to work out his nerves. With Nina.

My chest and face heat, boiling below the surface. I'd love to drive my heel into his balls. I try to take a calming breath, collect myself. There're enough rumors surrounding the past year of my life, the last thing I need to do is make a scene. As he opens his mouth, ready to make another sorry excuse, my palm cracks against his face.

Shit.

Blake clutches his jaw, clearly appalled. He steps back

and looks in his mirror at the fingerprints imprinted across his cheek, then snaps, "What the hell, Jolie?"

Other dancers exit their dressing rooms, heading toward the stage, some of them stopping in place, glancing between the two of us.

I force my feet in the direction of the stairs, hearing the patter of pointe shoes against the concrete as Lark catches up to me and turns me by my shoulder. "I had no idea they were together, but he's an asshole."

"Not arguing with you on that one." My chest heaves, and I slow my breaths, trying to steady the simmering beneath my skin and the vibrancy of my pulse. My hand throbs like a bitch. I clutch it with my other one.

Who knew smacking someone hurt so much?

"If you want to cut out, I understand."

"No way." I wrap my arms around her and whisper in her ear. "I wouldn't miss you dancing for the world. He's not going to ruin my night."

"You sure?"

Out of the corner of my eye, I spot Beth applying makeup to the asshole's face. The show must go on, I suppose. He doesn't look in my direction, doesn't care that I caught him. Meanwhile, a few grimaces from former colleagues have me flush with embarrassment.

"Yes. Now get yourself ready. Eat a few more O's for me and get to curtain call." I give Lark a swift peck on the cheek and nudge her back toward the dressing room. Pivoting away from her, I walk to the staircase as quickly as my heels will allow.

My mind spins over and over on what I just saw. I'm so foolish for thinking there was something real between Blake and me. The signs were there. Never staying the night. Never taking me anywhere in public. How was he even planning to handle things tonight? Hook up with Nina before the show and then meet up with me afterward?

Being slapped with the reality of how little I meant to him should sting more than my hand does. It hurts, but what is most painful is how much it doesn't. What hurts is that I hoisted him up on a pedestal, believing he saw me. Wanted me. Thinking he viewed me as some sort of prize. This was all a game to him, and I was desperate enough to let him play me.

I shouldn't be okay right now. I should feel like I've lost something. But other than regretting wasting years on him and hoping he'll trip over a swan tonight, I feel an odd sense of relief. I don't have to deal with him ever again. Not if I don't want to. I'm no longer at the Institute, and he obviously has someone else there who's happy to stroke his fragile ego.

Pulse racing, my fingers shake against the railing, still sore from meeting Blake's stupidly handsome face. I try to steady myself before heading into the lobby. A handful of patrons I recognize flash me pleasant smiles that I return. I even manage to make small talk with a few, though I can't recall what we discuss as soon as I exit the conversation. I'm moving with singular purpose in the direction of the ticket takers, fingers slipping into my purse to grab the ticket Lark had left for me on the counter.

"Jolie," a familiar voice calls from behind me. Delilah sprints toward me, wearing a pair of fitted black trousers and an oversized matching blazer. Her forehead is creased, lips pressed in a line. Lark must have texted her. "You okay?"

"No," I say, handing off my ticket before going through the turnstile. I shiver, clutching my coat around myself as I wait for Delilah to come through. Taking a few calming breaths, I savor the air filling my lungs. Once she's next to me and we enter the theater, I lean in and whisper, "But I will be."

"If you want, Lark will slip some laxatives in his water before opening night."

I can't stifle my laugh, and Delilah throws an arm around me, gesturing toward our row. She follows behind me, and we sit down.

"Think everyone here knows I slapped him?"

"Probably," she teases. "But I'm sure some of them are sad they didn't do it first."

As the lights dim and the curtain rises, she leans over and whispers, "The right person is out there."

Delilah is right. When I allow myself to think about the possibility of who that someone for me could be, only one person comes to mind.

Jax came when I needed him. And while nothing has happened between us, the brief time we've spent together has been much more intimate than the years of Blake falling into my bed.

But it doesn't excuse what Blake's done. Not by a long shot.

I glare daggers at him the entire time he dances. It's annoyingly in sync with Nina. While he doesn't trip over any swans, I get some satisfaction when I notice my dainty handprint is still visible when the spotlight hits him at certain angles. Guess he'll need to invest in some better performance makeup.

While I'm not heartbroken over tonight's revelation, I'm angry. However, it's more at myself than him. I convinced myself that we weren't together publicly because we were so passionate about our careers. I believed Blake saw me when he really just loved the way I doted on him. I was grateful for his parceled affection, but he didn't actually care about me.

I hate what he did, but I hate that I allowed myself to be something for him he would never be for me. He doesn't deserve me. He never did.

As soon as Lark emerges from the wings, I break out in a smile for the first time tonight. She's stunning, an ethereal swan moving across the lake with poised precision. My attention flits to Delilah. She stares at my best friend like she's the most magnificent person in the room. And to Delilah, Lark is.

I want *that*.

I hold back tears the rest of the show.

ONCE IT'S OVER, I nearly dash out of the theater, Delilah on my heels. "Jolie, you want us to get you home once she comes out?"

"That's okay, Lark should stay and celebrate."

"You're more important to her than celebrating," Delilah tuts.

"I know. Which is why I need you to stay and keep her here. Tonight is too big of an opportunity for her to waste. I'll metro back."

"At least call an Uber," she insists, typing into her phone. A minute later, I get a notification that she's sent me money. "Share the trip details with us and text us when you get home."

"Thanks," I say, voice a bit wobbly. I've never been more glad that Lark has Delilah than I am in this moment.

Giving her a quick hug goodbye, I scoop up my skirts in my arm and head toward the exit. I force a few smiles along the way at those who recognize me, avoiding any small talk. The last thing I want is to be here when the performers come out from backstage. I'm certain if I see Blake I won't be able to resist the urge to slap him again, and that would do neither of us any favors in front of all these instructors, benefactors, and columnists.

My breath fogs the air as I descend the stony stairs and wait near the valet stand. For the next ten minutes, I pace back and forth to combat my shivering. Whether I'm shaking from the cold or anger, I'm not completely sure.

A silver sedan pulls around the loop, and I match its license plate to the app. The window rolls down, revealing a young woman with cropped black hair and nails to match. "Jolie?"

"That's me," I confirm before gripping the door to get in the backseat.

Fingers fidgeting in my lap, I keep my attention out at the DC monuments, beautifully illuminated beacons in the starless night. It's easy with the daily hustle and bustle to forget that I live here. I rarely come to this area, tending to avoid the touristy attractions at all costs.

A gust of wind whirls through the car's interior.

"Brr…" The driver—whose name is Mindy, according to the nameplate at the front of her car—reaches for the temperature dials. "Let me get that heat going higher."

"Thanks." I smirk to myself, knowing that whatever she does won't shift the chill or stop our breaths from clouding.

Jax is here.

My gaze drops to my chest where my scar's buried beneath layers of lace and mesh. Did I unintentionally summon him?

"Hello, Tempest."

He doesn't say anything else, the comforting chill of him

sidled next to me in silence the rest of the trip. When I get out of the car, he speaks again. *"I was worried about you."* His voice is low and brittle. Hesitant. Like he—

"Did you know about Blake? Is that why you scared him off the other night?" I unleash the questions much louder than I intend to.

"Scared who off?" a voice shouts from my left. I swivel to find a homeless man seated on a park bench, a grocery cart full of clothes and items next to him. He gives me a pitying smile. "Sorry, fancy girly, but I think you're confused."

I guess *confused* is politer than calling me crazy.

Giving the man an awkward wave, I hobble on my heels that are now killing me and pull out a ten-dollar bill, wishing him a good night. When I move to offer him my coat, he waves me away. "I've got plenty, keep it and get yourself home safe. You'll catch a chill out here."

Little does he know that *chill* won't be leaving once I get home. Even if he blends in with the cold winter air, Jax's lingering presence remains, trailing me like an invisible shadow.

"What happened? I scared him off because I felt like it... Because..."

"Because what?" I snap, not having the patience right now to be met with riddles and half answers. I fumble for my key and open the door, kicking off my heels as soon as I enter the apartment. Hanging my coat on the hook, I turn when a flash of movement skates by my peripheral vision.

There, under the illumination of moonlight, is Jax's silhouette. He's barely visible, as if sculpted from ice, and there are no discernible features, but I can tell he's tall and muscular.

Gorgeous.

"Oh my god. Is that your true form?" My voice shakes from the shock of what I'm seeing—or *not* seeing. I take one tentative step after another toward him. "Your harbinger one?"

His head drops down, then tilts to the side. There's a hint of joyful amusement to his tone despite the fact that I can't see his actual face. *"Not quite... But it's something."*

"It certainly is." My brows furrow as I drink him in. The way I want to move toward him, discover how he fits around me... It's all consuming. A craving I can't explain. "What is this?"

"What is what?"

"What is this between us?" My breaths fog against his glassy form. Frosty swirls spread from the point of contact, and I watch them disappear, mesmerized. "How did you know to come tonight? I didn't call you, did I?"

He pauses a moment, and it's not the first time he seems to be choosing his words carefully.

"I sensed your pulse skyrocket. I dropped what I was doing and had to find you. I saw you watching the performance, though, and didn't want to interrupt, so I waited." His voice lowers an octave. *"What happened tonight? Your heartbeat was...erratic."*

"I found Blake with someone else before the show."

There's a growl, then a long pause only filled with the white wisps of my breathing.

"I'm sorry. He wasn't worthy of you, Tempest." His icy hand goes to my shoulder, and I jolt against the barely there touch. Even without any weight behind it, I can still feel him somehow. It's strangely comforting, and I find myself resisting the urge to rest my cheek against him.

"Honestly, I'm more mad at myself." My chest heats recalling the look on Blake's face after I slapped him. "I thought there was something real between us. How pathetic am I?"

"You're not pathetic."

"I was nothing to him."

"Want me to assist him with a well-timed slip?" Jax offers with a chuckle, although something tells me he's not completely joking. *"My skills are at your disposal."*

"That won't be necessary."

"What can I do?"

The sincerity in his voice disarms me. While I may not be able to fully see him, he *sees* me. Sees me more than Blake ever did. "Why do you care so much?"

He stills, taking his hand from me. Disappointment floods my veins until his near-translucent fingers brush my own. His touch isn't sturdy, but it's thicker than the icy breeze surrounding us. *"Like I said before, we have a connection."*

"Tell me more?" I ask, brows knitting together. "Please?"

His fingers interlace mine, gently guiding our hands over the spot between my ribs. *"We're mates."*

"Mates?" My voice wavers with the word. I don't know what it means, but beneath our palms, in the deepest recesses of my soul, it feels right.

"Mates were created by Fate to combat the loneliness that can come with immortality. Harbingers see it as a gift. It's not set when the bond will take shape, but once it does, it's a constant need to be with your other half. I can feel it. Feel you. Always."

"How come I can't feel you, though?"

"I'm not certain, but I suspect your instincts are tamped down because you're mortal."

There's a bittersweet quality to his tone. I wish I could see his face right now, not just the fluid outline of him. He ripples before me like a mesmerizing, moving sculpture. If I could, I'd freeze him in place and run my hand along every chiseled groove. It's my fault he's like this—not whole before my eyes. I haven't allowed myself to wrap my head around what he is. Even now that I know who he is to me, what he's done for me, I still can't bring myself to fully believe this reality.

To believe in him.

"What we have is unusual." He clears his throat. *"When my mate mark began to form, I was so excited to find you. I rushed to you, though I could sense something was wrong. Could feel your panic. Once I saw you trapped in that car, I realized you were mortal. I... I watched you die, Jolie. Held you in my arms until... It was the worst experience of my existence... Worse than my own death. Worse than the days I struggled with my transition into harbinger life."*

All the air pulls from my lungs and my knees buckle, nearly making me lose my balance. Jax steps closer, bracing me. It wasn't just my mother who died that day... I did too.

A frosty tear falls onto my chest, snaring my attention. I reach up, brushing along where I can make out his cheek before dropping my hands to his chest. "Tell me what happened."

Even though my fingers are met with resistance, he's not solid enough to hold. Not yet.

How I wish he was.

"You started to turn into one of us, but I begged Fate to stop it. To stop you from leaving this world. She hesitated at first, but eventually, she agreed. Brought you back. Afterward, I couldn't stop sensing you, wanting to be near you. It was agony, knowing we couldn't be together. So I begged Fate again... Begged her to make me forget."

My body stills as I take in his words. "Forget what? The accident? Me?"

"To forget it all. To forget watching you die. That I had a mate." His hands trail over my own. *"There's never been a harbinger gifted a mortal mate. But you weren't..."*

"I wasn't meant to be mortal when you found me," I finish for him.

"I thought if I forgot, it'd be easier to cope with. It was the last thing I asked for before hibernating for three seasons. My punishment for interfering."

Gently gliding my hands around him, I rest them on the nape of his neck as I take in the glistening pane of his face. He cradles my chin, those familiar eyes glinting through the darkness.

"The moment I woke up this winter, I could feel you. That thrum, the constant pound of your heartbeat in my ribs. I didn't understand it at first. I only knew you were mine. It wasn't until I asked for my memories so I could answer your questions that I realized what I'd done. And while I don't regret saving you, not for a second..."

"But?"

"Once I found you this winter, I needed to know everything about you. Was desperate to be near you." He clears his throat. *"I'd even watched you with Blake a few times."*

That admission makes me blush.

"I hated the fact that I couldn't bring myself to leave you alone. Even though I wanted you to live your life, it killed me to not be a part of it."

"I'm sorry." I can only imagine how much it hurt to see us together, especially after finding Blake and Nina tonight. To know I'd caused Jax pain, however unintentional, was like cracking my own ribs. Exposing something far too vulnerable.

"Don't be. I did this to myself and I wouldn't change the

choice I made." His piercing gaze holds mine. *"Your pulse is the most precious sound to me, Tempest."*

"Jax?" I press up to my tippy-toes. Gently gliding my hands around him, I rest them on the nape of his neck

"Yes."

"I'm really trying to process all of this."

His chin drops, and I can hear the disappointment in his words. He gave me the truth, one he's been avoiding. *"I understand. Tonight's been a lot for you, in more ways than one."*

"It has." I bite my lip, chewing over my request. Staring up at him from between my lashes, I imagine the rest of his features beyond the glittering gaze peering back at me. There's so much in those eyes. Icy-blue sadness, shimmering silver, bursts of gossamer hope emerging through the cracks. He's sacrificed for me before I ever even knew he existed, and despite how crazy it seems, how impossible, he keeps trying to reach me. Now here he is, wanting nothing more than to be seen by me.

"I need you to do something." I press up a tiny bit higher, until my lips are a snowy breath away from the silhouette of his. A thin slip of white curls between us and all I want is to breathe in the belief he has in me, in us, right back into him. To make it all a reality.

"Anything for you, Tempest."

"Kiss me."

Chapter Twenty-Three

JAX

She's so close.

So fucking close.

Our noses nearly touch, and my hand strokes her cheek. She barely notices as it subtly passes through her skin. Jolie's brought her ghost to life, given me form, but not fully. Not yet.

"Fates, I want to. More than anything."

Her brow arches in question. "But?"

"The way I want to kiss you, Tempest, you'll need to fully feel me." Her heart races within my ribs. *"I need you to believe in me. In us."*

It's a desperate plea but I'm not ashamed to make it.

"I want to." It's the truth. I can scent her desire wafting in the air like sugarplums and dark cherries. It's sweet and decadent. Absolutely mouthwatering. I also know I've never smelled it before, meaning she's only felt this way about me.

It's probably immature how happy that makes me, but I'll take my wins where I can get them, considering she can't even see my face yet.

"I believe you. But I'm not settling for a brief brush of my lips against yours. Not when I've waited months—years—for you."

It's taking everything in me to deny her. If this is what she smells like now, I'm certain when solstice hits I will shred through any space or season standing in my way.

Her palms come to my heaving chest, and I drop my hands from her chin, fisting them at my sides, ignoring the throb of my cock against my pants. Not that she can tell—thank Fate for that. If I let her see how affected I am by her, how badly I want her, I won't be able to leave when spring arrives.

Slowing my breaths, I step back from her. *"You're rattled by what you discovered about Blake tonight, but what if you hadn't? Would he be here now kissing you instead?"*

"I-I don't know." Her hands are shaking, and I want nothing more than to take them in my own, steady her nerves, and pull her to me. "Tonight...it was like a blindfold had been ripped away. I should have been more enraged with him. If I truly cared for Blake like I believed, I would have been. But I see now how pathetic I—"

"There you go using that word again, but you're the farthest thing from pathetic." I refuse to listen to her self-deprecating remarks. My mate is a goddess among mortals, and I can't help but close the distance between us, crooking her chin up to face me.

"I've watched you push your body all winter. You're allowing yourself to begin to heal inside and out, asking for help when you need it. I've watched you build a life—all I could ever fucking want for you." A tear slides down her cheek. I catch it on my finger, clasping it into my palm, releasing tiny, intricate flakes and letting them spin around us. Her pale-blue eyes draw upward, glittering in wonder. *"Every day you continue to amaze me. One day, when I get to claim you, body and soul, I'll show you just how much you do."*

The air sweetens and I stifle a groan.

Fucking hell.

"But you won't kiss me?" she rasps. Her body warms, melting me in some ways while crystallizing me in others. She doesn't even understand what she's doing to me.

"I'm not saying I won't *kiss you, Tempest. Just not like this."* I tousle her hair, the pins releasing to the ground and curls framing her face, wild and beautiful. *"I want you too much for that."*

"I'm so sorry, Jax." Her eyes drop. "You must think I'm horrible for having you stay with me and then finding me like *this.*"

"Never." While I don't want our first kiss tainted by the events of tonight, I've never been threatened by that idiot. Far from it. The connection we have transcends anything they ever could. Besides, it seems as if Jolie has finally figured that out for herself.

Her gaze is pinned to mine. My silvers, blues, and whites sparkle in her irises, reflecting back at me. It's hypnotizing, and I'm certain nothing could be better than seeing myself through Jolie's eyes.

"Will you stay tonight?"

"I wish I could," I grit out, fighting every instinct that wants to stay and nuzzle my mate for hours, *"but I have some things to take care of before morning."*

If I stay, I won't be able to stop myself from kissing her. And if I kiss her, I might never let spring come. The idea of being away from her for another three seasons is like being stabbed through the ribs with a dull ice pick.

"Oh."

The disappointment cracking through her voice almost shatters my resolve. I know I shouldn't, but I break down enough to offer the next best thing. *"Do you want me to come back tomorrow? Afterward?"*

"I have to be at rehearsal early, but if it's before I leave, then yes, I'd like to see— spend time with you. Maybe you can explain more about what the whole mate thing means?"

"Of course." I wince internally, unsure where I'd even begin.

"Goodnight, Jax." Her voice is small, delicate as hand-blown glass. There's too much at stake if I skip my Frost duties. I left in the middle of them to find Jolie, and there are things I still need to attend to.

"Goodnight, Tempest." I press a kiss to the top of her head, unsure if she can even feel it. Wishing desperately that she could. *"I'll see you in the morning."*

"See you then," Jolie says with a wave.

I glide out through the balcony window and into the night, smirking into the wind. I have a storm to brew.

Something sure to stir Fate.

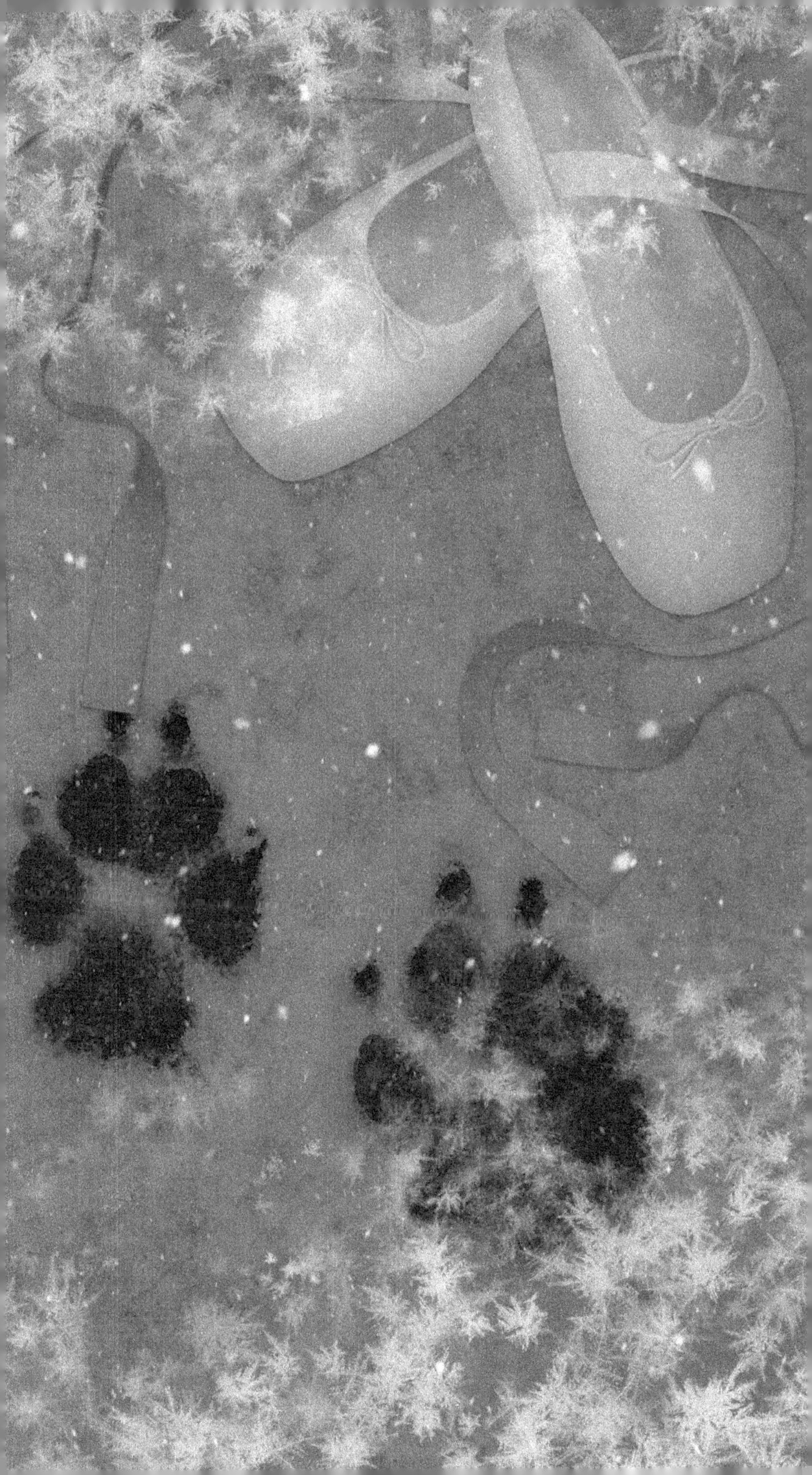

Chapter Twenty-Four

JOLIE

When my alarm goes off the next morning, I burst out from my covers, eyes darting around the room. Squinting, I make out Jax's shape in the darkness. Grabbing my phone, I shut off the blaring music, then notice a notification on my lock screen. A text message.

BALLET POTOMAC:

> Studio closed today for inclement weather. Will update once we reopen.

I scrunch my brows together. It was supposed to be getting warmer outside. How could there be inclement weather?

My eyes snap to Jax's. They glitter with mischief. "Was this what you went off to do last night?"

"*I needed more time with you,*" he says, like it's a matter of fact and not him personally deciding to mess with the seasons. "*I couldn't give up the chance to see you before I'm pulled away and spring steals the show.*"

I dash over to the window to see what he's done.

There are people slogging through a foot of snow on the ground, a few trying uselessly to dig their cars out. A few slip, falling on their asses. DC isn't equipped for weather like this. There's no way people are going anywhere today.

My gaze shifts to the balcony next to mine where a little girl and her mother are building a snowman together in its corner. She giggles, stuffing a mozzarella stick into the middle of its face, then takes a few small rocks, arcing them into a lopsided grin. The girl waves at me and I give her handiwork a thumbs up before stepping away from the window.

"So...you decided to kick up a blizzard?" I ask, turning to my frosty mischief maker. "How long will we be snowed in?"

"I'm hoping I bought us a few more weeks. Depends how much I've angered the Blooms and how long it takes them to thaw everything out." He shrugs. This one hundred percent interferes with the lives of mortals. He's already explained how it's the key tenet of his kind, so I don't see this going to go over well with whoever he reports to.

That's also a lot of missed rehearsals with *Giselle* right around the corner. After last night's revelations, I'm more motivated than ever to thrive at Ballet Potomac and shove my reclaimed soloist position in Blake's smug face.

I also don't want Jax to get in trouble on my behalf. What if he's punished again and I don't get to see him again? What if they take away his memories of being here and refuse to return them? I haven't been able to stop thinking about our almost kiss, and even though I'm slightly exasperated by him right now, it hasn't changed my desire for the chill of his lips on mine.

Unfortunately, I still can't see him anymore than I did in the moonlight.

"Okay, I feel like we have some things to talk about." I groan, swallowing down the part of me that already feels rejected. I had a lot of time while I couldn't sleep to think over my questions. Once the initial shock of Jax's news about our *connection* started to sink in, I wanted more details. "You said that I was your mate."

"*I did.*" He plops down on the bed next to me, and I drag the covers over my feet, tucking my knees into my chest. "*What do you want to know?*"

"What does all of this even mean? You can always sense me?"

"*Harbingers have heightened senses that come along with our earthside beasts. I can scent you, track you, sense your emotions.*"

"And feel my heartbeat?"

"*Yes, though that's unique to you and I.*" He holds out his hand, its outline beckoning to me. Once I slip my palm against his, shivering for more than one reason, he continues, "*Harbingers' hearts no longer beat. But your heart, your beautiful fucking heart, I can feel from anywhere.*"

"Even in your world?"

"*Yes.*"

I mull over his words, then my eyes snap up to meet the sparkling silver of his. "You said scent me... You can smell me?" My hands fidget against his as I try to maintain eye contact.

"*I can sense your feelings. Anger, truth, desire.*"

My body warms, and his attention drops to the pink spanning my chest.

"*Does that bother you?*"

"Um... Not really, though it's a bit embarrassing." I release his hand and cross my arms over myself, rubbing away the goosebumps peppering my skin.

"*Don't be embarrassed, Tempest. I love it.*" He swallows audibly, then his voice drops to a level that sinks deep inside me. A bone-level baritone that vibrates through me. "As mates, it is useful in finding each other, especially around solstice."

"Solstice?"

"The official changeover of the seasons. Once you've worked through the season, it closes at solstice. It doesn't necessarily coincide with the mortal realm's calendar. It's when the harbingers are set to transition before hibernation, a final way to reconnect with our mates before we rest and regain our strength to continue bringing the seasons."

"Your solstice isn't next month... It's sooner?" I croak out the words, my throat much too dry to form a full sentence without pausing to swallow.

"It is."

"What happens?" I ask, immediately wondering if I really want to know the answer.

"I'm only speaking on what happens to harbingers, I'm not sure if it will be the same for you. But you might find yourself having a certain itch that needs scratching."

"And my mate is supposed to scratch it?"

"I love seeing you blush," Jax says, and I somehow manage to heat even more, certain every inch of my body is beet red. He chuckles, and it shakes the bed, making my thighs clench. *"Usually, mates hole up for days together, savoring each other's bodies, reuniting souls before either turns in to hibernate."*

Hole up for *days*? My mind cannot comprehend, but my body wants to understand. Badly.

"Do the men— Do you have the same urges during solstice?"

"This will be my first mated solstice and no one else has a mortal mate, but yes, I assume so." There's a bit of a growl to his tone that he cuts off mid-sentence, as if trying to control it. *"I've fully prepared to handle things on my own, though."*

A vision of him *handling things* struts all too eagerly into my mind.

"Have I scared you off?"

I'm terrified. Not of him, though. My own intrigue scares me most.

He's sitting here and I still can't bring myself to believe it. Not truly. If I did, he wouldn't be slightly translucent, unable to fully touch me. When I realize he hasn't spoken because he's waiting for me to respond to his question, I blurt out my delayed response. "Just trying to wrap my head around everything."

"Well, now that we're snowed in, what should we do?" he asks, blessedly changing the subject. My skin stops prickling and gradually returns to its normal shade. Before I answer, he tosses out an idea. *"How about you show me some more of your favorite movies?"*

"Sounds great." It's the perfect excuse to keep him here but avoid more talk of mates or solstice. Or anything else that would make me blush.

We spend the rest of the day having a movie marathon, and I'm grateful for the company, especially when I head out into the living room, overhearing Lark and Delilah *enjoying* the day off from work. In between flicks, we talk about our favorite things. Jax tells me about Nivea, where he lives when he's not in the mortal world, and I ask about a million questions, trying to imagine what it must be like.

When night falls, he leaves for a few hours, promising to be back each morning to spend as much time with me as possible until spring forces its way in. He doesn't seem afraid of the trouble he'll be in. I still hate that he'll likely be punished because of me, though I can't help how much I savor our extra time together and the steadying weight of his presence.

OVER THE NEXT WEEK, his visits became fewer and farther between. The studio reopens. Occasionally, I spot his wolf watching from across the street, his glittering eyes and snout hovering just above the bushes. He never lingers long, though. Not that he really could. A wolf isn't a normal sight in DC, after all.

Then, one morning I wake to an empty bedroom, heat blowing strong and steady and stifling through the vent... And I just know Jax is gone.

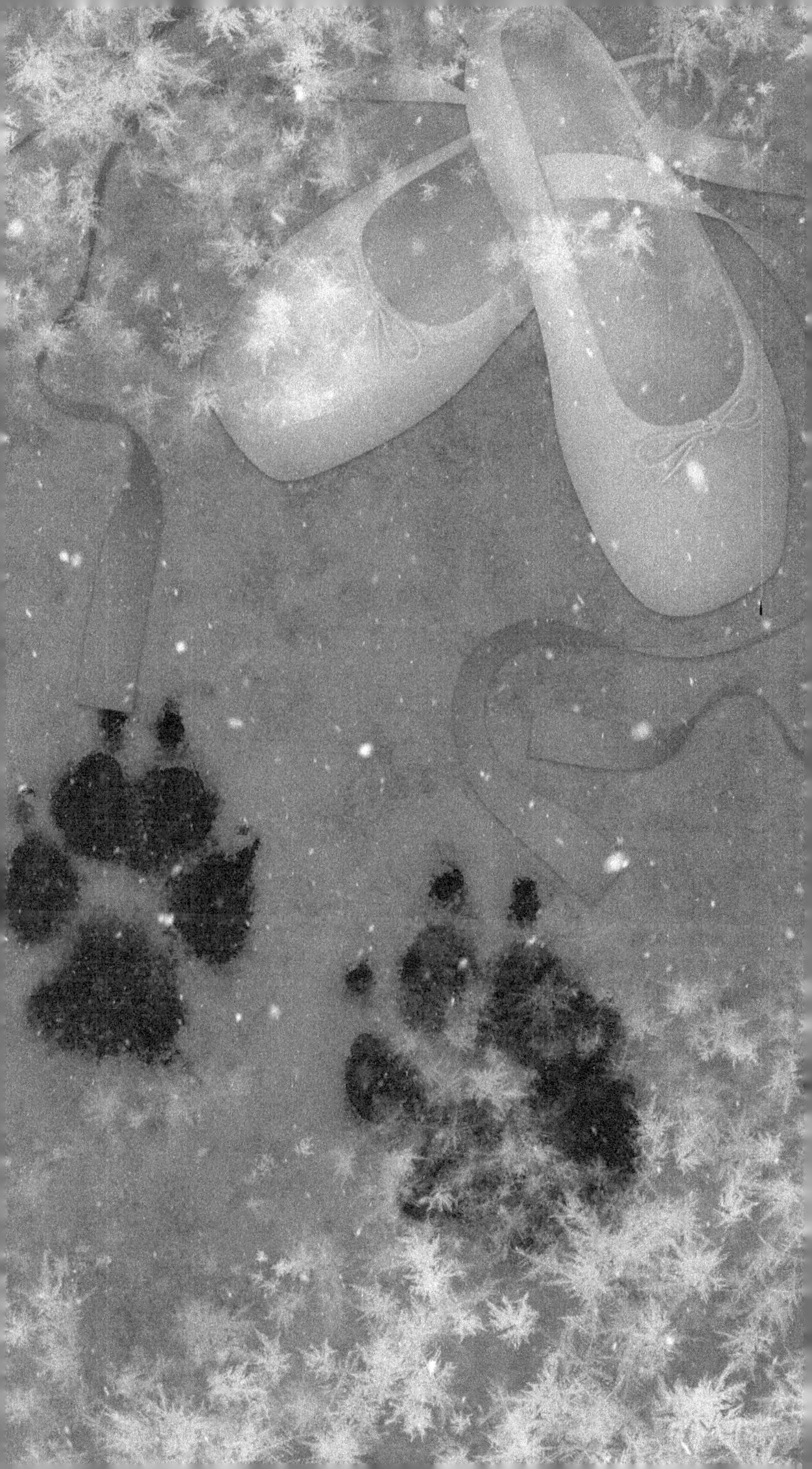

March
OCT
MO TU WE TH
10
17
24 25
31
2 3 4 5
9 10 11 12
16 17 18 19 13
23 24 25 26 20
30 31 27 28

Chapter Twenty-Five

JOLIE

It's been ten days since I saw Jax.

At first I'd hoped it was a fluke, but by day three, when ice dripped into pools on the ground, I was certain he had been called back to his wintry home. Was he being punished right now? He said it was worth it, but I couldn't help feeling guilty, especially since I never managed to catch a full glimpse of him.

Some days I wonder if I made it all up, but the dull ache in my chest is much too real.

I miss him.

I've been throwing myself into rehearsals, even more so than usual the last few days. My body itches to *move*. It's as if sitting still is the worst thing in the world.

I haven't gotten up the courage to join in for ice bath bonding with Evelyn and the other girls. Each time the pale shards float atop the water, it takes me back to the day of the accident. I still go to the recovery room to spend time with them, though, and I'm finally starting to feel like I'm finding my place at Ballet Potomac.

Once Evelyn, Veronique, and Sara are done with their ice baths and toweled off, I say my goodbyes and head to physical therapy. The pain from my injury is inescapable, my hip joint still a weak spot, but since I've started going to sessions, it's been more manageable on the longer days.

We go over a handful of exercises, and Heather shows me a few she wants me to do at home and between classes. At first, I was going to my sessions purely to appease Mistress Maral. Now I look forward to finding ways to work with my body instead of pushing against it.

Blake was bold enough to text me about our "misunderstanding." A full week after the fact. According to Lark, he and Nina have announced their relationship to the higher-ups at the Institute now that they've been together a few years. *Years*! I'd care if I didn't feel like I'd already wasted enough energy on him. Now his number is blocked and Lark's overjoyed at not having to see him outside company hours.

As I grab my bags and head out to leave, I pass by one of the small, empty studios used for the pre-professional students. A few times since Jax's disappearance, I've taken to dancing for an hour by myself, rehearsing different variations I learned at the Institute. I don't get to flourish my movements when I perform with the ensemble in the corps, so coming here a few times a week allows me to express the freedom I once had under the spotlight.

It's a sensation I hope to reclaim one day. Physical therapy may be helping, but I know my hip injury is permanent. There's no dancing without dealing with it, even if it's less of a burden now than it was when I'd been too stubborn to allow myself help.

Connecting my phone to the Bluetooth speaker, I throw on the Black Swan variation and begin to dance. I crave the breeze rushing against me as I leap and jump, kick and move. Warmth spreads feverishly through my limbs. After three times back to back, I can't shake the desire to dance *again*. I'm thirsty and hot, so I quickly grab my bottle, then step onto my towel and pour the water on my head.

What the heck am I doing?

After going through the combination a few more times, I crave the weariness that comes from a long day of rehearsals, but my body is having none of that. It's invigorated, wanting more, even as sweat beads along my chest. My limbs tingle and heat curls low in my belly. I pull at my damp leotard, moving it quickly to fan myself. For the first time since the accident, the idea of an ice bath actually seems appealing. So appealing that I nearly turn and sprint for the recovery room.

Holy cannoli. It's solstice.

Jax warned me. And now I know that solstice does, in fact, still affect me even though I'm mortal. I pace, clawing at my arms, wanting to claw off my clothes instead. Frantic need coils inside me, and I shove my hand down my leotard, palm grazing the silvery marking etched between my breasts. I squeeze my eyes shut, rubbing my thighs together while I think of Jax, wondering if he's as uncomfortable as I am right now.

He better freaking be.

Of course, that thought dominoes into the idea of him stroking himself. *Handling things.* I have no clue what that even looks like for him, but I whimper, stuck between wanting to control these impulses and give into them.

"I'm here, Tempest." Jax's whisper caresses my ear, reverberating beneath my belly.

A voice that's not in my head.

The breeze of his words curls over my shoulder, and I take two deep breaths and open my eyes. My icy-blue stare reflects back at me in the mirror. Frosted breath wraps around my cheek, puffed out from a pale-blue mouth that's framed by a chiseled jaw. Severe cheekbones glide up toward his eyes, twin panes of shattered glass that sparkle at me.

"Jax," I rasp, savoring the weight of him behind me, even though he's not touching me. But hasn't that been his way? I've felt him for weeks now. My very own gravity. "Y-you're really here."

"I am." His breath sends a shiver skating across my shoulder blades. I don't want to pull away from it, though. No, if anything, I want to lean into its chill, feel its bite against my skin. He hesitates a moment, eyes flashing up to meet mine in the mirror. "I've missed you so much, Tempest."

"I've missed you too." The words are a half-choked sob.

There's nothing imaginary about the way my pulse flutters beneath his icy stare. There's nothing imaginary about how his mere presence comforts me every time we're together.

"How did you get back here?"

"I may have bartered with a very understanding spring harbinger who's assigned to the East Coast," Jax says with a smirk. "I don't know how much time I'll have before they find out what I've done. I just had to see you. Solstice is hell without you. The idea of you being here, going through it alone..." He growled. "I don't want to waste this moment. Not when you can finally see me. Not when I can do this."

His hand skates up my throat, instantly sating the fire burning through my body. I feel each brush of the pads of his finger, pale blue and covered with small, feathered lines. It's like winter's claimed every inch of him.

Turning my face toward him, he lowers his lips to mine, kissing me so softly that it breezes over my mouth. I deepen it, exploring his tongue with my own, inhaling the rich, wintry pine that comes with the nearness of him. Each sweep of his tongue is decadent and refreshing. My body bows with his, like a willow on the breeze, pinned in place and blowing away all at once.

Pausing the kiss, he runs his nose over my cheek, grazing me with so much gentleness I feel more porcelain doll than woman.

"Is this how solstice always is?" I tingle, desperate for more as I zip my legs together. I don't want this to stop. I don't want this to be a dream. The way he treats me like there's no one else in the world he belongs to... I want to sink my teeth into it, consume and keep that feeling with me forever.

I want real, fierce passion. I want *him*.

"Yes." His eyes drop to the floor, tone thick and gravelly. "Though hopefully, one day, we won't be racing time."

Just like that? He's real and now he's gone? "You're going to have to leave?"

"I will. Temporarily. But I'll always come back to you, Tempest." He gives me a mischievous grin that lightens the air between us. Then he removes his jacket and shirt, and they disappear into nothing when he drops them to the floor. My pulse ricochets when he wraps his hand around my own, sliding them up his chest to between his pecs, settling them atop the identical silver swirls there. Only, he doesn't just have the one mark. There are hundreds of markings everywhere, spanning his chest, abs, arms. I move my hand, and he releases his hold, turning me so I can explore the panes of his body.

Each etched feather of frost creates a beautiful, delicately raised texture beneath my fingertips. He sucks in a breath when I trace along his stomach, the bulge in his dark-navy pants growing larger.

The need for him, for this, is too great. Maybe I'm crazy. Maybe I don't understand everything. But right now, I don't really care.

In dance, intention and perfecting the technique will only get you so far. At the end of the day, they are just the foundation for your instincts to take over. That instinct carries your body through the music. It's your signature. The wow factor that captivates the audience. And right now, I let my instinct carry me through this. "I want to see you... All of you."

The ball of Jax's Adam's apple rolls, and he nods, though he doesn't move, waiting for me to take the lead. I skate over the waistband of his pants before slipping my fingers under it and pulling them down. My breath falters. His cock is unlike anything I've ever seen.

I swallow hard, both from anticipation and a lot of intimidation.

It's covered in the same adornment as his upper body, the patterns wrapping around his thick length in beautiful invitation. What would those ridges feel like in my palm? Against my lips? I want to lower to my knees, take him in my mouth, and trace along each curved line with my tongue. And there, glinting at the center of its crown, is a silver ball with a snowflake stamped into the metal.

"You okay, Tempest?" Jax asks hesitantly.

I stumble over what to say, unable to look away. It's probably impolite to stare, but I can't help it. That piercing is staring back at me.

He frowns, then clears his throat, voice a bit deeper. "I'm not a mere mortal man."

"Well, that's obvious," I agree, gesturing at his very

unique erection. As if his flesh the shade of thick ice floating across a frozen lake, his markings, or his ability to shift into a wolf aren't already indicators of that.

I reach for it but he gently encircles my wrist before entwining my hand in his.

"Not tonight. There's not enough time and there are more pressing matters."

Are there? Because I'd really love to feel *that* pressing into me. Deeply.

I whimper with need, my thighs becoming slick.

What the hell? Did that sound just come from me?

His nostrils flare, pupils dilating until they nearly eclipse the prismatic irises holding me very willingly under whatever spell he's cast.

I'm spun to face the mirror, and Jax guides my hand up the glass. Touching the mirror is something we're taught never to do from a very young age. Nothing to mar being able to see every inch of our bodies as we move through the room. It feels both indulgent and indecent seeing my print stain its pristine surface. His textured palm skims up my arms, brushing over the scars at my shoulder before wrapping around my throat. His thumb directs my chin forward.

"Eyes on us, Tempest," he whispers. "Don't you dare close them."

I have no desire to blink now or ever again, for that matter. What if he's swept away and I'm left to wonder, once more, if he's all in my head?

Fingers skate along the top of my throat again, and Jax's whisper sends a shiver that has my toes curling against the burlap box of my pointe shoes. "You will watch everything I do to you. Understand?"

I nod wildly, gaze following his fingers down my neck. They loop around the strap of my leotard, dragging it over my shoulder. One, then the other. He presses a cool kiss to my shoulder blade, and my breath hitches, nipples pebbling against the periwinkle Lycra. The straps of my leotard hang, untouched, as he oh so gently pulls out each bobby pin in my bun. With each tug, stinging relief spreads from my scalp across the rest of my head. His brows knit in concentration until he's removed them all, taking my hairnet and mesh and tossing them on the ground.

"You're so beautiful, Jolie." My name on his lips is as worshipful as prayer. Sacred.

He kneels, taking his time to untie the ribbons of my shoes before slipping them off me and setting them aside. He does it so reverently, looking like he's worried he'll break me. Then his fingers skim up my tights, my body shivering beneath them.

This is real.

He's *real.*

Despite the fact that we've been communicating for weeks, seeing him brings a new level of understanding. It's Jax. He's whole, here, and he wants me.

Then he slowly peels my leotard down, along with my tights that are damp and clinging to me. I step out of them, and he brings them to his face and inhales deeply. "Fate be damned, Tempest, it's going to take everything for me not to come when I touch you."

"Touch me. Please." It's a whimper. A plea. This man is risking everything being here, and I don't want to miss a single moment of what he's offering.

One hand curves with my hip, the other glides up to my silver scar, my *mate mark.* He draws delicate circles over it, and every stroke feels as if he's doing the motion somewhere lower and much more sensitive. My legs rub against each other, desperate for friction.

The hand not drawing devotions upon my sternum taps my leg. "Wide second, Tempest."

"How do you know that term?" I ask, but like a well-trained prima ballerina, I do as I'm instructed and open my stance.

"Good girl." The praise hits me below my belly, and I wiggle at the kiss of cold air between my thighs. That is, until his fingers dip lower, spreading me apart. "I have been watching you for months. Maybe I picked up on a few things."

It really should creep me out that he's been watching me all this time. But the loneliness that's burrowed deep in my bones only feels comforted. Like he's been there, some unseen guardian angel wholly devoted to me.

I rest my head against him, giving into the pleasure.

"Eyes on the mirror," he tuts, and I cut my glance back up to the two of us, watching his fingers disappear into me. "So wet for me, Tempest. So fucking perfect."

His cock presses against my back, and I can't help but arch into it, the icy ball of his piercing grazing me. What would it feel like inside?

"I want you." When one of my hands leaves the mirror to reach for him, he gently but firmly guides it back to the pane with a kiss to the scars on my shoulder.

"I want you more." His eyes shimmer, darkened pupils staring at me from behind my wild waves that billow around my shoulders. He nestles into the storm of strands, words sliding down my body as his fingers slip in and out of me. "You have no idea how long I've waited for this, but I'll need *days*, not minutes, when I fully claim you."

Claim.

The word surges through my veins. I want him to claim me. Mark me in frosty promises and pleasure. Etch himself so deep beneath my skin that neither of us can exist without the imprint of the other.

Logically, it makes no damn sense.

My eyes remain locked on our reflection. In ballet, every part of our body is a carefully calculated equation of lines and curves that present a perfected picture. Every limb may look graceful and delicate, but each is held with immense tension and care. It's the beautiful illusion of effortless poise. Even when I was with Blake, there was always a part of me holding my core, wondering how I looked and if I fit the picture of what he wanted.

But I can't summon the urge to care with Jax. Not when his hand that's circling between my ribs sweeps over my nipple, each ridge of his skin making me shudder. The fact that all he's focused on is me makes me want him all the more.

I wish we had those *days*.

My body is keening, writhing. An uncontrolled tangle that's desperate to be undone. When my eyes begin to flutter, he takes his hand from my breast and slides it to my throat. "You're close, aren't you, Tempest?"

"Yes," I rasp. His eyes, sharp as glass, somehow soften when they scan over me. His cock jerks when his gaze slips to where his hand is between my thighs. Watching him watch us together has me moaning. "Don't stop."

My body trembles. Every part of me is coiled, leaning into his icy touch and begging for every twirl of his thumb around my clit, every plunge that curls into my center.

His fingers don't relent, spurred on by my sounds that filter up in white puffs. Frost swirls across the mirror, surrounding us, but my body is in an inferno, desperate to be soothed by his cool touch.

He skates against the sensitive nerves, and my knees buckle.

I'll surely break from the pleasure of this.

"Jax!" I cry out. I'm on the cusp of fracturing and floating away.

He holds me in place, supporting my body at its center. "Watch."

I hold back the urge to let my eyes roll skyward, to throw my head up. Instead, I take in his dark stare, the desire skating through his gaze as he drinks us both in.

"That's it. Ride my hand." His palm swirls my silver scar and presses into it while the fingers of his other hand twirl gracefully inside of me. My hips rock and my back is wet with smears of precum. His voice is gravelly, just above a rasp. "Look how beautifully you shatter around my fingers, Tempest."

It's my undoing.

My lips part, cloudy breaths blowing toward the mirror, and I scream so loud I'm sure some sort of studio alarm will sound. I'm unleashed, pleasure exploding from me in every possible direction. My knees crumble as I drink in the sight of Jax. His neck strains before he turns my chin to capture my mouth in a deep, unrelenting kiss. My pelvis continues to jerk wildly, riding out my orgasm.

Oh my god.

My eyes widen and surprise bolts through me. I've never been able to come with someone else. Thought it wasn't in the cards for me. I chuckle to myself, trying to catch my breath. How wrong I was.

The ecstasy of this, of him, will be the death of me.

As I come down from my ascent, Jax slips out of me, lowering us to sit on the floor. He tucks me into him, and I nuzzle against the panes of his chest. Bringing his fingers to his lips, he licks them clean. Maybe he can ignore the giant, glinting hard-on between us, but I can't. It's coated with glittering precum, and I lick my lips, craving to know how he tastes.

Before I can find out, he chuckles, crooking my chin and lowering his mouth to mine. Each kiss is long and lingering. "You have no clue how much my body begs for you. But I can't stay."

"When will I see you again?"

"I don't know." His voice is thick as he swallows down that truth. Like he hates it as much as I do.

"Will I have to wait until next winter?" My heart sinks, a heavy stone landing in my gut that has me nauseous.

"I will find a way, Tempest. One day, we will have the rest of time."

"One day." It feels like a brittle promise, but it's all I've got, so I cling to it.

"Kiss me until I have to leave?" he asks. Considering he just gave me the best orgasm of my existence, his tone is wildly unsure.

"Of course."

He strokes my cheek, then kisses, commanding my mouth. I nip his bottom lip, and he groans. I love drawing that sound from him. His cock rests between our stomachs, the deep-purple tip eager for release. I desperately want to feel its texture against my palm, but instead, I just savor how much he wants me; wants us.

Seconds or minutes later, he finally pulls his lips away, swollen from our kisses and this stolen time. The weight of his body recedes, skin becoming more translucent with each passing second. "It's time, Tempest."

"No." My lip quivers but I fight the tears. Fear begins to

close in, ready to choke me. "Can't you hold it off a little longer?"

"I can't," he says ruefully. "But I'll find a way to you in any season, Tempest."

It's the last thing he says before he disappears, leaving me naked and in a post-orgasm haze. When I glance at the previously frosted mirror, the final flecks of white slowly vanish. Like it never existed.

And once again, I'm alone.

Chapter Twenty-Six

JAX

I fought Nivea's pull as long as I could, not wanting to leave Jolie, especially not during a time meant to be intimate and soul-changing for us.

Uninterrupted.

Being able to bring Jolie some relief before I was taken brought me a small measure of solace. How beautifully she collapsed against me in pleasure. Her whimpers, her scent, the smoothness of her skin in contrast to the ridges of her mate mark—I've replayed them over and over the last two days. Those morsels have been my sustenance through my first mated solstice. I'm starved for her, and I'd thieve that time away all over again.

The problem for Fate and my fathers, in their capacity as Lead Albiduses, is they know that no punishment they deliver will make me regret my actions. I almost chuckle when they scold me.

"No frost marks for this winter's work."

"Very well."

There was a time when that consequence would have been a dagger to the gut. Prolonging my time from earning my place as an Albidus—it was the worst thing that could happen.

Nothing like finding your mate only to watch her die in the same breath to put things in perspective.

I still want to earn all my frost marks, but I want her too. The pulse of her heart thudding in my chest is a constant reminder that she's out there, that she finally believes in me and craves me like I crave her.

Thump-thump. Thump-thump.

My palm trails over her rhythm until it rests on my mate mark.

She hasn't tried to summon me since I left. Is she still thinking about our time together or was it all so fleeting that she won't think on it until I can get earthside again?

No.

I refuse to believe that. After everything we've been through, the weeks of messages, the things we've shared, she can't stop believing in me. In us.

The tapping of Dad's foot against the snowflake-tiled floor pulls my attention back to the stern faces glaring at me. We're in City Hall, their way to remind me how officially in trouble I am. Icy columns twist their way to the domed ceiling, a mural of Jack Frost painted across it in metallic silvers, pearly whites, and shimmering sapphires.

"You will be under our supervision until your next winter in the mortal realm," Pops says, his tone somehow both scolding and pitying.

Dad wastes no time adding, "You will be allowed earthside next winter for the southern hemisphere. You are not allowed back on the East Coast until it's winter there."

Six more months until I can see Jolie again. On the bright side, this means I'm not going to have to wait another three seasons to earn more frost marks. It stings, nonetheless.

"I'm sure this is incredibly difficult for you." Dad wraps an arm around me, eyes shooting to his mate. "But we want to help."

"Then help me find a way to make this work with her. There has to be something. A loophole of some sort."

Fate wrings her purple-and-green streaked hands, each nail painted a different bold hue. "There's a reason we have our rule about interfering with mortals. Even something innocuous can have ripples, affecting not just their fate but the fate of others. When I saved Jolie's life, the ripples of that were vast. Farther reaching than you can imagine. I'm still trying to mend the rift it created in the balance." She strides closer, a strange clacking rattling within her dress. My eyes drop to her hip. She halts in place, ignoring my curious gaze. "The Blooms called for your hibernation to be forcefully extended again. They were not thrilled with the stunt you pulled with Briar."

"Did he get in trouble?" My throat is scraped dry. Briar owed me a favor over a mishap ten seasons ago. While he'd never admit it from his seemingly gruff exterior, Blooms are a romantic bunch. When I told him about my mate, he'd let me use his harbinger magic to transport close enough where I could race to Jolie. I'd scented her approaching solstice with every pant of breath that billowed from my lungs as my wolf sprinted through the darkened DC streets to her.

I can't say that no one noticed, but I wasn't paying much attention. Only focused on one thing: finding Jolie and being with her for solstice.

"Of course Briar was disciplined. These things don't occur without consequence." Nausea churns in my gut.

"However, we explained the situation, and they've decided to let him finish out this spring, but he's on double duty to earn his flourish marks."

"I'm sorry."

"We're going to have to stay on top of you, aren't we?" Pops asks, arching a brow at Dad and then shifting his gaze to me.

There's something about when both of them come down on you, giving their full scalding attention. It's ten times more intimidating. Even though I'm grown—an immortal, for fuck's sake—I'm still not immune to the tinge of shame it brings.

But at the end of the day, I'd make the same decision all over again. No regrets. Those moments of seeing myself through Jolie's eyes, her watching as I brought her to the brink of ecstasy, they made me feel more alive than I ever have since being a Frost.

I loosen the corner of my lip into a lopsided smirk. "Things needed a little riling up around here, don't you think?"

They groan, shaking their heads.

Jolie's pulse clamors within my chest, a constant reminder she's with me even when we're separated by the veil. Without my harbinger magic, without an assignment within her vicinity, there's no way to her.

At least not yet.

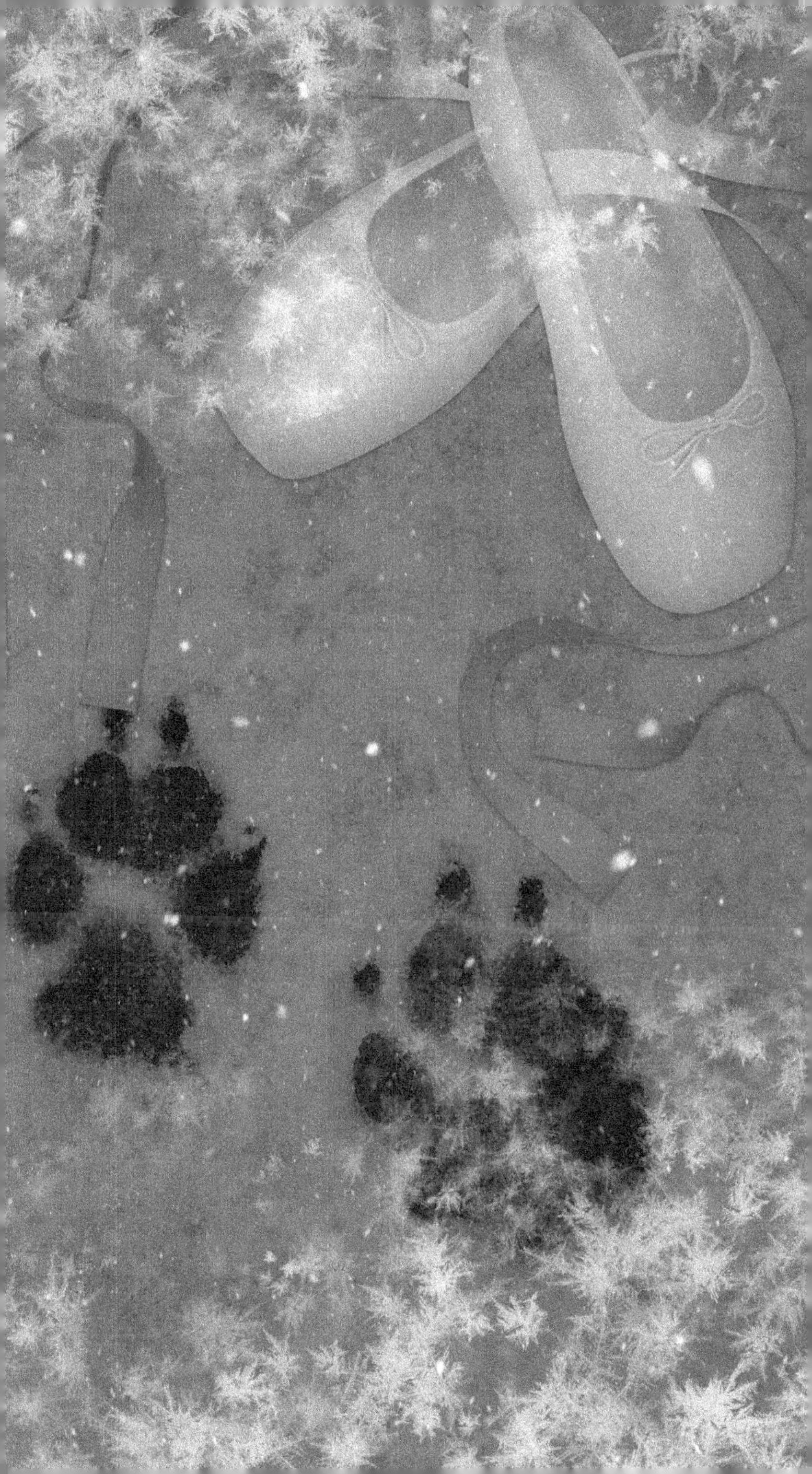

Chapter Twenty-Seven

JOLIE

When I wasn't at rehearsals, I tucked away at home with my hand between my legs or poised under a cold shower, which still didn't help much with solstice's effects.

After about two days, I was nearly back to normal. Though I couldn't forget Jax's cool breath on my skin, his fingers grazing the tips of my thighs, and that very hard, very specific, part of him. He'd watched every moment. Demanded I did too. Now that image of our bodies framed within the frosted mirror is imprinted into memory.

Luckily, *Giselle*'s opening week is finally here. The increase of rehearsals has been a welcome addition to my routine. At first, I worried Jax would distract me from ballet, now ballet is a much-needed distraction from him. It's been two weeks since that night at the studio, and I can't stop thinking about Jax and how we are mates.

Mates.

I am still wrapping my head around it. According to what he's told me, he still senses me, even now that he's practically vanished from my life.

But your heart, your beautiful fucking heart, I can feel from anywhere.

Does he hear my pulse ramping up its pace? Feel the nerves fluttering to life in my belly?

I press a hand over my heart.

Thump-thump. Thump-thump.

When it comes to Jax, there isn't much I wouldn't believe.

The other corps members and I line up along the curtain. Bouncing back and forth, I roll through the box of my pointe shoes, pressing up onto my toes to warm up my feet. No matter how many times I've done this, the nerves always arrive while I'm waiting in the wings. The blues and whites of the spotlights frame the stage in an eerie ambiance, and the thick red curtain is the only thing standing between us and the audience. Their murmurs filter over the top of it, a background hum amplifying my anxiety.

I remind myself this feeling is normal and the sensation will disappear the moment I emerge under the stage's inviting illumination.

Heading to the barre poised backstage, I hike my leg over the top rung and stretch out my hamstring one last time to prevent worsening my injury. Though the physical therapists are on standby, there's not much they can do for me while I'm performing. Once I'm out on that stage, I'll give it my all—no compensating. I'll push through the pain and check in with them during intermission. The most intense work, though, will be afterward, in The White Act, the second half of the ballet when the wilis are on stage. Even during the restful moments, we must hold our poses, exuding the picture of grace, framing the pieces taking place center stage.

In the corps, the last thing you want to do is stand out.

There are thirty of us out there. If each ballerina performed the piece individually, you'd notice the way Evelyn's arches extend her lines beyond reproach, the way Veronique's fingers tense when she turns swiftly across the floor, the way Sara perfectly tilts her chin with every step.

They claim no two snowflakes are alike. Each holds its own unique presence. It's a beautiful sentiment, but how often do we really appreciate the intricacies? When it snows, all we see is the wintry mix around us. The whole. Not each piece that creates it. The instructors, the audience, *that's* what they desire from the corps. The mirage of wholeness. We aren't individuals with years of sweat and suffering under our belts. We are a blizzard of motion. A storm of poise that moves and breathes as one.

Evelyn shoots me a knowing smile, switching her weight back and forth on her feet. I bring my leg down, finishing out my stretches before lining up behind her in the wings.

"Ready?" she asks, a slight shiver to her tone.

"Yes." It's half true. I'm always ready to perform. To be up on the stage in front of an audience, showcasing the talent I've worked hard for. But there are extra nerves that come with opening night. Something unexpected is bound to happen... And for the first time, the one comfort I've always relied on isn't here.

My mom.

When those curtains draw up, I won't find her smiling up at me, pride shimmering in her eyes. No moment where she's the only one I see, the rest of the audience merely a dark blur surrounding her glow.

However, Lark and Delilah *will* be here. I coach myself a few times to seek them out. But when the red velvet rises, I can't stop the pang of disappointment that floods me when my mom isn't there. Logically, she won't ever be, but no amount of reason can prepare me for the realities that come with the loss of her.

I grip my knees, gasping for air that's just out of reach. I'm drowning all over again, air shredded from my lungs. Helpless. Trapped in that car. Only this time, there's no piercing gaze. No mate to save me.

Mom is gone.

Jax is gone.

Evelyn kneels down, hand gently gliding up and down my spine. "You okay?"

It's enough to ground me and stop the theater from spinning. My gaze finally snags on Lark and Delilah in the front row. They must have paid a fortune for those seats. Not that they cared about that. I quickly sniff the tears away before I ruin my stage makeup.

I'm not alone.

"Yeah," I rasp, catching my breath and shaking out the last of my nerves.

The orchestra sweeps into the introduction. Wren's shoes lightly tap against the floor as she breaks into her first variation as Giselle. She's light and gorgeous on her feet, extending out into a stunning arabesque, unaware of the Duke watching her move gracefully across the floor. Her work is something to aspire to. I can't help the smile on my face when Rudolph takes her in his arms. Their bodies are instruments of storytelling, just as much as the ones made of brass and strings reverberating from the pit at the base of the stage. How beautifully they move together. Rudolph partners her with such synchronicity, the level of support that only comes from hours of dedicated practice and a foundation of trust.

I'm carried away for a moment, envisioning myself dancing out there. Picking flowers alongside my partner. Commanding the audience's attention.

Time slips by, and the next thing I know, I'm taking a deep breath and prancing out onto the stage alongside the other corps members to finish out the last section of the first act. For the ensemble, it's mainly acting to enhance the story being told. The real work comes in Act II.

We filter into the wings, hustling toward our dressing rooms to change into our wilis costumes—white leotards with long tutus. Quickly making additions to each other's makeup, we complete our costumes with darkened circles around our eyes. Then we pass out the chiffon veils, draping them over ourselves, transforming into the ghostly apparitions of the woods. Before we can take a true breath, we're behind the curtain once again, ready to go. My hip is stiff, so I wave over Heather, who does some dynamic stretches with me before the curtain rises once again on *Giselle*'s second act.

The lights darken to deeper blue. Mist creeps along with us as we drift out from the wings. Our entrance is slow, a series of ethereally elegant lines. Every so often I catch glances of my friends up on the stage with me and those in the audience. The ghost of loneliness still lingers, but each time my eyes connect with one of them, I'm comforted.

We dance for what feels like forever and an instant, until my limbs and toes are sore to the point of numbness. Until the performance is over and the thick, velvet curtain blankets us from the audience in a ripple of crimson.

We have a moment to catch our breaths before we're called over by Ballet Potomac's director. "Well done!" he says, clapping his hands together. "There are always hiccups the first show, but we couldn't have asked for a better opening."

My stomach unclenches. I inhale deeply, savoring the air dragging into my lungs now that my pulse is steady. It's not the type of feedback I expected—we never heard such a positive review on a first performance at the Institute. In fact, even by the last one, these meetings were something I looked to with anxiety.

The more time I spend at Ballet Potomac, the more I wonder if the loss of my position was a blessing in disguise.

The director turns things over to Mistress Maral and our choreographer, who talk us through a few spots they want us to focus on before tomorrow's matinee performance. Then we're dismissed to our dressing rooms.

After changing into my clothes, I hurry out to the lobby to meet Lark and Delilah. They each pull me in for a hug, handing me a lush bouquet of winter roses.

"You were amazing," Lark gushes. She loops her arm in mine, talking through the details of the performance. What she loved. Moments I stood out. I know she's doing it to appease me, but I savor her words, nonetheless. Brimming with excitement over my first opening night with Ballet Potomac and sharing it with Lark helps fill the gap left by Mom's absence. I miss her so much. She would have been so thrilled with my dancing tonight.

While Lark and Delilah talk about their plans for tomorrow during the Uber ride home, I listen to Mom's message again, comforted by the sound of her voice.

Once we're home, I shower quickly, finding myself disappointed when there's no message on the mirror. No mist when I breathe. No white wolf or handsome harbinger waiting for me. It's not just my mom's absence that leaves a void tonight.

Pressing my palm over the silvered mark on my sternum, I fall asleep and dream of Jax.

His words replay in my mind like a comforting prayer:

I'll find a way to you in any season, Tempest.

April
OCT
MO TU WE TH
10
17
24 25
31
2 3 4 5 6
9 10 11 12 13
16 17 18 19 20
23 24 25 26 27 28
30 31

Chapter Twenty-Eight

JOLIE

Lark bursts through my door. "What happened?" She clutches a pointe shoe over her head, eyes darting around the room until they land on me. "Are you okay?"

Oops.

I swivel my chair the rest of the way around to face her. "Sorry, just got excited."

My cheeks are sore from how hard I'm beaming, joy bubbling up from my belly like I've sipped too many sparkling waters.

This news is everything I need right now. *Giselle* was the perfect distraction, but now that rehearsals are dying down, the lack of perpetual motion makes the tender ache of missing Jax more raw. A partially healed wound scraped against pavement.

"Excited is good. I'm down with excited." Lark bounces into the room. Her arm drops by her side, but she still holds the shoe. "I thought something murdery was happening."

"Nope. Nothing murdery." I laugh, nodding toward her hand. "Though, I'm glad you were ready to fight...with your very dangerous shoe."

Her gaze hones on mine.

"Always."

I arch a brow at her. "What were you planning to do?"

"We both know the blocks of these babies can hurt. Figured I could swing 'em around a bit, maybe strangle them with a ribbon."

"You've thought about this in far too much detail."

She merely shrugs, then tosses the shoe onto the floor and comes closer. "So what's got you excited?"

"*Look.*" I swivel my chair off to the side, making sure she can see the email glowing from my laptop screen.

"Holy shit, Jolie!" Lark's leaning over me, hands on the desk while her lower half hops up and down. Her body is vibrating with all the excitement that thrums through me, and I love her for it. "Holy shit. This is huge! I'm so freaking proud of you."

"Thanks!" My cheeks heat. "I'm actually going to be *in* the Ballet World Summit. I can't believe it." I sigh, trying to freeze the reality of this moment. My mom and I always planned to attend the summit to celebrate when I finally made principal. Maybe that dream hadn't come true, not yet at least, but in a way, this feels like a sign from her. Not only will I be there, I'll be *performing.* "Have they sent out the list for the Institute yet?"

"No. Maybe they will before the end of the week? We both know who's going to be on it." She rolls her eyes. "Did you ever reply to his texts after the showcase?"

"Nah. I blocked his number. And honestly, there's not really anything else to say." I take one more look at the email, enjoying the serotonin boost it brings, then I release a sigh. "You were right about him."

"Maybe I was, but that doesn't mean I am happy about it... I'm sorry."

"There's nothing to be sorry about. It's easy to be blind to the things we don't want to see, even when they're right in front of us."

Lark wasn't trying to be right. She was trying to do right by me. Too bad I was so starved for a morsel of affection, I overlooked the obvious signs. The more I look back on our *relationship*, the more flawed patterns weave into my recollection. What we had was flimsy, awaiting the final thread to finally unravel.

And boy did it unravel quickly.

"CONGRATS, MS. WILDER," Mistress Maral says the next day, placing a gentle hand on my elbow to hold me back as the rest of the class exits. Evelyn is the last one out the door. She shoots me a curious glance, but I wave her on, pointing toward the recovery room where I'd meet her and the others. "I hope you're excited for this opportunity."

"I am. Thank you again for recommending me."

"Hmm." I can't tell if she's agreeing with or assessing me. Knowing her, probably both.

"I have to admit, I was a bit surprised. Why me?" My voice comes out hoarse between catching my breath at the end of class and insecurity over what she's getting at, despite not wanting to leap to conclusions.

"I had my doubts," she agrees. My stomach sinks, my nerves ready to rattle my carefully crafted composure in the name of professionalism. "But you've more than proved your mettle since coming to Ballet Potomac. I fully believe if you keep up the good work—and continue going to your physical therapy appointments—you'll be a strong candidate for promotion."

"Really?" I barely squeak out the word.

"I wouldn't have made the recommendation if I didn't believe you could do it." Her lips straighten into a thin line. "Now, you'll just need to do me a favor."

"Of course. What do you need me to do?"

The corner of her mouth quirks upward. "Prove me right."

I HEAD to the dressing room and change into my bathing suit, the one I've had tucked in my bag for weeks. If Ballet Potomac is finally embracing me, it's time I take the plunge and embrace them right back. It's a new season with the company, another fresh start. Mistress Maral's subtle confidence in me is the boost I need as I walk from the lockers over to the door. I inhale slowly a few times, peering through the slice of glass between the dressing and recovery rooms.

You've got this, Jolie.

I push the door open and smile over at Evelyn, Sara, and Veronique. The first two are still in the large ice-filled tubs while Veronique dries off with a towel. She furrows her brows at me, rightfully confused. "Are you about to do what I think you are?"

"I think so." My legs are a bit wobbly. I'm not sure if it's from my nerves or working so hard in rehearsals today.

"Ahh! Get on in, girl," Evelyn calls over, reaching an arm out to pat the basin next to hers. "I've got about seven more minutes left. Come join in for what you can of them."

I release a breath and shake the towel off my shoulders, showing off my navy one-piece halter swimsuit. Pale-pink flower petals descend from the neckline, scattering down my torso. I move to the side of the basin between Evelyn and Sara and hang the towel on the rack. I can already feel the temperature shift just by being so close to the water's edge.

I rub my hands together quickly. "Okay."

"Do you want some help getting in?" Veronique offers, extending her hand.

I almost tell her I can manage on my own but grip her palm instead. I brace myself for the sting of ice, along with any memories that surface with it. Every time I've even looked at these basins, I've been haunted by the memory of the accident.

My body submerged in the freezing water.

My mother's vacant stare.

The eyes that haunted me until I fully understood who they belonged to.

A small gasp escapes my lips as the tip of my toe plunges into the water, but I don't recoil. Instead, I sink it deeper into the tub until it touches the bottom, flattening out my foot. Veronique steadies me, and I swing the other leg over. *I'm ripping off a Band-Aid*, I remind myself, sitting down and scooting to the edge of the tub. Gripping the lip of the basin, my knuckles are white and tiny bumps cover every inch of me that isn't submerged.

My stomach twists, pulse races, and visions flood my mind. Each one drags me farther beneath the water despite how still I am, clutching the frigid basin.

This was a terrible idea.

Why did I think I was ready?

My body quivers.

"Cold, right?" Evelyn asks, giving a shimmy of her shoulders above the water.

I nod, but her words remind me that the cold is no longer my enemy. It hasn't been for months. Like the silver-white wolf that once startled me from afar, I no longer fear it. I embrace its sting and sink into the numb it brings. The cold is *him*. And when I think of Jax, I feel safe and loved.

Home.

"You sure you've never done this before?" Veronique asks, pursing her lips. "I literally screeched the first time I got halfway in." She chuckles, and the other girls join in. "You're doing incredible. Took me a full week to work up to a few minutes."

"And not even a jolt or jitter." Sara lifts her hands above her tub and claps a few times. Some of the other dancers stretching around the room look over at us, and my cheeks heat. Evelyn gives a dramatic bow of her head in my direction. "I'm in awe."

"Someone must be cold-blooded," Veronique teases.

I bite my lip and shrug, brushing off their words despite the questions that sink into me. "Must be."

My hand flies up to my sternum, moving the neckline enough so I can run my fingers over the scar there. It thrums, radiating through me. With each echo of its magic, my pulse slows, calm sweeping through my limbs until the icy water's threat begins to melt away. The memories spill from my mind, floating from the forefront of my consciousness as I think of *him*.

After a minute, I release my hold. My hands fall into the water and my shoulders are the only thing above its rippling surface. With each inhale and exhale, my body adjusts, first to discomfort, then a searing numb, and finally a welcoming embrace. Each lap of water, each graze of ice, wears away at the sharp and tender edges of my mind.

My fingers running through soft, silvery tufts.

The comforting weight of Jax's wolf keeping my toes warm in the night.

His chilling gaze raking over me in the reflection.

There's no water cold enough to counteract the warmth pooling within me.

I swallow, finally catching my breath.

Sara climbs out of the tub, and minutes later, Evelyn's timer goes off. Once they've toweled off, they come over to help me stand.

"Wow," I say, my body stinging as the warm air lashes my skin. Evelyn and Veronique each take a hand, supporting me while I get out. My legs quiver, and their grips tighten when my feet hit the ground. I'm like a newborn giraffe, stumbling a few feet with their assistance.

Sara walks over to the wall and grabs my towel, handing it to me to dry off. The three of them exchange quiet glances. I drop my gaze, scanning every inch of me that I can see, even craning my neck to try to peer at my back before I look at the three of them. "What?"

Evelyn's eyes dart between me and her phone screen. "You know how long you just went in for?"

I shake my head. "How long?"

"Almost 15 minutes."

"Wow." Usually it's recommended to work up to about five minutes when you've never done an ice bath before. Ten minutes isn't impossible. It isn't unheard of, but it's definitely not the norm.

I'm calm. Refreshed. And I can't help but wonder if there is some magic at play in this. Jax is still hibernating, probably after being punished for our last time together. Even with that knowledge, my heart races and my eyes dart around the room, hoping I'm wrong. That he's somewhere here.

Everyone is talking amongst themselves. I follow the girls toward the dressing room to change into warm clothes, but I can't help the final glance over my shoulder, full of hope only to come up empty.

No wolf. No frosty window. No soothing baritone billowing into my ear.

The only thing I find is that I'm pierced by the cleaving emptiness of missing Jax. Even though he's away, he still manages to bolster me with the strength I need to face my fears, and it fills that hollow space with pride.

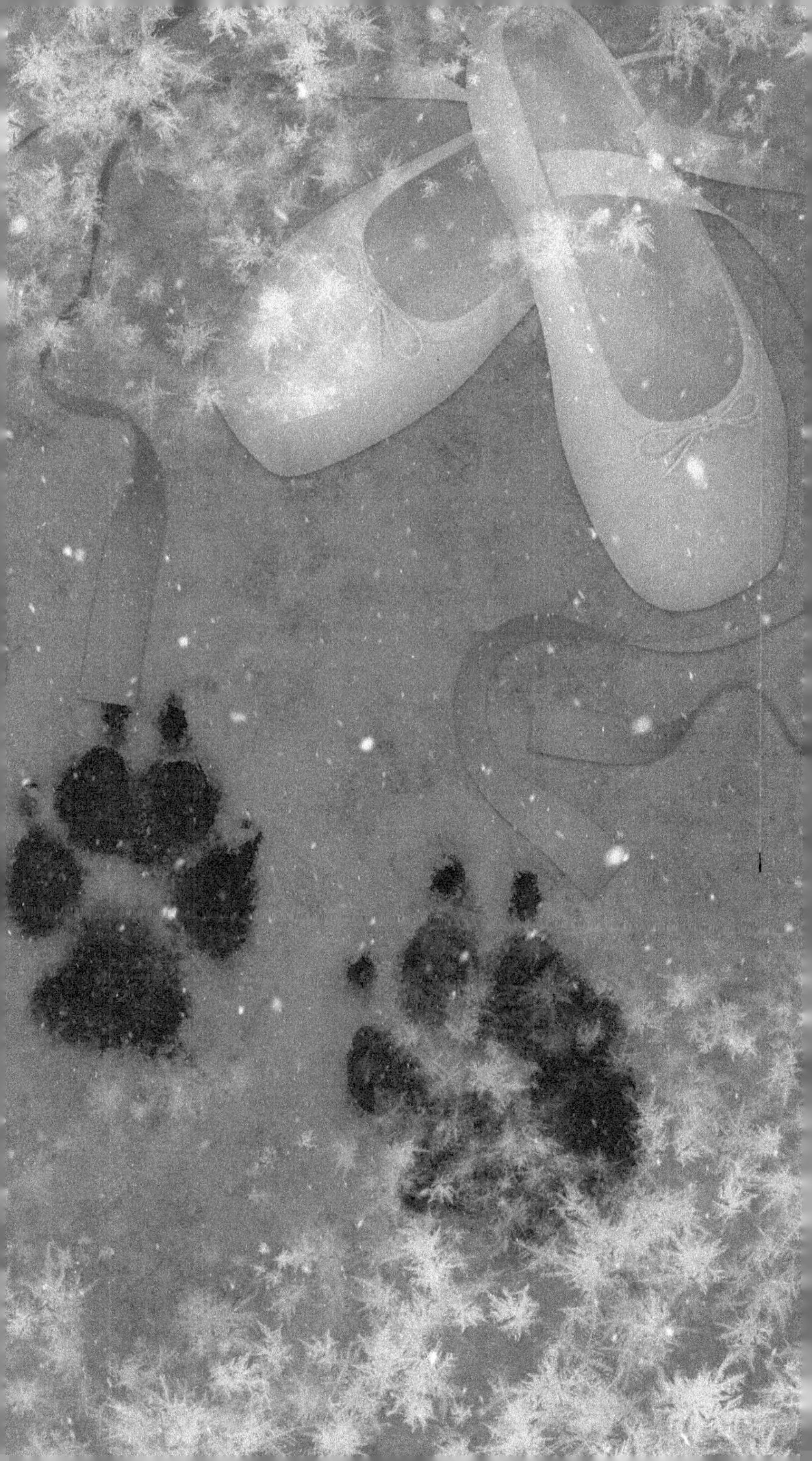

Chapter Twenty-Nine

JOLIE

Swinging the strap of my dance bag over my shoulder, I grab myself a banana before tossing another to Lark, who catches it up high with one hand. She twists to shove it into her backpack while I peel mine, taking a big bite.

"Ready to go?" she asks, reaching for the doorknob. I can only nod in response, mouth full of mashed-up banana.

I follow her out the door, but she halts so abruptly that I bump into her backpack, nearly spitting banana all over it.

"What the fuck?"

I peek my head out from behind her and my eyes widen. Perched on our welcome mat is a rabbit with a honey coat and large, white-tipped ears, one flopped over, lopsided. It stares up at Lark, seemingly startled.

"Hey, cutie!" she coos.

When the creature spots me behind her, it prances to the side, revealing a spray of ivory peonies. They're beautiful, delicately shining pale blue in spots where the sunlight reaches them. They remind me of Jax.

He had told me that a Bloom had helped him get back here for solstice. Could it be possible that this was a harbinger? The very same one? Of course, I can't ask the rabbit. That would be crazy, mainly because Lark is standing right here.

My how the threshold for what's *normal* has changed these last few months.

Lark's brows pinch. She bends down to pick the flowers up and hands them to me without drawing her gaze away from the rabbit.

"Thanks," she says, and we watch the creature scamper toward the stairs. "Look what somebunny brought you."

Her tone is teasing, and I can't help myself from chuckling at her pun, but unease settles through me. Lark talking to an animal doesn't surprise me at all. I swear she could've been a fairy-tale princess in another life, talking to birds and having mice stitch up gowns for her. But I still haven't told her about Jax. My best friend. The person who has a vintage Ouija board, talks to tiny creatures, and has seen me through my darkest days is the one I'm afraid will judge me most if I tell her the truth. A truth that I still find hard to believe, even as I stare at the peonies bunched between my fingers.

"Looks like there's a note too," Lark says, bending down one more time and handing me a thick piece of paper.

"Let me put these inside," I say, scurrying into the kitchen and getting water into a thin vase. I drop the peonies in it, then flip over the note with a shiny blue *J* on it. Jax's words are scrawled in tiny lettering across the glittering parchment in silver metallic ink.

"Better get going, Jojo," Lark reminds me.

I quickly tuck the note into my dance bag before I can decipher his scribbles and head for the door. Anticipation thrums through me to see what it says, but if I read it now, Lark will be more curious than she already is, and I'm not sure if I'm ready to divulge about Jax and everything that comes with him.

She ushers me outside, locking the door behind me. Should I be more shocked by how not weirded out she's acting or that I just had a delivery via harbinger post?

We finish descending the stairs and hustling toward the metro center. I am already sweating profusely. My hand comes to my forehead, wiping away a few stray beads of sweat. The sun is nearly blinding at this hour. Just a month ago, it would still be pitch black outside, the streets only illuminated by lamplight on this trek.

"Hold this a sec?" I ask Lark, handing my bag to her and peeling off my sweatshirt before tying it around my waist. She helps me loop it back over my shoulder. The cars are peppered in a thin coating of yellow pollen, and tiny white buds peek from the trees flanking the still-quiet streets. The morning blossoms around us, the sun rising with each step we take.

While it's been a gradual shift, it hasn't hit me until today that spring's officially staked its claim on the city. Winter is over.

The finality of it pinches between my ribs, but the note tucked away in my dance bag reminds me that Jax is still out there and thinking of me, spearing my hope for us a little bit further.

COMPANY CLASS FLIES BY. Before I know it, I'm off to another appointment with Dr. Tanner. I've begun to taper off my visits and even told her about Jax at my last one. He's become such a big part of my life that it's hard to always skirt around his existence. Not that I give her the full truth. That would probably be a progress-hindering revelation in her eyes.

I'm still counting down until I can read his note. While I technically could have done earlier, I want to savor each scrawled-out word. It's the first time I'm hearing from him since he left, and something tells me that messenger rabbit isn't something he'll be able to utilize frequently, considering the seasons stay mostly separated and he'll be hibernating.

"How is everything going since we last met?" Dr. Tanner asks, clicking and re-clicking her purple pen. "Did the extra week between appointments feel like a good amount of time or too much? We don't have to scale back yet if you're not comfortable."

"The extra week was great. I didn't feel the itch to come in sooner, but I have been looking forward to our session." My heels bounce against the carpet. "There's something I want to show you."

I reach into my dance bag, pushing aside my shoes and sweaty clothes from this morning's company class until I find what I'm looking for. I pass the white-and-black marbled notebook to Dr. Turner, then nod to her. "Open it."

She does.

She'd made it clear that the journal isn't for her to evaluate, it's for my own mind to process and unburden itself, but I wanted to share this moment. I follow her gaze as she flips through the pages in a few fluid motions. Her brows lift from behind her glasses, as if surprised.

"It's full," she says, the corner of her mouth quirking up as she hands it back to me. I fan it a few times. It's funny how light something carrying so much heaviness can be.

Months of grief, uncertainty, and healing all in one spot. It's a strange badge of honor, but the last half filled up quickly since meeting Jax.

"Those wins have been racking up." She repositions her pen against the clipboard balanced in her lap, eyes darting up to me. "Can you give me an example of your hard work paying off?"

"Well, I found out recently that my name was entered to perform in the Ballet World Summit." I can't hold in the giddy smile that bursts from me. "Mistress Maral thinks that if I keep up with the work and represent the company well, I've got a shot at promoting. I've just started rehearsing the choreography for my solo."

"What are you dancing?"

"Juliet's variation from *Romeo and Juliet*. The scene where she dances at the ball when Romeo first sees her."

"That's amazing, Jolie."

"I know. I can't believe it."

When Mistress Maral brought up Juliet's variation as an option, it just felt right. A ballet about star-crossed lovers separated by things beyond their control. A love that transcends life and death. I knew right away it was the piece I had to perform.

"Congratulations. That's a huge accomplishment. How do you feel about it?"

"Really good." My heels and fingers tap in unison, excited energy needing somewhere to flow. "Things are finally starting to come together. And I'm really liking my new company."

The more time I spend at Ballet Potomac, learning their processes and getting to know my fellow dancers, the better of an environment I think it is for me. Now that I've let go of the dream I'd envisioned of dancing principal at the Institute and partnering with Blake, on and offstage, my eyes are more open to the possibility of a future where I'm at. I adore Evelyn, Veronique, and Sara. I enjoy the class and rehearsal structure. And now, with this opportunity to travel to Sydney and dance at the festival, it's a sign they see a future for me there too.

"And how about Jax? How are things going since you mentioned him at our last session?"

My body goes very still at the mention of him, but I shake it off quickly, hoping Dr. Tanner didn't notice. Her pen meeting paper tells me that's not the case.

Crap.

"Good but quiet. His job takes him away for long periods of time." I bite my lip, trying to think of what I can strategically say. "I got a note with some flowers from him this morning." I leave out the part where the peonies were delivered via Bloom harbinger bunny.

Dr. Tanner smiles down at her paper and jots more notes. "How did that make you feel?"

"Valued... Loved." Though Jax hasn't said the words to me aloud, they are no less felt.

"I know being apart can be hard and sometimes lead to feelings of insecurity or resentment." She gives me a sympathetic dip of her head and waits. When I don't say anything, she continues, "But you feel good about things?"

"I do." Though I have to admit it's hard to feel like I'm fully living when I'm constantly straddling being present and dancing with a ghost just out of reach. It's not Jax's fault, but sometimes his absence tampers with my belief. "I'm counting down until I can see him again."

At least everything I've said is true.

"When will that be?"

My grin widens. "Winter."

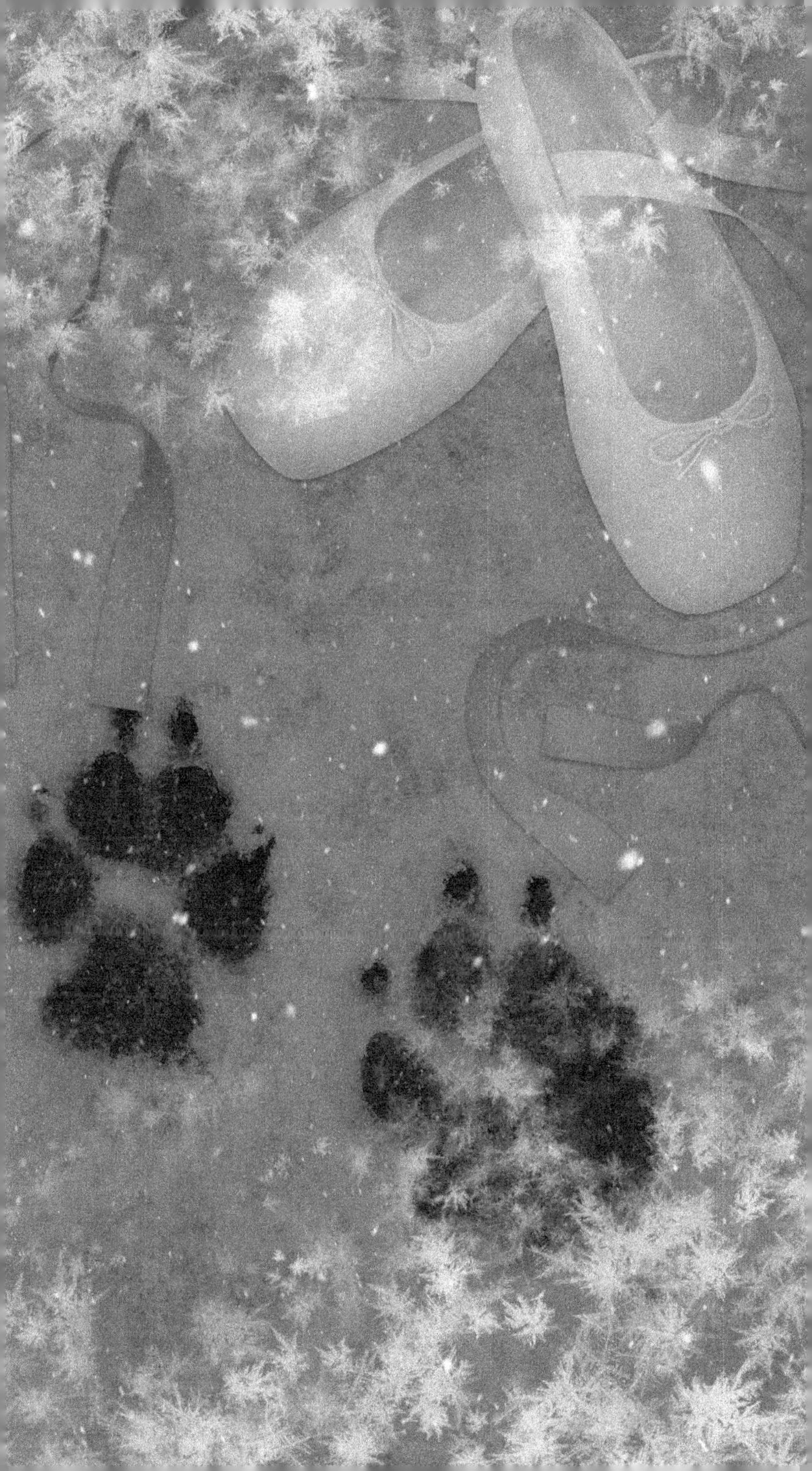

Chapter Thirty

JOLIE

As soon as I walk through the door to the apartment, Delilah's already yelling, "You're home in time to catch the last period!"

She ushers me into the living room, taking my bag and discarding it by the wall before she pats the couch. I almost hesitate, Jax's letter is still on my mind, but Delilah's enthusiasm draws me to her. *It's not like the note is going anywhere.* I hustle over and grab some Twizzler popcorn before tossing it in my mouth. I almost forgot it was the playoffs.

Delilah has been beside herself since her team made it. "The Redhots are up by two. Really hoping they'll score a couple more goals before the end of the game."

"How was your day?" I ask Lark, my hand fighting hers in the bowl as we both go for a big scoop of popcorn.

"Great!" Lark says between bites. "The Institute finally sent out the list for the Summit."

"And?"

"Looks like you'll have time to get sick of me in a whole other country!"

We both squeal, and Delilah ignores us, eyes glued to the television, her entire body is tense.

I loop an arm around Lark's shoulder. "Love that for us."

It'll be so amazing to see her dance again and have a buddy for the trip since my closest friends from the corps weren't invited. Plus, I'm always down for another Blake buffer. "Do you know what you're dancing yet?"

"Nope. I'm thinking of maybe the Emerald's first variation from *Jewels*. You know I love me some Balanchine choreography."

"Oh, you'd do amazing with that!" I'm already imagining her beautifully long legs sweeping with her tulle, moving gracefully through the fluid arm movements, spinning across the stage. Lark's body is naturally long, whereas I'm built more petite. Working for those impeccable lines took me years.

"Plus, there's a green corset-and-tutu ensemble I've had my eye on in the costume department."

"Of course there is." Leave it to Lark to pick her piece based on the costume.

"Well, if you're going to do it, you've got to do it in style. Right?" She nudges me with her elbow.

"Right—"

"Steal that!" Delilah shouts, and our heads snap back up to her. She's standing and jumping in place. "Go, go, go!"

Myles crosses the blue line on a breakaway. The defensemen speed toward him, trying to catch up, but they are not fast enough. Approaching the net, Myles dekes to the right and strikes it past the goalie's glove.

"Myles puts it top shelf, extending the lead to three!" the announcer shouts.

Delilah and the crowd roar as a crimson banner pops up on the screen with a close-up of Winston's face.

My blood runs cold.

That face. If you shifted the olive skin and green eyes and grew out his blond hair, he's the spitting image of...Jax. They could nearly be twins, minus Winston's crooked nose and the severeness of Jax's bone structure. It's so eerily familiar that on instinct I reach for my phone and pull up the search engine, typing in his name to learn more about him.

Winston Myles is from outside Boston, has played for the Richmond Redhots for six seasons, and is one of their best wingers. When I reach the part about a childhood hockey tragedy, my pulse skyrockets. The ice cracked under both of their skates, but his older brother shoved him out of the way, falling in before he could save himself. Winston was eight at the time, his older brother had just turned fourteen. When I read the name, the confirmation knocks the wind from my lungs.

Jaxon Myles.

Frantically, I type the name into the search bar, clicking on anything I can find to tell me more. A few youth hockey league clippings pop up, along with four articles about the accident and a local obituary. I read each one, on the verge of tears as I stare over and over again at the grainy photographs of a young boy with wayward blond hair and pale-green eyes.

Jax.

I rush to my room, heart pounding at the revelation of his story. He never told me how he died, and now I know why. He'd drowned in an icy lake, not unlike my own death.

My mind spins back to the fear I had of going into the ice baths at the studio. The idea of submerging myself beneath its frosted surface terrified me. Yes, Jax is dead. Yes, his memories have faded. But the courage he must have felt to get to me...then watch me die. The moment the light was snuffed from my mother's eyes, her lips parted, never to inhale or kiss my forehead again... It was still a memory I had to recall from a distance, otherwise I'd shatter. Watching his mate die in such a familiar way must have struck some deep part of him.

I wish I could hug him. Tell him about his brother. Talk to him about what I'd learned about his past.

My heart aches for the nearness of him.

I glance over at the peonies decorating my desk, and smile. Remembering the card, I grab my bag and pull it out, flipping it over and squinting to read his squiggled words.

> *Tempest,*
> *I miss you so much. Can't stop thinking about the last time I saw you.*

My mind flits back to the night at the studio, and my chest flushes with heat. Finally seeing Jax and his other-worldly glory would be ingrained in me forever. The chill of his fingertips grazing my skin. The texture of his captivating marks pressed to my back. The desperation of his kiss as we fought against Fate's constantly ticking clock.

> *If you're reading this, then Briar was able to get my message to you—hopefully he wasn't too grumpy about it. He's been working overtime after our little solstice stunt. I'm not allowed to leave Nivea until hopefully next season, after I hiber-nate. Until I'm allowed out, I'll be unreachable.*
> *In the meantime, don't stop believing, Tempest. I am counting down the days until you see me*

again. Remember: Even though the seasons keep us apart, I'm still here.

Always here and always yours.

Love your favorite Frost,

Jax

I chuckle at that last part. Even when he's hidden away in hibernation, it's like he knew I'd need these words. This reminder.

Him.

Maybe we can't be together right now, but he's no less with me. No less devoted. The least I can do is continue to believe in him. *In us.* If he's out next season, during our summer, there's a chance that I could be seeing him sooner rather than later...

I fold up the note and tuck it into my blank journal. Its pages have yet to be filled, every single one pristine. Empty until tonight.

I print off the articles about his life and, piece by piece, I begin to bring our story to life. Starting with his.

May

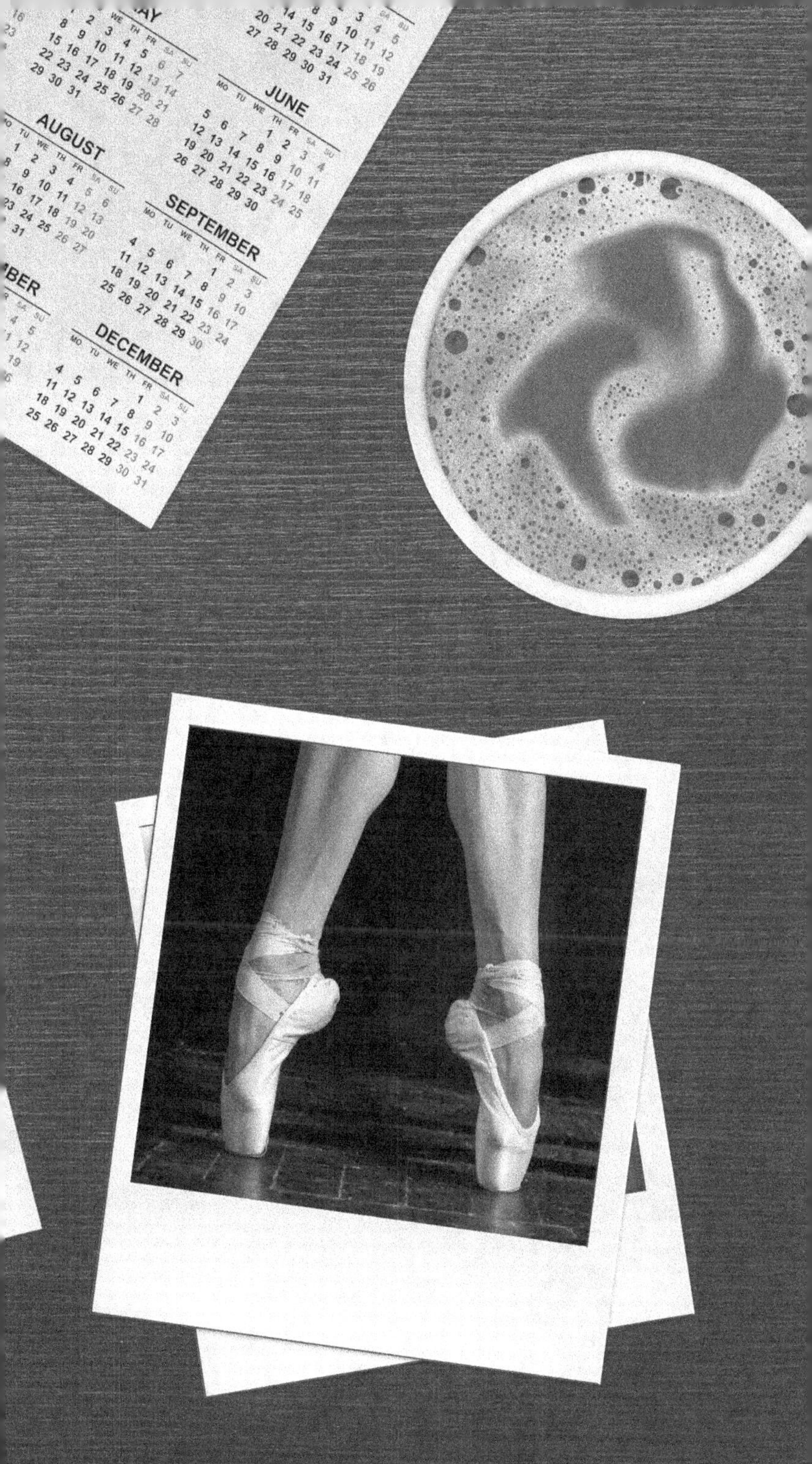

AUGUST
SEPTEMBER
DECEMBER
JUNE

June
OCTO
MO TU WE TH
3
10 18
17 18
24 25
31
2 3 4 5 6
9 10 11 12 13
16 17 18 19 20 21
23 24 25 26 27 28
30 31

July
OCT
MO TU WE TH

Chapter Thirty-One

JOLIE

The weeks of rehearsal become a blur of blisters, ice baths, physical therapy, and—of course—missing my favorite Frost. Before I know it, spring's turned into summer. While there's been no word from Jax since he went into hibernation, I do as he asked: continue to believe.

After two long flights—that thankfully didn't get delayed—and an Uber ride, we reach our hotel in Sydney. Lark contacted them ahead of time, so our rooms are across from one another. We drag our luggage down the hallway until we make it to the rooms, setting our alarms on our phones to grab some food in a few hours. We all need to catch up on some much-needed sleep. Despite all my efforts, I didn't get much rest on the flights with all the excitement of the trip.

Tomorrow, we jump right into rehearsals and the soloist showcase. Lark, Delilah, and I tacked on extra days at the end of the trip to sightsee and visit Australia's Hotham Alpine Resort before we return to DC. Delilah's really into skiing and wants to do the trip up thanks to a big bonus she got at her job. She's even treating us to box seats at the theater for the night we aren't performing after Lark told her how my mom and I had always planned to attend the Ballet World Summit. The night before we left, she gave me an envelope with the tickets inside and I sobbed.

Lark and I could care less about skiing. She just wants to do something nice for Delilah since she trekked all this way and took time off from work. I'll be there to keep Lark company and...there might be an unfounded hope wriggling at the back of my mind that I'll get to see Jax.

Even if there's no snow on the ground, it is technically winter in Australia. Jax said they worked year-round, all in different regions. He hoped to be allowed back to my world after hibernation. Was Australia's winter enough to warrant the Frosts' attention?

It might be a long shot, but I can't help my excitement over the prospect of seeing him. Wouldn't it be kismet for us to both be here? If he is out of hibernation, how close would I need to be for him to sense me?

I'd hoped I'd see his rabbit friend again before spring ended, but I never managed to run into him. I even had a note that I carried with me everywhere, just in case, telling Jax about my trip to Australia. Then maybe he could have planned to be here too.

As much as I wanted to tell him about his family in the note, I left that off. Not that it mattered since he never read it, but I figured it'd be best to tell him about it in person. While he doesn't remember everything about his mortal life, I'd want to know my family is still out there if I were in his shoes.

I lie in bed, staring up at the ceiling, still in my grungy travel clothes. My body's exhausted. The effort it would take to hunt through my suitcase for pajamas is more than I'm willing to commit to, so I curl up with the covers and fantasize about a future that seems much too far out of reach, maintaining my belief in the impossible.

But hasn't everything been just that since Jax came into my life—impossibility made reality?

A FEW HOURS LATER, we groggily grab dinner, so thrown by jet lag that we barely speak. Instead, we stare at our waters and food as they arrive at the table. I'm not even hungry. Nerves bubble up in my belly, riding on a tide of nausea. In less than twenty-four hours I'll be performing. In an unfamiliar city on an unfamiliar stage. It doesn't help that so much is at stake with my position at Ballet Potomac riding on tomorrow night's performance.

This is my biggest meal before then, so despite my lack of hunger, I ordered a soup, sandwich, and a salad, figuring anything extra I can store in the hotel fridge. The last thing I want is to be starving before the showcase. After I eat my soup, I nudge at my salad with my fork between bites, finally deciding to box up the rest and take it with me.

The sun hangs low as we walk back to the hotel. I snap some photos with Sydney's cityscape as we stroll, the theater and surrounding buildings illuminated under the hazy glow of streetlights.

"Get over there and let me take a picture of you."

When I don't move at her request, Lark nudges me forward and spins me by the shoulders to face her and Delilah. I force my best smile as she snaps pictures from different angles.

"Now, one facing toward the sign. Reach up and point your other foot behind you," Lark directs, kneeling low to capture whatever it is she's envisioning.

Bright-white lights beam down from the marquee, Ballet World Summit in big, block letters.

My chest pinches. I stare up at the illumination and hold my pose as my chin wobbles. Despite the bustle of people on the street and Lark and Delilah being right here, I feel utterly alone. There's an empty space beside me that's awaiting someone who'll never fill it.

The person whom I most wish was here to see this with me isn't.

I'm in Sydney without Mom, making this core memory that we should have been sharing, but instead she's gone. Just when I think I'm starting to pull myself together, I'm struck again by the harsh reality of her loss.

Lark doesn't say a word, just ends the mini photoshoot and pulls me into a hug. She holds me, letting me sob against her shoulder. Delilah reaches from behind her and places a firm hand on my back, patting it a few times.

"I love you guys," I sniffle out. I don't know what I'd do without them here with me on this trip. Delilah grabs a tissue from her Redhots fanny pack and hands it to me. Once I've wiped away my tears and snot, we head up to our rooms. I shower, then stretch, running through the variation a few times with music, then again in silence, waiting for sleep to pull me under. Tomorrow will be here before I know it, and everything needs to be perfect. Not just for me, but for the woman I wish was here to witness it firsthand.

Morning comes much too soon, and I wake with a shiver.

"Jax?" Popping up out of bed, I swing my legs over the side, gaze darting around the room for him or his wolf.

I stand up quickly, legs wobbling under me at the abrupt shift in my position. The thin carpet creaks beneath my feet with each step toward the window. Pulling the curtains to the sides, I search for any sign of him.

No breeze. No glittering eyes. No words frosted on the glass.

Nothing. The room is empty.

Everything is exactly how I left it when I went to bed. In the sunbeam from the slat between the curtains, I stride over to the desk, checking the hotel's stationary, then snap my gaze to the mirror, only finding my reflection. Disappointment begins to get the best of me, so I peek into the bathroom and do one final sweep before I admit defeat.

It's all in my head.

A few tears fall, and I grab a tissue from the nightstand to blot them away.

This is what you get for hoping, Jolie. Snap out of it.

I could reach for my mark, could try to summon him, but then what? I need to prepare for my performance. The future of my ballet career hangs in the balance. There will be time to chase Jax's ghost afterward.

I sniffle, attempting to stifle any more tears. Throwing on my solo music, I mark through the piece a few times, then start to get ready, putting on my warm-up clothes and a light layer of makeup. We're meeting an hour before our company's rehearsal slot to do some barre and stretching, going over the final details for tonight. Tossing my phone, room card, water bottle, and last night's leftover sandwich into my bag, I head for the door and take a last deep breath before everything flips into performance mode.

Soon, I'll be under those lights, and once I am, I need to dance like I've got nothing to lose, even if it's the furthest thing from the truth.

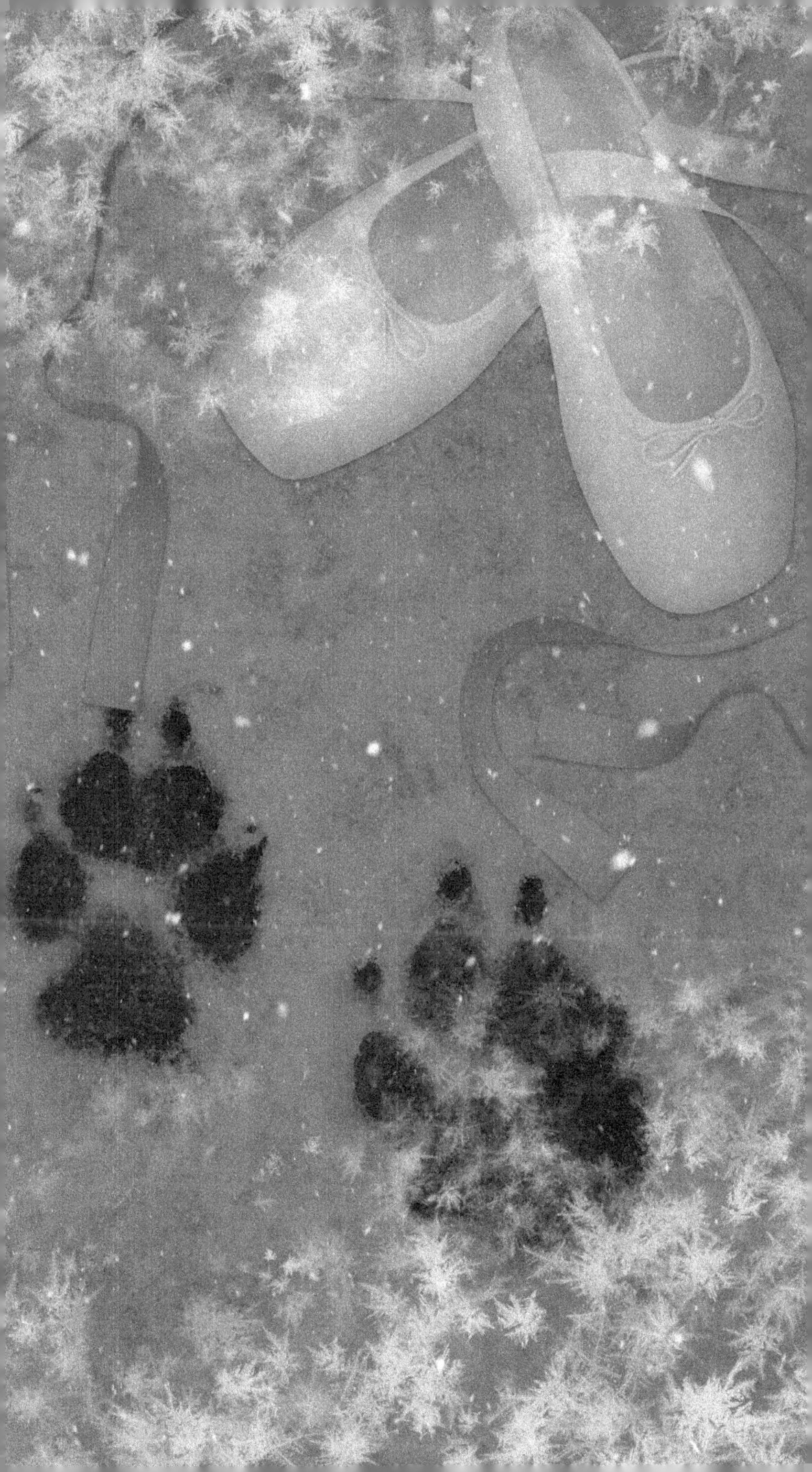

Chapter Thirty-Two

JOLIE

That night at the Summit, I slip my arm through the top of my dress and shuffle to the mirror. My body's still sore from rehearsal, but I do my stretches between things so I can go into the showcase refreshed.

The nerves continue to thrum through my body. They haven't stopped all day. I inhale, running my fingers along the creamy chiffon of my dress. Pale blue and gold trim crisscross my chest, looping over my shoulders and supporting a set of delicate, double-layered ruffles in the same material as the skirt that hangs over a matching leotard, falling to just below my knees.

I twist back and forth, and the scars slashed down my shoulder and upper back glint under the buttery dressing room lights.

"Did you want help with your makeup?" Lark asks.

I spot her reflection behind me in an emerald corset with sparkling rhinestones covering the entire bodice. Her attention trails along my scars, not in a way that's pitying, but one that says she genuinely wants to help me. There are some areas that are very hard to reach, so it's easier for someone else to do it for me.

Since summer has been focused on conditioning and preparing those of us going to the Ballet World Summit, I haven't felt the need to cover them up on a daily basis. Not like when I first returned to dancing. I normally had Lark assist with it when *Giselle* was in performance season, not wanting to stand out from the corps. Right now, though, I'm dancing a solo. There's no one else I need to match. No one else to be but myself.

"I think I'll leave them be today," I tell her with a smile that's reflected back at me in the mirror.

We stare at each other a moment, then I turn, taking in her full costume. The gem detailing is stunning, trailing down her ensemble and scattering onto the stiff, mint-colored tutu jutting out around her.

"You look incredible." I give Lark another once-over, admiring the shimmering elements that go all the way up to her emerald-encrusted tiara poised in front of her high bun. "I can totally see why you picked the piece."

She gives herself a nod of approval. "Right? So worth it." Lark slips her hands in mine and her tone softens. "You're going to do amazing tonight. Momma Wilder would be so proud."

"Thanks," I rasp. Not wanting to ruin my stage makeup right before the performance. "That means a lot." It means more than a lot, but I can't get the words out. It's a significance that cuts so deep, the only way I can let the emotions out is to let them bleed into my performance where they can't overwhelm me.

We lace our pointe shoes, Lark spending extra time beating hers up. The green dye makes them stiffer, needing more attention to get them supple. Giving each other a long hug, we part ways and head to meet our respective companies. Everyone is quiet once Mistress Maral and the director go over the order of the showcase, imparting their final words of wisdom.

My heart pounds so wildly, I can't retain any of it.

Once they finish, we split off into our own pre-performance rituals. I warm up my body a bit more, working through the stretches and exercises Heather gave me. With my earbuds popped in, *Juliet's Variation* plays over and over so I can immerse myself before I go on stage.

The next thing I know, they call the show and we are lining up in the wings. Lark waves to me from across the stage, and I wave back, my hand halting when Blake dares to smile in my direction from behind her.

Asshole.

His blond hair is slicked back, and he's dressed in just a pair of relaxed pants that cuff above his ballet shoes, muscles proudly on display. I don't return his attention, instead dropping my gaze to focus on the building crescendo in my earbuds. The fact that he can smile at me when I've blocked and ignored him for months just solidifies the fact that he's an arrogant jerk. The prince I once idolized is nothing more than an ant I look forward to crushing beneath my proverbial pointe shoe.

The burble of chatter from the other side of the curtain grows until the instrumental introduction plays over the sound system, hushing the audience. They announce the first piece to kick off the Summit, and the ballet dancer from the Royal Ballet takes his place on the stage.

I go back to listening to my music a few more times before tucking the earbuds into a small bag at the corner of backstage. There are only two more pieces until my routine. I'm grateful I don't have to wait long. Every passing minute my nerves riot, the routine slipping from memory, as if I haven't spent weeks preparing. Nausea mixed with the sudden urge to pee—all the usual pre-performance jitters—come out tenfold. Not that I'd expect anything less. This is how it always goes.

Come on, Jolie.

I wiggle out my fingers and toes, bouncing back and forth atop my pointe shoes before pressing them into the pile of rosin, cracking it into shards and dust until the tips are perfectly coated.

Something I love about portraying Juliet is her hopeful grace. This variation is from when she's dancing at the ball. At first, she moves by herself, showcasing her lightness. Her joy. It's such a stark difference from where she ends up at the end of the story, joining her lover in death.

This dance comes before all the tragedy, and if only for a moment, when I dance it, I can pretend I'm in the *before*.

Before my injury.

Before the accident.

Before each shattered piece of me was hacked into existence.

For these few minutes, I'm that young ballerina again and the world is bright and full of possibilities.

The stage manager ushers me over, nodding as she talks into the headset. I gracefully walk out onto the stage, arms carried softly in front of me as I set myself into my starting position. The lights are low, so dim that I know the audience can only make out my silhouette.

It's time. Everyone's watching.

Before I can finish one deep breath, the intro begins.

The lights come up, like the first burst of morning sun, and I move.

Each spin atop my toes is light and delicate. Each sweep of my leg reaches the skylights. Each brush of my arms moves through its arc, graceful and smooth.

There's no ballroom of spectators like in the ballet, so I carry myself around the stage, utilizing its entirety. I gaze over my arm, flirtatiously, admiring each line I perfectly execute. My confidence grows along with the music. It propels me into a grand jeté, and I leap so high that I might collide with the night itself.

I'm spinning and dancing my way to where my invisible Romeo stands. The one Juliet's been dancing for, hoping to catch his eye. It's an all too familiar feeling. Both in the weeks leading up to the performance and now. I stare off and extend my arm toward the corner of the room, picturing twin panes of glittering glass in the audience, reaching back for me.

How I wish he was.

I continue to dance for him. Continue to pretend. I strike my final pose, the moment Romeo has found Juliet, and I can't help but imagine it's real. That Jax is here, taking the form of the invisible man I'm embracing.

I barely realize the music has stopped. My attention is pinned to the back of the room and those eyes staring back at me.

In a flash, they disappear.

Snap out of it, Jolie. He's not here.

I don't have a moment for that to disappoint me, though, because just like magic, the crowd erupts in applause, standing before me in a wave of fancy suits and gowns. My smile widens as it echoes through me, vibrating deep in my soul.

I did it.

Chapter Thirty-Three

JOLIE

I'm still floating on cloud nine the day after my performance when my phone buzzes.

She tosses in a few sickly emojis for good measure. I know her well enough to know that's code for she won't be going anymore.

Well, I'm not missing out, even if I have to watch Blake perform. This is something Mom and I always talked about doing.

I carefully avoid the sequins of my champagne dress, tugging up the zipper slowly. The neckline hugs the slight swells of my breasts. One nice thing about being small chested—no need for a bra. I'm forgoing underwear as well, thanks to the slit of the dress slicing dangerously high on my thigh. Better to avoid underwear lines or a panty flash. It wasn't like anyone would be looking at me in the private box Delilah had splurged on anyway.

Grabbing my clutch, I slip my key and phone into it. Then I move into the hallway, waiting for the door to shut behind me before I walk toward the elevators.

The theater is only a couple blocks away, and the lobby is bustling when I arrive. I wave at a few of the passing ballerinas I hung out with backstage yesterday while I stand in line to get in. Whipping out my phone, I hold it out for the attendant to scan my ticket, then traipse to the bar to grab a glass of chardonnay. At least if I accidentally spill my drink, it'll blend in with my dress. I double check that my slit is in its proper place before walking on, enjoying how the sequins caress my curves, glittering like diamonds under the buttery chandeliers above.

The chimes ring, signaling the doors to the theater have opened. I spot the sign corresponding to my ticket on my right and steer away from the crowd. Gripping my skirt in the same hand that's holding my clutch, I use my other to stay balanced as I walk up the staircase to the upper level where the private boxes are. I follow the arrows until I come to the curtained-off box F.

An usher rushes over, holding the black velvet to the side so I can enter. "Anyone else joining you tonight?"

I give them a gentle smile. "Nope. Just me."

"Well, I'll be at the end of the hallway if you need anything at all, dear," they say, tipping their head.

"Thank you," I call over my shoulder before heading toward the front of the box and picking a seat in the center. There are two more boxes on my side and three across from us. I'm in the farthest right, closest to the stage. Curtains swag either side of the row, hanging like a set of long bangs, casting the intimate space in darkness compared to the well-lit theater. I sip my wine, watching people move between rows, finding their seats and making room for each other. I admire my favorite gowns and ogle a few famous faces. Famous for the ballet world, that is.

The emcee's voice booms over the theater, and the last of the audience takes their seats. They welcome us and remind everyone not to use flash photography, record on their cell phones, or walk out while a performance is taking place. Everyone, including myself, nods along. Each spectator is either a former, current, or loved one of a dancer. We know the drill.

First to take the stage is The Australian Ballet, performing the opening number with their two premiere principal dancers playing Carmen and her Don José, captivating us with their passion-filled pas de deux full of lifts and heavenly extensions. I watch, entranced, experiencing each step alongside them. It's a beautiful piece, a moment captured in a ballet about desire and how jealousy can turn to tragedy. The story of *Carmen* has been around for ages, told in a million ways. You know in the end that he will root his own destruction, but the way they are moving, vibrant and enamored, you can almost forget, can almost believe they will make it—even when the story never changes. The happy ending never comes.

I clap along with everyone else when it's over, then grab the program that's been left on the seat next to mine and flip it open to see what's coming next. With each piece, I am inspired. Reinvigorated. I'm caught in their spell, balancing between not wanting to miss a moment of their performance and wishing I was out there dancing it myself. Whenever I have a hard day at rehearsals, watching my favorite pieces online always rekindles the joy that the day-to-day can snuff out if you let it. Watching in person... It's a whole other level.

Mom would have loved this. I savor each performance, enjoy every moment, for her. For us.

The San Francisco ballet is up next with the Bluebird pas de deux from *Sleeping Beauty*. I've actually danced this variation before, and my heels tap out the steps of their own accord. I'm so glad no one else is here to see me embarrass myself, though I know Lark would do the same.

The curtains on either side of me jostle, an icy wind blowing in seemingly from nowhere. My chest and arms pebble and my body goes still.

Then I listen.

Ignoring the instrumental and the gentle patter of pointe shoes hitting the Marley floor, I try to see if he's here. Scared to get my hopes up.

Tiny white snowflakes trickle from above, pirouetting around each other on the breeze. Dancing just for me.

"Jax?" I whisper under my breath, eyes darting around the empty box. "Is that you? How..."

Not that I didn't already know the answer.

"We went over this before." Jax's comforting baritone strums through my core, voice drifting into my mind. *"I'm as real as the whisper of the wind, the cold settled in your bones, the flakes that fall outside...or inside, if I'm feeling especially inspired."*

The snowflakes encircle me along with the breeze. It's him. God, he's beautiful, even when he's more like sculpted ice than man. I want to snatch this moment before it flits away. The last time I saw Jax felt like barely a reality, his presence melting just as quickly as he'd solidified before me in that icy studio.

"I've missed you." The words escape me as naturally as an exhale.

"If you've missed me so much, then why aren't you letting yourself truly believe I'm here?"

After spending weeks together, curled up and talking night after night, he'd disappeared from my life, only showing up one brief time. I know he was in hibernation and couldn't get to me, but I can't help but fear another ephemeral visit. I'm scared to believe, scared to want this so badly only to have it taken away again.

What if one of these days he doesn't come back?

"I never stopped trying to get to you."

"I know," I say, a bit breathless. "It's not that I don't believe you're real or that I don't wish to see you. That couldn't be the furthest thing from what I want."

The sequins of my dress rustle, the fabric between my breasts lowering enough to feel the faint weight of Jax pressing a palm over the silvery streaks. My mate mark.

"How much time do we have?" My voice is a rasp. I'm almost too afraid to ask, but I need to mentally prepare myself.

Before I even realize it, frosty breath blows the tear streaking my cheek, freezing it in place. Barely visible fingers brush it away, the tiny flecks disappearing. *"I have to be back in the mountains by first light."*

"We'll be going to Hotham in a few days," I say as casually as I can, not wanting to sound overeager. "Will I get to see you?"

"Yes, you will. I'll work hard to make sure we have plenty of time to do everything we wish." My toes curl in my heels. *"Just call on me. It'll be easier once you're there. I had to sneak a little farther than I'm technically supposed to so I could see you tonight."*

"Were you here yesterday by any chance?"

"Of course I was." He gestures to the corner at the back of the audience. The exact spot I thought I'd seen him. *"You think I would have missed seeing you in your element, Tempest?"*

He cradles my jaw, pale-blue face finally taking form. His eyes sparkle under the dim light. "I came when I felt your joy. The moment you began to move under those lights. I've been trying to get ahead of my duties so I could return for a longer visit tonight."

"I'm so glad you were here. I thought you were, but I wasn't sure if I was just imagining it."

"Not your imagination, Tempest." His nose nuzzles mine, our eyes locked. "It was me."

He closes the distance and chills my lips with his refreshing kiss. It's tender, slow, and I just want to slip away with him.

The thundering applause ramps up my heartbeat, pulling my attention back to my surroundings. Lifting up from my seat, I peer over the theater box's golden banister at the hundreds of audience members standing up and cheering for the pair of ballet dancers bowing on stage. I flip through the program resting in my lap, drawing down the sheet with my finger, and spot the Royal Ballet's *Don Quixote* grand pas. Next up...

The emcee's announcement is muffled by the dying applause, but I don't need to hear it to know. Blake and his annoyingly charming smile take the stage alongside Beth, one of the other principals from the Institute. Lark mentioned that Nina's transferring to the American Ballet Theatre, and while Blake hasn't received an offer yet—from them or any of the other New York City ballet companies— they're hoping to move there together. We're both hoping she'll realize she's better off without him and leave him in the dust.

The air goes taut next to me, Jax noticing for himself who's taken the stage as the instrumental fills the space.

"Before you ask, I'm not here to see him." I turn away from the performance and thread my fingers through his hair. "Though I wouldn't mind witnessing him stumble."

"Just say the word."

"He's not worth it." I chuckle, shaking my head and then give him another kiss. "Besides, I don't want to waste getting to see you. Not when our time is always limited."

"What *do* you want, then, Tempest?"

The lights dim, and Jax's eyes twinkle like brilliant stars pinned against the darkness. Spring may bloom, summer may blaze, autumn may fall like the leaves, but my feelings for Jax don't shift with the seasons. They're steady through it all, eternal whether he's here or not. If winter never returned, I'd still be here, heart pounding wildly, waiting. Always.

Just as he'll always return to me.

If I have to steal a thousand tiny moments together, I will. I'll hoard them away, filling my journal with everything I recall, etching our story into its pages.

I'll stuff it full of new memories. New questions and possibilities. New wins.

"I want everything... You."

He smiles, and I lean forward, kissing him eagerly. Whatever being his mate entails, every aching part of me wants it. It's a gravity I'm desperate to fall into.

His icy touch grazes where my leg peeks from my slit, and I jerk.

"Sorry," he rasps, removing his hand.

I catch his wrist, guiding him back. "Don't stop. Please."

Whatever he's offering, I want it and I want it now.

He skims the slit of my skirt, sending shivers below my belly. I thumb over the feathery embossing along his wrist, wondering how each line would feel scraping against my skin. Wishing we were alone.

Splaying an icy hand at the top of my thigh, he waits a moment as my body relaxes, adjusting to his chill, tracing across my nose with his own. My breath hitches, coating the darkness in a mist of white, and I uncross my legs, allowing his fingers to dip between them.

He arches a brow at me. "Nothing but you beneath this, Tempest?"

"Doesn't work with the dress," I rasp.

The delicate crescendo of the music builds, and while the audience is turned toward the stage, I can't help but feel wildly rebellious with Jax's hand up my dress. Dipping, swirling, coating his fingertips. Twirling them around my clit. It's almost too much to handle. I shove my fist into my mouth to stifle my moan.

Jax's elongated canines glint with his smile before their sharp tips drag down my throat, nipping at its base. My breathy pants paint the air in thin smoke as I dig crescents into the chair's arm cushions.

"Tell me to stop or spread that skirt and let me devour what's *mine*," he growls.

My eyes dart frantically, the tiny, logical part of me screaming how crazy this is. We're in a full theater. I'm a ballerina. The picture of poise. Decorum.

But even as those reminders echo like a chorus in my mind, my hands grip my skirt, slowly inching it up.

He slides down in one smooth motion until he's kneeling before me, his prismatic gaze captivating my attention from the floor. It's brutally carnal and full of gentle reverence. Behind him, a swan bourrées delicately across the stage as the music starts to intensify.

Jax's hands trail over the pale-pink scar on the outside of my knee, one that has nearly faded completely. Pressing a long kiss there, he continues to pepper them up my hip and then across, toward my center. Each kiss is a promise of pleasure, vibrating through my whole body.

"Wider, Tempest." His words are wind, brushing up the inside of my thighs. Instead of snapping them shut to the cold, I let them fall open, spread before him. Bared. Obedient.

"So perfect for your mate."

I lean back, my shoulders digging into the cushions of the lush box seat. My eyes dart toward the few other boxes, but everyone seems to be enraptured by the ballet in front of them. Like I *should* be.

But then Jax's tongue laps at the apex of my inner thighs. There's only him and the sound of Tchaikovsky reverberating through me, making me bolder than the black swan moving silkily across the stage.

I bite my lip, copper bursting on my tongue. He swipes it with a finger, the chill of it soothing my mouth, then he brings the crimson drop past his lips and sucks it down with a groan. The silvery shards of his gaze almost vanish completely, swallowed up by his pupils.

His fingers disappear again, two of them pushing into me. My pelvis shifts and my sequins snag the fabric of the seat. Not that I care.

"That was a bad idea."

"Why?" I breathe, legs shaking.

"Because, Tempest, now that I've had a taste, all I want to do is bury myself deep inside you. Claim you in every way."

Whatever that entails, I'm in.

I jolt at the next flick of his frosty tongue parting me further. The cold is unusual but not unwelcome and each stroke against my center eases me into its embrace. My head snaps down to look at those holographic eyes radiating a rainbow of colors from between my thighs. His tongue spears into me, twisting and devouring, before he replaces it with his fingers. The music crescendos with my quivering body until I'm fisting the seat's arms, holding my upper body in place while my lower half, the part hidden from view, writhes against Jax.

Every limb pulls taut with a tension that threatens to leap out from me with nowhere to land. With a final curl of his fingers, I break apart, pulsing around him until he draws them out from me. For a moment, I mourn the emptiness, until his nose grazes my clit, tongue pushed inside me so far I wonder if that part of him is somehow magical too, deep and swirling within my body. It's as if he has to taste every ounce of my pleasure. Anything less would be wasteful.

My body becomes sensitive to each nudge of his nose. I grip his hair to ease him away, his lips glistening with my release.

"Are you okay?" His brows furrow, like he's worried he's done something wrong.

"More than," I sigh. "Just a bit...sensitive."

"Sensitive how?"

"I've just never..." I lower my whisper as much as I can, grateful for the applause camouflaging my embarrassment. "Finished. With someone else, that is. Solstice with you was the first time."

"I'll be the first and only." He smirks.

I almost huff out a laugh. From anyone else, I would have. Not with Jax, though. His expression is earnest. No cockiness flitting across his features. "And I plan to have you coming until the curtain closes. Unless you don't want—"

"I want it," I say hastily, biting my lip and debating if I should say more. His brows lift, a twinkle of mischief dancing in his eyes. His hands come up higher on my thighs, the slit of my skirt exposing me obscenely to the room.

"Yes," I rasp when his fingertips swirl inside me, coaxing me to give into the pleasure cresting again.

He kisses me deeply, a mix of ice, magic, and my release lapping against my tongue. Lowering onto his heels, he nips at my inner thigh. "Let me savor you."

I nod and stroke his sharp cheek with my fingers before looping them into his wild silver-and-blue hair, guiding him toward my desperate body. The crinkle of my dress and the strum of a harp are the only sounds I hear when the next dancers come begin their performance.

"They'll entertain you while I get the best show in the house." I blink twice, realizing that was echoed into my mind while his face is still pressed between my legs, licking and sucking. Sweat beads along my forehead and I try to catch my breath. I'm soaked, certain there'll be a huge wet spot on my dress when I stand.

Not that I care.

In fact, I'm certain I'll savor the stain, thrilled with any sign he could leave me with until I can be with him again.

I hold on to his scalp and ride his face, biting my own arm to stop from crying out when the second, third, fourth, and fifth orgasms quake through me.

He had promised I'd be coming on his tongue at curtain close. Not only is Jax very much real, but when he makes a promise, he follows through.

One of the many things I love about him.

Sometime after I've given up counting orgasms, the lights come up in the theater. I stand up and quickly adjust my dress. Jax flashes me a wolfish grin, guiding me out of the theater with one hand on my back. No one else can see him, but the brush of his fingers against the valley of my spine is all the support I need.

"Is there a spot?" I mutter under my breath, waving a hand at a few dancers I recognize. My legs are a bit wobbly from the orgasmic waves crashing through me for the last forty-five minutes.

"Do you want the real answer or for me to reassure you?" His tone is playful, and I elbow him.

As we stride among the crowd, I hesitate when people move close, not realizing Jax is there. They walk straight through him, a few tiny flecks peppering their formalwear, but they don't seem to notice.

"I'm used to it." He shrugs. "You see me and that's all that matters."

I keep him within my peripheral the entire time to ensure he's still there.

"Jolie."

I suck in a breath, turning my head to find Blake standing there, staring at me, his hands in his pockets. He looks eerily relaxed, but his tone doesn't carry its usual flavor of arrogance.

"Hey."

He goes to open his mouth, but I lift a hand. "You don't need to say anything, Blake."

"But—"

"No." I keep my tone calm, not wanting to draw any attention from the crowds of dancers, instructors, family, and friends piled into the lobby. "If you're about to say you're sorry, I know it's bullshit. You aren't sorry. If you're sorry about anything, it's just that you got caught and that your precious ego got bruised. So don't give me a half-assed apology or an excuse. You'll just be wasting both of our time."

Blake's lips zip shut, and I shake out my shoulders, continuing on my trek.

"Wow." Jax chuckles next to me. "You were magnificent."

"I gave him more words than he deserves," I whisper. We exit the theater, walking toward my hotel and I slip my hand into his. "Now, come with me. We still have a handful of hours until you have to go."

He lifts a brow. "Sounds like you have something in mind."

"I do." My dress is still damp in the back, and with each step closer, wetness slides between my thighs. The breeze lashes at my lady bits, and I check to make sure it doesn't kick up my skirt and flash everyone. "First, I'm going to get out of this."

"You'll hear no argument from me, though it's beautiful on you." His eyes shimmer as they scan over me, and he runs a finger along the cap sleeve of my gown. We cross the lobby toward the elevators that are surrounded by a mix of dancers still in layers of thick stage makeup and folks dressed to the nines from watching the performance.

"They missed the best show tonight, Tempest," Jax whispers. "One that I got to enjoy up close and very personally."

The memory sends goosebumps skating across my skin and my body shivers with an anticipation I don't have the patience for.

"You haven't even seen the finale yet."

Chapter Thirty-Four

JOLIE

I pivot right toward the stairwell, Jax following behind me. Luckily, I'm only on the third floor. Once we get to my door, I unsnap the magnetized clasp on my clutch, fumbling around my phone and wallet for my room key. I hold it up to the door.

Click.

My pulse skyrockets when it unlocks.

I spin to face Jax. The door shuts behind him with another *click* and groan of the mechanism. His eyes never leave mine. Not when I toss my clutch onto the desk, not when I balance walking backward on my heels, not when I grab the tiny zipper under my armpit and tug it down past my hip. "You said back at the studio that you're not a mere mortal man."

"I did." His voice is pure gravel, scraping at my composure.

I let the top half of the dress fall around my waist. "Show me, Jax."

I shimmy the heavy sequined material the rest of the way off until it's a glittering pool on the ground and step out of it in just my nude heels.

Under the beautiful, otherworldly etchings along his flesh, the wolf within watches me like a predator. But I'm not afraid. I'm prey, already devoured many times over tonight, and now I prowl toward him with my chest and head held high.

His huntress.

My heart rate slows with each stride. I channel my inner Carmen, trailing my fingers between my breasts, palm grazing a peaked nipple, the other brushing over my mate mark. Jax's jaw ticks before there's a not-so-subtle flick within his pants. My attention is pinned to the spot, eager to explore every inch of him as much as he's explored me.

"I can't fuck you tonight, Tempest," he growls out in warning when my fingers skim his trousers. "Not the way we both want and deserve."

"That's fine," I agree from under my lashes, blindly undoing the buttons with nimble precision honed through hundreds of quick costume changes. "You got to have a taste. Don't I deserve the same?"

My heel wobbles as I shift my weight, and I brace my core, kneeling down one leg at a time. Jax says nothing, frozen in place with his holographic stare beaming down at me. It sends a heady rush through me, like he's under my spell. Like *I'm* the magical one in this room.

"*Fuck*, Tempest," he says the moment my palm wraps around his shaft. He's huge, so thick my fingers are nowhere near able to meet, and I'm a little grateful I'm not trying to fit him inside me just yet. I pull his pants down the rest of the way, but instead of gathering at his feet, they disappear. My throat dries when I come face to face with his pierced cock that sits heavy in my hand.

He's got the Mount Everest of dicks. I want to scale its entirety, but it's going to take some work to get there. Just the idea of the trek has me growing wet. I zip my thighs together, as if it could stop him from sensing my want.

Giving him a few exploratory strokes, I savor the blend between the rough texture of his frost marks and satiny skin. His snowflake-stamped ball glints at me from atop his slit. I rub my thumb over the piercing, sending a pearlescent bead of cum skating down his tip. Leaning forward, I lap it up eagerly, a bit surprised when it tastes like decadent mint-chocolate chip. My gaze travels up the trail of silvery-blue hair, past his navel and mate mark, and I twirl the ball with my tongue before licking each sweet morsel that slips from his purpling crown. Jax tosses his head back, gripping his hair that I'd clutched only an hour ago, and groans, his hips bucking in response.

"Go easy on me or you'll be coated in frost before I get to really enjoy this," he rasps with a breathy chuckle.

That only encourages me.

Each movement becomes firmer, my fist tightening at the base of his shaft as much as I can manage. I wrap my lips around the head, tongue alternating between playing with his piercing and licking up every ounce of his desire. I bob up and down, using my hand to bridge the gap between my lips and his pelvis. Jax's eyes flutter and his hands come to my head, threading his fingers into my strands, moving with me.

No matter how hard I try to close the gap, he seems to somehow grow another inch, but that's not all. A large bulge encases the base of his shaft. I swear it wasn't there before, but now it's ballooned out, the heel of my palm running into it with each stroke of my hand. I blink a few times to make sure I'm not crazy before popping him out of my mouth, a trail of saliva and minty precum streaking down my chin. "What's *that*?"

"It's my knot." He says it like it's a fact, then snaps his mouth shut, brows crashing into each other. "It's not fully expanded, but completely normal for my kind."

My eyes widen.

Not. Fully. Expanded.

He clears his throat and then takes a step back, lashes dropping. "It's easy to forget you wouldn't know about this. I realize now it's probably scary to you. I'm sorry."

"I don't know about scary..." *Lies.* I'm terrified. My gaze trails back up to his face, the ball of his throat working as he appraises me. My chest aches at the sadness lacing his silver-and-blue eyes. I don't want him to be embarrassed, but I'm also trying to wrap my mind around this new discovery. Everest just got a whole lot steeper. But I want to do this, do it all, with *him.*

There are so many things standing in the way of us being together. A little—or not so little—*knot* isn't going to stop me. I straighten my shoulders and pull them back, giving Jax full eye contact. "How does it work?"

"Curious, are we?" His confident lilt reappears, and I nearly sigh aloud, grateful it has. I don't want anything to ruin the time we have together. "It'll probably be easier if I demonstrate."

He holds his hands out, and ice billows up from his palms, carving into itself until he's sculpted a near exact replica of the hard-on spearing out from his muscular body.

I swallow.

"Did you just make me an ice dildo?" I ask, eyes following its floating path down past my belly button.

"Sure did, Tempest. Want to prove you can take your mate's cock?"

I nod, at a loss for words, my eyes not leaving the perfect

model of Jax's thick body, minus the ridges I'm so desperate to feel inside me.

"Open your mouth and spread your legs," Jax growls out the command, and my knees scrape against the carpet when I widen my stance. He steps closer, and my lips wrap around his tip, tongue swirling eagerly over his piercing, making him hiss. The icy crown of his frost cock notches itself at my center. "Show me how good you'll take me."

Bobbing up and down his shaft, I use my hands to spread my saliva over its chillingly sensual length. I jolt when his icy replica enters me, and his jaw tenses, as if he can feel his magic pulsing inch by inch, driving deeper with each stroke.

I pop my mouth off of him, adjusting to the power that's currently plunging in and out of me, then I trace each line of his frost marks with my tongue. From root to purpling tip, I suck him into my mouth, bringing my hand around him, moving my body with the rhythm of his magic.

"Fuck, Tempest." His palm slides to my throat, thumb skimming over my pulse. "Think you can take me deeper?"

I'm not sure whether he means my mouth or my body. Splitting my attention, I grab his ass with my free hand. It's as cool as marble, and tug him closer until he hits the back of my throat and I sputter.

"That's it." His icy counterpart drives into me and I suck in a breath at the fullness of it. He cups my cheek, gently brushing it with so much reverence, you'd think he was the one on his knees before me. His words come out between gritted teeth, a harsh but devoted whisper. "Such a perfect mate. I can't wait to fill you with my knot. Mark and claim you from the inside."

Jax's knot teases at my entrance before inching and stretching me further. This time it stays there. His jaw is taut, veins bulging along his neck, as if he's holding on to every tether to watch everything I'm doing. To make it last.

To savor me as much as I'm savoring him.

"You're much too good at this. Maybe I should make another one of these so that tight little ass is good and ready for me too."

I clench around the ice, and it actually feels good. The frost soothes the throb inside, and I wriggle, wanting him to move it again, to keep driving it into me. "You'd like that, wouldn't you, Tempest?"

I suck on him vigorously, drawing out more mint-chocolate flavored precum as my hand makes long firm strokes. His breaths become pants, and I know he's close. It only encourages me to take him deeper, riding the frosted shaft beneath me, pulling him further into my mouth until he growls out his release, coating the back of my throat.

"*Damn.* Such a perfect needy mate," he says, brushing my hair as I swallow down the decadent mint-chocolate-milkshake taste of him. "Didn't waste a drop."

This isn't something I'm usually into. Giving head has always been more of a prelude to sex or saved for a special occasion like a birthday. With Jax, though, I've never been happier to get on my knees and learn everything about his pleasure.

Someone get me a cup and a thick freaking straw. Jax Frost is my favorite treat.

"Tempest, that was incredible," he says, drawing my attention. I lick the rest of his ecstasy from my lips with a pleased moan. He eases back, his expression odd, almost sheepish. If he could, I bet he'd be blushing.

"What's wrong?" I tilt my head to the side, spotting the still huge bulge staring back at me from the base of his shaft. *Fully expanded.* My lower body pulses around his ice. I've been so focused on the dick attached to Jax that I'm only just able to sense the one stilled inside me.

He's ramrod straight, cum leaking from his tip. I bite my lip, unable to look away.

"Tempest..." He warns, voice a low growl. "If you keep watching me like that I'm going to come again."

"Again?" My voice shakes with equal parts hunger and nerves.

Trousers appear on the floor, and he clears his throat, waving his hand. His icy twin slides out from me, but before he can remove it all the way, I wrap my hand around his shaft, my other fist squeezing his fully formed knot.

"Holy shit," Jax hisses, hips jerking forward. His ice plunges back inside me. "What are you do—" He can barely get out the words. I pulse my hand around his knot, mimicking my body's thrum around the icy one.

Taking him back in my mouth, I wonder if I'm doing this right. A mortal can hope. From the blissed-out expression on Jax's face and the glint in his eyes as he fights throwing his head back, I'd say that I am.

Look at me, being a good little mate and shit.

He chuckles breathlessly, crooking my face up to look at him. "Are you trying to kill me, Tempest?"

I slide down his shaft, replacing my mouth with my hand.

"I thought you were immortal," I tease, then flick his tip with my tongue.

His brows scrunch together, hips bucking with my silky strokes. "Let's see you give that snark when my cock's buried inside you, pumping you full of me for days."

Yes, let's.

I groan and clench around the ice, gliding up and down the shaft while it moves on its own again, giving me the friction my body begs for. A feverish need pulses through me. A desire to claim every inch of him until there's nothing between us. Nothing but him in me, on me, filling and fulfilling me.

Just the idea sends me over the edge. I'm falling for what feels like the millionth time tonight, my body weak from the repeated bursts of pleasure.

Thick streaks of glistening cum jet across my throat, collarbones, chest, and belly, cool against my skin. The knot starts to disappear as I swipe the last bit from his tip. It sparkles next to my silvery mark in the dim light. I once thought it was a scar of my tragedy, so much from that day was, but this part of me, it connects me to him.

My mate.

Jax gets down on his knees in front of me. "So. Fucking. Beautiful."

His eyes twinkle and his voice is raw—a shard of something so precious and irreplaceable it steals the breath from my lungs. He summons a washcloth and cleans every inch of me, taking his time and scattering kisses along my skin. The ice within me melts away on a drift of snowflakes, its chill felt even more now that I'm empty.

"Sure I can't convince you to stick around?" I ask, feeling guilty for even saying the words because I know if he could stay, he would. He doesn't want to have to leave me again. It's another crappy rotation on this never-ending cycle of seasons where Fate keeps us just out of reach from one another, occasionally letting our paths collide in the most beautiful harmony.

"I'm certain you can, Tempest."

It's oddly reassuring to know that I'm in this with him. Despite the pain of distance, we are etched into each other as much as the frost along his flesh.

He pulls a shirt out from thin air, guiding my hands above my head and slipping it over me. It hangs above my knees and smells just like him. I've already decided every moment I'm not out and about, I'll be cocooned in this. Wrapped up and enveloped in his perfect wintry scent. I lift the hem and inhale the rich, indulgent pine with the tiniest hint of juniper.

"I don't want to leave, but I need to get things in order so I can go undetected and give my mate the attention she deserves."

"I can't wait."

"Me neither." He scoops me up and carries me to the bed, tucking me under the covers and then settling in beside me. His body is cold against mine, a chilling reassurance that he's here as I lay my head on the pillow and fall blissfully asleep.

Chapter Thirty-Five

JOLIE

Sightseeing has been a blast, but when our long weekend arrives, I'm more than ready to get to the ski resort and relax. Thank goodness we decided to splurge and fly the hour instead of driving and worrying about tire chains. Too much of a hassle.

Lark and I packed pretty light, considering. Delilah, on the other hand, has all her cold weather and ski gear ready to go. When she looks like she might tip over, one of the lodge workers hurries over to take her skis and snowboard off her hands.

"Look at those hills! I can't freaking wait," Delilah says, rubbing her newly free hands together, cheeks pinked from the cold.

"Happy for you, honey. Enjoy those slopes." Lark gets up on her tiptoes and gives her a swift peck on the lips. "Happier for us, though."

She shoots me a grin, then pulls her beanie off, unleashing her frizzy curls. Combing through her locks, she tames it a bit, and I help her get the last few wayward pieces.

"Same," I agree, glad that Lark and I already decided to opt for a relaxing experience. I've booked us massages, facials, and pedicures, figuring we can indulge while her girlfriend skis. Between traveling, performing in the festival, and running around to fit in as many tourist spots as possible, my body is aching and exhausted. Besides, I've heard enough skiing horror stories to not want to do anything to jeopardize my career. Not when I'm potentially returning to Ballet Potomac as a soloist. The last thing I need is to get some new injury.

Nope. Massages, yoga, and hot cocoa are calling my name. Plus, we've booked an excursion for tomorrow night that I'm more than excited about, staying in ice domes near the resort. There's a hot tub Lark and I already booked for ourselves, and the overnight trip is more glamping than being out in the wintry wilderness. There's a fondue and wine experience around a bonfire and then private ice-encased domes with lush bedding to sleep on. When I first suggested it, Lark and Delilah thought it was strange that I wanted to book my own space... And maybe it was, but it was also a bit of wishful thinking on my part.

Jax did confirm he is doing his job here, though, and ever since the night at the theater and my hotel room, I haven't been able to stop thinking about him or his naughty promises. I'm addicted to him and this connection we share, already anticipating my next fix. The uniqueness of his body sends butterflies bursting through my belly. I'm both nervous and counting down all at once. I can't imagine how it will be to take his knot.

Despite my jitters, I want it all.

I want him.

"Look at that view," Lark says, gaze trained behind me. Delilah whistles in agreement.

I turn, instantly struck by the hills covered in mounds of snowy white. The mountains ripple, large and small peaks jutting up in the distance. Dark trees pepper the landscape, pops of color from Hotham's visitors decked out in their cold-weather garb, tiny puffs of white filling the space around them while they chat and enjoy the resort's outdoor amenities. "Wow. It's beautiful."

"It really is." Lark nudges me with her elbow. "How about we get our stuff to our rooms and then go get that spa time in? I'm sure Delilah is ready to channel her inner ski bunny."

"Sounds great!"

We walk through the lobby, thick stonework donning the walls surrounding an elegant and modern white stone fireplace that spans the length of the room. An oversized plush couch sits at the center of the main room where a few people are gathered, sipping at the mugs clutched in their hands.

I look down at my key card, following the signs until I've made it to my room. Dropping my bags next to the bed, I go straight for the balcony, unlatching the door and heading out onto it. I stare out at the view, hands gripping the ice-coated railing. The Frosts have turned this into a wintry haven, and I can't help but wonder how much of this is Jax's work.

If he hadn't intervened after my accident...would I be out there with him right now, painting the world white with a wave of my arm?

"Where are you, Jax?" I whisper to the wind. The scent of juniper and pine kisses my nose, and I breathe in deeply. I follow it to the right, and my heart begins to pound so fiercely I can feel my pulse through my fingertips pressed against the icy balustrade.

He's there in the distance, zipping along treetops with a hauntingly powerful grace that no human could ever capture. His body sweeps with the wind. He's the breeze itself, swirling around trees, decorating their branches. More movement catches my eyes, and I grip the railing tighter.

Not only can I see Jax, I can see more of them.

Frosts.

His fellow immortals flit on the breeze, between the trees, along every structure both natural and manmade, creating a wintry masterpiece right before my eyes. I lift a finger, pointing to each one as I count. They work so quickly, it takes me a minute to decide if there are four or five of them.

Four.

It's not far off from watching a ballet. From where I stand, witnessing them all move in and out of each other, they make up their very own ensemble. A small chilling corps. If any of them notice me staring, they don't seem to care.

Each one tends to a different spot, decorating with their own delicate flair.

One Frost glides closer, platinum hair whipping behind her as she pulls long icicles from the rooftop of the lodge. When her periwinkle eyes meet mine, she freezes in place.

"Hello," I say, wondering if there's an etiquette to approaching a should-be-invisible immortal when you're mortal.

"It's you," she says, focus floating back toward the other harbingers. "Jax's mate."

"Yes." I can't stop staring at the twinkle in her eyes. They are so different from Jax's but otherworldly in their own way. I wonder if every Frost looks so unique. Obviously, the transformation is stark. What did she look like in her mortal life? What would I look like if I had an immortal one?

"I'm Aneira." She gives me a gentle smile, tucking a lilac-streaked strand of hair behind her ear. "But you can call me Ani. Your mate does."

The way she speaks of mates both excites me and makes my nerves ratchet. Jax and I are mates. To Aneira, and potentially the rest of the Frosts, we are a forgone conclusion. A permanent partnership. There's no question of what I am to him in her glittering eyes.

I wish I felt that certainty when it came to a future for us.

"Do you want me to call him over?" Her attention darts to where the mate mark is hidden beneath my layers. "Do you want to?"

"That's okay. I have to be somewhere. But if you can give him a message for me, that would be amazing."

Knock, knock, knock.

"I better go," I whisper.

"Quick! What's the message?"

"Tell him I'm here." I smirk.

"Of course. That is, if he hasn't already figured it out." Aneira grins back and pulls down a few more icicles over my head at differing lengths. The closer she gets to me, the chillier the air is. "It was wonderful to meet you, Jolie."

"Likewise, Ani."

She waves goodbye, flitting away before she drops down into her chestnut-brown wolf form and sprints between the trees toward the larger silver-and-white one in the distance.

Jax's eyes sparkle, and the wind whispers in his comforting lilt. *"Looks like you were the one to find me this time, Tempest."*

Chapter Thirty-Six

JOLIE

After dinner, my body still tingles from three hours at the spa and having every knotted muscle rubbed before being pampered with facials and pedicures. I feel incredible, relaxed, refreshed.

Every step toward my room is far too slow. I pass the glass windows and their clear view of the stars and spot the faint outlines of Frosts moving outside. Blurs of graceful motion building their masterpieces, draping ice across awnings and spinning snow from the sky. I don't stop, though. None of them are Jax. While there's no logical explanation for the certainty, I can sense he's already waiting for me in my room.

As I lift the key to the door, Jax's growl from our last night together replays in my mind.

"I can't fuck you tonight, Tempest. Not the way we both want and deserve."

I pull the key back, clutching it in my palm. My gaze drops to my booties, and I adjust the sweetheart neckline of my navy-blue maxi dress, admiring how the swirled tip of my mate mark shimmers between my breasts.

While I used to opt for higher necklines, I've started

gravitating toward ones that dip lower, not minding it being seen. To everyone else, it's a silvery scar. To me, it's a permanent reminder of Jax. That he's real even when the seasons separate us.

And now he's just on the other side of this door, waiting for me. His chill and the gentle scent of spiced pine glide out into the hallway from under the door.

I shiver. I shouldn't be so nervous. Jax has seen me naked. Has witnessed how my body falls apart from his touch. His tongue. His magic. He watched me for weeks before I knew of his existence.

But tonight's different.

There's no race against the clock. There's only us.

My knees wobble, but I summon enough courage to finally bring the key to the door. It doesn't work the first time, so I swipe the key and try again.

Click.

I barely twist the knob and the door groans all the way open. The room has been transformed, glowing with buttery light where Jax stands before the stone fireplace. He's there in his fully solid harbinger form, just a pair of fitted trousers with his hands in his pockets. I actually think he's nervous too.

"Do you like it?"

"It's beautiful," I rasp out, taking in the cozy space.

White flower petals pepper the floor and bed. Quilts and blankets have been strewn throughout the room, and behind the thin curtains hanging in front of the balcony are strings of twinkling fairy lights crisscrossing over each other. "How did you—"

"I may have borrowed them from the florist shop," Jax replies. I can almost make out the tinge of a blush on his sharp, pale-blue cheek bones. "I've missed you."

"I've missed you, too."

The golden halo of lights hovering over Jax mutes his icy tones, and for a second, I can easily see the little boy in the grainy photos. The one taken tragically from this world.

I want to tell Jax that I've found his brother. Maybe he already knows Winston's alive. Maybe he's even seen him. But I know there will never be a normal time to bring up the subject, so I take a deep breath and begin.

"I know you remember bits and pieces of your mortal life, but did you ever search for your family after..." *...You died.* Somehow saying the words is like shoving an icicle into my own heart. "Do you remember what happened when you became a Frost?"

His brows lift a bit, then he crinkles his lips together to the side. "When you become a harbinger at a young age, it takes years of training. Not only to learn your Frost skills, but to also grow up and learn about the outside world." The ball of his Adam's apple bobs, and his voice cracks a bit. "Once I was done with my training, my first time back in the mortal world, I tried to find them. That's when I learned that you can only visit the areas you've been assigned. The leaders in Nivea purposefully don't let you go where your life was right away."

I think back to what Jax has told me about the Lead Albidus role in our past conversations. He's been working toward becoming one of these very leaders. "Why?"

"Look at what happened when I found you last winter." He kneels on the fur rug, and I match his stance, our hands coming together. His thumb skims the pulse point of my wrist, and I shiver, not daring to take my eyes off him. "Interfering with mortals is dangerous. It can alter destinies. Even with my memories removed, I still found you. Still interfered." The firelight tosses orange flares across his skin as his chest heaves. "They don't remove our memories after we die. It would be too cruel to wipe away the good things we experienced in life. The ones we loved. So they keep harbingers away for the first handful of winters. Once they know you'll follow the rules, that the mortal memories have loosened their grip, they aren't as strict.

"I found my family. Let myself get distracted by being around them for years. Then eventually, I stopped going. I think it likely happens to most harbingers that way."

The brittle resonance to his voice conveys the real truth: I've hit some fragile boundary Jax held within himself. But if this shatters him, I'll be right here to collect the pieces alongside him, no matter how sharp. No matter how deep they cut. He's read my journal, knows every ugly shard I've tucked away from the rest of the world. But not from him.

Never from him.

"Why?"

"What was the point? They couldn't see me." He tosses his hands in defeat, looking more like the teenage mortal than the otherworldly Frost he's grown into. "Wouldn't ever be able to."

"What about now? We both know there's a way. Your brother is still out there. I could talk to him. I could help him believe…"

"No."

"No?"

"What good would that do? Hurt him more after he's spent most of his life mourning me? I'm not the same person that built snowmen and played ice hockey at the lake with him."

The last words trail off. I stroke his cheek, hating that I've upset him. "You remember what happened, don't you? At the lake?"

"Of course I do." His voice lowers along with his gaze. "You don't forget something like that, Jolie."

"You never told me…"

"I didn't want to burden you with that." When his eyes finally reach mine again, the rims shimmer with the threat of tears.

"Is it because of what happened to me? When you saved me." I recall how painful it was just reading about the boy who took his little brother to play hockey at the lake and saved him only to never return home. Never to enjoy another winter by his family's side. "It must have been for you to find me like that. T-to watch me die."

"It was the worst pain I've ever experienced." A single tear tracks his cheek, and I brush it away with the back of my hand. "I hate that one day, if things work out as I hope, you'll have to go through it in your own way."

My hand stills at his temple. "What do you mean?"

"When harbingers are blessed with their mates, their lives become interconnected. As if they are one soul strung along a line between two bodies. You see everything. Their entire life bared to you."

"You saw my life?" I run my hand through his hair, toying with the silver and blue strands. What had he seen?

"Every beautiful and heartbreaking memory, Tempest," Jax says, crooking my chin. He leans in and kisses me once, slowly. Tenderly. "I knew the moment I did that, no matter how much I wanted you for myself, I couldn't have you. Not yet."

Not yet. "But one day?"

He brings our hands over the left side of his chest. "I hope so, with every beat of your heart that rests within me."

Thump-thump.

Thump-thump.

Thump-thump. Thump-thump.
Thump-thump, thump-thump.

My pulse scatters between us and the fire illuminates the frost marks in their beautiful, swirly patterns covering every visible inch of his arms and the strong panes of his chest. They sink into the divots of his abs and ascend all the way up to cradle his throat. I swallow thickly, remembering those marks against my palm and tongue.

Jax's pupils eclipse his prismatic irises. His nostrils flare and a low rumble works its way up his throat, echoing through me. I half expect the force of it to shake the room, but it's only my body that buckles, weak from it.

From *him.*

He pinches the bridge of his nose. "Sorry. Your scent is hard to resist."

"Then don't." I stand and lift the hem of my dress, pulling the scrap of lacy underwear past my knees and kicking it onto the floor. I want this. Him. I don't care if I don't fully understand all the intricacies of harbingers and their mates.

Mortal, immortal.

Life, death.

Mates, fate.

I understand enough to be certain that he's mine and I'm his in a way that's irreversible and all-consuming.

His chest heaves, fists balled at his sides. For a moment, his expression turns weary, as if weighing my words. Just when I think he's going to bring things to a halt, he prowls toward me.

"Fuck it."

He scoops me up into his arms as he stands. My legs wrap around his waist, dress bunching at my hips, forehead resting against his. I'm swept up in his gaze. In him. My thighs graze the marks along his stomach. I rock my hips eagerly, seeking friction, and with each curl of my pelvis, he grows harder beneath me, near bursting through his tight pants.

I reach between us, fumbling for his zipper. Gripping the small piece of metal, I tug it down, his cock bursting free. It's freaking huge. When my fingers trace the beginnings of his knot, they freeze.

Jax holds still, as if waiting to see what I'll do. Then he speaks, voice low. "It's okay, Tempest. We don't have t—"

A hiss cuts off his words when my fingers wrap around his base.

"Show me what it means to be your mate."

He growls, spurred by my words. In three strides, my back is pinned to the wall. His cock presses against me, drawing soft whimpers from my lips with each pierced graze of my clit.

"That's it, Tempest. Rub that perfect pussy against me. Take your pleasure."

I slam my hand against the wall, using it as leverage to ride along his cock. The angle is delicious, and my toes curl with each scrape of his frost markings on my skin. Desperate for more.

More friction. More pleasure. More *him*.

The pressure below my belly craves things I don't even know if I can express. My hips are frantic, bucking so wildly that I half expect to climb up Jax's tall frame.

The ecstasy is intense, almost too intense. He holds me through it, rocking with me, body following my rhythm and coaxing me on.

I'm losing control. Losing it to the swirl of that tiny silver snowball against my clit, the chill of his satin shaft between my lips, the delicately rough texture of his frost marks stroking my skin. The knot building at his base rubs up and down, spreading me further.

I moan, and my body spasms as it takes and takes its fill, the sound so guttural, so primal with need, that it nearly startles me.

Nearly.

Because then Jax plunges over the edge, and I'm certain there's nothing more beautiful. Hair mussed, lips parted, a low, rumbling growl erupts from him. He comes in hypnotic waves, coating my clit, dripping along the tips of my thighs. Thick and wet and deliciously messy.

Sharp canines graze my pulse, wet sounds building between us as he groans against my throat. I'm teetering on some dangerous line. One that I desperately want to cross. I lengthen my neck, savoring his frosty breaths.

"Tempest," he repeats, over and over, like a gentle prayer spoken on the breeze. His lips press to my pulse, peppering in a few playful nips. He rocks his hips, each glide is slow and intentional, as if he's trying to rub his essence deep into my skin. Then he runs his nose up the length of my neck and cradles my jaw, kissing me as he carries me over to the fur rug in front of the fire, laying me down with a restrained reverence that's almost painful.

His canines graze my throat and ignite something in me. Now that the haze of the mind-blowing orgasm is wearing off, I can't help but wonder why. "Can I ask you something?"

"Anything."

"When I...um...showed you my neck, I had this overwhelming urge for you to..." I trail off, not even knowing what to say, so I fumble for the closest comparison I can think of. "Is this mate thing like vampires?"

Jax barks out a laugh. My body flushes with embarrassment, and he quickly clears his throat, regaining his composure.

I frown. "Glad someone finds this funny."

He nudges my chin with his nose, so I lean my head away, exposing my throat to him.

"Vampires, from what I understand, like to drink each other's blood." As he speaks, he drags a finger up and down my neck, sending a shiver low in my belly. His chest rumbles against my back, and he moves a hand to splay over my hip. "Harbingers have the desire to claim their mates. To leave a mark and solidify the bond between us. It heightens the connection."

Jax reaches between my legs, smoothing his thumb across our release, rubbing it in until it's fully absorbed into my flesh. "One day, when you're ready to claim each other, just say the word and I'll happily sink my teeth into that sexy throat of yours."

He playfully nips me.

"Claim each other?" I crane my neck to look at him, understanding dawning on me. "As in, bite you back? Does it have to be your throat?"

He arches a brow. "Did you have somewhere else in mind?"

"I don't know," I backtrack. "I'm just trying to understand."

"A mate's bite is a full acceptance of the bond between them." I shiver against his cool touch. Savoring it and the scent of mint chocolate chip permeating from us. "We don't have to, Tempest. Not ever. Not if you don't want—"

"It's not that." I clamp my mouth shut, trying to find the words. "But my teeth aren't sharp. Won't that hurt you?"

I hadn't thought about it before, but all Frosts have those elongated canines in their harbinger form. Surely that made a claiming bite easier. Would it hurt me when he did it even though his teeth were sharp?

"Probably." He shrugs and pretends to bite my shoulder over the fabric of my dress. It's plastered to me, damp with sweat. "But it's a pain I'll gladly take."

Fingers drift up my center, hovering above my sternum where I can somehow sense his touch before he even does it. As soon as his skin grazes my silver mark, it echoes *everywhere*. "The bite is meant to be pleasurable. Even moreso than knotting since it's something exclusively shared between mates. Though that won't be the case for us."

"It won't?" I've been so focused on being able to take his knot since I first saw it, I didn't think about him with other people. A twinge of jealousy sinks into my gut, nausea at the idea that he's been with harbingers who are better equipped, better built to be his mate. Instead, he's stuck with me.

"Hey," he grips my chin and gently swivels it toward him until my eyes are reflected back in the cracked, glittering mirrors of his, "you'll be the first and only one to ever take my knot."

"Really?" I sigh, and he chuckles.

"I've always known nothing would ever compare to being with my mate." He dips down and kisses me, his minty breath invigorating me. Our tongues explore each other until he hardens against my back. "Now that I've found you, touched you, tasted you, I know I was right."

My skin flushes. The thought of the other night, when he was *preparing* me to take his knot, replays in my mind. It's like I'm some inexperienced virgin, not a woman that's had multiple men in her bed. But this, this is different. Not just because of Jax's *unusual* equipment, but because it's him. I want to blow his mind. Be everything he hoped for when he prayed for a mate for years.

I rub my legs together, feeling the remnants of our cum still slick at the top of my thighs.

Jax sucks in a breath.

"Tempest..." he warns, reminding me that he can scent how badly I want this.

"I don't want you doing anything you aren't completely certain of. Knotting, claiming—these are things I've understood for decades. Things ingrained into harbinger life. I know how strange it all is to you." His cool breath caresses my shoulder, tousling my hair.

"Are you hesitating because I'm mortal?" I ask. If I can't hide how much I want this, want him, then how come he's still cautious? How come our clothes are still on and we aren't wrapped up in one another?

"Yes." When my face falls, he quickly adds, "But only because I was taught about mates and everything it entails. You and I, there's never been anything like us. You might not experience the bond like I do."

"Tell me what it's like."

His eyes shut a moment, and he takes a steadying breath, as if weighing his words. He rests his head on my shoulder, the sharply crinkled corners of his eyes subtly soften. "My connection to you is a constant thrum. An electricity that never shuts off. You could be anywhere and I'd still feel drawn to you."

His hand drifts to my mate mark, fingers working until there's a *pop* of a button between my breasts. "The need to be with you. It's a want beyond wanting. To protect you from pain, love you, bring you pleasure—it is all-consuming."

Another *pop*.

Then another.

The buttons roll across the furs beneath us, and the fire warms the mark now fully on display. Jax's fingers swirl over my sternum, and desire pools at the top of my thighs. I clench them together, shifting for friction. He continues to play with my mark, and I can't help but wonder how it's connected to his own as his erection thickens against me. "In my world, there is no question once you find your mate. You witness their entire lives, hopes, and dreams in an instant. Fully seen, fully cherished."

"And that's how you feel about me?" I rasp, clinging to every word.

"My words barely do it justice."

He huffs out a laugh. Rolling to face him, I cradle the sharp angles of his cheek.

Staring at him, I can almost imagine what he'd look like if things had gone differently. If he'd lived a full life. If he'd never met Fate. Maybe we would have found each other under different circumstances, though I doubt it. All I know is that I can't imagine a life where he's not part of it. Not anymore. "Ever since you came into my life, before I even understood why, I saw you in my dreams and in my waking hours. At first, I thought I was crazy. I couldn't understand everything that was happening. But I do feel this tether between us. It's as real to me as you are. I may just be mortal —"

"You aren't *just* anything, Tempest," Jax says, platinum brows drawing together, tone deadly serious. "You are *everything*."

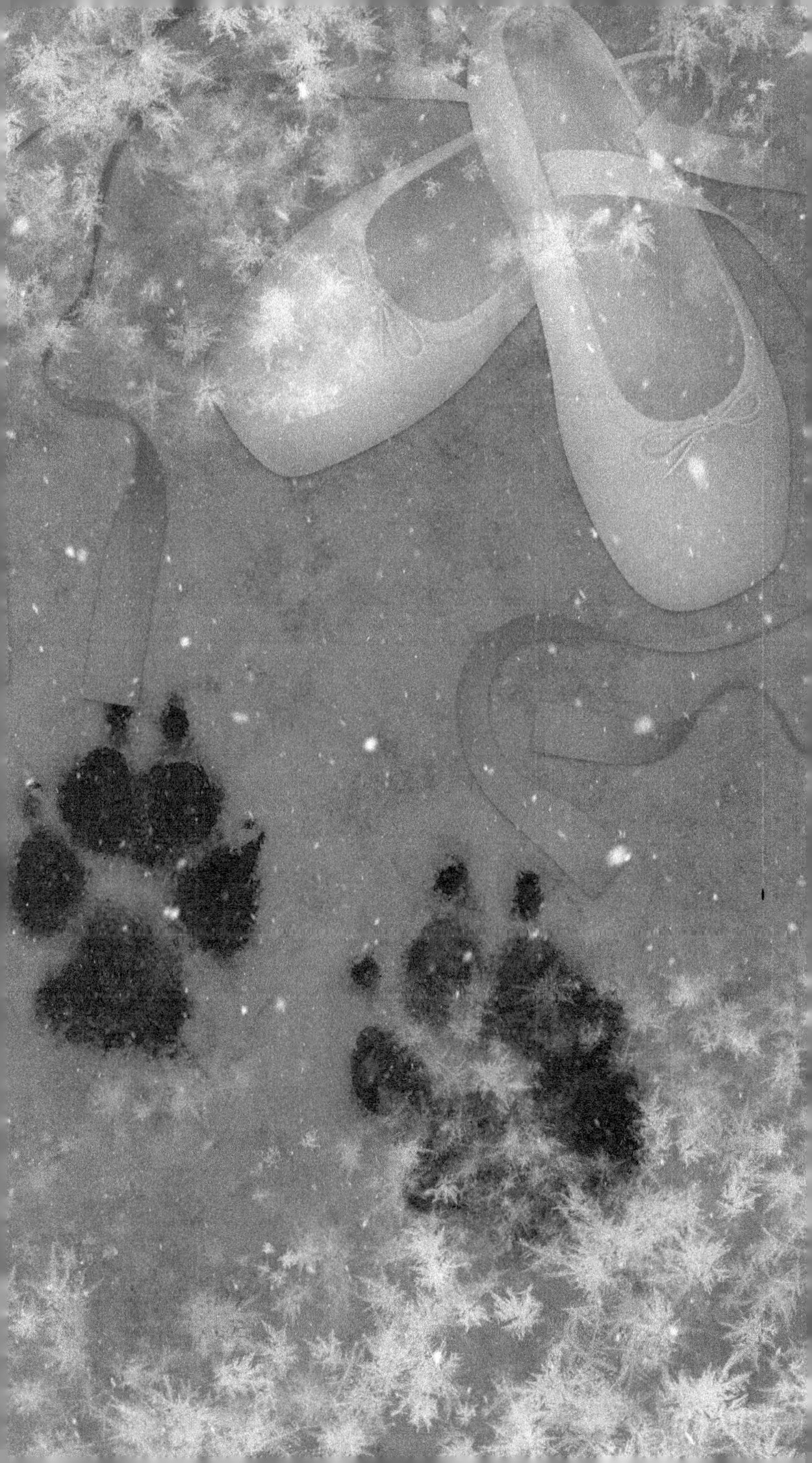

Chapter Thirty-Seven

JOLIE

*Y*ou *are* everything.

I close the distance and kiss him. With each brush of our lips, my confidence grows until every part of me that fears the unknown drifts away. Taking his hand in my own, I bring it back to my buttons and guide him so every achingly beautiful part of him looms over me. His pants are still unzipped, the tip of him poking out above the waistband of his briefs, a pearlescent line of cum leading away from the ball of his piercing. I thumb over it, rubbing his release over his tip. His groan is music to my ears. The sounds of his pleasure, of his want for me, makes me want to dance with him like this for the rest of time.

I tug down his pants until his erection springs free to rest heavy against my stomach. I drag my gaze back up to capture his, the eyes I've memorized piercing me so deep they see straight into my soul.

Sitting back on his heels, Jax shifts his weight to remove his pants the rest of the way. They disappear from view. As he strokes himself from root to tip, I bite my lip in anticipation.

My heart thuds wildly in my chest, the only sound in the

room outside of the crackling embers in the fire beside us. I rock myself to sit upright, coming to my knees until we are face to face, then I loop my arms around his neck and move in close. My lips are a breath away from his. "Jax?"

"Yes, Tempest?"

"Knot me like I'm made for you."

Half a beat passes before Jax's fingers grip the seam of my dress, then he rips it apart as if it were a piece of tissue paper. Buttons pop in all directions. His eyes go to the mate mark, then trail over every inch of my exposed skin. His marks dance across his flesh under the flame's movement. I run my palm over them, savoring every peak and divot, wanting to kiss them. Imprint them onto my own skin. My fingers come to the center of my bra, twisting to unhook the clasp. Jax watches, his stare intense as the lace falls to the ground. I press up onto my elbows, my knees knocking with my nerves.

What if he changes his mind? What if I'm not able to do this? What if—

The anxiety is blown away by a gust of wind and snowflakes. My nipples pebble and Jax's hands grip beneath my knees, dragging me toward him. There's a possessiveness in his eyes that has me aching for him to claim me with his bite. I suck in a breath as a pillow is shoved under my ass. I'm completely exposed with my knees notched on either side of his hips, bared to his icy gaze and the chill of his breath as he appraises me.

"Your body." He trails his hands down my thighs, and I clench on instinct, only feeling the emptiness. "Your pussy." He sets his hands on either side of my chest until he hovers above me, and his silvery ball glints at me from between my legs. My hips wriggle, desperate to rub it against my clit. Even more desperate to discover how it feels inside me, pressed against the bundle of nerves deep within. Jax shifts his weight, one hand trailing the underside of my breast and sliding up to my mate mark. "Your soul." I whimper, near bursting from the anticipation. "They're *mine*."

"Yours," I agree. Because it's true. I'm his. Every beautiful and broken shard of me.

He palms my breast, lips encircling the opposite nipple. My entire being thrums to life beneath his touch, and I reach between us, thumbing over the head of his cock. Swirling the precum streaking his tip, I run it up and down my slit until I bring him to my entrance. "Mine."

"Yes," Jax rasps against the shell of my ear. He steadies himself above me, inching into me with a hiss. His silvery brows scrunch together, like he's summoning every ounce of control to not plunge right into me. He lowers his face to mine, and just before he kisses me, he whispers with a frosty breath, "Everything I am and everything I will be is yours, Tempest."

I cradle him with my thighs a moment, then lower my knees toward the ground as I take him deeper. When I think he's reached the depths of me, his piercing grazes that delicious spot inside, and the thick base of his shaft where the knot is partially expanded bumps against me.

"I-I don't know if it'll work."

Jax shushes me, running a hand through my hair. "Relax, Tempest. We'll get there."

We kiss, tongues tangling together. The spicy pine of his body envelops me. Pulling out just a bit, he makes small thrusts that make me pant for him with each graze of his snowflaked ball. I spread my legs wider, grateful for my flexibility, and dig my heels into the ground. The pillow angles me perfectly, his piercing stroking my insides until it sends me over the edge of ecstasy. He's so thick, so deep, it's hard to imagine him going any further, but I'm desperate to take him in.

All of him.

Pressure coils below my belly, and I wrap my arms around him, tugging his hips closer. I gasp, nails digging into his back. His body quivers against mine. The vibrations, and the blissed-out expression on his face, have me clenching and drawing him into me even more.

"Fuck," Jax growls out.

My body stings when his partially inflated knot is finally captured within me. Pride swirls in my chest as I cling to him.

We rock together, on the cusp of ecstasy until the pressure becomes unbearable, until I'm whimpering. The dam within me crumbles.

"Jax!" I shake and writhe, clawing his back, savoring the scrape of his frost marks beneath my nails. Each tiny curl of his hips has me feral. I embrace the overwhelming fullness of him, wanting to draw every drop of his pleasure into me.

The veins in his neck strain. He grits out my name and a string of curses, some of which I've never heard before. His cum floods me, and I tighten my legs around his waist. He peppers kisses along my throat, whispering low in my ear. "You feel incredible."

I'm throbbing around his knot with each dose of encouragement he spoons me.

His nose grazes my neck and then he bends his head down, sucking a nipple into his mouth, making me cry out again. I'm a pleasure-filled mess, panting with each stroke of his tongue. It almost is enough to distract me from the ache between my legs.

Almost.

"Oh my god," I gasp, nearly biting Jax on instinct,

shoving my fist into my mouth instead. When his knot fully expands and locks into place, I hiss, stifling down a scream.

"That's it." His thumb strokes my clit and my hips jerk in response. "Knew you—could take me—Tempest."

Each move of his tongue over my nipples, each circle of his fingers over my clit, makes the painful numb become bearable.

"That feel good?" he asks, genuine concern lacing his tone.

"Yes." I barely rasp. "More."

"You sure?" His lips press into a line, eyes scanning over my body, as if he's worried he's done something to break me. But if this is what being shattered by Jax entails, I'd gladly let him break and piece me back together for the rest of time. "I can just hold you if it's too much."

Jax hisses as my hips buck and I draw figure eights against him. Moving helps the discomfort ebb, and my body begins to adjust to the fullness. I swirl and shift, Jax continuing to suck and stroke me into a ball of tension ready to burst. When I do, he growls his satisfaction.

Another gush of cum paints my insides, his cock jerking within me. The ball of his piercing nudges the nerves within as I pulse around him. I crest again, pleasure hitting me in a deep wave. Now that the dam has crumbled, each orgasm unleashes more rapidly than the last, feeding off of Jax's. His attention is wholly poised on my body, working us into a delicious cycle of my ecstasy dominoing into his.

He fills me over and over, our bodies locked and rocking in front of the fire until I'm covered in a sheen of sweat despite the chill of his skin.

Hours later, my eyes flutter, spent by the ripples of our pleasure. When he goes to move, I tighten my legs around him. "Not yet."

It's not lost on me that these days are the last few before I return to DC. To summer.

I want to imprint this into memory. His body weight against me. The chill of his breath tousling the wisps of my hair. The fullness of him in the deepest parts of me. Every second we get together is precious. A snowflake cradled in my palm. Something to admire, to memorize each delicate line before it melts away.

Jax's hand comes to rest over my mate mark, and I interlace my fingers with his. I focus on every crackling ember of the fire and every spot where his skin meets mine. I draw the details across the pages of my mind, then tuck them away.

He kisses my shoulder at the start of my scars, trailing his fingers along my body, and I can't help but wonder if maybe he's doing the same, just as scared of these memories fading.

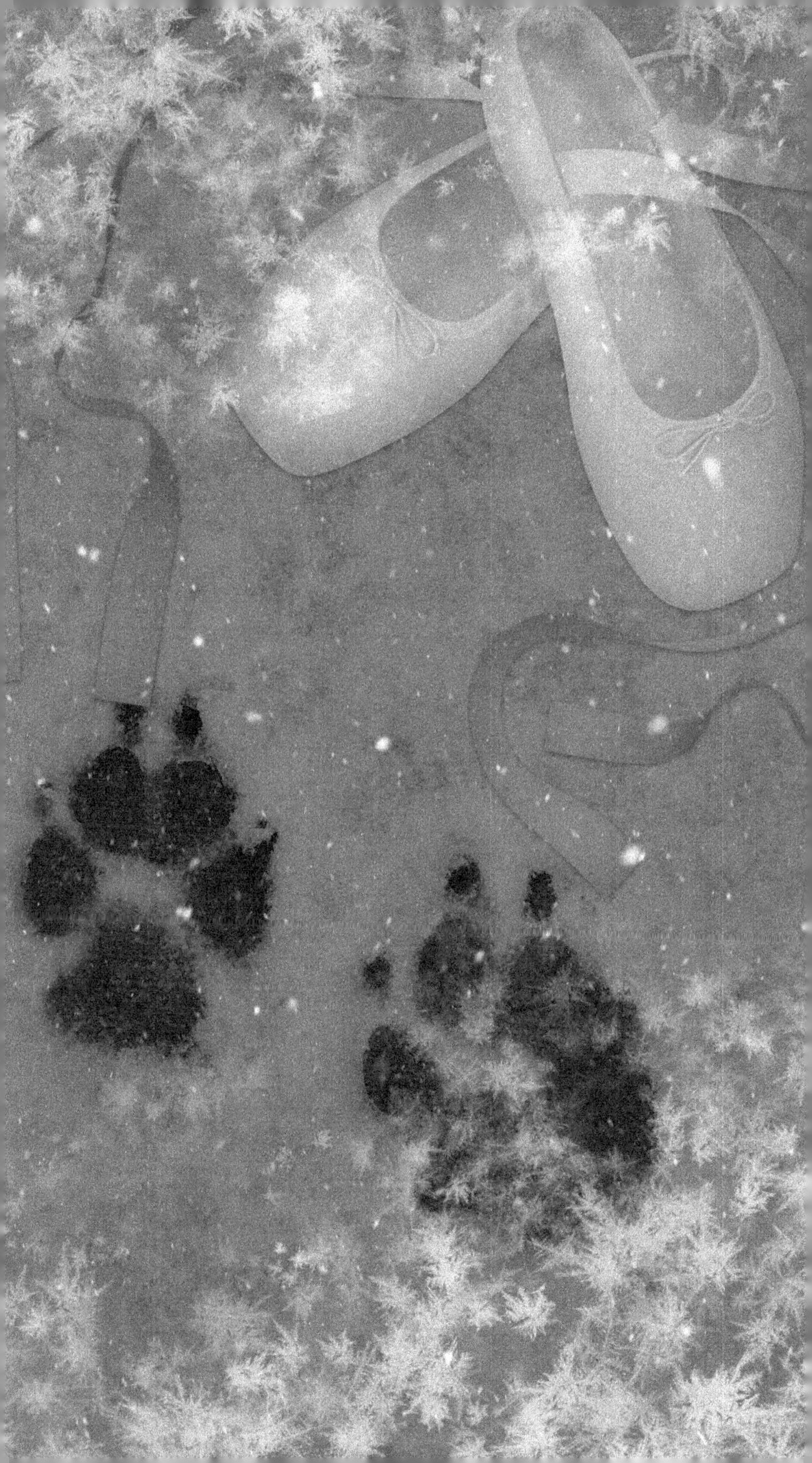

Chapter Thirty-Eight

JOLIE

I spend the night in Jax's arms, the warmth of the fire beaming on me while he's cool on my back. My body aches. A glorious throb between my thighs that he soothes with his icy magic. Every so often I wake, kissing him, pulling him on top of me to feel him solid against me. I need these reminders that he's here. Real.

Mine.

Buzz, buzz, buzz.

I crane my neck over Jax to see who's calling. The last thing I want to do is leave his arms, but Maral's name flashes across the screen.

Buzz, buzz, buzz.

I ignore the slickness between my legs, some of it seeping out from me, and I get up to hurry to the phone vibrating on my nightstand. "Hello. Mistress Maral?"

"Hello, Ms. Wilder." Her tone is firm with a brush of something lighter. "I wanted to inform you that the director and I spoke after your performance at the festival. We both agree that you're ready to take a more prominent position within Ballet Potomac."

My throat quivers and my heart pounds wildly. "Really?"

Jax's arms wrap around me, dragging me backward until I'm flush with his chest. The ridges of his frost marks graze my shoulder blades, and I sink into the sensation.

"Yes, really. You've worked hard all season, continued to show that you take your career seriously. Gone to your physical therapy appointments," she adds, tone a bit sterner. "You'll start rehearsals as a soloist once you're back. And will continue your appointments with Heather."

"Yes!" I squeal, then clear my throat, trying to train myself into regal calm. "Thank you, Mistress Maral. I promise you won't regret it."

"Continue to impress us, Ms. Wilder, and I see big things in your future."

I see them too. The beautiful ache of long days at the studio. Floating above the audience, gliding gracefully across the stage in silks, tulles, and chiffons. The thunder of applause beneath the heat of the spotlight. They're flashes of dreams buried deep in my soul—ones I thought would be made reality at the Institute. Instead, those dreams have been saved for the place where I truly belong.

"Thank you, Mistress Maral. For everything. See you when I get back stateside."

"See you at rehearsals, Jolie."

I knew I danced my heart out. Left every piece of me under those magical lights. But being proud of your own performance doesn't mean anything will come of it.

I didn't dare hope for more.

Now it's happening. *Really happening.* A reclamation of the soloist I was. Only this time, it'll be better because I'm stronger. Not just physically with the help of my PT sessions, but mentally and emotionally too.

I've spent my ballet career wanting to be seen. To show my worth. To be valued. But I've learned so much over the last year and a half. No matter how much I've sought their validation, the only one who can truly give it to me is myself. I know my worth. Know the blood and sweat and tears I've given season after season. Mistress Maral and the director have recognized it too, but at the end of the day, no one can believe in me more than myself.

I hadn't been the first to see it. There had been others to breathe life into my belief. First my mom, all the years she supported me. Then there was Jax. His sacrifice gave me this chance to not only do what I love but love myself doing it.

Turning to face him, I cradle his sharp cheeks in my palms. "I did it. I got soloist."

The smile that spreads across his face, the joy that bubbles from him, they're expressions of raw hope, bottled up and shaken to burst.

"Thank you." Tears streak my cheeks. I don't bother to wipe them away. "Thank you for saving me."

The rims of his eyes shimmer, highlighting the glittering shards of his irises. He's beautiful, persistent, and eternally mine.

Pressing up to my tiptoes, I kiss him. Slowly. Gently. Then possessively and deep. His hand threads through my hair and he guides me to the bed, nestling between my thighs. We celebrate the future the best way we can: tangled together with our bodies surging as one.

Not long after, Lark knocks on the door. I kiss Jax goodbye for the day, watching him bound through the snow. His wolf runs into the far hills, ones I'll be heading to today with our excursion. While I miss him already, I know he'll find me there.

And I'm already anticipating the next time I can have him.

I never knew sex could be like this. Otherworldly. An

out-of-body experience. My body heats at the memory. Not just because it's mind-blowing, which it is, but because as much as I want to unravel him, watch him lose control under my touch, he equally wants that in return. His pleasure doesn't exist without mine, and I don't ever want my pleasure to exist without his.

The night replays on a loop in my mind the entire ride to our excursion: A night under the stars full of delicious food, drinks, and relaxing. It's the closest I'll ever get to actual camping. While I've booked myself an ice dome for one, I fully intend to have company with me all night.

I can't wait.

Tonight is about much more than the opportunity to see Jax and to spend time with him. There's something else I want from him before we're left to say goodbye once again.

When we get to the campsite, our guides point out where our domes are located. I'm across from Lark and Delilah, so we part ways, agreeing to meet back at the bonfire's central area in twenty minutes. I head to my ice dome, finding a lush bed with blankets and pillows, along with a nightstand. I throw my pack on the ground and rifle through it, making sure I packed the good underwear for later versus the long johns I'm rocking beneath my clothes right now. Thermal underwear is not part of my seduction plan. Not that I think he'll need much seducing, but I don't want any hesitating when we talk tonight. Every minute that passes reminds me of the looming months apart once I leave. I hate that we'll be separated again.

Before I know it, my alarm goes off, and I wander out to the bonfire to meet Lark and Delilah. A few Frosts flit into my field of vision, and I search for Jax, wondering if he's among them, disappointing myself when he's not.

"Who's ready for s'more fun?" Our tour guide Gail

chimes over the loudspeaker. We follow the other excursionists into the large tented dome. Long tables span its width with different s'more fixings, cheeses, meats, and fruits.

We all load up our plates and exit the tent to gather around the bonfire, sitting along a bench that looks like it's been dug straight into the snowbank.

"*Brr!*" Lark says at the same time Delilah curses under her breath. I sit next to them, giving a dramatic shiver, though I'm not really bothered. Yes, my ass is chilly, but the cold isn't an issue for me anymore. In fact, I sink into the numb, savoring its bite.

"I have news," I say, voice bubbling over with excitement. "Ballet Potomac is promoting me to soloist."

"Holy shit, Jojo!" Lark puts her plate down, nearly knocking me over with a hug. "I'm so happy for you. Selfishly sad you won't be at the Institute with me, but I cannot wait to see you take center stage next season."

"You know we'll be in the front row," Delilah adds, holding her fist out until I bump it.

We grab our hot cocoas and cheer with them before spending the next hour eating and taking turns toasting marshmallows on the fire. Once our bellies are full, we hang out and talk. Picking up the deck of cards, Delilah shuffles and passes them out. We play a few rounds of crazy eights. It's nice, quiet, and kills time before it's our turn to have the hot tub.

Lark and I part ways, throwing on our bathing suits and meeting at the tub. The sun sinks beyond the hills, painting the sky in silky shades of pink, purple, and gold.

It's stunning, and I can't take my eyes off of it as I climb in.

The warm water engulfs me, and I lean back, continuing

to admire the sunset while Lark pours us each some white zinfandel. Cupping the stemless glass in my hands, I take a few sips, enjoying the warmth of the sun on my face. Lark shoots me a grin, and the two of us sit together in perfect silence, enjoying the view.

I've been itching to tell her about Jax. About *everything*. It's so hard keeping this secret from her. She's held my hand on the hardest days of my life, is happy to talk through my struggles or sit silently with me like she is now. And I haven't been able to be honest with her.

Bringing the glass to my lips, I gulp the rest of it down before I pour myself another. That catches Lark's attention. "What's going on, Jojo?"

"I have something to tell you, but I don't want you to freak out."

"Okay..." Lark's brows furrow, then she eyes my empty glass before chugging her own, holding it out for me to top her off.

I tip over the bottle and begin to talk, my hand wobbling a bit. "After the accident, I kept remembering these eyes. Sparkling silvers and blues. Not like anything I'd ever seen before. I couldn't figure out why at first. I figured it was some strange way of coping with the trauma of what happened. Then I saw those very same eyes on a wolf watching me from a window the first day at Ballet Potomac. After that, I started noticing strange things around the apartment. The thermostat being low, messages left for me... I thought it was a ghost."

"Does this have something to do with the brand-new Ouija board shoved in my closet?"

"He broke it," I blurt out before adding, "on accident!"

"He?" Her lips press into a line. My heart races, waiting for her to nod along with mock understanding or suggest I check myself into a facility. "So he's the spirit you were communicating with?"

"Sort of." I take another sip, the wine burning as it slides down my throat as I search for the right words. "He's not a ghost. Well, he's dead but also...not. He's a harbinger, a winter one."

She sets her glass on the side of the hot tub. "So less Casper and more Jack Frost?"

"Yes! Exactly." Steam rises up around us, highlighting the slowly darkening sky. I put my empty glass next to her partially drunk one. "Funny story... Jack Frost is actually real. He's retired now, but the idea is similar enough. Jax has only met him a few times."

"Jax?" She cocks her head to the side, as if testing the name in her mind.

"Yeah. That's his name."

The seconds stretch on for what feels like forever, only the sound of the jet spinning bubbles through the warm water filling the silence.

"And you and Jax are still communicating?" Each word is slowly enunciated, like she can't decide how she feels about what I'm saying. Not that I can blame her. She should be more panicked right now. Shouldn't she?

She places a hand on my shoulder. "Come on, Jojo. You've gotten this much out."

She's right. I've already told her most of the crazy parts, what's a little mate chat between friends at this point? I clear my throat. "We are still communicating, but it's a bit more complicated than that."

"How complicated?"

I grimace. "Complicated enough that I'm pouring us each one more glass."

"Then you better get pouring, Jojo, because I need to

know everything," she says, lifting her glass up and nodding toward the half-empty bottle of wine.

I spend the next thirty minutes talking her through everything until we're out of wine.

"So you can call him?" She blinks at me. "Do it."

"I mean, it's not always immediate."

"Just try it. I want to meet him!"

Is this some sort of trick? Does she not believe me?

"Um. Okay." Sliding my hand to my mark, I glide my fingertips over it. "Jax, are you there?"

For a few moments, all I hear are the sounds of my breaths. My pulse kicks up beneath my hand. Then, in a rush of wind, he appears, pale-blue skin glimmering against the dimming backdrop, the moon faintly glowing within the dark-purple sky scattered with stars.

"Hello, Tempest."

"You came."

"I said I would." His gaze turns to Lark who's staring at him. Like she...

"Do you see him?"

"If you're talking about this very attractive guy with plat-inum-and-blue streaked hair, yes."

"Nice to meet you, Lark," Jax says with a small bow.

She smirks at him, slipping a hand under my chin to shut my mouth that's hanging open. "Likewise."

"How?" I gape at her. It took me months to see him and here Lark is, chatting with Jax in a matter of minutes.

"You said yourself that you needed to believe." Lark shrugs like this is just a casual hang out between friends. "I followed your lead."

"So you see him. You agree he's real. And you don't think I'm crazy?"

"Well, we're all a little crazy," she says with a chuckle,

putting an arm behind me on the hot tub's ledge, her brown eyes meeting mine. "But yes. I believe you."

Snapping her attention to Jax, she waves him toward one of the empty seats opposite us. When he sinks down into the water, I still, half expecting him to melt or freak out by the heat. Instead, the temperature just lessens in intensity, as if he's cooling it, but not enough to bother Lark. Leaning back in her seat, she gestures at him with her hand. "Now, tell me all about yourself, Jax. Jojo's given me a quick rundown, but I want to know what your intentions are for my bestie."

When our time's up in the hot tub, we head back to our respective ice domes to change into fresh clothes. Jax follows, sitting on the edge of the bed while I peel off my wet swimsuit. I pull a towel from my bag, and he grabs my wrist as I walk past. "Let me."

"Okay." He guides me between his knees, his face level with my breasts. He pats down my body gently, covering my skin with kisses until I'm completely dry.

I put on my thermals, navy blue with snowflakes swirling across them.

"If I didn't know any better, Tempest, I'd think you picked these out with me in mind."

"Maybe I did."

"Then maybe I look forward to stripping them off of you later before I have you sit on my face."

For someone so chilly, how did it just get so hot in here?

I swallow hard, pushing down the vision in my mind.

The one I really want to make happen. But we promised Lark we wouldn't miss stargazing. While she isn't telling Delilah about Jax or what I told her, the idea of not keeping it a secret and having him there with me makes me smile.

Jax presses a soft kiss to the nape of my neck, then hands me the rest of my clothes, jacket, and beanie. If he wasn't blue, didn't just stroll in through the ice wall, or transform into a giant wolf, this would almost feel normal. "How come you can touch me and move the things around us now so easily? You didn't seem to be able to before."

"Your belief solidifies me," he says, stroking my cheek with the back of his hand.

I take his hand and fold his arm around me, wriggling my ass against him. He growls. "You do that again and we won't make it out to meet your friends."

"Fine," I whine, giving him one last playful swish of my hips, "but I expect you to ravage me thoroughly afterward."

With a snap of his fingers he's dressed in full cold-weather gear, like the cold somehow affects him. A dark jacket and matching jeans with a peek of a light-blue shirt. He smiles, and I swear it always manages to make me melt. "Oh, I'm counting down the minutes."

So am I.

I spend the next hour and a half listening to Gail talk about the stars while thinking only of the harbinger at my back. I can feel his presence the entire time, and I wonder how close he was before I could see him; how often I didn't realize he was right there, waiting for me to believe. Waiting for me to find him too.

We say goodnight to everyone and head back to my ice dome. Each crunch of snow beneath my feet makes my nerves bubble closer and closer to the surface. Barely inside, my hands find Jax, stripping away his jacket, shirt, pants, and briefs. They all disappear before they hit the floor.

I crash my mouth to his, and we're a tangle of teeth and lips and tongues. Skimming the hem of my shirt, he peels it over my head before unclasping my bra and palming my breasts in his hands. I moan against his mouth. Gripping my waistband, I pull my bottoms down, stepping out of them before pushing Jax back onto the bed.

I climb up his strong body, admiring every dip, curve, line, and feathered frost mark. He gives me a firm smack to the back of my thigh. "Get up here, Tempest, I've been craving your taste."

I turn, moving backward. Lowering my hips, I hover just above his face.

"Lower."

"I-I've never done this. I don't want to suffocate you."

"Not possible." He chuckles. "Though I'd gladly let you."

He gives me a tug down to his lips and I yelp. His tongue feels like it's everywhere as he licks, and laps, and spears into me.

It's incredible.

"Oh god, Jax." I quake above him and watch his body come to life, cock hardening with each messy stroke, and I grab his chest to steady myself. His mate mark stares back at me, and I give into the instinct to touch it, grazing the pads of my fingers over each silvery ridge. He groans beneath me, his cock lengthening under my gaze. Pearly streaks slip from the slit on its head.

I lick my lips.

Then lean forward, thumbing the silver ball. More precum weeps out. It'd be a shame to waste it…

I bend forward and lap up every morsel leaking from him, savoring his sweet taste and the chill of it against my tongue. I moan as he worships my clit, sucking in pulses that have my hips jerking, out of control. Mint and chocolate slip down my throat as I wrap my lips around his tip and sink lower on his shaft until my chin meets his pelvis. The ball taps the back of my throat, and I swallow against it, choking a bit, tears rimming my eyes.

"Fuck," Jax growls against my clit, the sharp tip of his canine nipping where I'm most sensitive. And I want it. I want those teeth to sink into my skin while his knot pumps into me over and over. I want to know what it feels like to tether myself to him completely, to sense him as much as he senses me.

Just say the word and I'll happily sink my teeth into that sexy throat of yours.

My hips writhe on his face, and I cry out, the orgasm whipping into me so hard that I can't even focus. All I can do is moan around his cock. My heart pounds, and pounds, and pounds, until I finally release him from my lips.

I am pure instinct. Want and need. As Jax continues to consume my soul through another earth-shattering orgasm, I bottle up the pressure building in me, take a deep inhale, and sink my teeth into the inside of his thigh.

Mine.

Copper hits my tongue, followed by a fiery ice that floods my veins. It fills me with a wildness I don't care to tame. One that will only be sated by my mate's bite, his knot...

His claim.

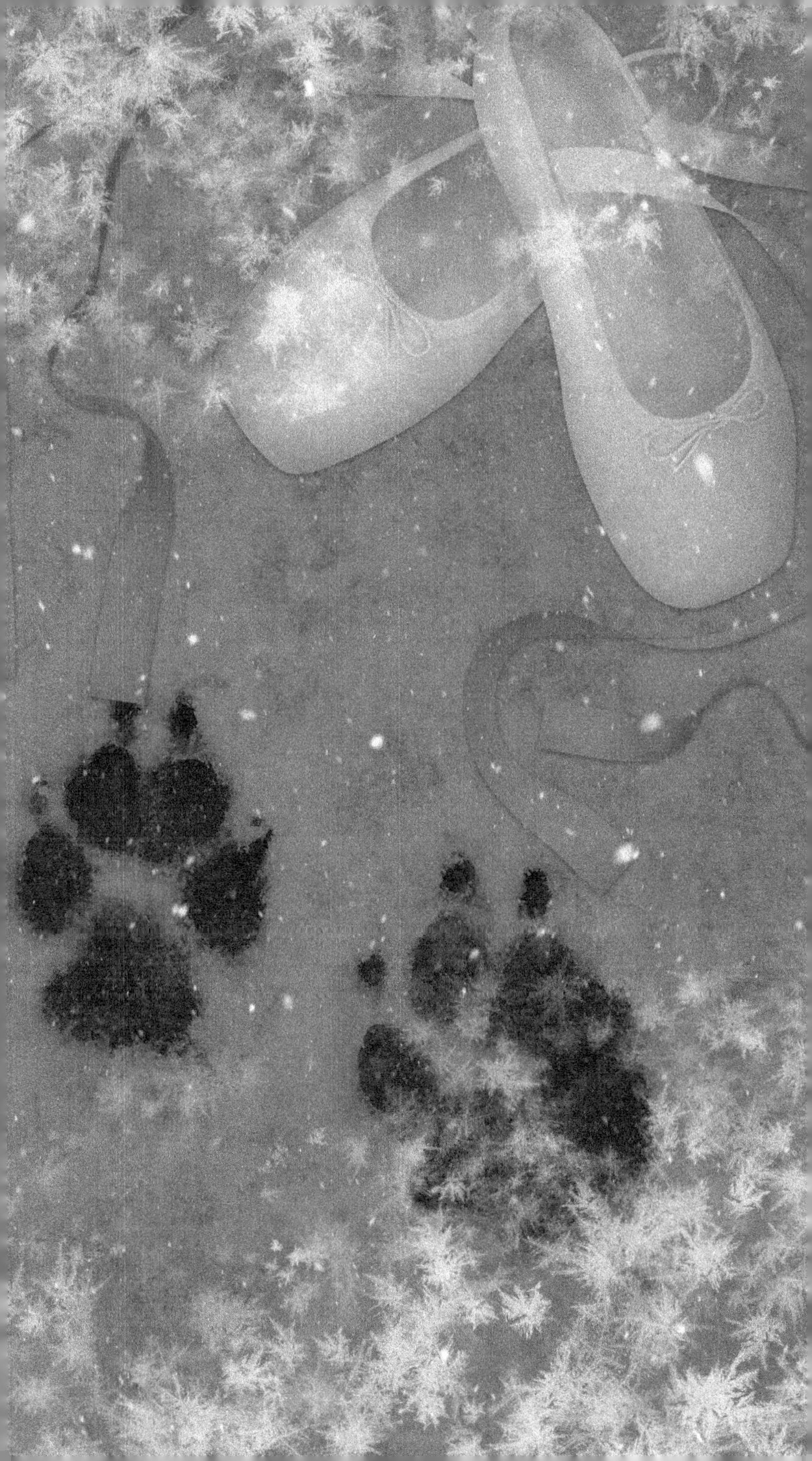

Chapter Thirty-Nine

JAX

Jolie's teeth break my skin, and I freeze beneath her. Face covered in her release, I'm suddenly fighting the urges rising up in me. I want to give into them so badly. The pain in my thigh is searing, but Jolie licks at her fresh marks with her tongue, soothing them.

It's the hottest thing I've ever seen.

"Tempest," I say, keeping my voice low. I fist the comforter, fear holding me back. "Is this—" I hesitate, unsure what to say. I don't want her to regret this. On the other hand, I've waited all my immortal life for this bond. For her. "Did you mean to do that?"

She looks over her shoulder, tongue dragging over her lips. "Yes, Jax. I want you to claim me."

Her icy-blue eyes flash at me with so much certainty. In an instant I'm sitting up and repositioning us, kissing up her back until I reach the base of her neck. My body curls around hers.

"You want my knot?" I whisper into her ear, my cock pressing against her pussy. She gives two quick nods, getting on all fours in front of me. Baring herself to me. I lick my lips, tasting the remnants of her desire, then run the tip of my cock along her slit, rubbing my piercing against her until her hips wiggle. I line myself up and thrust inside her, and she pushes back, meeting me with a gasp.

Someone's eager.

She moves to sink further down, but I grip her hips, holding her in place. "Beg me for it."

Her chest heaves, nipples peaked into hardened nubs. I thumb over one and then the other. "Please, Jax," she whimpers. "Please give me your knot."

"I think my mate wants more than that." I nip the shell of her ear and her pussy clenches around me. She releases an unsteady breath, white painting the air, and I pull out an inch before sliding back in, teasing her until her arms are shaking to keep her on all fours. "Don't you, Tempest?"

She groans, panting as I continue to pulse against her. "I —"

"Don't be shy. Tell me."

I need her to say the words. To let go with me. If I'm unleashing with her tonight, claiming her in return, then I want her to relinquish herself to our instincts. She may not be a harbinger, but she's my mate, primed to fully solidify our bond.

"Fuck me. Bite me. Claim me. Please." She bites her lip, and I can't stop myself from nipping at it, kissing her feverishly until it's swollen. Hearing the desperate inflection as she confesses each desire, it's the final confirmation I need.

I bury myself in her, and she cries out as her pussy grips me like a fucking lifeline. "I'm going to take you so hard, when you come on this cock, I will be drenched. Then I'll bite you. Fill your sweet pussy. Do it over and over again until I'm leaking down your thighs." She whimpers at that, and fuck if it doesn't do something to me. "You want that, Tempest?"

"Yes, Jax. Please." That's when I really start to thrust, driving my hips in and out of her. Her plea makes my knot expand, and she hisses. I wrap her chocolate strands around my fist and pull her up to me, my other hand cupping her breast, thumb stroking her nipple.

"I love you, Jax," she breathes out. "Make me yours."

Her body shakes against me. I plunge into her hard and fast, our bodies slapping in a frantic rhythm that echoes through the small dome. "I love you so fucking much, Tempest."

I want to make her scream. For our bodies to be so loud they shake the walls down. So destructive the world tremors with the depth of my want for her. Causes an avalanche.

The aching need I have when it comes to my Tempest, it's been cultivated by months of desperation and my sacrifice that got us here. One I'd make over and over again.

Her vibrancy is what I cling to every minute of every season we're apart. I hate that it'll happen, that spring will come, but there's also beauty in the seasons. They're constantly changing. Some may break us, but then they'll make way for the next. Eventually, winter will return, just as I'll always return to Jolie.

I want to fill her, coat her in my scent, cover her in my frost. Ingrain myself so deeply into every inch of her that every harbinger who crosses her path knows that this mortal is fierce and perfect and *mine*.

Jolie arches, taking me deeper. Then she reaches behind her, stretching her neck before me. Her fingers thread through my hair, and I graze my teeth along her throat. She smells so goddamn good. I arc one hand over her hip and find her clit, and her pussy pulses violently around me as she comes.

Pleasure spears down my spine, and I growl before

sinking my teeth into her neck. Copper coats my tongue. *Her.* It's a rush nothing compares to. My mate mark glows with silver luminescence along with the one between her ribs. They flare as one, pulsing with the beat of her heart. The one that beats for the both of us.

Our hips move in unison, seeking more, locked together. My fingers work expertly over Jolie's clit, and her pussy draws out every ounce from my knot. I come, and come, and come. Minutes turn into hours. Moonlight spins into dawn. There's only my mate, our bond, and this inescapable pleasure. I clutch each moment with her. They're the lifelines I'll cling to through the coming seasons.

"Jax?" Jolie asks when morning is in full swing, the other campers making their way out of their dens. "What happens next?"

"Now that the bond is accepted, you'll be able to sense me just as I sense you. I don't know how you being mortal will impact things, but you should be able to at least sense my emotions." I press a kiss into her hair. *"You'll be able to contact me through our mind connection."*

Her head cranes back to look at me, brows lifted in surprise. "How—"

"Place a hand on your mark and think what you want to say."

I guide her hand to her sternum, its faint glow reflecting into her palm before I press it against her skin. "Now try."

There's silence for a moment. Then I hear her voice faintly in the back of my mind. A sound I'll treasure forever. *"Jax?"*

"Tempest."

"I did it!"

Giddy bubbles fill her words, and pressure builds behind my eyes. I blink away the tears and bring my hand to my own mark, certain if I try to say the words aloud, my voice will crack under the weight of my joy. *"You're a natural."*

"It's easy to be when I'm yours."

Yours.

I was someone's. A belonging I've craved for as long as I could remember. I loved my Frost family. They embraced me when I'd been lost to the mortal world, lost to my mother, father, and brother. But once I was old enough, I watched each season as everyone paired off, finding their mates, building a life beyond their lifetime.

And I was alone.

Well, not completely.

Hope's been my constant companion, beating within me along with each glorious thud of Jolie's heart. And while I still don't know what our future will bring beyond her mortal years, our mate bond is real and whole.

"I love the way that sounds on your lips, Tempest."

"Want me to say it again?"

"Always."

She stretches and wriggles her hips, shifting so I come out of her. The moment the air kisses my sensitive skin, I miss being engulfed in her warmth. Pearly streaks coat her inner thighs, dripping down as she rolls me over to straddle me. I swipe some up with my finger and bring it to her clit, circling it in a wreath of pleasure. In a fluid motion, she wraps her fingers around me, then sinks down onto my cock. I watch our bodies join fully, my knot spreading her lips wide so I can see her taking in every inch of me.

Her voice pulls my attention to her icy-blue eyes. "I'm yours, Jax. And you are mine. My mate. My love. My *life*."

JOLIE

We finish out the trip abroad, and while Delilah hits the slopes, Lark and I hang out. Jax joins us off and on between his Frost duties. It's so odd to have her see him, but I'm grateful not to have to keep the secret any longer. To share the blessing and burden of being mated to an immortal. It's also nice to be with someone who doesn't earn an eye roll or glare from her every time he's around.

Jax seems to enjoy the company too. He and Lark goof off together like they didn't meet days ago. She asks to see his magic, and he proudly shows off for her, making snow fall over our heads, drawing obscene pictures with ice on the lodge's windows, sculpting ballerinas in elegant poses on my balcony. They're so detailed, eerily capturing our likeness. I recognize the flare of my chiffon skirt and the stiff tulle of Lark's emerald ensemble. He really was there that night. Not that I didn't believe him, but the icy proof makes my heart melt even more. If that's possible.

Joy radiates off of him with an otherworldly glow. I know he has a family of sorts within the Frosts, but it must be lonely being surrounded by mortals who can't see you. A world that doesn't know you exist. The lightness to his tone, in his gait, it's something I want to freeze and carry with me long after this trip.

The time to leave arrives, but I refuse to say goodbye. I just can't. Instead, we talk through our bond off and on, keeping each other company if only in our minds. It's a comfort unlike anything I've ever known. When my flight crosses over the ocean, I nearly panic, worried I won't hear him once I'm stateside.

"You still here?" I ask tentatively, scared I'll only be met with silence.

"I'll always be here, Tempest." His low chuckle vibrates through my mate mark. *"Remember that cute little bite you gave me? You're stuck with me now."*

"Cute? Little?" I say in mock offense, taking a quick glance at the subtle silvery glow coming from my sternum. It's faint but there in all its reassuring glory. *"I happened to feel very ferocious when I did that."*

"Oh, you certainly are ferocious." Without seeing him, I can tell he's smirking, and I wish I was there to kiss and nip at his bottom lip. *"I'll make sure to warn the other harbingers to stay wary now that they're on your radar. My perfectly feral mate."*

"Only feral for you," I chime back.

His silky growl simmers below my belly. I'm certain if he were closer he'd be able to scent my desire, and that thought brings with it a slew of memories:

My handprints smeared across the studio mirror.

Delicious mint chocolate coating my tongue.

His skin stamping frost marks upon my own.

The searing stretch of my body around his knot, locked together for hours.

A low rumble vibrates through our connection. He's remembering too.

Our stolen moments are small treasures I'll pull out and admire until winter brings Jax back to me. He'll still need to hibernate. There will be times of radio silence despite our newly formed mate bond. But hearing his voice from thousands of miles away is better than nothing. It's a reminder that even as he fades back into the veil of his world that he's real.

That he is, and will always be, mine.

August
OCTOBE
MO TU WE TH FR
3
10 11
17 18
24 25 26
31
2 3 4 5 6 7
9 10 11 12 13 14
16 17 18 19 20 21
23 24 25 26 27 28 29
30 31

September

Chapter Fourty-One

JOLIE

It's been over a month since I last saw Jax. The distance sucks, but we manage to talk each day while he finishes up winter in Australia and I kick off another season with Ballet Potomac, only this time as a soloist.

Evelyn, Veronique, and Sara are thrilled for me—albeit envious, which I totally understand. They aren't any less supportive of me, though. It's all I could ask for, and at least we get to see each other at company classes and rehearsals for Act I of our fall showcase. We'll be dancing Kingdom of the Shades, an excerpt from *La Bayadere*.

The tips of leaves shift from green to rich ambers and maroon, rustling with the breeze, signaling fall's arrival. It was Mom's favorite season, and I always think of her when they begin to change.

As Lark and I head toward the metro, movement pulls my attention toward the trees lining the streets, and I spot two golden-skinned harbingers. They swirl in and out of each other's way, tapping at branches, working so quickly I nearly miss them. It's crazy to think how unaware we are of their existence. How easy it is to take their harbinging for granted.

The mugginess of summer remains, the heat more stifling than it should be in September. Sweat beads along my chest and brow, and I wipe it back into my hair, using it to slick the wisps around my bun.

After tucking my dance bag between my feet as soon as Lark and I sit down, I strip off my loose t-shirt, desperate for air. You'd think the metro would be filled, but it's earlier than the commuting rush. Only five other people are spread out along the empty seats in our section.

"You okay?" Lark asks, not looking at me. I follow her gaze to the front of my leotard that's mottled with sweat, turning the pastel-pink hue into deep-mauve splotches.

"Yeah," I reply, though my tone's a bit breathless. Pulling up my phone, I swipe to my camera, inspecting my pallid skin and the droplets peeking from around my hairline and the base of my neck. Could it be—

"Tempest?"

My heart pounds at Jax's voice, and I cross my legs, body warming all over. Lark stares at me with her brows bunched together. Her thick sweatshirt has me grabbing my water bottle. I twist off the cap and chug down a few sips as I reach back out to Jax. *"Hey."*

"I'm so sorry." His lilt is low and gravelly, scraping along my skin like the canines I wish were dragging down my throat again. Claiming me all over.

Oh no. This can't be happening...

"I'll talk to my fathers and Fate. Maybe they'll let me come to you for a few days to see you through sols—"

"Shit."

"What is it?"

Double shit. I didn't realize I said that aloud. A few of the other passengers glance in our direction but quickly return to their business.

"Tempest, are you there?"

"Solstice," I reply to Lark, ignoring him. "It's happening."

Her previously pinched brows lift in surprise. I'm so glad she knows about Jax. The last thing I want to do is explain what is going on right now in public. "Oh, so this is what being horny is like for harbingers?"

"Stop laughing!" My eyes dart around the metro car, skin prickling with embarrassment and probably something more.

"Do we need to get off at the next stop?" Lark points up to the metro map, chuckling as I glare at her. "Oops, poor choice of words."

"It's not funny," I grumble, crossing my arms over my sweat-stained leotard. Thank goodness I always pack a spare. I'll need it.

"You have to admit, it's a little funny." Lark's face softens with something akin to pity.

"Tempest, you there?" Jax's voice calls through our connection. *"Hold on. I'm going to talk to them."*

"No, Jax. Don't."

He pauses a moment. *"Don't?"*

"Stay where you are. Please." I take a few deep breaths, not wanting to sound stressed and cause him to do something stupid like start a freak blizzard or swap in with some autumn harbinger. *"It's not worth getting in trouble. Not when we are so close to winter. I don't want to do anything that could jeopardize that."*

I've been counting down to winter, my winter, ever since I left Australia.

"But—"

"No," I warn. It won't take much encouragement from me to have him doing something reckless. That will only wind up with us separated again—more than we have to be. *"Not*

when you're going to ask to get assigned back here. We'll have the next solstice."

I'm already slick just thinking about it.

Or maybe that's the solstice talking.

Fighting the urge to tell him to screw it and come hold me, engulf me with his presence and fill me, I take a few more steadying breaths, pinching the bridge of my nose.

"What can I do?"

"Why do you sound so calm when I feel like peeling off every layer of clothing right here on the metro?" If I have to be hot and bothered, he should be too!

"I'm far from calm." There's a sharpened edge to his tone, but on voice alone, it doesn't sound like Jax is about to sweat out of his skin—not that I think that'd be possible for him. *"And if you strip off those clothes, I'll break out of here and show you how* not calm *I am."*

"I wish." The words are out before I realize they might set off another chain of events. According to Jax, Fate's very concerned with the effects of him saving me and the ripple of what she's had to do to fix it. They are leery of the consequences from us solidifying our bond but haven't gone so far as to forbid him from coming here this next winter.

"Tempest... Do I need to come there?"

"No." I keep my tone firm, using the hand pressed over my mate mark to refocus my breathing and slow my heart rate as much as I can. *"Stay where you are, Jax. I mean it."*

Would this experience be different if I were a Frost? I have the distinct feeling that if I ask him, he won't tell me. Any mention of if he hadn't interfered, if I had become a Frost, is quickly met with silence or a change of topic.

"Are you two doing that weird mind-speak thing?" Lark groans, pulling me back to the present. The tracks rumble beneath our feet, and I glance out the window, noting that we are nearing Lark's stop.

"Give me a second."

"I'm sorry, Lark. I'm listening." I try not to talk to Jax when I'm around other people, otherwise I tend to look crazier than I already feel when I think about being bonded to an immortal that will be bringing us winter in a few months.

"Are you going to be okay for rehearsals today?"

"I have to be. We're working on the pas de deux choreography for *Petite Mort*."

"Ooh la la." Lark fans herself dramatically.

Petite Mort is a contemporary ballet, choreographed in the 1990s by Jiří Kylián, that plays on the French translation of *la petite mort,* which means "the little death," a euphemism for orgasm. Lark's been teasing me ever since I told her we were performing it, but honestly, I think she's a bit jealous because the Institute prefers to only do classical ballets. She would kill to do more contemporary work— which is why I'm slowly trying to woo her to the dark side to join me at Ballet Potomac. "You know...you could always audition and next time you'd be dancing alongside me."

"Yeah, yeah, yeah," she replies, blowing me off, though I notice she's never given the idea an outright rejection. "Anyway... Why don't you take my extra towel today?" She pulls it out of her bag and tosses it to me as the metro screeches. "I feel bad for your partner. You're going to be sliding all over them with all that sweat. Who are you partnering again?"

"Vincent Rollins."

"Ah yes, the adorable, curly-haired ginger."

"That's the one."

The car stops moving and the doors *whoosh* open to the

platform. Lark stands, resting her hand on the back of my seat.

"What time are you done today?"

"Should be home by five or six, why?"

"Just curious." She walks out onto the platform, turning around and calling out right before it shuts. "I have a short day today, so text me if you need anything."

I give her a nod and a wave through the glass while the metro groans to life. Normally, we don't ride together, but Lark doesn't have rehearsals until later today, so she's going shopping before she meets Delilah for lunch.

"Jax? You still there?"

"Always, Tempest." His voice comforts me, but I wish he were here, that his arms were around me, the chill of his body balancing the heat of mine. Missing him is a constant ache, but since we bonded—since I've given in to believing in who he is and what we are—the throb has gotten more manageable.

At least, until today.

Right now, I just want to summon him here, kiss him, and press my body to his...but if I say the words, it'll only land Jax in trouble. He's proven to be charmingly persistent when it comes to me. So instead of telling him how badly I'm craving him, I turn the tables. *"How are you doing with solstice? Are* you *going to be okay?"*

"I'm more worried about you. At least I can hole up at home."

My mind conjures an image of his hand wrapped around his cock, stroking himself until cum jets from his pierced tip. I clench my thighs together. The metro rumbles beneath me, only making the sensation worse. I may combust if I don't do something about this soon.

"I'm guessing you still have to dance today?"

"Yep." I croak out, trying to wrangle my thoughts. The

metro screeches and slows to a stop at my destination. Finally. *"With opening night less than two months away, every rehearsal counts. It'll be alright. I'll just ice bath afterward."*

"Well, if you want some company, you know where to find me."

"I do." I get up and head out the sliding doors, then hustle up the stairs to the street. Why did I choose today to wear a pale leotard? I'll have to wear my warm-up leggings the entire day, even if I sweat my ass off. *"And you'll probably hear from me."*

"If something changes and you need me to get to you, just say the word."

"Okay." Though I know I won't summon him. No matter the circumstance. *"I love you."*

"I love you too." I'll never tire of those words from his lips. *"Looking forward to chatting with you later, Tempest."*

"Same," I reply, and push open the doors to the studio.

I'm sweating profusely through all the combinations, to the point where even Mistress Maral tells me to take a break to get some water. When we finish company class, I use the thirty minutes between to do cold compresses all over my body and change my leotard and tights. Then it's back to back *Kingdom of the Shades* and *Petite Mort* rehearsals. The first goes by quickly, thank goodness, and before I know it, I'm waving goodbye to Evelyn, Veronique, and Sara.

While all the soloists are performing *Kingdom of the Shades*, only three of us have been selected alongside the three principal female ballerinas to perform *Petite Mort*.

Despite all the sweating, my energy thrums with the increased solstice boost. I need somewhere for the tension to go.

There'll be no pointe shoes, no frilly tutus or bedazzled costumes. Instead, a dozen of us, six women and six men, showcase our lines in skin-tone, corseted leotards. Stripping down from baroque dresses we wear like armor to nothing but lines and energetic partnering as we *duel* with our fellow dancers. We're meant to look naked, and right now, I wish I was because I've already managed to sweat through my second leotard of the day. My body is sticky and gross. I think about my friends enjoying their ice baths while I'm rehearsing and jealousy swims through my veins.

"*Petite Mort* is meant to be bold, sensual, and, at times, aggressive. It was Kylián's ode to how in the moment of pleasure, we are reminded that life is ephemeral. Death is never far." Our artistic director, Luke Fantome, shares with the class. Then he calls up Wren and Rudolph, asking them to demonstrate a few lifts for us to practice.

I sit down, and Vincent extends his arm out to me. His eyes scan over my body. "You feeling okay?"

"Yeah, just working extra hard." I titter before grabbing his hand and letting him pull me up. I push from the floor, clutching his shoulders for support. He catches the tops of my legs and we hold the position while I brace my core, arching my back, extending through the tips of my toes. All these lifts need to look seamless. Effortless. To get there takes practice, lots of blunders, and loads of muscle control. Partnering for *Petite Mort*, where it blends modern into the classical ballet style, our bodies must hit every line and then, just as smoothly, transition into a fluid lift or jump.

Outside of the things I can practice and hone on my own, trust is a huge part of whether a pas de deux looks graceful and swoon-worthy or clunky and awkward. Vincent is a seasoned soloist, most likely promoting to principal within the next year. I've seen him lift other dancers numerous times, but trust doesn't come from repetition. It comes from every time he checks in with me, each moment he's made me feel welcomed since promoting, the fact that he doesn't complain about how sweaty I am right now while he's stuck pressed against me.

An hour and a half later, we break for the day, and I say my goodbyes before quickly shuffling to the dressing room. I'm so ready to peel myself out of these damp clothes. I change into my swimsuit then head for the ice baths. Vincent and Wren join me for about ten minutes before they go about the rest of their recovery. I don't leave the basin, though. It feels too good. And I miss Jax. I miss his scent breezing over me and the comfort of his chill. Every part of my body burns, and the ice brings me solace.

After thirty minutes, I get out and throw on my clothes to go home.

I'm already sweating again before I reach the metro.

I consider touching base with Jax on the ride back but decide not to. For some reason, I have the feeling as soon as I talk to him, the effects of solstice are only going to get worse. Each step up the stairs to the apartment, my thighs rub together, and I'm already becoming damp again.

As soon as I get to my room, I'm contacting Jax. I can't have him come here, can't risk him being punished again on my behalf, but I need to talk to him. Need him in whatever way I can get.

When I enter the apartment, Lark's standing up at the couch, a basket sitting atop the coffee table.

"What's this?" I ask as she waves her hand at the basket, taking a dramatic step back.

"Just a little something." A grin streaks across her cheeks. "Ran some errands on your behalf this afternoon. I put together a solstice survival kit."

My jaw drops when I spot a big, blue, semi-translucent dildo, its thick veins climbing along its shaft. Nestled beside it is a smaller vibrator to match.

"Someone decided to be an overachiever in the best friend department today."

There's a bottle of wine, a pine-scented candle, a box of mint-chocolate cookies, and peppermint patties. When I pull out the mint chip-flavored lube, I'm certain that I'm seven shades of pink.

"I may have had a little fun. More than a little." Lark chuckles, then comes and gives me a hug. "Hope it helps." I'm still processing my survival kit when she heads to the wall and grabs her dance bag and her overnight one, looping them both over her shoulder. "I'm going to Delilah's for the next forty-eight hours so you can have some privacy. I'll have my phone if you need me for any solstice-related injuries. The thermostat's been set as low as we can go without getting in trouble with the landlord. There are snacks in the basket, ice packs, and special ice in the freezer I made just for you."

"Thanks, Lark." I may have the weirdest best friend on the face of the planet, and I wouldn't have it any other way.

"Don't mention it." She blows me a kiss, then heads for the door, calling over her shoulder, "Say hi to Jax for me."

"Will do."

As soon as the door shuts, I run to open the freezer, on the hunt for an ice pack and finding a silicone mold that's been labeled *Jojo*. Peeling up the top, there are about a dozen life-size dick-shaped ice cubes. If Lark were here, I'd glare, but I have to admit, part of me wants to pop them out and run them along my feverish skin.

Maybe I will...

"Jax," I call, hand above my glowing mark. *"I need you."*

"Are you okay?" His voice is low and frantic, concern hovering over each syllable.

"I will be," I say, not wanting to concern him. I swallow, trying to think of what to say. *"Lark got me a survival kit."*

There's a beat of silence, then Jax's smooth voice fills my mind. *"A survival kit?"*

"Yeah... For solstice."

"Okay. Color me curious... What did she give you?" I can picture him arching a silver brow at me, and goodness, I miss his face.

I'm suddenly shy, which is funny after the things we've shared. But maybe it's because we haven't done more than talk and flirt through our bond since I returned from Australia. Sadly, talking and flirting aren't going to cut it right now.

I need more.

"I'll tell you what's in it, but you have to promise me something."

"Anything, Tempest." If those two words don't stir my libido to life even more than it's already kindled... No ice bath can sate this fire within me. Only him. *"What do you want?"*

"I want to feel like you're here even if you're not... Tell me what to do." I'm trying to sound smooth, but I can't deny the plea in my tone. Having him in my heart, in my head, this last month has been incredible, the bond giving me constant reassurance, but soon he'll have to hibernate, and with each conversation we've had, I can sense his weariness. Until now.

I want to tip over the edge with him, despite the distance. *"Let's do solstice together."*

Jax's low growl rumbles through me. *"Oh, Tempest, I hope you know what you just unleashed."*

"What should I do?"

"We'll get to that. But first, tell me what's in this kit?"

I imagine Jax's lazy smile, eyes sparkling with mischief, wrapping a hand around himself and stroking so deliciously slow. The vision floods my veins, pooling between my legs. Every part of me tingles with desire.

It's all the courage I need as I go through my basket with him and begin to undress.

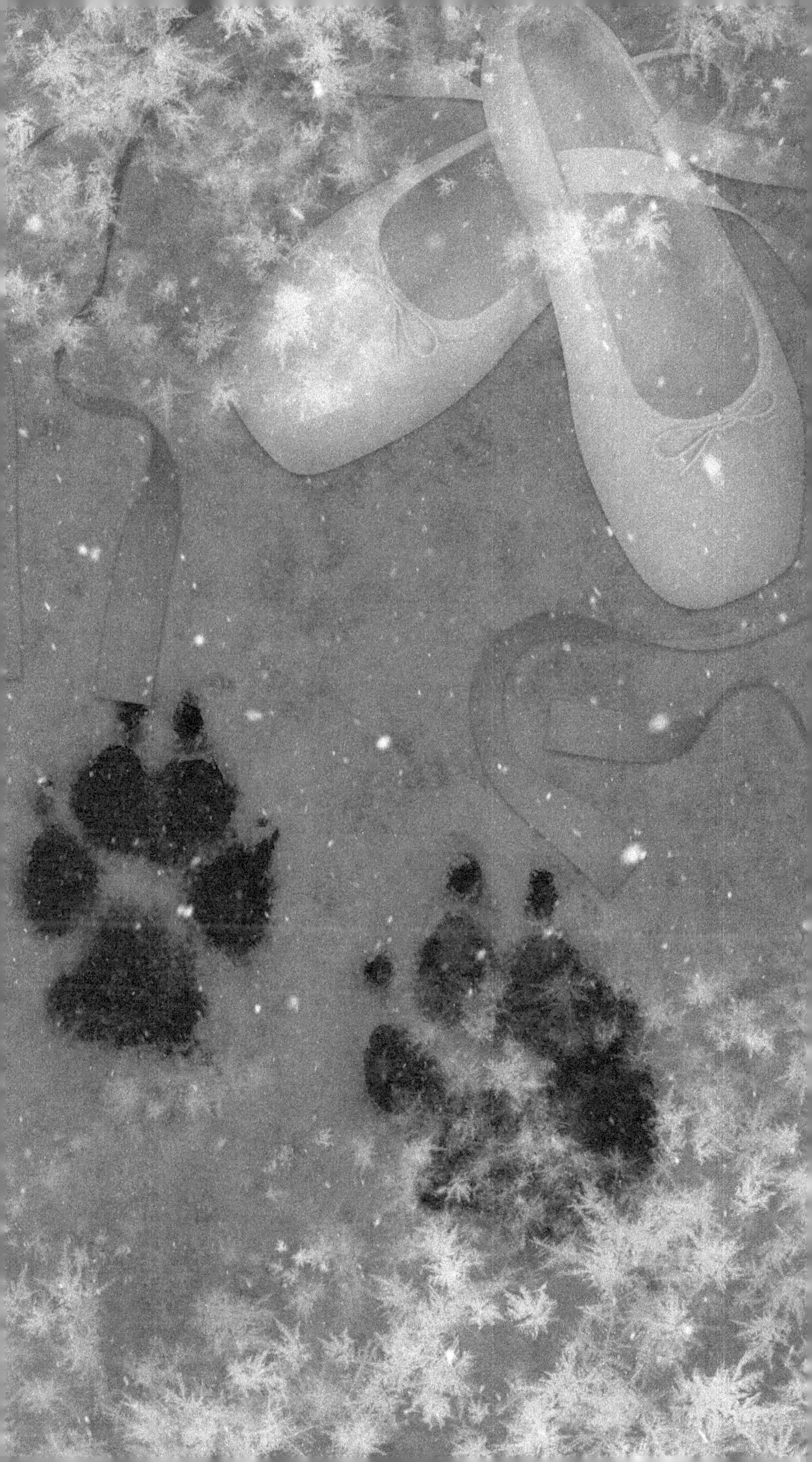

October
OCTOB
MO TU WE TH FR
2 3 4 5 6
9 10 11 12 13
16 17 18 19 20
23 24 25 26 27
30 31

JUNE
AUGUST
SEPTEMBER
DECEMBER

JOLIE

It's opening night and my first performance as a soloist with Ballet Potomac.

I loop the last section of my chiffon drapes around my pointer finger, then sweep through a few port de bras, admiring how the fabric follows the circular curves of my arms. The other two soloists are doing the same, each of us taking turns pinning our hair pieces in place, securing them to our buns. The three of us are the only ones dancing in both acts tonight, first with the corps in *Kingdom of the Shades*, then afterward in the second act with *Petite Mort*.

Knock, knock, knock.

"Ten minutes," comes the muffled voice of our stage manager.

We move in a flurry around the room, setting out our corseted costumes for Act II, tying up our pointe shoes, and painting our lips a rich mauve. Then we're off, floating toward the wings. Resin crunches beneath my toes.

"Break a leg, Tempest."

I nearly topple over. After solstice, Jax joined his other Frosts in deep sleep, resting and replenishing their energy. I wasn't expecting to hear from him until closer to winter. Not that I'm complaining. Jax's pride flares to life in my chest, and I slip my hand to my mate mark that's hidden beneath my leotard. *"You have impeccable timing. Aren't you supposed to still be in hibernation?"*

Bouncing in place, I shake out my arms, as if that would somehow release the nerves ping-ponging around my body. I can't predict when he'll be in my head, but I start most of our conversations since my schedule's been hectic. Besides, Jax doesn't want to distract me when I'm dancing, which I appreciate.

"Well, I set my alarm a little early." I savor the low rumble of his chuckle as I move upstage, tucking into the wings behind Veronique. Evelyn and Sara line up behind me. *"Besides, the nervous flutter of your heartbeat mixed with your anticipation was a pretty big giveaway. Don't think I could have slept through that. How much longer?"*

"The curtain's about to go up."

The lights are low, which they'll remain for the entirety of tonight's performance, only the pale sheen of blue lights casting an eerie glow over our white costumes.

"I know you'll do incredible." It's a beautiful reassurance. One that I need right now. At least until I see Lark and Delilah in the front row, cheering me on. *"I sent you a little gift since I can't be there. Wish I could see you tonight."*

"Same."

"Looking forward to hearing all about it later tonight. Love you."

"Love you, too."

"Merde," Veronique calls back to us.

"Merde," we all say in unison, shooting each other excited smiles when the orchestra begins to play.

One by one we step forward, sweeping our legs behind us into an arabesque with effortless control before our arms float up, the drapes creating a ghostly wing-like effect. Veronique's pointe shoe lifts up to my chest as she enters the stage. That's my cue. I join the dancers ahead of me, hazy-blue light turning me into a shade descending from the afterlife. All of us move down the sloping entrance until twenty-four ghosts haunt the stage with our ethereal elegance.

With no bright spotlight to dance under, it's hard to make out the audience. They are nearly a sea of black. Nearly. I bourrée, arms floating above me, and catch the blue-hued faces of Lark and Delilah smiling up from the front row. I stifle my smile, focusing on the movement and my fellow dancers within my peripheral vision. This piece is all about lines, grace, and execution as one captivating unit. When we break off, heading to the side of the stage, the three principals come out to the center, and I notice a flicker of movement.

It can't be...

My heart beats wildly in my chest and tears threaten to spill from my eyes and ruin my makeup, but the dance keeps me moving, second nature from rehearsing it so many times. I could do this piece in my sleep. But right now, I'm doing it in front of the woman who supported and sacrificed so much for me to be on this stage.

My mom.

She looks just as she did in life, but now her skin gives off a golden halo, the only light source coming from within the audience. Her hair has burnished streaks through its previously brown tresses, falling around her shoulders and looking wind swept.

The dance continues and I don't miss a beat. The smile on my mom's face widens with each passing phrase of music, warming me more than any spotlight could.

She's here.

I'm bolstered through the rest of my performance, and before I know it, it's intermission. I don't even want to exit the stage, worried that she'll disappear like a leaf on the wind, but when I turn to the wings, she's there, waiting for me. Following her out into the hallway, I look around to make sure no one else is there.

We have fifteen minutes of intermission and I need to get changed into my costume for Act II, but I won't miss the chance to see her. I pull her into a long hug. She smells of sweet apples and cinnamon, and on her neck is a single imprint in the shape of a maple leaf.

"You're a harbinger."

"I am."

"How?" I rasp. "I thought they were only mortals who didn't live fulfilled lives."

We pull apart and my mom clears her throat. "I fought the pull beyond the veil. Not when I couldn't be certain you'd be okay."

"I'm not." I don't know if I'll ever be.

"You will be." The corner of her lip turns up in a smirk. "A mother knows these things."

"So you're a harbinger because of me?"

Her lips pull into a line, as if weighing the question herself. "That's part of it...though I'm sure there's more to it than that." She takes my hands in hers, thumbing over my skin. Her touch is like the autumn breeze, delicate and comforting.

"They don't tell us why. Maybe we are meant to learn that on our own. But while you and your dreams were my priority, I stopped dreaming for myself." There's no resentment in her words, only honesty.

What had my mom wanted out of life? Did she ever wish

to fall in love again after my father left? Were there goals she never realized? It's funny how this is the first time I'm wondering about it, looking at my mother and seeing her as a person with her own wants and needs.

She swallows thickly. "Whatever the reason, I'm grateful for this chance to dream after death... Who knows, maybe I'll be blessed with a mate of my very own?"

She brushes my cheek and pulls me in for another hug.

"You were incredible tonight, sugarplum. I'm so proud of you," she whispers against my ear. I can't fight the tears, not when hearing her voice for the first time since she was alive. Not when I've spent months savoring her voicemail over and over.

"I miss you so much, Mom." My voice shakes, and she swipes away the tears with a gust of autumn wind.

"I miss you too. More than you'll ever know."

It's really her. Changed but still the woman who helped me try on my first pair of pointe shoes, took me to *Swan Lake*, told me time and time again that everything would be okay—until she couldn't.

Until things weren't okay anymore.

I push away the image of the last time I saw her. A horrific shell of who she was. Even though she's transformed, her harbinger form still somehow captures the comforting light she was for me in life. I'd much rather think of her this way. Staring at me with pride and joy and all the love I could ever wish for.

I guess some loves transcend life—taking us far beyond mortality.

"How? Have you been here all fall? How am I only seeing you now?"

"I'm still going through my training, not out in the world yet. Fate showed up and gave me transport here tonight."

Fate.

"She's here?"

"She's everywhere. Always." Mom smooths my hair against my head. "It's so good to see you, sugarplum."

I pull her in for another hug, savoring the solidness of her, that she's not just in my mind—a wishful thought turned reality.

"You better get ready for the second act." She presses a kiss to the crown of my head. "I can't wait to see you up there again. So beautiful. So happy." A golden tear streaks down her cheek and I wipe it away.

"I'm happy because you're here." I don't want this moment to end. I don't want to go and not see her again. It might break me.

"I'm here," she says, placing a hand over my heart. "Even when you can't see me, you carry me with you always."

"Will I see you again after tonight?"

"Yes, sweetie. You will." She squeezes me tightly, and I close my eyes, locking my arms around her, not wanting to let go.

The air shifts, cinnamon sweeps away on the breeze, and before I open my eyes, I know that she's returned to the audience, ready to support me, even in immortality. I sniff back tears as I head toward the dressing room, reminding myself of her words.

Even when you can't see me, you carry me with you always.

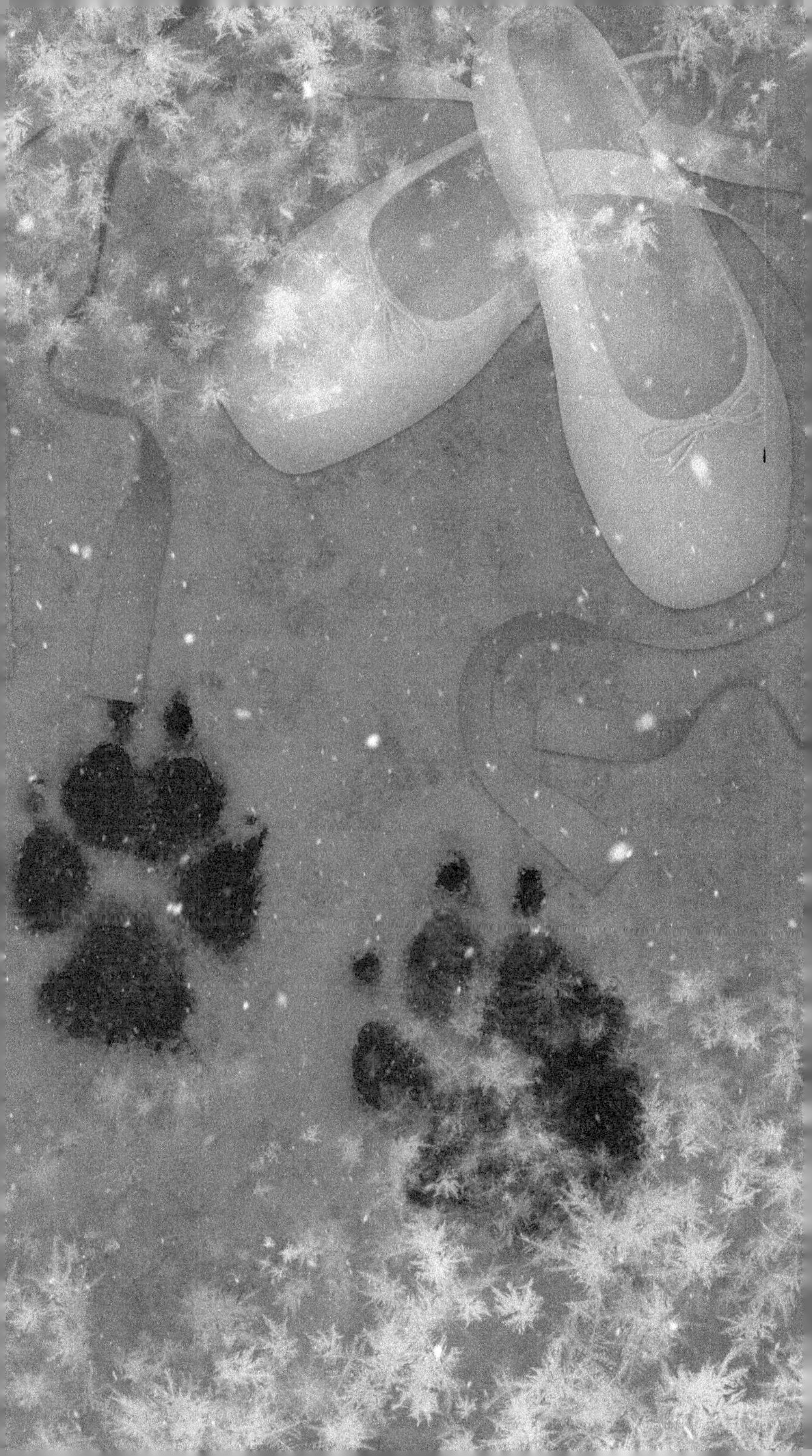

December
ОСТОБ

Chapter Fourty-Three

JOLIE

I've always loved winter, but the first sign of frost has never made me giddy. Not until today. It creeps around the windowpane, curving along the finger-drawn letters.

I'M HERE. TEMPEST.
SEE YOU SOON.

I'm still in bed, "Ice Cream" blaring from my phone. My eyes dart over to the thermostat, noticing it's dropped a few degrees. A smile peels up my lips and my hand goes to my mate mark. *"Where are you?"*

"Good morning. I see you got my message." His smooth baritone is every comfort I need. Even though his tone sounds calm, the excitement thrumming through my chest doesn't belong solely to me.

"Yes. You came by already?" I can't believe I missed it. *"Why didn't you wake me?"*

"You're so peaceful when you sleep."

I groan, wishing as he chuckles that he was here so I

could smack him with a pillow. *"You know, you're lucky you're my mate. Otherwise that would be a lot creepier sounding."*

"If I remember correctly, you still fell for me after my initial creeping."

"I'm pretty sure that sort of wooing only worked on Bella."

"Are you comparing me to a sparkly vampire?"

"If the stalkerish behavior fits," I quip, but before I make another snarky comment, it flits away, replaced by a realization. *"Wait. You actually know the reference?"*

"Yes, we learn about it during our Frost training. It's useful to know about how the mortals view anything related to our culture before we send new Frosts into the world... Though I have to admit, we tend to focus on Jacob. The better choice of the two. Obviously."

"Says the wolf."

"We'll see how much of a Team Edward fan you are the next time you want your feet warmed or are desperate to be stretched and quaking around my knot."

Well, damn.

I swallow hard, thinking far too much about Jax and his very special anatomy. How much I really do want to be quaking around him.

"Tempest..." His growl shakes through me. *"I need to get winter started before I get started with you. Otherwise, I won't get anything done."*

It's a sensual warning I have no intention of heeding. Once I'm done with rehearsals, that is. *"How much longer?"*

He groans and, god, I missed that sound. I can't wait to hear it up close, rasped against my skin. *"What time are you done with rehearsals?"*

"Four."

"I'll walk you home."

"I'll be counting down the minutes."

"Same, Tempest. See you then."

I jump out of bed and get ready at lightning speed. The fact that I'm running late to class is the only thing distracting me from freaking out over seeing Jax later. I'll be able to kiss him, hold him through the night. We got our wish to have him back on the East Coast. As much as I wanted to torment him into coming to me right away, I don't want to do anything that will have him sent elsewhere. This will be our first full season together.

Besides, I still have classes to attend.

When I get to the studio, I have about five minutes to warm up before company class hits the barre for pliés. Mistress Maral decides to mix things up, changing the combinations—which she does annually. It's nice to be learning them alongside everyone this time, not having to catch up. We're all a little lost together, but we get through the new changes with a shorter center and across the floor section of class. We're between performances, so after a short break we work on conditioning, followed by pas de deux technique where we practice different lifts. It makes the time go by swiftly, which I'm grateful for.

I'm lifted over Vincent's head, leg extended and back arched. We set the position, and once he feels steady, he walks in a circle around himself. My gaze passes the window, and I catch a white furry snout and captivating eyes peeking from an all-too-familiar spot.

"Focus, Tempest," Jax tuts. *"If he drops what's most precious to me, I'll have to get some icy retribution on my mate's behalf."*

I drag my attention back to the lift. Vincent sets me down before we continue the rest of the class. When everyone hits the ice baths and recovery room, I do a quick stretch and then grab my things, heading out the door.

Thank goodness today wasn't one of my PT days. I'm pretty sure I'd end up ditching poor Heather.

When I get outside, Jax is waiting for me, no longer in his earthside form. He puts his arm around me and we head to the metro. Though he seems a little unnerved sitting with me for the ride, he does.

"You know, you could just zip back to my place and meet me there."

"And miss another minute with you?" He crosses his arms. *"I don't think so."*

I rest my forehead on his shoulder, not caring if it looks a little odd. Everyone else is focused on the hustle and bustle of their own lives, I'm going to enjoy every moment of mine.

The entire walk back to the apartment, we talk while Jax continues to spread winter around DC. He sprinkles frost over the grass, wrangles the breeze with a blow of air from his lips and a swish of his arms. As we ascend each stair up to my floor, he draws ice along the rail and pulls down icicles from the awnings. It's so effortless and second nature. Little details I easily overlooked before.

Then we're in front of my door, my breaths painting the air white when his arms wrap around me. His bulge presses into my back. When I open the door, I have half a mind to jump him, but instead I'm met by Delilah's loud cheers. "Get over here, the game's about to start!"

"Umm... I know I said I'd watch tonight, but I actually really need a shower." Lark's got another *Nutcracker* performance tonight. In a few days, the show is closing for the season. Delilah and I have become a steady source of company for each other. It's been nice, but of course my mind is wandering to the things I'd like to be doing with Jax alone in my bedroom right now.

"Oh, okay. If you get done in time, come check out the rest!"

"Sounds good," I say, leading Jax toward the bedroom.

Delilah continues to cheer in the background. "Let's go Redhots!"

When I get to the door, I realize he has stopped, attention pinned to the screen Delilah's currently bouncing around in front of, clapping her hands.

I backtrack and nudge him with my elbow. "Want to stay and watch?"

"No, that's okay..." But there's something cracked in his tone.

"Actually, Delilah, I need to cool off before I shower."

She steps back and pats the couch. "Get on over here, then, Jojo."

I nod toward Jax, and he follows me to the couch, putting his arm around me as we sit together behind the Redhots' number one fan.

"Yeah, Winston, get around 'em!" Delilah cheers at the screen. Jax's arm tenses, but he doesn't look at me or say anything. "Go, go, go!"

"She's very enthusiastic." Jax laughs. He watches her reactions, the beautiful sound echoing throughout the room, though I'm the only one who can hear him. I memorize the way every piece of his silver-and-blue hair shakes with his vibrating body. It sends a heady buzz through me, joy spreading along our bond.

"You have no idea," I say, grabbing some Twizzler popcorn and tossing it into my mouth.

His brother skates toward the goal, smacking the puck into the net. We cheer alongside the crowd on TV as Winston Myles does a celebratory fist pump and his fellow players glide over to join him. Then he skates toward the bench, bumping gloves with each of his teammates down the line.

Jax's eyes glitter as he takes it all in.

We watch the rest of the game. Delilah's yelling makes up for Jax's silence. When it's over, he follows me to my room, holding my hand. The thermostat drops as soon as he enters.

So many emotions muddle our bond, a flurry of feelings I can't read. Whatever he's thinking, I want him to remember he's not alone. He'll never be alone again. Neither of us will.

I wrap my arms around him, pulling him close to me.

"You okay?" I ask, glad to finally not have to speak through the link.

"He's good. Older," Jax says, voice quieter than usual, laced with a sad sort of pride. "I knew he played, but I hadn't seen him in a while."

"How old was he the last time you visited him?"

His brows draw together. "Twenty, I think, give or take a season."

Based on the articles I've found online, Winston Myles is thirty-three years old. It's been almost thirteen years since Jax has last seen his brother. I had done the math when I learned about them both. If Jax had lived beyond the accident, he'd be about thirty-nine now. I cross the room to my drawer and snatch out my journal, handing it to him. "Here."

Stepping backward until he can sit on the mattress, Jax flips to the first page, then the next. Each one's filled with articles I've compiled about his life and his brother's. Page by page he continues to read, a few tears tracking down his cheeks that he wipes away. When he gets to my entries with long, bulleted lists of wins and paragraphs cataloging our moments, together and apart, I hold my hand out for him. "I'll take that back now."

"Worried about me reading something in particular?"

"There's nothing in there you haven't experienced first-hand." It's our story scratched onto the pages, words and doodles I return to when Fate and the seasons keep him away. A physical reminder of my belief. "It helped me cope while I missed you. I wanted to know about you. Your life. I also thought maybe you'd want to know too. I meant to show it to you in Australia, but you were so angry when I brought up your brother..."

"I'm sorry. I wasn't angry." He kisses me, deepening it a moment before he rests his forehead on mine.

The blues and silvers of his eyes glint with their mesmerizing, prismatic flecks. I'll never tire of letting them hypnotize me.

"Sometimes it's easier to keep that part of my existence separate. Even if it's a part of me. I don't want to forget my mortality, but sometimes it just hurts too damn much."

"I understand." I cup his cheek with my palm, his chill seeping into the pads of my fingertips. "It's how I feel about the accident. It's easier to pretend it didn't happen, but eventually, it catches up to me and I'm hit with the pain that my mom is gone all over again. Or at least I did, until I saw her." I give him a small smile, thinking back to seeing her as an autumn harbinger. While I didn't want the night to end, I carry her with me like she reminded, and I hold on to her promise that she'll see me again one day. "Thanks for that."

"You already thanked me." He nuzzles my nose with his own, then traces it up to press a kiss to my forehead.

"Well, there are many things to thank you for." He saved me, revived my life, turning my story into something beautiful despite the tragedies that could never be unwritten.

Jax sucks in a breath, and though I can't articulate the words, I let him feel the weight of them through our bond. I press up onto my tiptoes and drift my lips along his, then nip the bottom one before kissing him with the force of two lost seasons. I kiss him like we have all the time in the world and no time at all, savoring and devouring him all at once. "In fact, I'm very eager to show my gratitude in person."

"Is that so?" He arches a brow. "What did you have in mind?"

Pressing my palm to his mate mark, I lower him to my comforter. I straddle his waist and his hands grip my thighs. "If I remember correctly, you mentioned something about quaking around your knot earlier?" I reach for the hem of my shirt, lifting it over my head. "Think you'd be up for a demonstration?"

My mate mark glows between us, and his chest heaves, pupils blowing away the prisms of his irises. His body comes to life beneath mine, and I rock back and forth over the bulge, wanting to taste him and feel the fullness of him settled within me.

Jax cocks his head at me, a mischievous grin spreading across his face. "I think I can manage that."

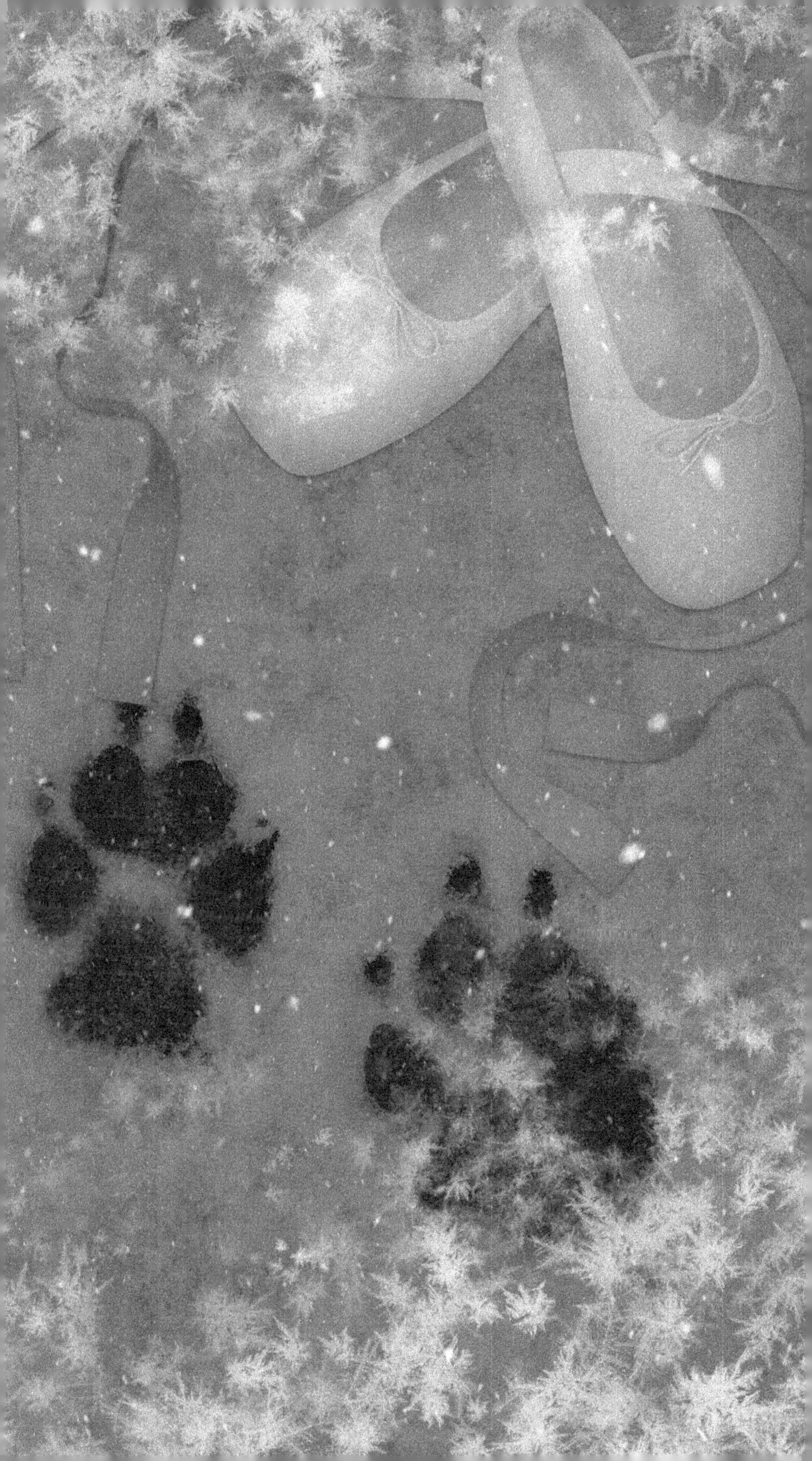

MO
3   4
10   11
17   18
24   25   26
31
MO   TU   WE   TH   FR
OCTOB.
2   3   4
9   10   11   5   6
16   17   18   12   13   14
23   24   25   19   20   21   22
30   31   26   27   28   29
January

JAX

Pajama-clad children peek through windows, pointing their tiny fingers in my direction. Their eyes are alight with merriment. One jumps back from the windowsill, returning a few moments later with their mother, gesturing with grins across their face. I love kids. Their joy is infectious and they are usually the most appreciative of my work.

I spin, whipping up wind and zipping around the dimly lit Dorset cul-de-sac. White flecks erupt from my palms, spraying into the sky in all directions before they dance and scatter toward the ground.

"Jax. I need you."

Tempest.

She doesn't need to summon twice.

I throw more bushels of snow, giving an invisible bow to my audience, then I shoot up to the cloud line, releasing a flurry from my fingertips.

Waving over to Aneira, she gives me a quick salute, already knowing where I'm heading.

It's been a little over a month since I came out of hibernation and returned to my mate. Together, we've celebrated my first holidays since being mortal. I've burned my tongue on hot cocoa, built a snow family, danced under the moon-light with Jolie. When she's not busy at rehearsal, we are always together, cramming in as many memories as possi-ble. It's a strange sort of normal I wish we could get used to.

But we can't.

I press my hand to the mate mark, going to her, and finding myself inside a large, brightly lit building. People walk past and through me, but I don't see her. Something pitches in my stomach. Just then, I spot Delilah. I draw closer until the crowd parts and there she is.

My mate.

"What do you need?" I ask her, only Lark noticing outside of the two of us.

Her tone had been urgent, but here she is with a big smile on her face.

"I'm so pumped. Thanks for the tickets, Jojo!" Delilah's loud voice carries over the crowd. She throws her hands up in the air. "Redhots are gonna dominate tonight!"

I freeze in place.

That's when I notice it. Everyone around us is dressed in red-and-white jerseys, beanies, and hoodies. Colors of the Richmond Redhots. A few are wearing a blue-and-green combo, representing whatever team they're playing tonight. Jolie gives me a half-apologetic smile.

"Of course! You spoiled us in Australia, figured it's the least I could do," she says to Delilah with a shrug.

Lark looks between the two of us, then puts an arm around Delilah. "Why don't we grab some drinks?"

"Sure thing."

"Want anything?" Delilah asks Jolie.

She shakes her head. "I'm good."

The pair stroll toward concessions, leaving Jolie and I standing there in silence. I barely feel the people passing through my body, too focused on her and why she brought me here.

I know the reason, but I need to hear her say it. "Tempest…"

"Hear me out." She puts her hands up, not even using our connection. No one notices her talking to seemingly empty air. They're too busy shuffling into the arena to catch the game. A game *my brother* is playing in. He's somewhere in this building. Within reach.

"We're just going to watch. I know how long it took for me to come around to the idea of believing in you. If you decide you want to try that later, I'll help. But let's go in and watch." She waves me over. "Come on."

"Fine." I'm shocked, but I can't deny her. She's at least made it clear she's not going to force me to do anything. I sigh, resigned, and loop my arm around her as we move inside with the crowd.

I follow Jolie to her seats, waiting with her until Lark and Delilah show up with their treats.

"These seats are awesome!" Delilah cheers, and I'm fully prepared to enjoy her hoots and hollers during the game.

Jolie takes the seat at the end of the row and I hang out in the aisle. Lark smiles over at us both. I'm nervous, but there's something reassuring about being here with them. Even though Delilah doesn't know about me, she and Lark have taken care of my mate when I couldn't. That means everything to me.

The players skate out and the announcer introduces the starting line-up. My eyes are glued to the number 12, MYLES staring back at me from my brother's jersey.

It's him.

He's right there.

His face is hidden under his mask, but I've seen the articles, watched the games. Witnessing Winston as an adult is like someone pressed the fast-forward button on my life. For a moment, I can almost pretend that I never died. That I didn't memorize the crescent scar beneath his glove down to the last faded tooth mark. That I just forgot the middle of our story and I'm here now, watching my little brother play hockey.

I have to remind myself that I'm in the arena. An immortal. Because the past threatens to drown me all over again right here on the ice. It's where my mortal life ended. For a while, the pain of what I lost was unbearable, until I found a focus. A way to cope. My frost marks, becoming Lead Albidus, they were goals—something I could work toward that would help other lost Frosts like myself.

I did my duty. I brought winter to the mortal world and I was damn good at it. Then one day, without warning, the ache I'd learned to exist with became bearable. I was grateful and angry at myself for it. But then I'd see my family and that old wound reopened. It did each time I tried to see them until I stopped. A flimsy Band-Aid over a deep, gaping wound.

And tonight, Jolie ripped it off. Only this time, she's here with me, watching from the stands, knowing I need her for this.

The game kicks off and Delilah doesn't disappoint. Her wild antics soften the emotional blow of seeing my brother. She stands the whole time, waving her arms, no different than she does at home—only maybe a smidge louder. Not that anyone cares. There are tons of people around us screaming and cheering as well.

Winston sweeps the ice with the other players, faster and more strategic than his opponents by leaps and bounds. "He's amazing."

"Yes, he is."

I can't stop watching him. It's like seeing Jolie on stage, experiencing the joy of her doing what she loves. They're ignited. My brother loves hockey. He wasn't as obsessed with it as I was when we were kids. He went along with it because I dragged him out to play with me. Now he does. I can see it in the gait of his strides, the lift of his chin, the tension held in his grip. The power behind his celebratory fist pump when he scores.

"Go on," Jolie urges me in a whisper. "Enjoy your invisibility and get the best seat in the house."

"You're sure?" Excitement, along with a heavy dose of nerves, floods my veins.

"I'm sure."

I flit closer. Pride fills my chest, remembering all the days playing together, our dad teaching us and pretending to make calls in a booming voice as if he were an announcer.

Then I'm skating alongside Winston.

I'm the wind propelling him forward. The ghost cheering at his back. When he scores again, I fly up and bump his fist with my own.

He brings it down, halting his skating. I almost think I see him stare at his glove afterward. Like he can sense I'm here.

Logically, I know he can't, but I'm by his side whether he believes I am or not. My passion became my brother's, and every time he glides out onto the ice, he takes a piece of me with him.

I press my mark and fly back to Jolie, kissing her temple and holding her while we watch the rest of the game. The crowd roars, the arena full of rabid Redhots fans. It's a high unlike any other. Since becoming immortal, I don't think I've been more surrounded by love. But this feeling has nothing to do with the crowd of thousands.

It has everything to do with him and *her*.

She's given me the most precious gift. Tonight, I realize I haven't been as invisible as I thought.

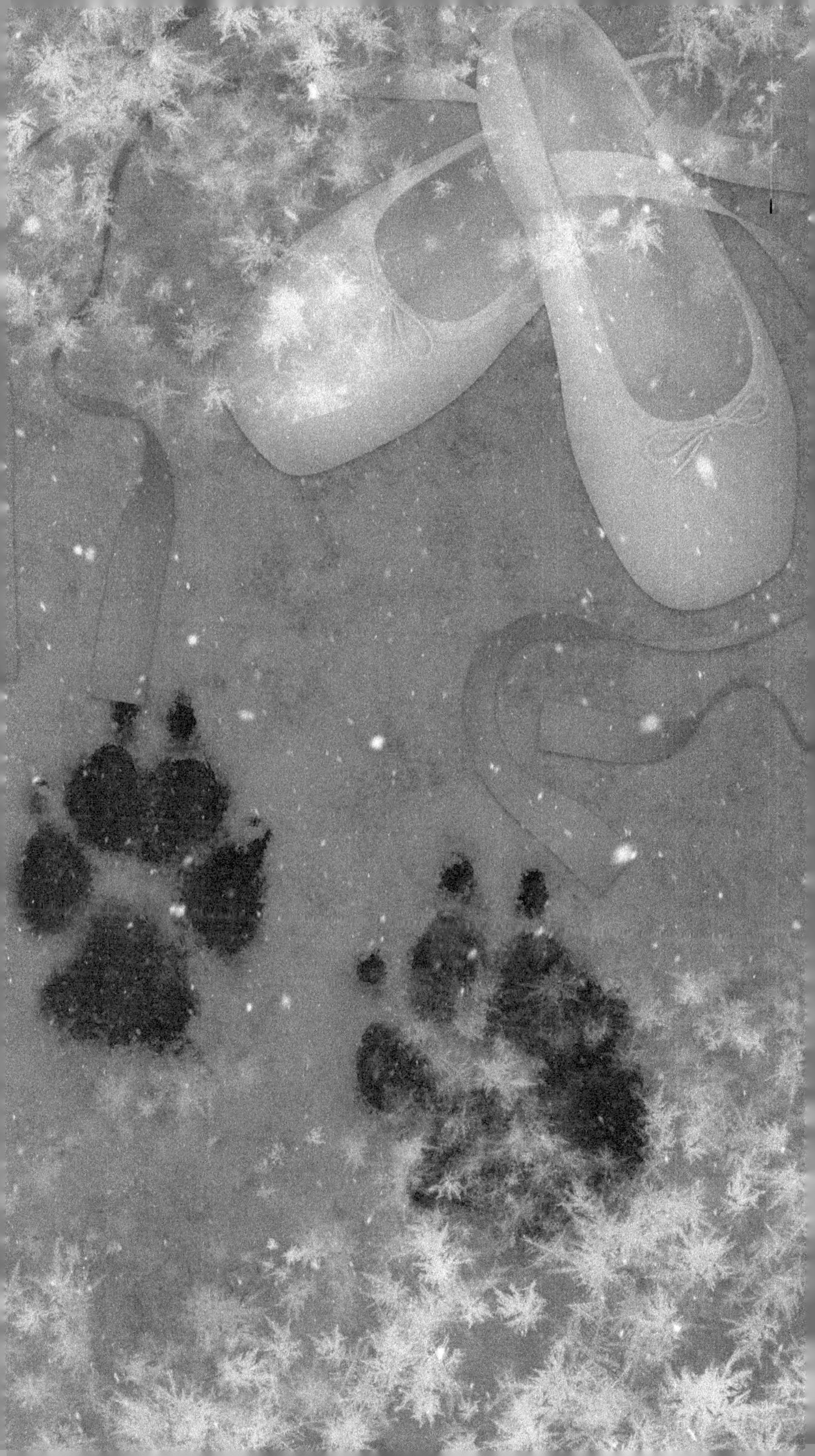

February
OCTOB
3
10 11
17 18
24 25 26
31
MO   TU   WE   TH   F
2   3   4   5   6
9   10   11   12   13
16   17   18   19   20   14
23   24   25   26   27 28 29
30   31

Chapter Forty-Five

JOLIE

The pot hisses, steam billowing into my face. I lean into the chill pressed against my back, Jax's arms wrapped around me while I stir the macaroni.

"Looks like Phil missed his shadow once again." The newscaster's voice filters into the kitchen from the TV. Delilah's doing a sudoku while the news plays in the background. "Spring's coming early."

Their voice is excited, trilling with anticipation for the new season ahead. But all I feel is dread. A stone sinking into my gut, rippling into acidic waves. I crane my neck to look at Jax, but his expression gives away nothing.

"Be back in a few hours, Jojo," Lark calls over, rushing out of her room and putting the backs onto her oversized art-deco earrings. She waves a silent goodbye to Jax. I'm not sure why she's never suggested letting her girlfriend in on my secret. But I do know that as amazing as Delilah is, she tends to scoff at anything that goes beyond facts and logic.

"See ya." I keep my tone casual, not wanting her to worry.

Delilah flips off the TV, standing up from the couch and following Lark out the door for an early Valentine's date.

"You knew about spring, didn't you?" I say as soon as the lock clicks behind them.

Jax swallows audibly, and I turn to face him. "We were summoned back to Nivea for a meeting."

"When?"

"A few days ago." His prismatic gaze drops to mine, all the sorrow I'm feeling reflected right back at me.

"Why didn't you tell me?"

"Because leaving you is already hard enough." He sighs, then brushes back some strands of my hair and cradles my jaw. "I'd rather enjoy every moment we get until I have to."

"Wouldn't I eventually figure it out when solstice hits and I'm rabid for you?"

"Well, yes, but then I'd have an easy way to distract you," he says with a growl. He leans over and nips the base of my throat where the scars of his claiming bite remain. It sends a full-body shiver through me, my underwear becoming damp.

Stupid, sexy harbinger and his mate magic.

He'd actually be here for this one, able to sate my need for him in person. As much as I was looking forward to a solstice together, I hate that it also means Jax will be returning to Nivea for at least another season. And he'll need to hibernate for some of that, meaning he'll be unreachable. I've been much too spoiled having had months where we could talk all day, even when we were separated. That's going to end soon. There's no plan in place for after this. We've just been savoring this winter together.

"I don't want you to go."

"I know. I hate it too," he says ruefully. I open my mouth to speak but then clamp it shut. Jax arches a brow. "What is it?"

I blurt the words out, something I've wondered during

our time apart but have been too scared to give voice to. "Do you ever regret saving me?"

"Never, Tempest. Not even once." There's no hesitation in his tone. It's hard as steel and twice as sharp.

"But we wouldn't ever have had to be apart. I'd be a harbinger like you, like my mom, even if we were designated to different seasons." My heart thuds loudly in my chest, and Jax's palm rests over it until its rhythm slows. "It would be easier."

"You're right that things would be easier, but I wouldn't have changed a single thing," he says, thumbing my mate mark. His glows back at me from his bare chest, and I reach out to touch it, not missing the twitch beneath his waistband. "Other than maybe getting stuck watching you with that idiot, Blake. I could have done without that."

Oof. I glare and punch him gently for that one.

"But I look at everything you've done, how much you've grown. Maybe I would have had you already, but I'd be missing out on the incredible person you've become." He kisses me softly—once, twice, three times—before reaching past me and grabbing the wooden spoon, stirring the water on the stove before it boils over.

I quickly grab the potholder and strain the noodles, finishing up my macaroni and cheese while I talk. It's the only thing keeping me from breaking into tears. I don't want to cry right now. I want to be able to discuss this. "How long will we do this, Jax? How many seasons will Fate keep us apart?"

Jax nudges my bowl closer, and I dish my lunch out and grab a spoon. He follows me back to my room, sitting on the bed while I sit in the desk chair, spinning it to face him. I know if I join him on the bed, he'll become too distracting, so I keep a healthy distance and shovel some macaroni into my mouth.

Clasping his hands in his lap, he taps his foot nervously on the floor. After a minute, he sighs, expression becoming serious. "I don't know how long. But whatever time I bought you when I begged Fate to bring you back, I want you to have. I don't want you to miss out on a single thing that life can offer." His eyes drop to the floor and his lips press into a thin line. "Even when you can't see me, can't reach me, I'll be there through it all."

My chest aches. I don't want him to think I'm ungrateful that he saved me, for being able to dance again, for the time we've gotten together over the last year, I just hate the circumstances. The way our love is constantly racing against a ticking clock that neither of us has control over. "Promise?"

"Of course, Tempest," Jax says, crossing the room in two strides and kneeling at my feet. His strong hands slide to the outsides of my thighs, and I set down my macaroni. Taking my hands in his, he kisses each knuckle, then cups them in his own. His hypnotic irises peer up into mine, and he holds my gaze like he refuses to ever let it go.

"It's never truly goodbye. Not for a love like ours."

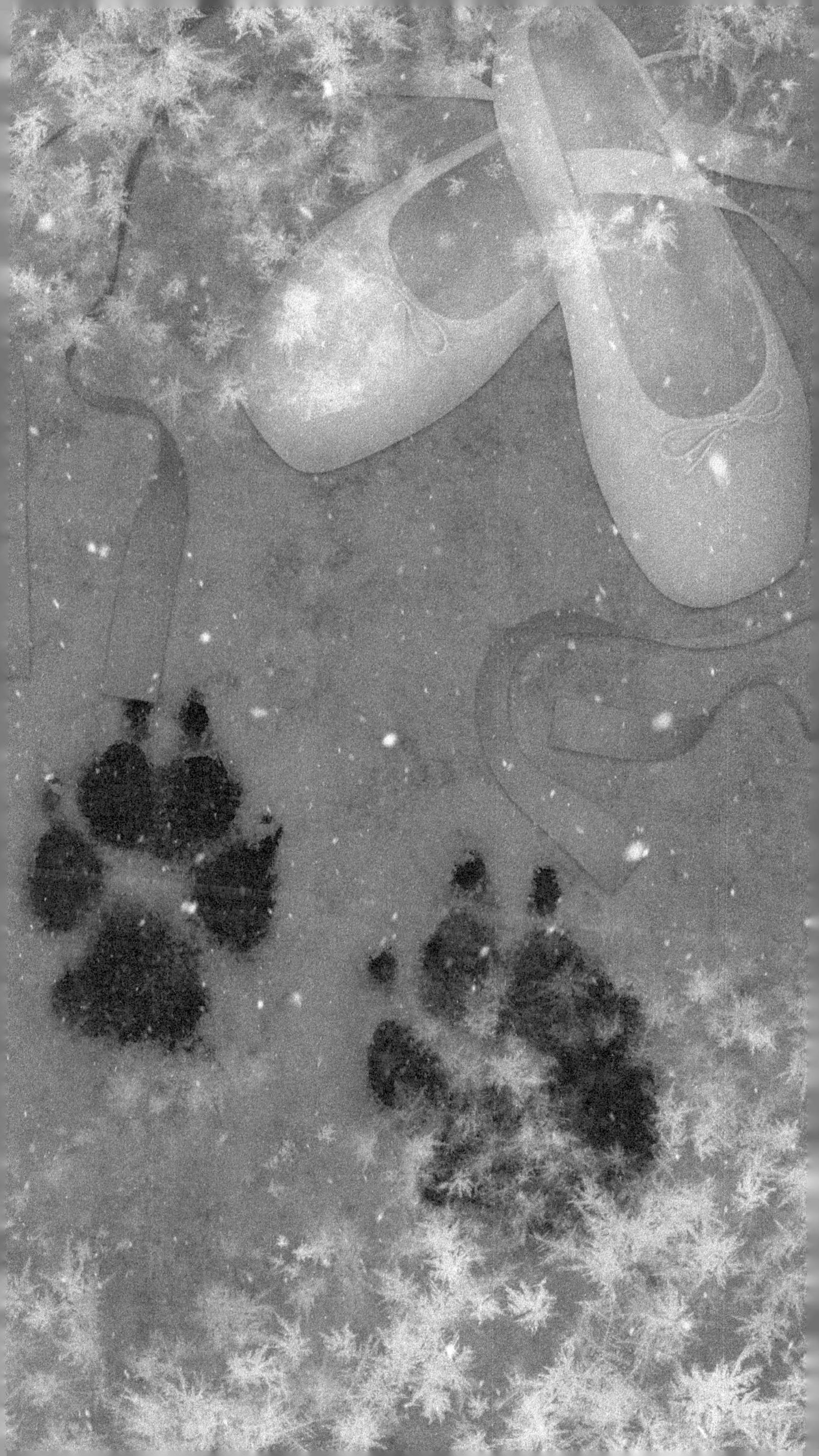

15 seasons
later
OCTOBE

Chapter Fourty-Six

JOLIE

Fifteen seasons come and go, but we never say goodbye. Not truly.

Every moment we've had together I hoard away, collecting them in my journal until it's filled, replaced, filled again. Our love captured between the pages for no one but myself.

Lark joined Ballet Potomac as a soloist with a guaranteed track to principal. We promoted side by side two years later. I indoctrinated her to ice baths, and she continues to provide me with solstice survival kits. We watch hockey with Delilah, and Jax goes to every Redhots game he can when he's earthside.

Despite the distance, our love continues to grow. Even when he's away and unreachable, I can feel him. He's the whisper of the wind, the cold settled in my bones, the flakes that fall outside. The sun can be shining, the windows clear and untouched, and the flowers in bloom, and he's still here with me.

Always with me.

He's the silver-glowing scar spun at my sternum, cradled between the neckline of a feathered corset. The patter of my pointe shoes when I run to my spot, adjusting my headpiece one last time before springing onto the tips of my toes. The caress of fog as the scenery opens and reveals me to the audience.

My steps slow and falter, carrying me across the stage in a series of beautiful extensions. Desperate sways and arches. He's the breeze that kisses my skin when I take that final tragic leap into an unforgiving pond. The one who'd truly follow me there.

Already has.

He's the roar of applause when the sea of swans part and Vincent leads me to the front. The warmth of the spotlight as I curtsy, and curtsy, and curtsy, savoring every moment until the thick velvet curtain drops on closing night.

He's the standing ovation earned from a dream built on borrowed time.

This last year as principal has been incredible, but my leg throbs as I cart three overstuffed bouquets of roses toward my dressing room.

"I don't want you to retire," Lark says, pulling off her black-feathered headpiece and setting it on the vanity. "I'm really going to miss you."

"I'll miss you too, Lark." I hand her one of my bouquets. "I'm just grateful we got to dance together again. I'm grateful for it all."

We finish getting out of our costumes, go out for celebratory drinks with the company, and cheers to all our hard work before we dance our way home. It's a beautiful night. A stunning finale. Everything I could ask for.

After Lark tucks herself into bed, I wait for the gentle sounds of her breathing to filter under the door before I head for the balcony, admiring the autumn leaves carried along the breeze. Wrapping my arms around myself, I recall my mother's words and wonder the truth of them.

She's everywhere. Always.

"Fate," I rasp out to no one but the moonlight.

And I wait.

And wait.

And wait.

When a hand grips my shoulder, I spin around, half expecting to find Lark awake and ready to drag me back into the apartment.

Instead, a woman in a striking rainbow-hued dress is there. Rose gold locks billow around her, colorful streaks embedded in them. She reaches for me, her outstretched palm shimmering beneath the moonlight.

"You're beautiful," I say, a bit stunned. I imagined Fate to be older, less...vibrant. But the woman before me is timeless, a walking dream, one I could never conjure up on my own. "You know why I've called you?"

She nods but says nothing. Betrays nothing.

My legs are numb, fingers quivering as they grip my sides. I don't know where I'm going. What will happen. Regardless, there's one thing I'm certain of: Dance may be the love of my life, but Jax is the love of my existence.

That courage propels me forward. I slip my hand into hers and whisper so softly that my words could be mistaken for the breeze.

"It's time."

And with a featherlight brush of Fate's lips against my temple, the cold comforts me in its chilling embrace.

Chapter Fourty-Seven

JAX

Brown strands tugged between my fingers...

Icy blues engulfing my very being.

Tracing along her cheeks with my nose, inhaling her sweet, spiced scent...

Flushed skin quivering against the panes of my chest.

Soft lips, a sweet tongue, and the playful nip of teeth...

Even in hibernation, Jolie's with me. She's always on my mind. I can always sense her joy, sorrow, and strength, thanks to the mate mark emblazoned on my chest. Every time she dances, the music echoes through her bones, pulsing within my own, just as her heart beats within my chest with its comforting thrum. A metronome I use to measure the months apart.

Thump-thump, thump-thump.

Thump-thump, thump-thump.

Thump-thump.

Thump-thump.

Thump.

Thump.

I TOSS AND TURN.

Waiting.

Silence.

I continue to rock, fighting my deep slumber as I wait for that pounding. That pulse. A melody that's etched itself between my ribs.

But it doesn't come.

SOMETHING'S WRONG.

DRAGGING myself out of hibernation is always a struggle. I've worked extra hard during the winters I can see Jolie, not wanting to do anything to lose more time with her. If that means doubling up my icy workload as I deliver winter up and down the east coast, then so be it.

She'll always be worth it.

My eyes snap open. Popping up in bed, I bring my palm over my chest, waiting for the steady thud... Even a faint one...

Silence.

I spring out from the covers, padding across the room—

That's when I see the curls of words woven between frost along my windowsill.

I'm here.

I'm. Here.

Fuck.

No, no, no.

This can't be happening.

I stagger out of my room, my body adjusting to the

drastic movements after sleeping for weeks. When I see her standing before me, I freeze.

"Tempest?" I rasp.

Rich navy locks with a large chunk of silver frame the left side of her glittering porcelain face. Those icy-blue eyes still hold their same shade, only now they shimmer in captivating facets like two aquamarine gems. She's beautifully ethereal in a way I could never imagine. Wouldn't dare to. A cream-colored tulle skirt hangs just below her knees with a matching cropped sweater exposing an inch of skin. There are no marks adorning it like mine.

Not yet.

The corner of her mouth lifts, a sharpened canine glinting back at me. "You said you'd always find me, so I figured I'd return the favor."

I take two weak steps toward her, my feet dragging across the floor, until my forehead rests against hers. Our chests heave in unison, her faint periwinkle lips only a breath away from mine.

"Why?"

Fate stands behind her, and I shoot her the pain I can't bring myself to show Jolie right now. How many times have I dreamt that she'd be here by my side? Envisioned our life raising young Frosts and dancing among the mortals, building flurries and blizzards and marvelous winters.

"Did I do something wrong?" I knew her time was borrowed. Fate had warned me all those winters ago when I'd sought her out. But I thought she'd have more of it. "When I saved her, you said there was no guarantee she'd become a harbinger. That I might have doomed us both."

"You didn't do anything wrong," Fate says, tone calm and silvery, like she's talking to a wounded animal. In a way she is. "You were willing to wait forever."

Jolie grips my chin and directs my gaze back to her. "But I wasn't." Her palm sweeps along my cheek, no longer leaving a trail of fire, but my skin still tingles beneath her touch. "I called on Fate, not the other way around."

"But how are you one of us?" I swallow down the last bitter dregs of fear. She's mine and she's here, and that fills me with a joy I don't deserve. She should still be out there, doing what she loves. "I sacrificed to give you more time. A full life." *Something I'd never gotten the chance at.* "The day I found you in that lake, I saw your wishes, your hopes and dreams. I wanted you to have all of them."

"That's the problem. Those dreams, those wishes, changed." Jolie lifts to her tiptoes and nuzzles her nose against mine. "There is no full life for me without you, Jax." She reaches for my hands and folds them into her own, bringing them to her mate mark. Then her lips brush along my jaw, my cheek, grazing the shell of my ear. Her whisper hums through every part of me. "*This* is my full life. *Our* full life."

Visions of skating along the city center, sipping frozen cocoa, burying myself within her for hours with nothing but the breeze kissing our skin, all dance through my head. We'll do it all. And more.

Time is no longer borrowed. It's as infinite as we are.

"*Ours,*" I repeat.

And though we've already claimed each other many seasons ago, the word has never been full of more promise.

More hope.

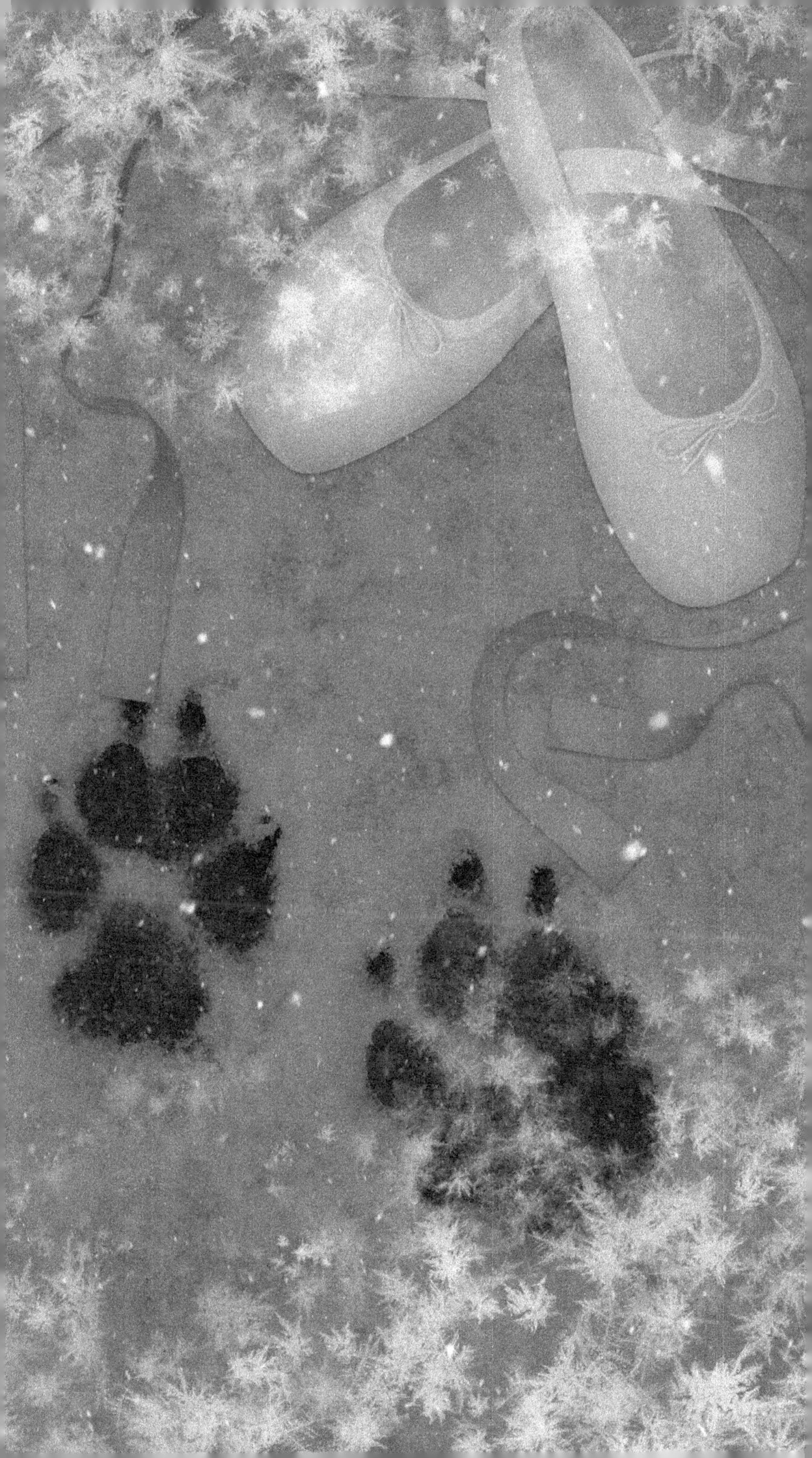

Epilogue

The wolf chases his mate between the trees, her silver tail swishing with each leap through the snow. She growls playfully, turning around to face him, jaunting back and forth on all fours. The moon highlights the white tips of her gray fur as he sprints for her. This time, she doesn't run off. The pair roll across the snow, nipping at each other, nuzzling under the stars. No one enters these woods in the winter, making it the perfect playground for these Frosts to leap and bound through.

She's still getting used to this form, along with her immortal one, but her mate is captivated by her beauty in them all. He growls, pinning her down by her throat, his canines grazing her fur. He licks her face before darting away, and it's her turn to chase after him.

As the sky brightens, the wolves disappear from mortal view and tend to their Frost duties. The harbinger paints each oak he passes in a shimmering white until every tree in the forest is under winter's spell. Icicles hang from branches, glistening around the mouths of caverns, and a light layer of white is scattered through the grass.

Hiding behind a deadened tree trunk, he crouches down and watches her.

His mate.

She twirls along holly bushes, flicking delicate strands of ice atop their pointy leaves. She prances, gliding across the snow on her tiptoes, waving her arms, brushing the wind with such force that it rattles the plants surrounding her.

Always his tempest.

Her laughter chimes along the breeze, unnoticed by the families strolling through the park early this morning. She knows he's near, it's impossible for her not to sense him. The mate mark in her chest glows brightly.

Popping out from the trees, she dashes out of reach, and he follows, giving her a bit of a head start before capturing her in his arms. He spins her away, then back in, snowflakes flurry out from her fingertips. They dance for no audience, unworried about the steps but completely in sync—as if their shared heartbeat never faded away. All they see is each other. The world merely exists around them, a blur of silver and white.

Fate watches from her ledge, admiring her handiwork. Ripples across a rainbow-streaked pond, some she set in motion, others beyond her control. The silvery stone appears beneath the whirls of colors as she stirs it with her palm. She knew she could get them here, even if the path had been washed away—or crushed within her grasp. They'll never know the lengths she went to, but watching them together fills her with pride that can only be achieved through struggle. Enduring.

Catching the rock, she lifts it out of the pool and presses a kiss to it, feeling the biting chill of frost nip at her lips. She slips it into the pocket of her skirt, letting it clack against the others.

Waltzing to the scale, she furrows her brow and leans closer to inspect each nook and cranny, checking for any fissures that could throw things off balance with her latest additions. Once she's given it her seal of approval, she reaches into her dress and pulls out the silvery stone between two fingers, marveling over the nearly imperceptible feathered markings giving it a rich texture. Holding her breath, she thumbs over them as she slowly sticks the stone on the right side, knowing before it happens that it'll sink, lowering an inch as the other side lifts higher. And higher.

That won't do.

Luckily, she has a plan. A way to balance the scales. Drawing three rocks out from her pocket, she swirls them in her hand, listening to them scrape against each other. Spinning back toward the left side, she rises up on the balls of her feet, placing them on the flat surface one at a time. First the lavender, then the seafoam green, and finally the gold. They clatter, one after another, and the scale groans as it shifts.

Perfect.

Pride blossoms in Fate's chest at the sight of her harmonized creation. Her assistance with Jax Frost proved to be more meddlesome than she'd planned for, but with a few tweaks, everything should balance out soon enough...

Starting with spring.

Thank You

FOR READING

It brings me so much joy to finally have Jax and Jolie's story out in the world. I figured I'd share some backstory as to how *Etched in Frost* came about…

Before the broody Jack Frost from *Rise of the Guardians*, there was *Jack Frost* the adorable claymation movie made in 1979. I grew up loving to watch the holiday classics every winter and his movie always stood out to me. It was my favorite, for whatever reason, even though it made me cry because Jack Frost never really got his happy ending.

While Jax is his own magical character, his inspiration was borrowed from facets of these two Jacks that came before him. I've known for a few years that I wanted to do a Jack Frost reimagining but it was still too early to do anything with the idea.

Then about a year ago, I was talking to my friend Thea. We were reminiscing about dancing growing up.

If I wasn't in school, you could probably find me at the studio rehearsing or at home stretching or practicing. It was as necessary to me as the air I breathed. I continued to dance through college and eventually stopped, due to a long-standing permanent hip injury (yes, the very same one Jolie had).

Thea asked if I would ever write a dancer into my

stories. At the time I didn't have a clue if I would. I was wholly focused on finishing out my *Blaze Legacy* dark fantasy series. The problem was, after a series of setbacks and rejections in author life, I was having the hardest time getting the story down.

I was in a huge mental funk.

It felt like no matter how hard I worked, no matter how many books I published, how much of my soul I poured between the pages, that nothing I did was enough.

About a month later, in December, I was watching a dance performance on TV and two kernels popped into my head: ballet and Jack Frost. I couldn't get Jax and Jolie's story out of my head. *Etched in Frost* had carved its mark into me.

At first I hesitated because we were getting ready to move cross country. I didn't know if I could add an extra book to my 2024 publishing schedule. Luckily, I had some of the most incredible people in my corner. They encouraged me to follow my frosty muse and write the story that nagged to be told.

I'm so glad I did. The few months I spent writing *Etched in Frost* pulled me out of my mental slump. It was the story I needed to write for myself.

It's a story about love. About sacrifice. But at its heart, it's a story about being seen, not just by others, but by yourself.

I hope this story reminds you of the impact you have, even when you might not see it.

If you have a moment to leave some stars and a review on Amazon & Goodreads, even just a few words makes a big difference! Share with anyone you think would love *Etched in Frost*. You are the way fellow readers find indie authors and their work.

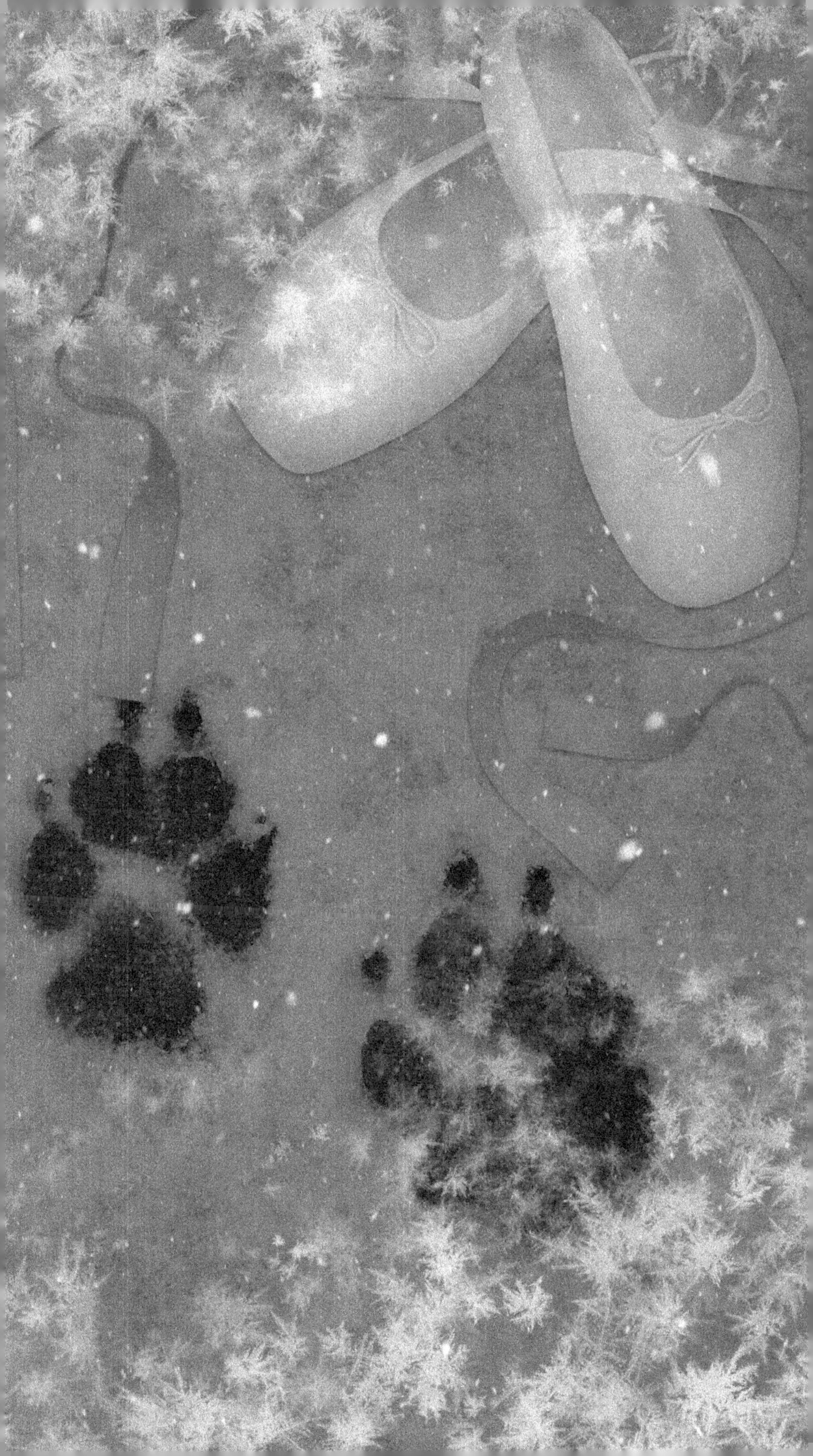

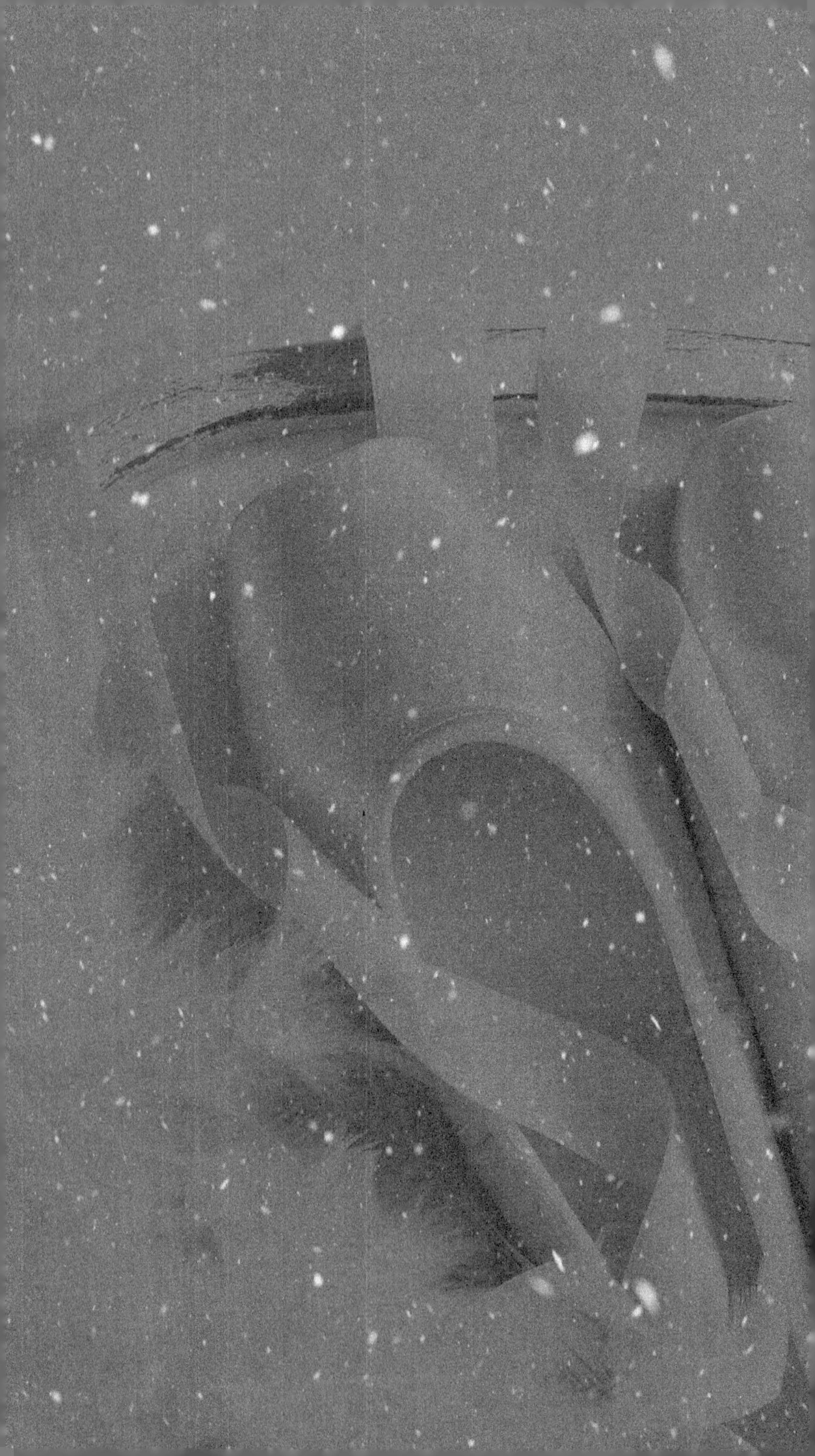

Acknowledgments

First off, I'd like to thank all the readers who have taken time to escape to my worlds. To everyone who has shared about Etched in Frost and has helped hype this story— it means so much to me to finally get to share Jax and Jolie with you.

Thea - This story wouldn't exist without you. Thank you for seeing me and these characters and for bringing them and me to life through your beautiful cosplays.

Emmerson - Your friendship will always be what I hold most dear but you were the lifeline I needed to get Jax and Jolie's story told during an extremely hard season. Thank you for reading the words dumped from my mind and helping me make sense of them.

Mom - My love of old claymation movies and Jack Frost is because of you. The love of dance I have is due to all the time and money you put into my passion. Thanks for reading my words, no matter how messy, and for always encouraging me to tell my stories. You're simply the best.

Chinah - Thank you for bringing your usual magic touch to this story. It means so much to be able to put my book babies and complete trust in you. Eight books down and more to come—thank you for helping me get through the onslaught of deadlines to get here. Your friendship, support, and pep talks have saved me more times than you'll ever know.

Angelique - I have loved working with you on all these books together. Thank you for being such an incredible sounding board and friend. We finally got our Jack Frost the HEA he deserved!

Fedy - Your messages when you beta read absolutely made my day. Thank you for loving these characters and reading my early words. You're amazing.

Kaitlin - You've been here from the beginning it feels like and I'm so grateful for our friendship. Thank you for sharing about these stories, supporting me through writing all these books, and my move cross country.

Sam - The best PA I could ask for. Thank you for helping coordinate things and keep me organized so I could focus on the move and getting these stories written this year. I'm so glad we finally got to hug in person and I cannot wait to celebrate more milestones to come!

Savanna - You always bring such beautiful insight to the beta reads. Thank you for lending your artistic brilliance to help make Etched in Frost shine.

Sydney - Thank you for your friendship and support while I worked to get this story out. I'm so proud of you for everything you've accomplished this year.

Vanessa - Our friendship means so much to me. Thank you for reading this in the early stages, your feedback, brainstorming ideas with me, and for all the support you've given me over the years since the beginning. You're amazing.

Sarah, Ashton, and Aubrey - Thank you for helping me give myself permission to write this story. Rearranging my publishing schedule so I could tell Jax and Jolie's story is in large part because of you and your support. Love you!

And finally, thanks to my husband for always supporting my dreams and loving me through every season.

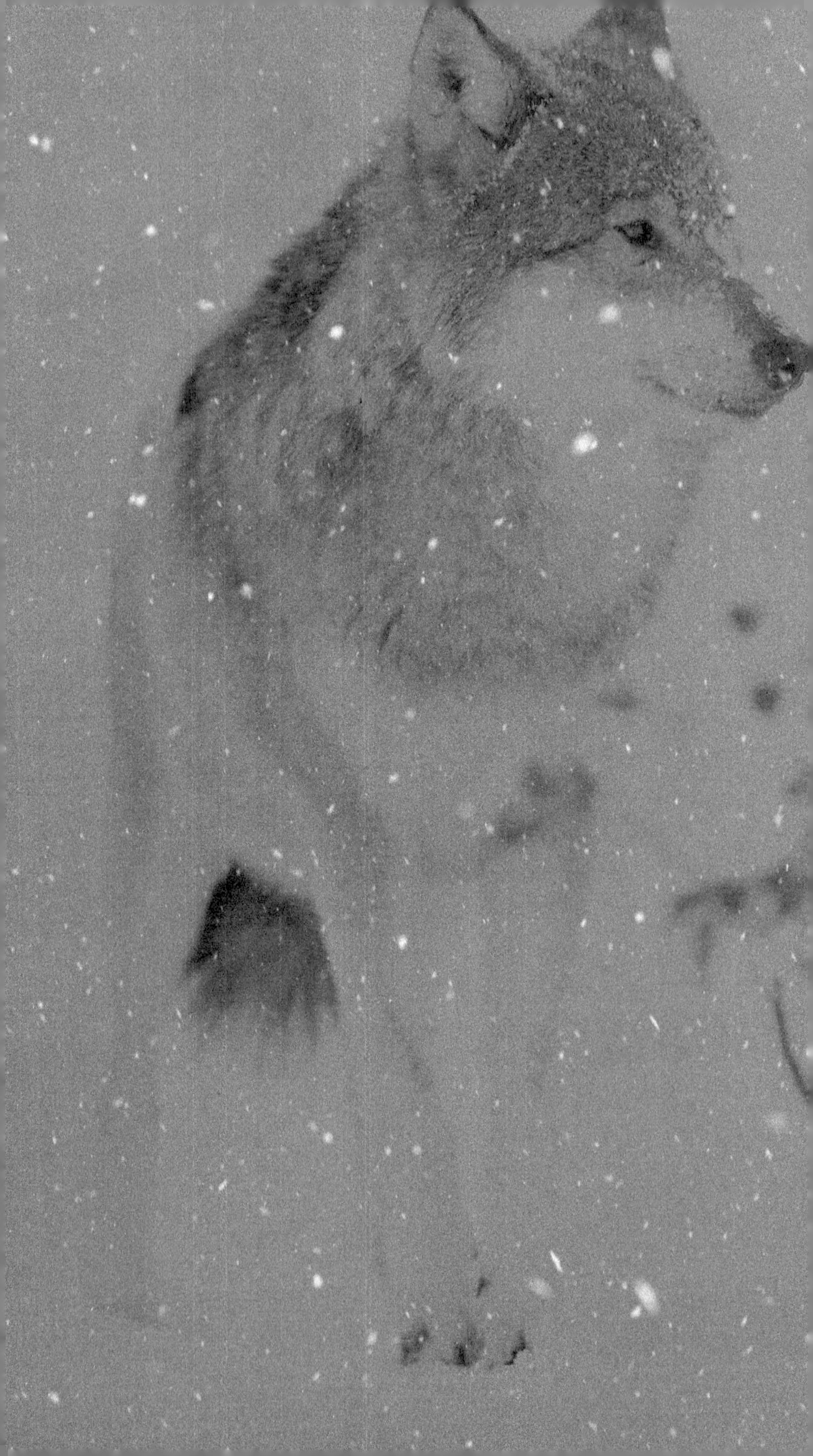

About
THE AUTHOR

Author L.R. Friedman loves curling up with a cup of coffee while diving into the romance of magical worlds.

She currently lives in Virginia with her husband and three children.

When she's not writing, you'll find her enjoying tacos, dark chocolate, and the occasional glass of whiskey.

The girl that grew up trying to find a hidden realm in her closet, she hopes to transport readers to beautiful, sexy, dark, and enchanting places through her stories.

For updates about upcoming releases, please visit http://www.lrfriedman.com, and sign up for her newsletter or join her group on Facebook at Books & Brews with L.R. Friedman.

www.ingramcontent.com/pod-product-compliance
Lightning Source LLC
Chambersburg PA
CBHW060603300726
48975CB00005B/1426